SACRAMENT

ALSO BY SUSAN STRAIGHT

Mecca
In the Country of Women
Between Heaven and Here
Take One Candle Light a Room
A Million Nightingales
Highwire Moon
The Gettin Place
Blacker Than a Thousand Midnights
I Been in Sorrow's Kitchen and Licked Out All the Pots
Aquaboogie: A Novel in Stories

SACRAMENT

A Novel

SUSAN STRAIGHT

COUNTERPOINT

CALIFORNIA

SACRAMENT

This is a work of fiction. All of the characters, organizations, and events portrayed in this novel are either products of the author's imagination or used fictitiously.

Copyright © 2025 by Susan Straight

All rights reserved under domestic and international copyright. Outside of fair use (such as quoting within a book review), no part of this publication may be reproduced, stored in a retrieval system, or transmitted in any form or by any means, electronic, mechanical, photocopying, recording, or otherwise, without the written permission of the publisher. Additionally, no part of this book may be used or reproduced in any manner for the purpose of training artificial intelligence technologies or systems. For permissions, please contact the publisher.

First Counterpoint edition: 2025

Grateful acknowledgment for reprinting materials is made to the following: Paulann Peterson, "A Sacrament" from *A Bride of Narrow Escape*, Cloudbank Books, 2006, by permission of the author. Marcel Proust, excerpt from *The Guermantes Way*, 1913. Lucille Clifton, excerpt from "won't you celebrate with me" from *The Book of Light*. Copyright © 1993 by Lucille Clifton. Reprinted with the permission of The Permissions Company, LLC, on behalf of Copper Canyon Press, coppercanyonpress.org.

Library of Congress Cataloging-in-Publication Data
Names: Straight, Susan, author.
Title: Sacrament : a novel / Susan Straight.
Description: First Counterpoint edition. | California : Counterpoint, 2025.
Identifiers: LCCN 2025021098 | ISBN 9781640097131 (hardcover) | ISBN 9781640097148 (ebook)
Subjects: LCGFT: Novels.
Classification: LCC PS3569.T6795 S23 2025 | DDC 813/.54—dc23/eng
  /20250512
LC record available at https://lccn.loc.gov/2025021098

Jacket design by Robin Bilardello
Jacket images: light leak © Getty / DrPixel; landscape © Getty / Cavan Images
Book design by Wah-Ming Chang

COUNTERPOINT
Los Angeles and San Francisco, CA
www.counterpointpress.com

Printed in the United States of America

10 9 8 7 6 5 4 3 2 1

For all we lost

For all who saved us

And for all of our beloved

✦

In memory of Art Laboe, who brought love and dedication to millions of listeners—a California soul; Dorothy Allison, my sister in spirit and narrative, who is with me every time I write; Lucille Clifton, grace and lyric, who once read a poem aloud for my mother-in-law; Douglas McCulloh, genius and generous photographer, who spent twelve years adventuring with me through our homelands; and all those souls who left us during the past five years.

Writing is how I pray.
It connects me to the voices above.

HELENA MARÍA VIRAMONTES

PART ONE

ONE ♦ Take the Wet from Water

LARETTE WOKE UP HEARING THE SONG. HIS FINGERS WERE pressed into her palm, not even the whole hand because Rudy Magana's hand was too big, so she held his four fingers while she sang to him. The song his wife, Norma, had requested.

She kept her eyes closed. She could feel the weight of his knuckles.

This one was hard. Mary Wells had one of the most beautiful voices ever, the purity of the 1960s, when each dip and quiver and hesitation was clear. No vocoder or electronic help back then. Only the lovely voice. Larette had practiced the song in the trailer for an entire afternoon. Memorized the verses. *It would be easier to take the . . . wet from wa-ter . . . or the dry from sa-nd . . . than for anyone to try to . . . se-pa-rate us . . . stop us from holding hands . . .*

Last year, when she was still onstage, everyone said Larette's fingers were long and elegant as she lifted her hands to the air. *So graceful! Like Lena Horne!* they'd say, if they were older women. *You were the best witch ever in The Wiz! We saw you at the Rialto Players, but you should be on Broadway.*

Now when she walked through the hospital parking lot, some people would seek her out. They'd say, *We've been sleeping here in our truck because of my uncle. My sister was over there smoking, and a lady told her about you. She said you sing for people so they know they aren't—alone. Please, can you sing for him? My dad?*

Larette sang for one person at a time now. No stage. No practice except in the bathroom of the ICU for maybe three minutes, while she threw cold water on her face and rubbed at the deep line on her forehead from the protective gear and the multiple caps over her hair. The line perfect as if a tiny fairy had dragged a tiny plow across her skin.

She was half awake now, in the Mallard. The little trailer with the AC roaring overhead. The queen bed wedged at the front. The tiny window like a porthole and the sun lowering into afternoon. She closed her eyes again.

Rudy Magana's hand big as a baseball glove. She felt it in her palm again. Like it was really there. She cradled it from underneath, holding knuckles huge and swollen from work, fingers bigger from all the fluid in his body. She had practiced in the trailer for a whole day, to sing it as close to Mary Wells as she could.

He would slip away when they let him. His wife and four daughters.

"But sing to him one more night, mija, please. The one he used to play in the park when we were in high school. I was sixteen and he was seventeen, he would do anything for one kiss. *Solo un besito, Mami, I'm gonna die.*" Norma Magana sank down onto the asphalt on her knees and sobbed, and two of her daughters looked fiercely at Larette.

Larette had said, "I'll text you five minutes before I go into his room. Probably close to midnight."

"Please," Norma had said in the parking lot. "Just one more time to see him."

NOW LARETTE LOOKED out the trailer window to the big block wall of CamperWorld. She made herself get out of the bed that felt like it was in a cave, took three steps to the small kitchen sink, drank a glass of water. Sunday, August 16, 2020. Her phone said 3:39 p.m. Shift started at 6:00.

She didn't even sleep in pajamas anymore. Definitely not a sexy cami set for her husband. She wore a tank top and shorts, in case someone banged on the trailer door for an emergency.

She didn't wake up on her side, with her palm on her husband's chest, hard as armor under her fingers. She hadn't told him anything about the hospital and her patients. Holding their hands.

She opened the narrow door and went down the two metal steps onto the street. Hers was the second Mallard RV in the line of four parked in the cul-de-sac, in front of the CamperWorld of San Bernardino. They were only three blocks from the hospital. One ICU nurse in each trailer. Marisol Manalang's was the first trailer. She was from Sacramento. She had two pots of herbs beside her wheels—lemongrass and mint. A card table set up outside, with a blue tablecloth and a mason jar full of crape myrtle blossoms, where they ate dinner before they went to work.

Larette had nothing, because she kept thinking she'd go home. Only rogue baby palm trees like green butter knives, sprouting from the crack in the asphalt near her feet.

She and her cousin Cherrise, in the third trailer, had been here since July 2. Pam Ott, in the last trailer, had come on July 8 from Morocco, Indiana.

Larette and Cherrise weren't traveling nurses—they lived right here, in San Bernardino. But they came to the trailers to keep the virus away from their kids. Larette rolled her shoulders back and forth. Scapulae. She felt those bones while her patients were on their stomachs, and she massaged their backs to help them breathe. *Stretch them angel wings*, her mother used to say, her mother who had worked at Our Lady all those years ago. Who called them shoulder blades? Nobody wants two axes under their skin.

Larette woke up feeling ghost fingers more often now. Cherrise woke up in her trailer on her hands and knees, doing chest compressions on the mattress. Marisol woke up shouting because she heard the *beep-beep-beep* of a reversing truck and thought an IV line was empty. Pam wasn't used to the dry heat of San Bernardino—she'd wake up with one cough from the Santa Ana winds, and then she'd panic and they could hear her coughing and coughing, like she was replicating the sounds of the hospital hallways. Marisol had made Pam some strong herbal concoction she learned in the Philippines, and Pam would take sips until she calmed down. She'd play a video on her phone of her son, Jonah, laughing and chasing their dogs in the yard back home until she fell asleep. The tiny barks blended in with the crickets in the grass along the sidewalks near CamperWorld.

Larette went back inside and lay on the bed again. Closed her eyes.

Ghost fingers in her left palm. Her right hand holding the phone on FaceTime for the wives. The husbands. The children who were grown. The sisters. Brothers. Tias. Primos. Los nietos y las sobrinas. All their faces. Stoic. Weeping. Biting their lips so hard it was like seeing people from another planet on the screen when they wavered and moved and disappeared for a moment and she heard screaming. The biker covered with tattoos, his face crumpled. The dogs—Lisa Valenti's mournful huskies, their twin faces in a kitchen howling into the phone held by Lisa's sister. Larette could imagine this woman, with her perfectly streaked caramel hair and pink nails, her chest rising and falling with the ventilator, doing dishes and singing along with her dogs.

You just call out my name, and you know wherever I am, I'll come running to see you again . . .

The song Lisa Valenti's sister requested was from James Taylor. "She sings it with the dogs, and it was our song when we were little. Can you please do that one for her? She'll hear it. I know she will." Then she broke down. "It was my baby shower. That's how Lisa got it. I thought we were out of the woods."

I haven't told my husband anything, Larette thought again, hearing the other trailer doors open and close. He doesn't know how it feels to hold their hands. I know he holds animals when they're dying, but it's fur and claws and . . .

No, she thought. It hurts him, too. He always told her about their eyes. Burro eyes with eyelashes. Dog eyes blue from old age. A beautiful blue, he said, and their owner is homeless in a tent down by the Santa Ana River, crying about how the dog is leaving him. Telling me, *My best friend's heading up to the sky with them blue eyes, bro* . . .

"Larette. Larette!"

The voice came a few feet from the hitch. They learned early on not to put your face up to the little windows or you'd scare the shit out of each other.

Larette cranked open the window. Cherrise moved into her vision. "You okay? You were . . . making noises."

Larette rubbed her eyes. "Well, you weren't for once. But it's so hot, girl."

Cherrise said, "Like our mamas used to say. So hot the devil is frying us up like hush puppies. But you gotta get ready."

Cherrise was already dressed in her scrubs. Her hair in a bun. "I'm up. I'm up."

Cherrise opened the door of the RV. They kept the doors unlocked in case one of them got sick. They didn't want to find one another passed out on the little beds. But Larette had Covid in July. She'd been in the ICU three days, and Cherrise had tended to her. Cherrise was the only one of the nurses who hadn't gotten sick yet.

"Come on, cuz. It's four thirty. Gonna be the vespertine hour before you know it. According to your son. He's right over there."

Larette sat up, dizzy. The heat. Her favorite sheets from home damp with sweat. The slanted ceiling of the trailer just above her head. Her hair wrapped in the satin cap.

"He's here?" she said.

Marisol Manalang poked her face around Cherrise's shoulder in the doorway. She wore her magenta scrubs, her lipstick matching, her eye makeup perfect, her straight black hair gleaming damp from the shower. "Dogcatcher here, too. I cook for him."

Marisol called him that as a joke, because Grief hated the word. Larette's husband, Grief Embers, had worked eighteen years for the San Bernardino County Animal Control Service Division. "The largest county in the U.S.," he'd tell people. "Bigger than New Jersey, Delaware, Connecticut, and Rhode Island all put together. I track mountain lions. I rescue bobcats and burros and bears, but people still wanna to call me the dogcatcher."

But he'd never tease Marisol Manalang for the nickname. She was the queen of the four trailers. Queen of the ICU at Our Lady. She was the first traveler the hospital had hired in April, when corona overwhelmed the wards. She was born outside Manila, in the Philippines, but moved to Sacramento when she was fifteen. By now, countless traveling nurses had come and gone, but Marisol was still at Our Lady. She ran the world.

Larette could smell the chicken adobo Marisol had cooked. She said, "Okay, capitana."

Marisol came inside and slid a small plastic bag onto Larette's bed. "I get contraband for you. Go outside—Grief have a bag, too."

Larette got up and stood on the small metal step, looking down the block, where her husband had parked the truck. He was carrying plastic bags from Staples. Her son, clutching his phone, stared up at her, and immediately her phone pinged.

She pivoted and sat again on the bed she hated so much.

U look tired Mom.

Never say that 2 a woman, baby. Even UR mama

She hated the trailer. The bed. The phone. The typing. The sounds of it.

She went to the tiny bathroom and stood for one minute under the shower, cold mist stinging her face and collarbone. The four nurses showered at work, showered the minute they got back from shift. Her hands were raw from gloves and sanitizer and disinfecting. Larette dried herself fast, then smoothed her hair into a wet twist onto the top of her head. She put Olay on her face, dipped her finger into the pot of bronze eyeshadow and sparkled her eyelids, drew black kohl liner above her lashes, and pulled on a new black mask. She took clean scrubs—she was teal—from the pile of three on the little kitchen table.

By the time she stepped outside, pushing the flimsy door closed, her back was already dripping with sweat. Fluids, she thought. Every fucking minute is all about bodily fluids. If it would just be October, and the first cool day, and I didn't have to go anywhere but sit in my garden at home and feel the wind, I'd cry, too. I'd hold my own hand and cry.

THEY WERE STANDING at the corner, near Grief's old truck. Her husband was still in his uniform. Lieutenant Grief Embers. His belt heavy with equipment—Taser, pepper spray, flashlight, all of it. County of San Bernardino cap. His boots covered with dust—he must have been wrangling dogs or even a horse in the dirt. His wispy mustache and goatee clean gleaming black. He'd washed his face even though he couldn't kiss her.

Dante in his Dodgers jersey and jeans. His hair longer than it had ever been during a summer. No Little League. No science camp. Nothing.

It was the clumsy braids that made her want to cry when she came to six feet and stopped. Six feet distance or six feet under. People said that all the time now. Dante had texted her in the beginning, when corona started, **6 ft distance feels like random. The virus could go further. Who made up 6 ft 2 bury people? Was there a scientific reason?**

"Mom," he said. "There's no school this year. They decided virtual."

The braids. Five of them, and she could see Grief's fingers parting and twisting but not able to do it right.

Grief had Covid back in May. May 9 to 25. Dante had found him, in the hallway, at night, while Larette was on shift. While he was waiting for the EMTs, Dante had whispered to her, "Dad was crawling. He had sweat on his whole back, Mom. Like it was raining inside."

He was terrified. Her baby. He'd called 911, the EMTs arrived in white hazmat suits, and Dante was left alone in the front yard. She called Grief's best friend, Johnny Frias, to come take care of Dante, while she stayed at the hospital.

Larette got hers on July 5—and two days after she got home, the hospital asked some nurses to move into the RVs, to keep their families safe.

Her husband and son stuck in the house without her. Every day, she saw Dante on FaceTime, at 8:00 p.m. and then once more at 10:00 p.m., when he was supposed to go to bed, but she knew he stayed up half the night researching. Getting ready for high school.

He stood on the sidewalk staring at her, holding the bag.

He hadn't had the virus.

"I'm a freshman," he said. "We don't get to do anything." He wasn't going to cry. His eyes the same as hers, topaz and green. His face not sun-dark, because no baseball no swimming with his best friend, Manny III, no hikes no nothing.

"No nothing," she said, sending the words as softly as she could across the six feet. "That's what you used to say when you were little. No nothing! When I went to the store and didn't bring you snacks. Now y'all brought me snacks. Right?"

As jaunty as she could. But it wasn't working.

"I brought you markers. Dad got me three more whiteboards. I have a whiteboard for each class, and you do, too. English with Mrs. Hua, and she says we have to start with poetry. Bio with Mr. Espinoza, and we're starting with anatomy. He's crazy and I like him. He has a cactus tattoo on his arm."

"Virtual forever, baby," Grief said across the void shimmering with heat. The sidewalks were shaking. The asphalt on the cul-de-sac a black river rippling just a little with mirage as if thousands of fish were underneath. "The school district just emailed us. While you were sleeping."

"Okay," Larette said, keeping her voice steady, the fish swimming underneath her beloveds, the fingers of a stranger imprinted in her palm, the man she loved staring at her, the man she'd met when she was sixteen, just like Norma Magana. Grief had come around the Madrigals' practice room at San Bernardino High still in his baseball uniform and said, *I could hear you all the way from first base and I had to see what you looked like. You're like—the stars or something.*

But Dante, the product of baseball and stars, never sang. She and Grief had sung around him since he was born, but their act was appallingly hilarious and he hated it. He was thirteen. He put the plastic bag on the sidewalk between them and said, "Mom. You have to help me with the poetry. Because you know a million lyrics, and they're like poetry, right? Mom. I never thought I'd say it, because you and Dad embarrassed me forever, but I miss when you guys sing. Even though everybody laughed in the bleachers."

He ducked his head and turned around for a minute. Like a dog chasing its tail. He was chasing his composure. But Larette was allowed to cry. She was allowed saltwater.

"Fifteen days, baby," Grief said. "Too long. And you went to the Launderland—you coulda got robbed, Larette."

She hadn't been home for that long. She and Cherrise had

worked straight shifts for nine days, and on her day off, she'd washed her scrubs at the laundromat to be safe.

"Nobody wants to get near me when they see my scrubs, baby," she said. "The plague."

Grief stepped forward with a tiny bag. "Hooks," he said. "For the whiteboards. My offering so you don't mess up the Mallard. But I'm tired of this shit, Larette. I can't take it much longer. You didn't even get Sunday."

"No," Larette said, the tears cooling already, though they were thicker and more gelid than sweat. All the secretions of the body. Sweat was useful. No other animal with tears. Fish with their big eyes, and cats and dogs with their eyebrows—no tears. Even corgis like Marisol's on her FaceTime, a dog whose huge eyes looked outlined with kohl and so expressive—no tears. The burros Grief had sent her videos of yesterday when he had to rescue five from the freeway not far from here—big eyes with ridiculous lashes, and they were terrified, but no tears.

When Dante turned back around, she could see he had smeared his own eyes. "Fifteen days, Mom."

She said it for the first time. "It's war. Okay? We're in a war. That's what Mariah Ball says. Remember her? Our charge nurse? She came to your games a few times. Her kids are all grown. She says we have to look at it like battle and if we were soldiers nobody would say shit. I'm sorry, baby. I'm sorry."

Dante said, "But then you'd be in, like, another country. It's, like, worse that you're three-point-four miles away from home. For reals." He pointed to the four trailers parked at the end of the cul-de-sac. "And somebody could break in there. Dad and I see homeless people all around here in the alleys."

"We're safe," she said, hating the word more deeply each time she said it. "I'm safe, you and Dad are safer away from me, and you're safe doing virtual school. Just . . ."

She was talking to them like patient families. Strangers.

Crocodile tears. Nobody was crying crocodile tears.

"Be patient," Dante said, angry again. "Have *patience*. You got *patients*. Dad's gotta be patient to get the burros off the freeway, and then one asshole comes down the shoulder and hits them and drives off! I'm fucking tired of hearing it."

But Grief was staring at Larette. Not at Dante, to tell him no cussing. Grief said, "You're right. It's war. But you gotta think about quitting, Larette. We didn't sign up for this. CamperWorld dude, he's seriously watching over you all while you sleep? You trust him?"

"He's obsessed with us." Wait. Not the right word.

Grief's eyes narrowed. She had to think of a song to distract them both. Comfort them. Like everyone else. Larette took two deep breaths. Like she did before she sang to the strangers who weren't strangers because she'd wiped down their faces and cleaned out their ears and she and Marisol had changed their catheters, being gentle with the manhood of strangers in the depths of their coma-dreaming.

Larette looked straight into Grief's eyes. She knew because of how he moved that corona lingered in his joints and lungs but that he didn't want to tell her. And she wouldn't tell him about her headaches, how she couldn't breathe going up and down the stairs in the hospital. She wouldn't tell him about Rudy Magana.

She sang, *The moment I wake up* . . .

He shook his head. He sighed. But then he sang, off-key and way out of practice, *Before I put on my makeup* . . .

She sang, *I say a little prayer for you* . . .

Her mother's favorite. The first song Larette had ever learned, when she was four, watching her mother put on pale green eyeshadow and her hospital uniform. Her name stitched in black thread over her right breast. *Topaz*.

Larette said, "I have to go. It's the vespertine hour, right, Dante? What stars are you watching tonight?"

But he didn't answer. He dropped the Staples bag on the sidewalk and walked back toward the truck.

Grief called, "Dante, we got dinner coming!" But their son was already in the cab, looking down at his phone.

Marisol walked down the sidewalk with a container of GladWare full of food for Grief and Dante. Marisol made a big pot of adobo chicken every Sunday, and rice in the rice cooker, which didn't heat up her trailer at all. Larette was the only one with a husband and child who came to see her—so Marisol always packed some for them.

Her son was giving up on her. Her husband knew she wasn't telling him everything.

Grief looked past her. "Lieutenant Manalang," he said. "I know—you running a tight night shift here, and I gotta go."

"Five o'clock," she said, her accent and consonants precise. "Lieutenant Ember." She put the bag on the sidewalk like an offering to the gods and backed away two feet.

The smell rose fragrant and powerful, and Grief said, "I would crawl on the cement for your food, madam."

Larette would have been offended if she wouldn't have crawled with him.

"I don't call you Dogcatcher every time," Marisol said, suddenly serious. "But tonight, you take care. For who you find."

Because Marisol told them about dogs. Ghost dogs that had once been people, leaping into the windows of her trailer. Big birds, the size of ravens, that had once been humans, flying down to land on her trailer, above her bed.

She said something to him in Tagalog, and then pointed to the truck. "Starcatcher? He not hungry?"

"He's mad at me," Larette sighed.

"Tell him eat," Marisol said, and went back toward the picnic table.

Then Grief said, "You got somebody new coming. To the flock. I can't believe you're in a Mallard."

Larette turned around. The owner of CamperWorld, Rick Schneider, had opened the big wrought iron gate and was towing another trailer with his blue Silverado. He bumped down onto the cul-de-sac and pulled slowly around until he was behind Pam's trailer. Pam poked her head, wrapped in a towel, out the door.

"Another duck," Larette said.

"Those green feathers. Green is always the most beautiful, right? Like the fig beetles? The mallard feathers in the sun?" Grief held the food but didn't move.

"Peacock," Larette said.

"Yeah. Emerald. Jade."

She said, "Marisol wears that green jade buddha around her neck. She says it saved her life. Twice. Her mom brought it from the Philippines."

"You took off your wedding ring when you were sick." His voice slow. Measured.

"Cherrise took it off. In case."

In case her hands swelled up like those of so many patients—and the ring had to be cut off to prevent gangrene.

"But you haven't put it back on yet," he said.

"Because of the gloves, Grief. With the gloves and the sanitizer, my hands are peeling every night. I don't want to wreck my ring."

He held up his own hand. His wedding band. "Maybe you need a better ring. We got that one a long time ago. Maybe everyone needs to see how married you are, baby."

She closed her eyes. A half-carat diamond engagement ring, a plain gold band. From the wholesale jeweler in downtown L.A. "I love my rings," she said through the mask. "But the solitaire was cutting up the gloves, Grief."

"Cherrise still wearing hers," he said.

Cherrise had been widowed now for eight years. She never took off her wedding band.

"Grief! We peel off gloves fifty times a night. You have no idea."

"Larette."

The adobo between them, releasing its magic.

This was the moment she should step forward and take his big scarred hand in hers. Forget the six feet. Cradle his four fingers and run her own fingers into that palm, tickle him, kiss the center of his hand like she used to, when they were sixteen, when she made him shiver and close his eyes. Hug him for just a moment and speak into the side of his throat and whisper that she held people's hands for hours, that she had only a song to offer them by then.

But she was afraid to be too close to him. She blew him a kiss, like a stranger.

TWO ✦ Power Rangers

THE BREEZE TOOK MARISOL'S SUNDAY DINNER UP INTO CamperWorld, they all knew, and the big wrought iron gate would slide open any moment so Rick Schneider could come down in his truck and get a container. The adobo smelled like some version of heaven, Cherrise thought, the garlic, peppercorns, bay leaf—Cherrise held a chicken wing. Marisol was serious about her GladWare. She had everybody's name printed in black marker on the bottom, little perfect letters. Rick was so thrilled to have his own GladWare that he carried it like a church offering basket when he walked toward them.

This afternoon his Dodger-blue Silverado was towing another Mallard. He pulled in behind Pam's trailer, got out and disengaged the hitch, then parked the truck across from the two picnic tables in the grass parking strip.

"You all are a sight for sore eyes," he said. "Four beautiful girls in four beautiful colors. Like . . . Wonder Women."

Raquel said into Cherrise's Bluetooth, "Oh my God, he did *not* just say that. He can't talk like that."

Cherrise couldn't say anything, of course, because she was trying to eat her dinner. She had to put the wing down, wipe her fingers, and text quickly, **Yes, he can, he's just happy 2 C us & he talks like that**

Inapropro mom

He's a 50yrold man living in a big RV & we don't know his past so don't judge

No reply.

Of course she heard Raquel switch to voice. Raquel said into her earpiece, "So overly eager, Mom. He's a stalker."

Cherrise refused to put down the wing again. The sauce so complex. Like gumbo. Like the chicken stew Pam had made from her grandmother's recipe. Hungarian. With paprika and sour cream. They all made chicken, once a week, except Cherrise. Cherrise didn't cook. Her husband, Ronald, had loved tacos—all varieties of tacos. After he died, she and Raquel had lived on tacos, beans, and rice for years. Except when she bought Rosie's chicken and waffles.

She had ten more minutes to eat and then get ready for the fourth floor. She texted, **Have 2 go.**

Raquel said, "You always have to go."

Yeah. Or people die.

A fly sensed that she was distracted from the chicken and rice. Marisol grabbed the container of food she always packed for Rick, who stood on the sidewalk at a respectful distance and said, "You got a new Wonder Woman comin' tomorrow."

Raquel said, "They die anyway, Mom. All I read is people dying."

Cherrise wiped her fingers one more time and took a deep breath. Down the block, Larette was talking to Grief, who held his arms up like goalposts. Damn. Those two never argued. Never. Her daughter had just turned fifteen. She never calmed down.

"How do you know that guy doesn't have the virus? You're supposed to be staying safe there, and he could go to the store and get it," Raquel hissed.

"He doesn't go anywhere," Cherrise hissed back. "He watches over the trailers and the street, and apparently he had a freezer full of frozen dinners in his RV and now he at least gets home-cooked food from everybody but me because I can't cook, okay?

Are you happy? None of us have a life and I have to walk to work now, so please, please, just do your homework and help Auntie Lolo. Hydrate out there in the desert."

Raquel was silent.

Cherrise could hear Grief's truck turn the corner, could hear Rick saying, "The whole block smells like a restaurant I could never afford!"

Then Raquel said, "You know what, Mom? You could have said no. You could have said I'm quitting until this virus is gone. You picked strangers over me."

"Raquel! You don't get to talk to me like that just because we're on the damn phone."

"You send me out here to the end of the world and you're gonna get it anyway and then I'm gonna be an *orphan*. Yeah. Stupid word from, like, Dickens. See? I'm doing my homework."

The pop of disconnection. Silence.

RICK SCHNEIDER SAT in the bed of his truck on a beach chair. He ate the chicken and rice, drank a Coors Light. "Great company," he called eventually. "Maybe you guys are like cool Power Rangers in your uniforms. Yeah. That seems better."

People had been buying RVs online—trucks came to tow them to buyers all week. Pandemic. Rick said off-the-grid was an obsession. His business was booming.

But he wasn't going anywhere. He loved San Bernardino, and this was his contribution to the war effort, he'd told them when he first offered the trailers to nurses at the hospital. He'd read about the travelers, how they needed safe places to rent. The four of them stayed here for free. Rick hitched up each trailer once a week, at night when they were working, and pulled them inside CamperWorld, where he had a dumping station. He emptied the black water, as he called it. Cleaned the tanks. Checked the propane. Washed the outsides with a power hose. Brought them back dripping and clean.

When Cherrise came back on the mornings her trailer had been serviced, there were hundreds of tiny circles in the dust of the asphalt, where the last drops of water had fallen and evaporated in the night. Like a strange protective spell.

"Who's coming?" Pam said, finishing the last bite of her rice. When she first got here from Indiana, she'd looked dubiously at the adobo, the gumbo. Then she had leftovers the next day, and she said, "This is like church at home in Morocco. Saint Ingrid's, when all the ladies bring their casseroles. I think I have something that will work." Eventually, once she learned the tiny stove, Pam made Hungarian paprika chicken stew, red and smoky, and the flavors melted into the steamed Calrose rice Marisol made in her rice cooker.

"Somebody from Texas," Rick said, standing up in the truck bed, his beer belly high and hard in the Route 66 T-shirt he always wore. "She's driving all night because she doesn't want to fly. The germs."

They didn't correct him anymore. Viral particles. Germs. Whatever.

Marisol said, "You have enough for lunch?"

He held up the big GladWare and said, "I'm the luckiest man in California. Gotta get my exercise now." He sat down on the tailgate and launched off awkwardly, then went back to the new trailer and bent down to adjust the blocks.

Larette had been quiet all during dinner. Not on her phone. Just staring up at the mountains. The white rockslides of the San Gorgonio Range turning faint pink in the lowering sun.

"Dogcatcher eat his chicken now," Marisol said gently.

Larette only nodded. *Grief givin' you grief?* was the joke they said sometimes in the hallway, if he sent her pictures of tranquilized bears or bobcats, texting, **Everybody lying down on the job.**

Not tonight.

Cherrise said, "All the chickens that died so y'all could live. Remember your mom used to say that, Larette? We'd be sitting out there in the courtyard of the apartment in the summer eating fried chicken. All five of us cousins. All girls. You, me, and Merry. Matelasse would come from Rio Seco. Saqqara from L.A."

Their mothers had all come from Louisiana to California over the decades. Some came in 1955, but Turquoise and Topaz, their mothers, had come in 1986 after three hurricanes in a row. Topaz was twenty-two, and Turquoise was nineteen. *I take my chance with a damn earthquake, oui? They ain't got fool names like them hurricane*, Cherrise's mother always said.

No, Mama, they call the earthquake here a name, too. Look. Northridge. Whittier. They call them for the city.

Well, that's better than Danny, Elena, and Juan. I hated sayin' stupid names like that. Kicked our ass and made us leave for California. Tired of gettin' flooded out. Tired of that cane field. Look here, we on the second floor of Las Palmas Court. Swimmin' pool. Ain't even no rain here.

She and Larette had grown up in adjoining two-bedroom apartments, and if they complained about anything, their mothers would say, *We slept four to a bed in Houma, we slept on pallets on the floor. You both spoiled.*

"We gotta go," Larette said.

Cherrise shut her trailer door, brushed her teeth, charged her phone. She stared at the damn thing plugged in, lying on her own small bed. All the Mallards facing north, Rick said, to keep the afternoon heat from broiling them. The new trailer lined up the same way, for whoever was coming from Texas.

If there was another traveler coming, the hospital expected summer to keep getting worse. And maybe fall, too.

Cherrise put cold water on the back of her neck one more time. The travelers made $4,200 a month. Staff nurses who'd been at the hospital for years averaged $2,900.

"You guys are angels!" people in the parking lot called to the nurses who walked into the hospital each night. The families had no idea who lived here and who didn't. Everyone wore scrubs.

It was a traveler who had saved Grief. She was only here for two weeks. Karli LeBlanc, from Lake Charles, Louisiana. She had a daughter who was twelve, and they fought on the phone all the time. Karli left Cherrise a card with a sunflower on it, and she'd written in tiny, beautiful cursive, *You got this! Maybe? Almost? For sure? Yeah. You do.*

Three doors slammed. Cherrise got up and almost didn't bring her damn phone. All night it pinged—families of her patients, respiratory therapists and nurses, Raquel if she couldn't sleep.

She texted Raquel one more time. **Hydrate, plz! I promise when I come out there, I'll bring a whole case of Takis.**

Cherrise packed Raquel's old JanSport backpack with extra scrubs in a plastic bag. She added a bag of Vicks Honey Lemon, for the smell; two PayDay bars, lunch of truck drivers; and her 1:00 a.m. dinner in the blue GladWare. Leftover tamales from a street vendor.

Raquel texted back. **U haven't come all this time. U never took me 2 C dad. U just left that day. July. His BD is Wednesday & U prolly won't come.**

She sat back down fast. She hated fighting via text. **Srsly. I'll try 2 come. I'll take a short nap & head out there. Promise.**

If U don't come I'm going. I have a ride.

Cherrise texted, **What? Lolo doesn't drive.**

No reply. Cherrise tied her sweater around her waist, like in high school, and opened the thin metal door. Who would drive Raquel? Maybe one of her aunts? But they were working. Who would her daughter even meet out there in Oasis?

A boy? Online? Shit. Couldn't be a kid from STEM—they were all San Bernardino. What if one of those boys had driven out to Oasis to see Raquel?

Raquel didn't text back. Cherrise slipped the phone into the scrubs pocket and went down the steps, a strange prickle of unease between her shoulders. Different from work. She looked south, to her house, only five miles away.

Rick shouted, "*They sally forth into the night!* What my dad used to say. When we would all go hang out at the park. Have a good shift, Power Rangers."

They waved at him and headed down the cul-de-sac toward the avenue. Only three blocks to the hospital. They each had backpacks with thermoses, lunches, snacks. Plastic-wrapped masks, caps, gloves in case there weren't enough in the supply closet. PPE was getting harder to come by.

Sally forth! Not angels or mercenaries, Cherrise thought. We walk to work like kindergartners holding a rope.

Marisol wore her magenta scrubs and magenta scarf over her thick black hair, cut in a shag that feathered toward her perfectly blushed cheeks. Her lipstick was magenta, too. Her clipped, dismissive voice was hilarious. Whatever happened in the ICU, Marisol would give someone side-eye and say, *This? This not bad. Not like the forest. Where I live.*

Even now, when the ICU was crowded and out of control, Marisol just took over and said, *Give him to me. Move.* She'd nudge a slow EMT out of the way.

She had no children—she'd helped raise her three younger sisters, by her stepfather. Every single adult in their extended family of eighteen was a nurse or a respiratory therapist. Marisol was forty-two, and her youngest sister, Jasmine, was twenty-eight, also a traveler, but she was home now in Sacramento, watching all the dogs, including Marisol's corgi.

"Listen," Marisol said now, holding up her phone. "He sing for me." The dog was beautiful, his big eyes outlined with black as if he wore liner, looking directly at them, howling gently. *Awooo, awooooo.*

Pam was next, her long brown hair with bright red streaks she touched up every week. For Indiana football. Her husband had played football in college and now sold tractors in a dealership. But no one was buying during the pandemic, so she came here. Pam held up her phone so her son, Jonah, who was five, could see everything in California. "Here are the noisy dogs. Listen. What are their names?"

"Chuy and Chulo!" he said.

The two German shepherds were guarding Grandma's Attic Storage, all the sliding metal doors gleaming in the setting sun. Armando Garcia, the night watchman, waved at the parade, like he did every night.

Pam continued, "Here are the trees with flowers! This one is crape myrtle. See the pink? Like a beautiful jungle here, Jonah. All the flowers."

Cherrise waved at him when Pam turned the phone to her. So nice back then—when Raquel was five and Cherrise could just list things, their names and their existence, and that was enough.

Larette caught up with Cherrise. "Try that voice with a teenager, right?"

Cherrise laughed. "I hate the phone." Then she said, "You and Grief. Never seen you with friction. Never, Larette."

Larette held up her left hand. "My rings."

"And he just now noticed? You left them at home, like, three weeks ago. He thinks you lost them?"

Larette shrugged. "He thinks I'm not wearing them. For a reason."

Cherrise was astonished. "You? He must be out of his mind."

Larette grabbed Cherrise's hand. "You got yours on. As he pointed out."

"The wedding band's smooth, so it doesn't snag! Ronald and I didn't have time or money for the engagement ring. Remember?"

They'd decided on a Tuesday to get married. On Friday, the

four of them drove an hour to Laguna Beach and went to city hall. They walked on the beach for hours that summer night in their dresses and suits. The joke was that since Ronald and Cherrise both worked at San Manuel Casino, they sure as hell weren't driving three hours to Vegas to get married in another casino.

"I was twenty-one, girl," Larette said. "I thought I knew everything. And you were pregnant."

They followed Marisol and Pam around the corner and turned north, toward the mountains. The hospital rose ahead of them, windows lit and reflecting mellow gold from the west. All summer, there had been fewer cars on the road in Southern California, and everyone remarked on how, with no smog, the sunsets weren't deep, heated crimson. Just quiet slipping into darkness.

"We went to Indio for two nights for our honeymoon," Cherrise said, remembering the hotel room with a balcony, and all Ronald wanted to do was head out to Mecca and ride the horses on his parents' land in the date palm gardens. She'd only ridden twice before, so she sat behind him, arms around his waist, her cheek against his long braid, the Salton Sea shimmering blue at the end of the rows of tree trunks.

"We didn't get to fight," Cherrise said. "That's the thing. When the man you love dies like that, you don't know if you'da had friction. So I'm not judging, Larette."

"Yeah, but I've known you longer than anybody else in the world. Remember?"

Cherrise nodded. Both their mothers were gone. The cousins had visited Houma only once, when their grandmother died. They stayed for two weeks. They were still children then.

Larette said quietly, "So you better tell me when I'm messing up. I'm messing up right now with Grief and Dante."

"Well, damn, Raquel's hating on me." Cherrise felt the prickle again. Like a fingertip.

"She wants to come home."

"She wants me to quit. She says I'm putting strangers over her. She's right, Larette. I haven't been out to Oasis since I took her. Six weeks. It's just, we haven't had a night off, it's two hours each way, all I want to do is sleep."

"I know," Larette said. "I know."

Cherrise said, "Ronald's birthday is Wednesday. He'd be thirty-eight. Damn. I'm gonna go out there. Bring her some Takis, take a new Dodger hat and a six-pack to the cemetery."

They crossed at the first light. Larette said, "Grief wants me to quit, too."

"You gotta tell him how it feels. When we're in there. In the land of—"

"I know."

They stopped across the street from Our Lady, to wait for the next light. Marisol had put away her phone. She was humming like she always did. A song from her grandmother back in the forest, she always said.

Cherrise said softly, "Larette. When I get it, don't let me—"

Not the intubation. No.

"Girl," Larette said. "Stop."

THREE ✦ Oasis, California

RAQUEL TOOK HER FLASHLIGHT AND SAT WITH HER LEGS over the edge of the top bunk bed. She shined the light on the floor, on the walls, around the windowsill. Looked out the top pane, above the swamp cooler, at the rows of palm trees that came all the way up to the edge of the yard. It was still so hot, but the starlight made the fronds and trunks silver, and that looked cool. Even if it wasn't.

She looked for the tiny headlights of the white truck that would be moving through the palms so late. The two men who might be walking. One following the other.

Her mother didn't know anything about her now.

It was 10:18 p.m. Her mother had been on shift four hours. Auntie Lolo's snoring was a low hum from the other room. Her great-aunt went to bed at 8:30 every night, because she woke up at 4:00 to be in the date garden with the workers, before the desert heat went crazy. She made Raquel get in bed that early, too. Like Raquel was in kindergarten.

Because she didn't want her wandering around at night. Lolo knew Raquel had met Joey Ortiz in the dates. But now that Raquel was doing virtual school in the packinghouse, she saw him in the afternoon, too, when classes were done.

The ceiling fan was clacking five feet away from her face, the window cooler roaring, in the only bedroom in Lolo's house. It was 109 degrees in Oasis today. Forty-two days she'd been out here. Away from her mother, from San Bernardino, from decent internet so she could do her summer school assignments for STEM Academy. Now virtual school all year. That meant she had to set up her Chromebook in the packinghouse, the only place with Wi-Fi. Her background was a fucking tablecloth draped over some boxes. It was a beautiful tablecloth, with palm trees and an old-school truck that said LOLO'S DATE GARDEN. Some lady from Australia had made it and sent it to her aunt way back in the 1950s.

But Raquel was still in a storage room, with a bare lightbulb over her, for Zoom.

She hadn't seen any of her friends—Akisha, Leilani, Marshall—in real life since March.

Raquel would have written the days on the white walls of the bedroom—like guys did in solitary confinement in the movies—if she hadn't been freaked out about what might be inside the walls.

The mother scorpions. Waiting for their babies to be born.

WHEN SHE FIRST got here in July, she couldn't believe her mother had forgotten the story of them coming out of the walls. The baby scorpions all crawling toward the baby girl in the crib here? In this room? Or was it the other room, where Lolo was sleeping?

It didn't matter that there were probably ten coats of paint on the walls. White. The little house was, like, a hundred years old. When Raquel's grandfather took the window AC out to put in a new one, there were holes in the wooden windowsill. Scorpions wanted to come inside to be cool. Lolo's mother and her husband had made these adobe bricks themselves. They had holes in them, from where the straw had turned to dust. That's how the scorpions hid inside. Pregnant.

How could her mother have forgotten the story?

Raquel stared at the big wooden beams in the ceiling. She'd pulled the bunk bed away from the wall, inch by inch, so there was a two-foot space between her and the adobe bricks. Her father had slept here, with his brother, in the summers when they worked in the dates and the grapefruit. They never got stung.

At least, her dad never said he got stung. He'd been dead for eight years. They'd only had seven years to talk.

One night, sitting with Raquel in the dark backyard at home in San Bernardino, with the flashlight he used for work making a moon on the wooden fence, her dad told her about how when Lolo was a baby girl, she could have died. He let Raquel hold the beam into the dark and the moths came like tiny white birds.

He said scorpions in the desert were like aliens. They glowed in the dark. Ghostly blue, if you shined a light on them. "At least you can find them because of that." Had he said exactly that? She hated that there was no record. No record of the things he'd told her, when they sat out here under the palms. Because she was so little. You didn't know to remember when you were little. And you couldn't write yet. No phone. No voicemail. No text.

Now she closed her eyes. He said they carried their babies on their backs. Like possums.

Her flashlight also functioned as a stun gun. Grief had gotten it for her—they'd practiced holding the button on one side for the light and then the other side for the stun gun. She didn't know if it would work on scorpions. She sat up on the bed now and aimed it at the walls and the floor. Nothing glowed.

She didn't want to ask Auntie Lolo. Lolo was her grandmother's sister. She slept in the big room that held the kitchen and couch and bookcase and TV and dining room table. When Raquel first arrived, she couldn't leave this bedroom for six days. Her mother said she had to isolate. The virus could be anywhere on both of them.

The Fourth of July had made everybody sick again. Her

mother said, "Hell, it was on a weekend, and everybody partied hard. What makes people happy is killing them now. Raquel, baby, you have to go out to the desert. Just for a few weeks. Until this surge is over."

Auntie Lolo was eighty-two but could hear everything. Every cry of the peacocks in the date garden. Every owl at night. She said old people didn't have to sleep the same way as teenagers. Old people slept like animals—floating just above, but still listening. And teenagers slept like they were under the earth and they had to pop their heads out every morning.

Raquel wasn't asleep now.

She never got any sleep because she was waiting for the scorpions.

Her mother had told the story again, a couple of years ago. They were at a birthday party for a nurse, standing in a backyard, talking about the desert. Her mother was holding a tequila paloma. Her favorite drink.

Nurses could party.

"My husband's great-grandmother built that house in, like, 1930. Out in the middle of twenty acres next to her sister's place. Near the Salton Sea. Her sister built a wooden house. But the great-grandmother and her husband made their own adobe bricks. I guess it was spring. And at the end of summer, all these baby scorpions came crawling out of the walls. And their baby girl, Lolo, was in her crib."

"Jesus Christ!" her mother's supervisor, Mariah Ball, said. "She died?"

Raquel's mother had laughed. "They had a dog. The dog went crazy and was trying to bite all the scorpions. Hundreds of them. They woke up and got the baby out."

Mariah Ball said, "But how did they kill all the scorpions?"

Raquel's mother had shrugged. "No idea."

During the last week of summer school, Raquel had written

an entire report on scorpions for Mr. Espinoza, for extra credit because she'd lost the week of quarantine. Scorpions jabbed their prey with that tail, held it over their own head and sent that stinger down hard, paralyzed the bug or whatever, and then ate it. The acid dissolved the exoskeletons of their meal.

Top bunk. Every night she climbed up like a little kid. Like her father used to be. And heat rose, so she was suffocating now. Oasis. The fan pushed the hot air into her face. Her eyeballs dry like grapes in her skull.

She was a teenager, but she wasn't sleeping under the earth.

TOMORROW MORNING SHE would work in the date packinghouse from 7:00 to 8:00, then have coffee and burritos with her aunts for fifteen minutes and then log on for class at 8:30. She wished her mom could see her arranging the Medjool, Deglet Noor, and fresh Barhi dates on the platters for Muslim New Year. Al-Hijra. Her mom didn't even know about these holidays. Raquel had learned them all, the entire year of Ramadan and holy days.

She couldn't sleep like this. She had to call her mom, out in the trees where there was service. Swear to God, if her mom didn't answer soon, she was going to call Larette and ask if her mom had the virus.

She grabbed her boots from the foot of the bed. No way she'd leave them on the floor. She went back down slowly, using the flashlight to check all the baseboards. No blue scorpions. She slid her bare feet into the boots, put her phone into the pocket of her shorts, and went into the hallway. In a bed in the corner, by the window, so she could see the tops of the palms, Auntie Lolo was breathing deep.

Quietly, Raquel went into the bathroom, where the window was open.

She moved quickly into the first row of palms, heading toward the packinghouse, where cell service was best.

No call from her mother. No text.

She missed every single thing about home. Back in April and May, her mother had tried to be cheerful, texting Raquel that she was on the drive home, so please, baby, shake out the spiders really good and then get out the way. Raquel would go into the backyard, take the blue silk robe off the hook on the porch post and whip it six times into the hot spring wind, then sit in the wooden chair by the lemon tree. Her mother would come in through the gate, walk straight to the back porch, strip off her scrubs, and put them into the washing machine they'd moved outside. Her mother stood in her underwear, the boring white cotton Hanes bra and panties she'd ordered from Target so she wouldn't have to wreck her Victoria's Secret with all the bleach to kill the virus. She poured Tide and Clorox into the machine, and then she quickly took off the Hanes and threw them in there. Her hipbones stuck out like tiny baseballs on top of her legs when she moved fast to put on the robe. She never got to eat lunch now. She saluted Raquel and went inside to shower.

Once Raquel said, "Why do you even have Victoria's Secret? Why get all fancy?"

She meant her mom didn't go out anywhere. And her mother looked like she would break the steering wheel. She said, "I can have what I want. You're a baby, Raquel. You don't know anything yet."

And then that night, when they were eating Takis and watching Trixie Mattel, her mother said, "Okay. Because nurses gotta wear scrubs. Clogs. We gotta have something for ourselves. Even if no one sees it."

Back in the spring, while her mother disinfected, Raquel had to stay outside with her laptop, even though the Wi-Fi was weaker on the small cement patio with the ramada covered with palm fronds for shade. She always looked up at the brown fringes of last year's fronds. Her father had built the ramada when she was five. It was one of the few things she remembered about him. He had long black hair held back into six blue elastics. Dodger blue. His ponytail reached halfway down his back. He'd told Raquel to sit in her Dodgers canvas chair, safe under the eaves of the house, and he'd gotten out a machete and trimmed big fans of green fronds off the palm trees in the yard. Then he climbed up and spread them on the wooden structure. Together, they watched a game on the TV he brought outside, but Raquel remembered the magic: the light that shimmered through the green skin of the fronds, sparkled when the hot summer wind blew the fringes and sun got through.

Her mother worked evenings back then, at San Manuel Casino. She was a nurse there, for people who got sick because they forgot to take their heart meds, or drank too much, or fainted because they got scared, or pretended to faint so they could try to take money. Her father worked day security. They met getting coffee between shifts. They got married, and Raquel was born, and six years later, her father and his friend Benny went straight from San Manuel to Dodger Stadium for an evening doubleheader. The second game didn't end until midnight, and on the Golden State Freeway coming down toward the San Bernardino Freeway, a drunk driver going the wrong way hit them head-on.

Along the back fence, he'd grown those three palm trees for the fronds. Every year, she and her mother hoed out hundreds of baby palm seedlings like green knives along the sidewalk. On IG Reels and TikTok, people always made a big deal of filming in front of L.A. palm trees, the tallest, skinniest ones in Beverly Hills and Venice. Those weren't useful for anything. These were Washington palms, the ones native to here. Her father had grown them like corn or tomatoes.

He was born in Mecca, where date palm trees were crops in a field. He took her out to the desert when she was five, rode around with her on his horse, which still lived in a corral at Auntie Lolo's place. He held her up to the bunches of dates on the youngest trees and they looked like golden bubbles floating in the air.

After Raquel's father died, her mother never went back to the casino. She got a job with Larette, as an RN at Our Lady. She worked day shift—ten hours, four days a week.

Until corona.

School had closed March 17, and the district finally gave her a Chromebook in April. Raquel had freaked out until she got caught up by May 1. At STEM Academy, the end of freshman year was six weeks away and how the hell would they take finals?

HER BEST FRIEND, Akisha, loved virtual school. She did all her work. Then she made her TikToks. Her three Chihuahuas going crazy about all the UPS and FedEx trucks on their street, and she played "Please Mr. Postman." Akisha lived up near the Cajon Pass, in a big new two-story house, and her bedroom was upstairs. She had the whole setup for TikTok and IG Live in her room, with a walk-in closet for all her clothes, and a big mirror for her dance practice. Her dogs danced insane circles, skittering on the shiny black wood floor, like Akisha had trained them, while she played "My Lovin' (You're Never Gonna Get It)." They got 2.3 million views.

Her other close friends, Leilani and Marshall, loved virtual school, too. They had their rooms set up beautiful. Raquel's room was dim and brown. She kept her screen black when she could.

Raquel spent hours watching Akisha's TikToks. One day, she went into the backyard and sharpened her father's machete with the little diamond file in his toolbox. She put her phone on a chair and recorded herself cutting off palm fronds with as much flair as she could imagine. She sent it to Akisha, who replied, **U look like baby Gina Torres in some weird jungle movie with The Rock. Not a TikTok brand that's gonna get U followers! Stop!**

I'm tryin.

U look so good & U don't like 2 dance.

I got my dad's feet. I'm working on science. I don't have time 2 dance.

Everyone has time 2 dance now.

Mr. Espinoza, her bio teacher, worked them hard in May. One week, he gave them overviews of four different viruses—West Nile virus, SARS-associated coronavirus, hantavirus, and SARS-CoV-2. He told them, "Find the physical transmission methods and the humans and animals affected most. I will not condescend to you because you are home. I want you to think about careers in the medical field. Next week you will draw detailed illustrations of two of these viruses. Be prepared."

Her mother would come outside in her favorite pajamas, her wet hair in a towel, holding a Corona with lime wedged into the neck. That was their joke—she and Larette each drank one Corona at night.

"Mr. Espinoza?" her mother said, smiling.

"Mosquitoes transmit West Nile. Hantavirus was mice."

"So a mosquito bit a bird and then bit a human. But what did the mice do to the humans?" her mother said, looking at her. "For transmission?"

Raquel googled hantavirus; in 1993, there was an outbreak in the corners of New Mexico, Arizona, Utah, and Colorado. The Navajo Reservation. "Poop," she whispered. "It was in their poop and then in the dust, and when the wind blew people got it in their lungs."

"Jesus," her mother said. The sky was turning the darker blue of dusk. "Mr. Espinoza's trying to give me different nightmares?"

Raquel typed in *feces, mouse and rat.*

"The man doesn't play around," her mother said. "I put the rice on." She held out her hands. "Come on in. I'm clean."

ON JULY 5, Raquel had hosed off the patio, careful not to get her mother's robe wet. But that night her mother rushed in through the back gate, threw her uniform into the washer, and slammed down the lid without adding Tide. She grabbed the robe and began to sob. Her face collapsed. Raquel stood up by the lemon tree, but her mother put up her hands. "This fucking virus! Jesus help me. The cases are surging. They're asking us to stay in these trailers. To keep our families safe from the virus, and to keep us close to the hospital because we're so tired."

"A trailer? Like, we have to move?" Raquel said.

"No. Like, parked near the hospital. It's good—I can't bring this home to you. You're all I have, Raquel. But if I'm not here, that means you can't stay here."

"I'm fifteen!"

"You just turned fifteen last month! It's not safe. You have to go out to Lolo's."

Her mother showed Raquel pictures on her phone. Four little trailers parked fifteen feet from one another on a cul-de-sac. Donated by some guy. So the ICU nurses could live isolated and safe only three blocks from the hospital. "RVs," her mother said to someone that night, on the phone. Like they were giant houses on wheels, driven by old white men in the far lane of the freeway. The CamperWorld guy would keep an eye on the nurses, and they could walk back and forth to work, not touching anything, not falling asleep while driving. A nurse in L.A. had worked four twelve-hour shifts and died when her car drifted off the freeway.

"I'd be fine here," Raquel said desperately. "There's Mrs. Ralphine." The next-door neighbor had lived in her little house for her entire life. She was eighty-eight and looked out her window at the street all day.

"No, baby," her mother said. "Too many eyes to notice you here by yourself. Who's Mrs. Ralphine gonna chase down? It's safer in Oasis."

"I haven't been there for years. They still think I'm a baby." Raquel remembered her grandmother Sofelia and Auntie Lolo crying last time—saying she looked just like her father. Raquel had stood in the hot desert yard feeling like she'd stolen something.

Her mother couldn't come close to her. Couldn't put her hands on her shoulders or smooth back the hairs that always sprang up around Raquel's forehead when she was sweating. Her mother swayed in her robe and closed her eyes for a long time. Then she opened her eyes and said, "You're five-six already. They'll say you're as stubborn as your dad and as pretty as your mom. Go pack."

They drove through San Bernardino, Calimesa, and Morongo, through Cabazon, where Raquel's mother used to always stop at the dinosaurs.

Raquel fell asleep. She didn't wake up until the bumping of the car into the dirt parking lot. The big sign that said LOLO'S DATE GARDEN. All the palms were dark towers along the edge. Past the sign was the packinghouse, and then the adobe house. Auntie Lolo and Grandma Sofelia, wearing white T-shirts, sat like ghosts in the doorway of the house. Then her grandmother stood up, put her hands on her own face. Like that meme people made for the painting. *The Scream.*

"Cherrise," Grandma Sofelia said.

"Raquelli?" Auntie Lolo said in a muffled voice, and her mother started crying.

They stood ten feet apart, like a force field from a movie about aliens had fallen onto the front yard.

Her mother said, "You know she's gotta isolate six days. I coulda brought it home today. It could be in the car. In her hair."

Then her mother said to Raquel, "They say we're gonna get it under control. I'll be back to get you in August. That's what they told us. It'll be better in August."

For the first time in her life, Raquel wondered whether her mother was lying. Her mother never lied to her. She described how nasty the appendix looked in the surgery tray, how breasts looked when plastic surgeries got infected, how one patient with yellow eyes had jaundice and looked like a wolf at night in the dark of the hospital hallways.

"What I guess a wolf looks like," her mother said, that time, looking past Raquel into the backyard. "Your uncle Grief sees coyotes and even mountain lions. He said bobcats and lions' eyes are green in the dark. But this man had eyes so yellow around the iris, I got scared."

They'd always had an agreement. Only the truth. Raquel had never had anything to lie about. She went to school. She did her homework. She looked at everyone else's Instagram and TikTok. Snapchat back in the day.

Raquel said, "August? Seriously?"

"Yes," her mother said. Then she got back into the car.

Her grandmother and aunt moved away from the house. And Raquel took her suitcase inside, alone. Remembering there were only two rooms. She went into the darkness of the bedroom and closed the door.

SHE HAD SLEPT for an entire day. Woke at night with the heat pressing the breath from her. Or corona. She lay very still in the top bunk. Like a cave. Raquel held up her phone, only a few feet from the ceiling fan that clacked above her. No service.

Isolate. Intubate. Immolate. She wrote down vocabulary words on her legal pad. No Wi-Fi or data in the old adobe house. Raquel cried. She'd be six days behind in summer school. She read the poems in the book Mrs. Hua had assigned them. *Poetry of Nature and Resilience*. A poem about a fish with scales. A poem about an oak tree.

Three times a day, Auntie Lolo knocked on the only window in the bedroom. From outside. Her silhouette through the glass. She put foil-covered plates on the wooden shelf that used to hold the window cooler, outside. Her grandfather had lifted off the AC unit and set it on the ground, so Auntie Lolo could leave the food there. Raquel lifted the sash and took her meals inside.

Her aunt would come inside from the date garden, wash up in the bathroom, and say to her through the door, "Raquelli. Don't worry. Don't worry. If you are me, you've seen everything. This too shall pass. That's from the Bible."

Then Auntie Lolo would go to sleep, snoring like the low rumble from Raquel's street when Mr. Garibay left his truck on to warm up.

For three more days, Raquel opened the door once a day, after her aunt left. She took a bath in the tiny bathroom, spraying down the tub with Clorox, putting her wet hair in a bun and hoping that would help her stay cool.

She stared out her window at the date garden, the trees right at the edge of the yard. The silver palm trunks glowing like hundreds of IV poles in her dreams. One night she heard beeping like a heart rate machine and she freaked out until she found it. An old clock radio in a drawer.

She was so hungry she couldn't sleep. The plates were big: eggs and bacon and tortillas, enchiladas and tacos and carnitas with beans and rice. But she missed all the things she and her mother ate in bowls on the couch, watching *RuPaul's Drag Race*. Takis, Cocoa Puffs, the cinnamon twists called rugelach. Hot Cheetos.

On the fourth night, she couldn't stand it. She went out the window, crouching on the sandy earth near the window cooler. She nearly crawled to the edge of the date palms and sat there looking at the packinghouse. There had to be internet there—Lolo's Date Garden did mail orders.

A dish on the roof. She walked at the edge of the palms and sat behind one, near enough for a signal. Her mother had texted during her breaks. Twenty-two times. Raquel read them all.

Miss U my sweetie

Hope UR hydrating

Hot here today so it must be like hell out there I know but be patient

Larette had a little relapse. She has 2 get fluids so she's been in ER the whole day. She's better, tho. She can't get it again. We don't think. I'm ok. The trailer is tiny.

Raquel looked up at the sky. So dark in the Coachella Valley that she could see all the stars. The Milky Way. She'd forgotten this was the only place she'd ever seen the Milky Way, so long ago. Her cousin Dante was obsessed with stars and constellations. He'd told her the Milky Way was a long trail of trash. Debris. Space junk.

Raquel reached into the pocket of her sweats. She had stolen her mother's perfume. She touched the bottle.

When things were normal, her mother fell asleep in her scrubs. When things were normal, Raquel would watch one more show and finish her homework while her mother slept with her mouth open and her head on the back of the couch, and the smell of her JLo rose up from her throat. The traces left even after work. Then she'd startle awake and say, "Raquel Marigold Martinez, you better give me that phone, 'cause you're not staying up all night looking at stupid shit."

Now Raquel pictured her mother in the trailer. Was there even a couch? The tiny shower. What if the water pressure didn't get the corona out of her mother's hair?

Her aunt Larette had corona on July 5. Relapse? Shit.

Raquel read all the way to the last two texts.

I know UR safe because I haven't heard a thing.

I know UR in the little room with no service so I'm sorry about school, baby, UR a genius U catch up fast.

Raquel texted back. **The bunk bed is tiny. My feet R at the edge I feel like I'm sliding off. My teachers R prolly so mad but I'm gonna make up all the homework. When can I come home?**

Her mother texted back immediately. It was 9:50 p.m. Almost her mother's lunch. **Where RU?**

I just came outside 2 breathe. No 1here.

Go back inside. PLZ

THAT NIGHT, RAQUEL didn't go back inside. She held up her phone. Sound off. Data out here. All those dogs racing around houses. Lip-syncing. Akisha had posted seven TikToks of her Chihuahuas dancing to songs. Drake's "In My Feelings." Raquel watched until she was dizzy.

She had three voicemails. Akisha the first two, laughing about the weird poems Mrs. Hua had sent, about fish and chickens and camels, then asking where the hell Raquel was. The last one was her mother.

Crying. Saying clearly, like no mask: "Girl, I should get it. I want to just lean in and breathe that shit. Larette. You should just give it to me. Fucking virus. Then I can get it over with."

Her mother must have misdialed.

Her mother said, "I miss you, girl. I want to hear your voice on shift. Get better. These trailers are shit without you singing."

Raquel felt the tears like an explosion. She stuffed her T-shirt into her mouth. She waited until the spasms slowed down. Her mother missed Larette. Not her.

She stumbled into the palm trees, heading down one row

toward the glittering Salton Sea way in the distance. Black diamonds of light. Her phone was an aqua slice of light in her hand. Between the palm trunks, the long dirt hallways were dim.

A shadow moved through the trees, a white straw hat floating like a small planet. Stopping, sailing away again. He went down one more row and then disappeared. Raquel stopped.

But someone was following him. There was movement about six feet behind the white hat. Someone wearing black. A black baseball cap. He disappeared.

Raquel stood close to a palm trunk. The smell of water and metal lifted from the earth. Irrigation was at night, because the days were so hot the moisture would evaporate.

"Why you out here?"

She jumped. A black Raiders cap. Black T-shirt. A guy. Not that much older than Raquel. He stepped out from the other row. His eyes glittering. Bandanna around his mouth.

"I fucking live here now," she said. She backed away. Six feet. Seven feet.

"Don't lean against that tree," he said suddenly, voice even lower.

"What the hell?" Raquel had been reversing to lean against a palm. She turned around. A dark triangular stain seeped into the gray trunk.

The boy pulled down the bandanna. He took off his cap and rubbed his forehead with his arm. "Mi abuelo. He keeps peeing on the trees. I mean, we all gotta go. We figure it out while we're workin'."

Raquel rolled her eyes.

But he said, "He keeps pretending like he's checking the bark. But he's tired all the time. And he's peeing all day. He comes out here at night to see the irrigation and it's, like, every half hour. I been following him for a couple weeks. In case . . . I don't know."

"That's prostate," Raquel said without even thinking. The

pictures her mother had shown her of the gland, saying, *Well, women have ten things that go wrong when they get to be sixty, but men just have this one, and damn, they cry like babies about it.*

He sat down on the cement cistern a few feet away. "How do you know?"

"My mom's a nurse." And then she started to cry. She had to wipe her eyes with her T-shirt. The ground around her feet was black and shining with the recently run water in the long furrows.

"Wait, you're Señora Lolo's—"

"My dad was her nephew. Ronald Martinez."

"I remember him."

"He died. After a Dodgers game. A car accident."

"I remember," he said. "I'm sorry."

She went down on her knees for a minute. She couldn't stop crying. He thought she was crying about her dad.

He took off his shirt. "Here. The ground is wet. You can sit here."

He put the shirt on the cistern and then moved away into the row.

"This isn't some stupid Netflix movie," she said.

"No shit," he said. "In Oasis?"

She sat on the shirt. She wouldn't look at him now. His bare chest and stomach. "So he's afraid to go to the doctor?"

He shrugged. "Nobody wants to go near the clinic, ey?" He stared into the palms. "Everybody's getting sick in the Brussels sprouts and the beets. Because they have to be right next to each other. My cousins work in the fields."

"Your grandpa is Señor Ortiz," she said, remembering him now. The little white truck.

He nodded. "Gonzalo. My dad's Joseph. I'm Joey. I started here four years ago but only summer 'cause of school. But fuck it, corona, ey? I'm not going back for senior year. I gotta make some money." He lifted his chin. "What are you, like, a junior?"

He thought she was sixteen. Fine, she thought. "Yeah. STEM Academy in San Bernardino."

"Oh, so you're gonna be a doctor?" He raised his eyebrows.

She shook her head. "Research biologist."

"Damn."

"I had to come out here until—"

The wind blew between the palms, the smell of the Salton Sea like iron and fish. She was six feet from him. Her father was six feet under.

She drew up her knees and laid her cheek on the bones. Patellae, her mother had taught her years ago. Smelling the faint scent of Axe coming up from his shirt. Akisha was brutal about guys and Axe. His breath was quiet and watchful. The first coyotes sent up cries short and experimental toward the bright silver sky, and then one long howl that circled around and around for what seemed like forever.

He said, "What's your number?" He held out his phone, old and so cracked it looked like tree branches on the glass.

She hesitated.

"You can text me if you, like, need something. Or you want to talk. I'm out here every fucking night. Following him. Next month is harvest, and we work all the time. I sleep for, like, a few hours, and then I'm up in the trees."

Raquel put her number into his phone, and he texted her. She saved his contact under *Raiders*. Then she went back down the row and he picked up his shirt.

HE HAD TEXTED her once. August 1. **U cool?**

She sent, **I guess.**

Most nights, she could see the headlights moving like tiny blurry stars through the palms, and she knew Joey was out there, but she stayed away.

NOW SHE STOOD in the hallway of palms leading to the packinghouse. Texts pinged in from Akisha, from the group chat, spam about clothes and jewelry.

Nothing from her mother.

Where R U?

Mom. They said Virtual school 4ever. I need 2 come home. I cant handle 1 more week I swear

2moro I start work in the packinghouse.

U don't even know how hard it is

Auntie Lolo says she's proud of me 4 working

????? Srsly

Fine I'm going 2 the cemetery Wed 2 see dad don't worry about it

Raquel kept walking, toward the smell of the water. The harvest had started this weekend. The crew was working in the Barhi date palms, near the Salton Sea. Now she could hear music, and voices. It was cooler to work at night. Joey was probably out here with his grandfather.

She headed down the corridors between palms, crossed one work road. The music came from the older part of the gardens. Lolo said these were Deglet Noor, over sixty years old, the first hundred trees Lolo's mother had planted. Their trunks were tall and straight, with ancient wooden ladders nailed to the top half. Raquel stopped to listen. A thread of music. Oldies, like her neighbors played back home in San Bernardino. Someone laughing. She moved into the next row, stepping over the damp weeds that grew between the palms. Not the white truck—a big black pickup. A pair of white boots dangling off the bed, like that was the person laughing. Raquel stepped across the water in the furrows, stepped through the grass growing between the trunks, and hoped Señor Ortiz wouldn't be startled by her.

But Joey's abuelo wasn't there. A guy sitting in the truck bed, wearing a black uniform. White rubber boots. He was laughing at Joey, who was on a tall metal ladder that met up with the old wooden ladder. Joey was putting brown paper over a big bunch of dates that dangled heavy. He tied it with string and then climbed back down the ladder, jumping the last four feet onto the ground.

She stepped forward.

He said, "Shit, don't scare me like that! I thought you were a ghost."

Raquel stared at Joey. "Did something die out here? It smells like death."

He laughed. "That's his truck. Fish death."

The other guy said, "Who the fuck are you?"

Joey said, "Raquel. Señora Lolo's family." He took two steps toward her, then looked back. "This is my cousin. Beto."

His boots were bright against the dark night. How could he climb ladders in boots? she thought.

But Beto said, "This motherfucker gotta tie paper around every bunch. Five or six bunches on every tree. That's a lotta climbing, monkey boy."

Joey lifted his chin. "You gotta throw fish food into the ponds at midnight. That shit stinks."

Raquel looked up at the chandeliers of golden dates, and suddenly she saw them, when her father held her in his arms, lifted her toward them. Gold bubbles. She bent to pick up one that had fallen. No bubble. Hard and unripe, of course. All the dates coming down the conveyor belt in the packinghouse. She was thinking of anything so she wouldn't cry. They'd think she was weak. A stupid sad-girl meme. Her mom hated those memes.

Then she was sadder about her mother. Focus. Focus. Science. Science is immutable. Dante always said, *The stars don't change unless they blow up.*

Raquel took three breaths. She said to Joey, "What does the paper protect from?"

He looked surprised. "Moisture on the dates. Bugs. We don't harvest these till last. October for Deglet Noor."

"What kind of bugs?" she said.

"What the fuck kinda question is that?" Beto said.

"Extra credit," she said.

"Oh, extra credit." He even made that sound bad. "Two high school sweethearts."

Joey started up the ladder again. "Fuck you, bro. I'm done with school. The Wi-Fi at home doesn't even work half the time, fool."

Raquel said, "You can tell me about the specific insects another time."

Beto hopped off the truck and said, "You a brainiac, eh? But you look good. Primo here says you're gonna be a fuckin' scientist. But you could be a model."

Raquel said, "Models don't get to talk."

Beto cocked his head at her. "I gotta get to work. You see the truck, eh? I got my own place. This fool ain't got shit. But he can climb."

Joey said, "You used to climb, too." He moved the ladder around the trunk.

"Not now," Beto said. He looked at her again. "I work security for Coachella in April. People tip me, like, two hundred dollars to let them cut the line. So you're a junior, eh? We could kick it sometime. Go to a party or whatever."

Raquel didn't like his eyes on her shirt. On her legs. She went fast to the first rung, and headed up the trunk, before Joey could say no. Four rungs up, someone called, "Vamos al pescados, cabrón."

Señor Ortiz came down the row, his creamy straw hat glowing, his face invisible. He pointed to Beto. Beto headed toward the parking lot.

A glint of gold when Señor Ortiz smiled at her and pointed at the top of the palm.

She went up a few more rungs. Joey and his grandfather held on to each side of the ladder. The Deglet Noor trunks were trimmed into perfect diamond patterns, by Señor Ortiz's machetes all these years, she knew. Did she remember him slicing off the thorns of the new fronds, too? So long ago? She went higher and higher, the sugary smell of a few early dates ripe already.

How did Joey do this all day and night? The backs of her thighs were already burning. They better not be looking up at her ass. In the sweats. Glad she'd been afraid of scorpions.

But she'd reached the top of the metal ladder. "How high is this?" she called, not looking down.

"Thirty-two feet," Joey called up.

She wasn't going to touch the ancient wooden ladder nailed to the top of the trunk. He didn't go all the way up those, did he?

She put her hand on the bark. Don't look down.

Deglet Noor. The bunches hung just above her. These weren't the golden bubbles like Barhi. Deglet Noor were longer, pale green, dangling heavy from the end of bright orange stems. They were her mother's favorite—dark capsules of dense sweet that looked like wrinkled cigar stubs.

My dad used to climb up here, she thought. Maybe he climbed this tree. She put her hand on the bark. Maybe he put his hand right here to rest for a minute.

She lifted her head. Down the rows was the Salton Sea. Glittering black. The mountains dark purple on the other side. The rows and rows of shorter palms—the Medjools and Barhis, their fronds like hundreds of feather dusters.

And the cemetery was to the east. Only seven miles away. She'd googled the location. When her mother brought her, they were both so scared they didn't even think to visit his headstone.

She steadied herself. Then the loud vibration of an engine

starting. Revving. She held tight to the top rung and looked toward the packinghouse. Beto's truck. He spun the tires, left veils of dust hanging in the air when he raced out toward the road.

Raquel took the first careful step down. Beto could give her a ride to the cemetery on Wednesday. If her mom didn't come.

Her friends all wanted her to take pictures in Coachella, because they thought she was right next to the music festival. Maybe Beto could give her a ride there, and she could take pics where Beyoncé had stood.

Joey was there waiting at the bottom rung, and he held out his hand, but she jumped down.

He said real low, "You don't want to hang out with my primo. For reals, though."

She looked away from his angry eyes. He didn't know anything about her.

If her mom got corona, Raquel could pay Beto for a ride. She was going to make $12 an hour this week packing custom boxes of dates for Al-Hijra. And she had $128 in her room, back in San Bernardino.

If she had to run away.

No.

If she had to run home.

FOUR ✦ Gone the Sun

LARETTE DIDN'T SEE THE CRAPE MYRTLE BLOSSOMS IN Pam Ott's hair until they were almost in the hospital parking lot. She said, "Wait up, Indiana!"

Two circlets of pink blooms. Ruffled and delicate, one resting on the top of her head and one on her shoulder, bright against the blue scrubs.

Larette plucked them off and handed them to Pam. "It would scare me if I took off my PPE and something fell into the sink."

Pam took a picture of them in her own palm for Jonah. "These were in Mommy's hair from the trees, baby! See you tomorrow, my love!"

He murmured, half asleep. She kissed the screen and put the phone in her pocket.

Over the blue surgical masks, they put on their second masks—the black N-95s.

They walked through the families parked on the street leading to the hospital, people camped out in cars, sleeping with the seats back. On the grassy hill near the main parking lot, people sitting in lawn chairs, children on blankets, separate islands of humans talking on phones, playing games on phones, staring at the hospital windows waiting for their loved one to be able to stand with the help of a nurse and wave. Signs lying next to the lawn chairs— DAD WE LOVE YOU. GET WELL SOON. Hearts and flowers drawn with markers. American flags, Dodgers flags, Angels flags, Raiders flags, Rams flags. All the tribes camped like they were waiting for a parade. They wanted their loved one to be able to look down and see them.

The big white tents of the triage area like a circus.

When the four nurses made their way through the parking lot toward the ER entrance, a woman said, "There they are!" She motioned to her son, who stepped forward and lifted a box of doughnuts and two four-packs of Starbucks coffee. He bowed his head, the part in his blond hair pink. The security guard motioned for him to leave the food at end of the check-in table.

Larette bowed back. A crowd of people lined up six feet apart.

Then a woman hustled up to them, saying, "You're Larette Embers, right? That lady over there, Dolores something, she said you're the one who sings."

Larette saw the quiver of flesh on the freckled arm when the woman raised her finger and pointed toward the parking lot. Dolores was Crescencio Sotelo's wife.

Marisol stepped forward and said, "You the daughter, yeah? Of Beverly. Mrs. Ember will call you later. Thank you."

Cherrise came up behind her. "I'll take the doughnuts to Aparicia in Housekeeping. Go. Just take five more minutes by yourself. The rock maze. Go."

LARETTE WALKED AWAY from the crowd. Walked fast toward the physician parking lot, on the side of the building. Past that were three cement benches, set apart. The only place to sit. Two of the respiratory therapists were there, talking across the space, holding cold sodas. Past them was the small gravel lot with a circle of stones arranged for meditation walking. No phones allowed.

Three women pacing carefully, slowly, distanced, their heads down.

She stood in the physician lot, stared up at the sky through the old jacaranda trees here. Vespertine hour. It was Grief who taught Dante that. The hour when the small animals come out for the cool, and the predators come out half an hour later to find them. When the day birds make their last sounds, and the night birds make their first sounds. The last butterfly. The first cricket.

A car pulled into the lot but didn't park. Dr. Yoon's black Audi. He got out from the passenger seat.

He'd come to Our Lady last year, to be supervising physician in the ICU. When they met in the nursing station, he said to Larette, "My first name in English is John. When I came to America, I was six. My father told me that was the best name to have here. Because you could be anyone."

Now he walked around to the driver-side window, which slid down, and he leaned in to kiss his wife. All Larette could see was her pale perfect cheek, and her fingers on his shoulder—her nails painted light blue. Then the back window slid down, and another hand lifted, frozen in the air to wave. The last two fingers missing, and a big diamond ring on the middle finger.

Dr. Yoon lifted his hand, and the car slid away. He turned to nod at Larette, but he didn't speak until they started back toward the hospital entrance. He said, "My wife and my mother are going up to Pearblossom. In the desert. They will not come back until—" He rubbed his eyes.

His hair was glossy and black, combed back severely from his forehead; he wore a perfectly ironed long-sleeve blue shirt and dress pants. He felt he should look professional under the layers of protection.

His English was always formal and correct. "I heard you speaking with your son last night. About meteors."

Larette usually called Dante here, just beside physician parking. Dante had been fascinated since he was five with constellations, meteor showers, black holes. This summer, he was obsessed with which insects and animals would survive nuclear annihilation. "I missed the Perseids ten days ago," she said. "But the Epsilon Perseids might show up early September. He's hoping for optimal conditions."

Dr. Yoon smiled, always the same considerate flash. He rarely showed his teeth. He said, "Ten years ago, my parents bought twenty acres up in Pearblossom. They have an orchard. Thirty pear trees like they had back in Korea, in the 1950s. They like the cold winter. Some snow even. You can see every star so much better than down here." He looked up at the hospital. "My mother and father were very young and just married during the war. They had to walk through the snow for days, hiding from the North Korean and Chinese troops. My mother lost four fingers and three toes to frostbite. But she loves to sit out in the snow here in California. She says she can let it fall on her until she decides to go inside her house with the heated tile floors. Every night, I think that I paid for her floors with these floors."

They went inside.

IT WAS LIKE trudging underwater all night, in a movie where people wore special suits to traverse the bottom of the ocean. The nurses on shift lifted their feet only a few inches and shuffled forward, the refrigerated air swirling around them.

Larette texted Dante to ask him the name of the deepest part of the sea.

U could google it URself

She couldn't respond to say she could barely see, for most of her shift, except when she was FaceTiming with families. That would scare him. Anyway, she never chose the right combination of words for what she wanted to know.

U can say it to UR phone

She couldn't text him back: **I just wanted to know. It doesn't** matter. She was on the second flight of stairs. She stopped and tried to breathe.

Mariana Trench. Between Guam and the Philippines. Other kids ask their moms stuff. U always ask me.

She was coming back from a ten-minute break. 9:17 p.m. She'd ducked into the corner of the stairwell on each floor, waiting to catch her breath. Catch it. Like it was running. She'd never catch it, because she could barely walk some nights.

At certain hours, she still couldn't breathe. She made herself take the stairs to the third floor, over and over during the night, even though she could feel her lungs as pocked and dry as the green florist foam blocks from all the dead bouquets trashed outside in the courtyard. The gift shop full of gurneys and beds. Gurneys crowded at the chapel doors like goats trying to get into the corral at her neighbor's ranch.

She pushed open the ICU doors. The Mariana Trench. The hallway. She was so tired, dragging her feet along the ocean sand in the PPE always too big—the coveralls baggy over her scrubs, the cap over her hair, the elastic riding down her forehead, the two surgical masks, the plastic face shield, gloves and booties. Each window looked like an aquarium, showing patients intubated, as if snakes were sucking out the air rather than giving it.

The first window—Marisol bending over a patient, Pam crouching to reach a catheter bag. Both patients face down to help them breathe. Naked under the winding of sheets. Their soft white or brown or golden shoulders covered with hair or smooth as satin. Their butts big and soft or flat as nopales cactus. The soles of their feet like pale slugs glowing in the greenish light.

The third door opened and Cherrise came out with a sheet soaked in sweat. Stan Earley's room. Behind the three masks, Cherrise said, "Fucking bin is full again. He's drowning."

Inside Larette's head, her own heartbeat still whooshing in the middle ear, the brain ache constant like too-tight braids when she was a child. When Larette had corona, Cherrise did not leave her side for days. Cherrise's long fingers in latex tracing Larette's jawline, her temples, when she woke.

She had not been intubated. She'd prayed every day that Dr. Yoon would try everything to avoid that. She'd stood countless times beside someone's bed when the sedative was added to the IV line, watching the faces blur and go slack, the mouth drop open. All these years of singing onstage, shaping her lips and tongue around the lyrics and feeling the vibrations of her vocal cords, standing in front of the mirror to practice and seeing the thin ropes rise along her throat when she sang hard. Watching the rigid plastic forced down past the magic that made humans able to hum and lie and whisper and moan scared the shit out of her.

It had been a messy intubation, failed, that got her sick. She knew. The mask had been slipping, one substandard mask with a strap that kept loosening, and the patient was very large, and the throat muscles lax, and the sedative not enough—he coughed violently and the tube flew from Dr. Yoon's fingers and the spray of saliva and mucus terrified them, the three in their face shields like welders and the sparks invisible. Two days later her fever was 105 and she slid down the wall in the break room, where Cherrise found her.

SHE WENT INTO the nursing station. Mariah Ball, the charge nurse, left her chair only for the bathroom, and for her lunch at midnight. "You need coffee?" Larette asked, but Mariah lifted her elbow to the Dodgers thermos on her right, never stopping her fingers flying over the keyboard. She was fifty-five, started at Our Lady when she was twenty-one, knew everyone and everything about the hospital.

The whiteboard covered half the wall. Fourteen beds on the

ICU ward. Two new patients, two hours ago. Because Julio Hernandez and Bob Shoemaker had died just as the shift began. She and Cherrise had disconnected their IVs and pulled the needles from the protesting skin and the catheters from their sad penises and the breathing tubes from their throats. She and Cherrise had used wipes to clear the dried foam and saliva from the corners of their mouths and the deep wrinkles in their cheeks. They were men who had worked hard. Hernandez missing two fingers on his left hand, at the second knuckle. Shoemaker with calluses that had turned white and soft during his ten days here, so that when Larette turned over his palm, it was as if small shells had been glued at the pads below his fingers.

Tonight she had Crescencio Sotelo. And Beth Beverly.

BY 12:20 A.M., Beth Beverly was failing. She'd come in at 7:40 p.m. the previous Sunday. Those stubby little feet older women had, flopping to the side while the EMTs rolled the gurney up. Thick-soled brown clogs. The women—their sensible work shoes, their swap-meet sandals, kitten heels if they'd been at church, huaraches if they had been in the garden when they fell. Beth Beverly was still mildly animated that night, lying on the gurney with enough energy to hold on to her glasses. Larette walked alongside, seeing the high hump of stomach under the sheet.

Now, outside the nursing station, Dr. Yoon was waiting for Larette. Nancy Kriele, the anesthesiologist, was headed down the hallway toward 3009.

"She came in Sunday night, correct?" Dr. Yoon said.

"I saw her. She was pretty good."

"Yes, she had symptoms, but she had fallen and hit her head. That's why the daughter called EMT," he said.

Larette followed him down the ICU hallway, crowded with crash carts and IV poles. A terrible glittering forest. They put on new PPE outside 3009, the gown and gloves and extra mask, mushroom cap and face shield. The rush of negative pressure in the room sucked at Larette's chest under the uniform and gown.

Beth Beverly was gasping for breath, her mouth open like a baby bird's, like all the other mouths, the animal impulse to throw back the head as if the air would slide down better. Coyote and lion and bird with tongue to the sky. Nancy Kriele looked up at them; when they were ready, she added the sedation to the IV line. Larette held up the roof of Beth Beverly's mouth, her two gloved fingers hooked and pushing up on the hard cartilage. Her face shield misted, and she held her own breath so it could clear for two seconds, long enough to see the epiglottis heavy as a baby pear.

Pearblossom, the stars, flakes of snow on Dr. Yoon's mother's feet. What shoes did she wear when she sat in her high desert yard with her own face lifted to the falling sparkles of California that belonged to her?

The vocal cords alongside the exposed throat, and Dr. Yoon held the stiff curve of tubing and waited for exactly the right moment to slide it down the tiny channel of this woman's whole existence if she were anything like any of us who needed to speak and laugh and sing and whisper to someone, anyone, and the plastic entered her body and the machine whooshed and began to breathe for her.

AN HOUR LATER, Larette called the first number on the file. Lisa Beverly. The daughter. The woman who'd come up to her in the parking lot.

"Oh my god, thank you for calling, I've been going crazy, how is she, how's my mom?"

Larette told Lisa all that had happened in the exact shorthand she used for everyone, the basics she could use unless the family member was in the medical field and knew too much and wanted more specifics. Lisa Beverly was a preschool teacher, had lived with her mother in Calimesa for the last ten years since her divorce. "My mom was a Girl Scout troop leader for thirty years," she said. "I grew up in the scouts, we went camping all the time in Big Bear."

Beth Beverly was seventy-two, her weight was 187, and she had diabetes. Larette closed her eyes, envisioning the hundreds of Thin Mints she had eaten herself, bought from all the daughters of housekeeping and nursing staff. *An entire box of chilled Thin Mints, with coffee, for breakfast*, Mariah Ball always said. *Possibly the best tradition of the American woman.*

Larette said, "I bet you all cooked in those foil packets over the fire—somebody told me that. In high school. They said it was the best dinner they ever had."

Then Lisa Beverly began to sob. "Hobo supper," she said. "That's what we called it. Can you imagine saying that now? We taught the girls to cut up the potatoes and carrots on a board out there by the fire."

Larette said, "I'll be taking good care of your mom all night, okay? Probably tomorrow, too, because I have the same shift. I will be right beside her."

"Can I see her on FaceTime?"

"You don't want to do that yet," Larette said smoothly. "She needs the rest, and so do you." She paused. It would be astonishing if Beth Beverly lasted two more days. "You asked me to sing? Keep her company? What's her favorite song?"

Larette looked at the whiteboard covered with black marker, Mariah's old-school cursive beautiful and slanted on each name for each room.

"You won't know it," Lisa Beverly said, crying harder. "It's 'Taps.'"

Larette rolled her eyes. She knew it instantly. "You mean the song where y'all say goodnight?" She sang some of the words softly.

"Yes," Lisa Beverly said, almost inaudible through her sobbing.

Larette said, "I will update you in the morning, before I go home, okay?"

"Unless something happens," Lisa whispered.

"We're gonna make it through the night," Larette said.

SHE DRANK COFFEE from her thermos, using a paper cup. Wiped her face with a paper towel, hating the smudges of lotion and oil and sweat from her forehead, translucent on the rough white. She went back toward room 3009.

New white coveralls, then the thin blue gown that covered her front and shoulders. New gloves. Face shield. The door hissed shut. Beth Beverly's feet and calves white in the fluorescent light. Her belly rising and falling hard, like always when the ventilator breathed for a human. Temp still 103. Corona's ravaging assault on the tissues and organs, and the body affronted and angry sending back its heat.

"Like *The Avengers*," Dante would say, even two months ago, when she could watch a Marvel show with him on a Sunday while her clothes rumbled in the dryer.

She loved *The Avengers*, even though *Guardians of the Galaxy* had the music.

Dante would wait at least an hour into a movie, then ask casually what a few bodies had done that week, how each human was different in response. "So the virus attacks the lungs for some people. And, like, kidneys for somebody else. Like, it throws whatever power it thinks will work?"

"Right," Larette said, her feet bare and up on the coffee table. Not swollen and hot inside sneakers and booties. She used to paint her toenails on that day off. Essie's brightest gold.

Now she used cooling wipes on Beth Beverly's swollen calves and feet, because fever was partially soothed there, not just the forehead. Larette's face shield fogged up immediately when she bent and lifted the sheet.

Dante listed the powers for her. "Ghost Rider has the hellfire chain," he said. "Storm has, like, the weather. She can bust your eardrum with atmospheric pressure. And Blade—" He didn't look at her. "His mother got bitten by a vampire when she was, like, having him. He's got so much shit he can do."

She always said the most basic things, she knew. She just liked all the movement on the TV screen, all the colors, Dante's leg near hers.

"It doesn't matter because Thanos just kills everyone," Dante said softly, staring at the blocky figure on the TV.

Now she put her gloved hands on Beth Beverly's forehead, the skin so pink it looked like a child had gone crazy with blusher. "I'm going to swab out your mouth, Beth," she said, close to the earlobe bright red. "I'm sorry if it's uncomfortable." She maneuvered a new moist swab around the mouth, the corners of the woman's lips vibrating with the pulsating machine. *Hiss, thump. Hiss, thump.* Sometimes Larette woke in the trailer in the middle of the morning panicked, hearing nothing, thinking the power had gone out in the hospital and each person would suffocate while she slept.

She checked the ventilator tubes, IV lines, the catheter. Very little urine, dark as tragic Kool-Aid, the color Larette always saw when the body was dehydrated. She held her phone. She only knew the first verse by heart. *Day is done, gone the sun, from the lake, from the hills, from the sky . . .* She sang the verses five times. Earworms that would stay in her head for hours. *A star gems the sky, gleaming bright.* Now she missed Dante even more.

She said, "I'll be back, Beth." She went outside, stripped off the PPE, breathing hard herself after the singing behind the two masks, the sweat above her lip. She threw everything in the huge square plastic bin; all night, the containers filled with plague were taken to the basement. Marisol lifted her hand, two doors down, entering 3005. Cherrise had just come out of 3002.

Across the hallway, she looked into the window at Crescencio Sotelo. At his feet. He'd been in a coma for six days, but he'd wiggled his feet. Opened his eyes briefly. She stood beside his bed. Not intubated—he had a tracheotomy, the tube springing from his throat. His mouth open. She swabbed it with moisture. He was coming back, though. His fever down to 99. His body recovering. He was thin. His wife, Dolores, said he'd always been a fighter because he was flaco, and his arms were still roped with muscle.

She touched the baby finger on his left hand. Still pale green with car paint. Still a few sparkles on his skin from the paint sprayer.

When he awakened, Larette would have to tell him about his best friend. The one who'd helped him paint his 1964 Impala for a car show. They weren't supposed to be in the driveway together. But they had worked on the car for four days.

They were admitted one day apart.

Rudy Magana.

She'd have to tell Crescencio that Rudy had died. She swabbed his mouth out once more, checked all the lines holding him in the bed like Gulliver, his feet splayed apart, his big toenail on the left foot still black from where he must have dropped a hammer or tool, back when they were in the garage laughing.

FIVE ✦ The Benches

FROM THE FOURTH-FLOOR WINDOW, SHE COULD SEE MILES into Southern California, all the cities laid out in a grid of jeweled lights, the freeways lacing through like rivers. Larette kept thinking of all the hospitals, named for saints and places and mountains and people, holding thousands of humans tethered to the beds by tubes. Pulling in the refrigerated air, trying to breathe, while everyone in the parking lots below felt the heat linger in the night. Waiting.

Tonight the lights of the city looked like shallow waves lapping at the edges of the San Bernardino Mountains. Our Lady was the tallest building here, and Larette always looked at the gleaming shape of the white arrowhead etched into the slopes. A rockfall centuries ago that left behind pale stones. Every night, when she left the hallway of icy controlled air, the constant whooshing of machines and gurneys, and descended the stairs, the first thing she touched outside was the warm stone wall that led to their secret place in the far courtyard. The original chapel building and the hospital, built in 1900, were edged with stones, and low stone walls led to the edge of the complex, where she met Marisol at 2:00 a.m.

"Contraband," Marisol said. She took the pack of Lucky Strikes out of her scrubs pocket.

Larette handed her two fives. "Thanks."

Marisol took out her single Swisher Sweet.

They had started one night in July, during the beginning of the surge. At the 2:00 a.m. break, Larette was walking in the rock maze, and Marisol stood at the edge, saying, "Where we can smoke?"

No tobacco allowed anywhere on the hospital campus. She walked with Marisol across the small lane separating the hospital from the old nuns' quarters, now offices, and the cemetery, which was public. She showed Marisol the tree.

Four cement benches were set in a square under the ancient sycamore tree, the white-barked branches horizontal and thick with golden-green leaves big as baseball mitts. The statue of Our Lady of Sorrows, her palms held to the sky, watched them pull out their lighters.

That first night, Larette sat with Marisol. "My bad secret," Marisol said, lighting the cigarillo. The smell faintly sweet, perfect, dry, and brown. Larette held out her hand for one.

"At home, my sisters find and take away," Marisol said, lighting Larette's from her ember. "But I smoke this one every night, for my grandmother. She have a pipe, when I am a little girl. When we walk in the forest, she keep the smoke around us so we safe. The spirit know we are come." She took a deep drag and let out the cloud. "I smoke this one same reason."

The only time they saw each other's mouths all night. Larette missed her makeup kits and the mirror in her bedroom at home, with the bright bulbs. Her costumes and shoes. Her boas and gloves. Her scripts. To sing behind the masks now, to sing inside her head, to sleep in the tiny trailer and wake up remembering the lyrics to songs from *Kinky Boots*. Which she wouldn't sing, because the 2020 show had been canceled.

She looked at Marisol's lips around the cigarillo, that first night, and breathed in deep.

Marisol told her she was born on a tiny farm in the forest, outside of Manila. She said her mother and grandmother had enemies, and when she was a girl, walking home through the trees, two women came to attack them. A black dog and a black bird, their souls transformed into things that swept down from branches and appeared from behind vines. Real animals that bit Marisol in the calf, bit her mother in the arm. The bird pecked a hole into her chest. She pulled the neck of her scrubs to show Larette the scar. A deep dent in the tender skin above the clavicle. A divot. Larette shivered. Meat taken away in a beak.

"Maria," Marisol said. "My mother take the man Maria want. Before I born. She punish me for punish my mother. My blood to make cry."

Larette tasted the sweet tobacco. Grief wouldn't believe she could be this foolish. But she saw the beautiful sudden sparkle of her mother's Lucky Strike. In the Las Palmas complex, they had lived in number 17, on the second floor. Cherrise and her mother lived next door. In the summer, like now, Larette's mother used to walk her down to the rectangle of lawn behind the wrought iron gate, near the pool, and say, "Long as you got a patch of grass, you can lay down and listen."

Larette could hear tiny insects moving in the blades. The gurgle of the pool. The thumping bass of cars passing by on the street. But filtered through the grass, the music was like the earth's heart beating. Then brief moments of nothing—nobody laughing or shouting, no cars—when the grass glistened with dew coming up from underneath, somehow. Coming from the center of the earth. Her mother's lips on the cigarette. The hiss of breath and then smoke rings above her like the rings of Saturn.

NOW THERE WERE four of them, under the tree. Near Our Lady of Sorrows.

"So many ladies," Mariah Ball said, lighting her Marlboro. Taking the first deep inhale. "Perpetual Help. Hope."

"Succor," Natalie King said. She was a phlebotomist. She lit up a Virginia Slim. She said that was what her mother and her aunt had smoked, when they worked here years ago. They'd smoked with Larette's mother. Larette's mother used to mention them. *Two ladies from Bowlegs, Oklahoma, loved them some fried chicken and Virginia Slims.*

Back then, they didn't have to come all the way out to these benches. They had picnic tables just outside the maintenance area. But this tree and the benches technically belonged to the city, though the hospital chapel was only twenty feet away, across the narrow dead end. Since Covid, it was where patient families sat during the long days to smoke and cry and pray.

Louie Lozano, the night security guard, always patrolled here—the staff who smoked came out at 1:00, or 2:00, or 3:00, and Louie played his flashlight on the tree. He washed down the benches, the tree trunk, and the surrounding cement every night when he came on shift.

"Happy Monday already," Louie said now. "Them benches, they're like the trenches, eh? Like my dad said he was in the trenches somewhere. With his homeys. At night."

"Where?" Mariah called.

"Korea." He walked off to patrol the hospital entrance.

Marisol said, "Our Lady of Lourdes." She lit her Swisher Sweet. "That where we go in Manila, when we go to town."

"Where did you go to church at home?" Larette said, getting out her pack. One Lucky Strike. One.

Marisol laughed. "We go to the forest. We have a shrine. We smoke the cigar—bigger than this. To call the spirit for good. And make the bad go."

They were quiet then. Blowing out the smoke in opposite directions so it didn't go into their faces, eyebrows, skin. Their hair was covered with caps, their scrubs with the paper gowns. The smell lingered on them, of course, but they sprayed lavender Febreze that Mariah Ball kept in her bag. She and Natalie King had joined Larette and Marisol the third week. If there was no patient crashing at the moment of the 2:00 a.m. break, Mariah left Pam and Cherrise in charge for fifteen minutes.

"Did you see the tattoos on Bill McInnis?" Mariah said finally. "He survived World War II and the Korean War, and fucking Nineteen takes him out."

Larette hadn't heard her like this. The tattoos—dark blue insignia of the Marine Corps and some names, blurred with the fall of his crepey arm skin. "His wife told you?"

Mariah nodded.

Natalie said, "I used to see Mr. McInnis in the lab. He would always joke about his heart, after he had the bypass."

Mariah said, "They'll never call this a war. We can't be fucking soldiers because, A, no guns. B, we're female. And, C, they don't believe in the enemy. Nothing to shoot. Just a fucking cartoon floating around on their TV or whatever."

Mariah kept her elbows on her knees, head down. She sat like a man. The ember of her cigarette pulsing.

Mariah always said she couldn't tell her kids anything about the ICU. "My son would want to break something," she said. "Because he's twenty-four and all they do is break stuff. My daughter would be mad at me. No matter what. Because she's a twenty-two-year-old college student majoring in fuck-you-Mom."

None of us are telling anyone we love about anything, Larette thought. I met Marisol in April, and she knows everything about me right now.

Natalie's feet in her black Crocs. Mariah's K-Swiss sneakers. Marisol's Dansko clogs that her younger sister Jasmine had gotten free from promoting them on her #nursetagram and #scrublife. Jasmine was @nursebabyqueen; she had 24K followers and had just started working again tonight at a hospital in San Francisco.

Larette's Pumas. Grief and Dante had bought her new Pumas for her birthday.

She hadn't told Grief anything true for weeks.

She'd known Natalie for years. Natalie had a firefighter husband. She wasn't telling him shit, either.

Larette said, "Your mom was a legend in Neonatal."

Natalie nodded, blowing out a smoke ring. "She taught me to do this. She smoked one cigarette a night, her and my aunt Minnie. Just one. *My only vice,* she used to say. *But don't take that half hour away from me.*" She laughed. "They had half an hour. We're lucky to get fifteen minutes."

"Don't look at your phone," Mariah said. "Or you'll get five."

Larette stared into the branches of the sycamore. *Only one,* her mother used to say, when Larette was small. *I smoke out there to keep me company, when I miss my grand-mère. I had to work in the cane field with her, when I was twelve. She smoke a pipe, she still did. Her mama smoke a pipe. Back in slavery time.*

Larette drew in one last drag. Why did we call it a drag? Not a breath? Who made up *drag?* Probably some soldier, during some war. She pushed the ember into the bucket of sand at the edge of the cement square.

She said to them all, "My mom used to say only one thing nobody can snatch from you, baby. Can't snatch your smoke. Can't catch it."

Then she stood near the river rock marker with the empty rectangle. The bronze plaque about the tree, the chapel, the statue—stolen last month. For the second time. Melted down in some recycling place. For a smoke of fentanyl or meth. A breath of high.

The sweetness of Marisol's cigarillo spread into the breeze. Kept the spirits away.

"We carry the baby through the smoke when they born," Marisol told Larette the first night they came out here. "The mother, she sit over another smoke. Keep the spirit away from her body."

When they came back, after that first night at the benches,

Mariah froze as they passed her desk and the whiteboard. She smelled them. Mariah said, "Well, hell, if you two are gonna partake, I'm going out there, too."

Now Marisol left the last half of the cigarillo in the sand. She never finished one. She said, "Somebody come get. They watch from the street. They see the lighter."

Mariah said, "Come on, you gotta start throwing those away. They're covered with virus."

Marisol said, "You don't see me put there. Those men go in the trash. They need this smoke, too. Why I make them touch nasty?"

Larette went last, single file, the kindergarten line again. Six feet apart or six feet under.

Eight feet to cover in booties when they got through the parking lot where the blue lights of phones floated everywhere in the hands of people staring up at the windows. When the four women went inside carrying dust on their shoes, from the sycamore leaves into the cold, cold hallways.

PART TWO

SIX ✦ Cabrón

IT WAS JUST AFTER 1:00 A.M. WHEN I PUT ON MY FLASHING lights and pulled over a woman who scared me more than anyone else had in the last six months of deserted freeways and lunatic kids racing Kawasaki motorcycles across all lanes. Brand-new white Cadillac Escalade like a heavy ship, but going exactly one hundred miles per hour for the seven minutes I followed her.

Sunday night into Monday morning? Where was she speeding to?

She never slowed down. Not like most drivers when they saw me in the rearview—the patrol Harley every driver hated, the way people put on their brakes like they hadn't been speeding, the way they got over into the slow lane immediately like, *Cut me a break, man, I'm not going eighty-five now.*

We were on the 91 through Yorba Linda—on a summer night, all four lanes could be streaming with cars coming back from the beach or the desert. But this August, people were freaking out that summer was almost over and no one could go anywhere still.

I walked along the freeway shoulder to the passenger window. The vapors of her idling engine were like smeared gold in the night heat, heading up to the stars. The tinted black glass slid down. I hated it every single time. *What surprise awaits?* my friend Rob, who worked night shift with me, would say. *A smile? A Glock? A little kid holding Goldfish?* I'd grown up on a ranch with an old truck with a window crank, and that's what I drove when I wasn't on patrol.

Blond woman with her long nails painted pink reaching my way, her wrist with the green veins. Creamy leather interior. The AC blasting like Alaska into my face. License: Joan Beverly Dimian, fifty-four, Balboa Island. "Should I confess?" she said.

I held her driver's license, looked at her in the overhead light. Her hair in a fancy high bun, like a movie star. Black dress. Long diamond earrings sparkling from behind—the sun rising in the east.

She said, "I'm coming from a party in Palm Springs that should never have been held. More than a hundred people. A secret. My husband drove in his own car. He's staying for two days—with the girl I'm not supposed to know about. I want to go directly into my house and upstairs to my stepmother's suite. The most horrible woman in the world. My mother died on fire in her bed. When I was eleven." She stopped.

I said, "I'm sorry, Ms. Dimian."

She looked right at me. "I'm sure your mother is perfect."

I never said shit to people in their cars. But I said, "My mother died when I was seven. Pneumonia. It was freezing in our house."

She said, "Wait—you're not in uniform. Are you Highway Patrol? Or is this military? Who are you?"

Because of corona, we weren't wearing our tan wool uniforms and dress boots. Dry cleaning during corona was too hard. Since May, we'd been wearing the dark blue utility jumpsuit. Cotton, so we could wash them ourselves. Keep the virus away from our families. Tactical boots. I had on my helmet but also a mask.

I didn't even think—I said, "We're wearing this uniform during Covid. Easier to disinfect cotton. So everybody stays safe."

She bit her lips so hard they disappeared into those two ledges of our skulls that hold our teeth. She said, "I can't believe we're telling these things to each other."

I waited ten seconds, like I always had since I was a rookie, trained by my senior CHP officer, a guy named Melt Olsen. If you waited ten seconds, people usually started to tell you the truth.

She said, "My mother was smoking in bed. She fell asleep. Our entire house burned down. My father married an even richer woman. She lives upstairs. She has hated me since she first shook my hand. She shook my hand! I was eight. She has never touched me since. You can see how old I am. Now I want to go upstairs and hug her. Because people were coughing on me all night and I'm sure I have this virus. I would like to kiss her on the cheek. I want her to die." She turned her head toward me, and her earrings moved across her neck like baby horse tails. "That might be the new way to murder someone, correct, officer? Officer J. Frias?"

I shook my head. "I don't know, ma'am." I knew from the tilt of her head she was trying to see my eyes above the mask. Her face was bare—she had matched her lipstick and her nails, like some women always did. Her eyes were glittery with makeup.

I dropped the citation onto the seat. I didn't want her to murder me.

LARETTE EMBERS TRIED to call me every day at 2:00 a.m. so we could stretch together. She knew my back was bothering me, from all the double shifts. Her husband, Grief, had been like my brother since we were eighteen and played on a semipro baseball team out of San Bernardino. When we were twenty-one, we went to the CHP Academy up in Sacramento together, with my friend Manny Delgado. But Grief and Manny left the academy in week 7, after some gabachos came after us and wanted to fight—white rookies from Huntington Beach. Grief went to community college and then the training academy for Animal Control, and Manny went to work with his dad, restoring custom classic cars.

I was patrolling the 91 freeway when Larette's voice came through my Bluetooth at 2:14 a.m. "Johnny. Back break."

I pulled into the parking lot of the bike trail along Green River Road. It was so quiet that when I called her four minutes later, I could hear other nurses talking behind her. Somebody said, "See, Larette ring stay up in the air. Don't move."

"Like a fucking halo," somebody else said.

"Larette," I said. "You smoking?"

She said, "No," in that tight voice people had when they just let out a long breath and hadn't taken in enough air. "Officer Frias."

She and Grief made fun of me for paying attention to every tiny detail, every minute. I couldn't help it. It's how we stayed alive. Her, too.

But if she didn't want to say she was smoking, that was on her. "I got five minutes," I told her. The jumpsuit let me move a little better than the wool pants and long sleeves. I grabbed each boot from behind and stretched my quads. Like when Grief and I used to play baseball. He was first base, I was third, we made those long perfect throws.

Grief and Larette met in high school, in San Bernardino, and he built all the sets for her theater shows. Back when we were eighteen, Larette was the most stunning girl I'd ever seen in my life, and she was still that way. Even in her scrubs she looked like a famous singer. Their jokes were all songs, their secret languages were lyrics to really obscure shit.

Now she said, "Put your hands on your hips and let your backbone slip, Johnny. Okay. Now lift up that right knee and hug. Like you want to hug whatever girl you're hanging around with. Wait, who were the last two?"

"Hilarious. Leti, she could have been the one," I said. "I was thinking about a ring."

"How'd you meet her? I forgot."

"She was teaching a class I took. Then I saw her in traffic court. Interning for a lawyer. She left for Stanford. Law school."

"Grief said the last one was a model. Like, gorgeous."

"Esme Portillo. That was, like, two weeks. She moved to San Francisco to be an Instagram influencer. Santa Ana wasn't working for either of them, okay?"

"*You* weren't working for them, Johnny," she said, laughing. "Or they woulda stayed."

I put my left boot back on the ground. Balanced.

Larette said, "You're almost forty! Don't be that guy waits until he's fifty to have a kid with a twenty-five-year-old. Grief will talk more shit to you than I would."

Their son, Dante, was a great kid, obsessed with galaxies and space. I ever got married and had a kid, I'd want one just like him, smart and watchful and generous. When his parents both had corona, I'd stayed with Dante for weeks, putting food outside his bedroom door. Larette worried about him every night since she'd gone to live in the trailers near Our Lady.

Coyotes were farther down the river, in the brush. Chatter-yipping soft. Probably about me.

Larette said, "Three minutes. Think angel wings, baby. That's your scapulae. Shoulder blades. Rotate them around. Ten times back. Okay. Ten times front."

"Shit," I said. I could feel the cartilage in my right shoulder blade crackling like Rice Krispies when you put on the milk. All the years roping calves, throwing the reata my father taught me to make in the barn. All the practice at the shooting range every month, with the rookie I was training, Justin Pham, trying to get him as good as me. He'd never had to shoot rabbits for dinner.

But his father, Tony, had come from Vietnam when he was nine. Tony usually stood on the other side of his son and said, "We shoot twenty quail on a Sunday to eat, remember? Out in the desert. Focus. Focus like you hungry."

Larette said, "Two minutes, Johnny. Hang your head down by your knees, right? Helps your spine. Lower and lower."

Touch the ground, she always said. With my weapon, flashlight, Bluetooth, all the gear on my belt. Lower. Lower. My fingers touching the sharp little foxtail seeds all golden in the asphalt. Four fingers.

I said, "Larette. I got the second knuckles down. Far as I can go."

And her voice got all sad. I swear she started crying. "Those knuckles," she said. "Grief says his knuckles hurt like hell. All those joints and their stupid names. Shoulders, elbows, knees, and toes. Remember that shit? Phalanges."

"You okay?" I said, standing up too fast.

She whispered, "I'm worried about my cousin Cherrise. I think you met her a long time ago—at one of Dante's games."

I had a flash of memory—she had long curly hair? She rolled her eyes when Grief and I talked shit about the ump calling strikes wrong.

Larette said, "Her daughter, Raquel, just turned fifteen, and she's out in the Coachella Valley with family to keep her away from Covid. But she's been so mad at Cherrise."

"Teenagers," I said. "I pull over twenty speeders every night going a hundred, a hundred and twenty. They're all twenty and under."

"Yeah," Larette said. "Cherrise keeps missing Raquel's calls, and tonight she has this bad feeling something's wrong."

"Where's her husband?"

"Johnny, she's a widow. You don't remember? Her husband got killed after a Dodger game—one of your CHP friends got to him first. A guy named Tom Leslie?"

Damn, I remembered then. A drunk driver. *Widow*. What a strange, sad word.

Then my Bluetooth went off. Dianne in dispatch. "Frias, you ten-eight?"

I told Larette, "I gotta go. Watch your front." Corona wasn't coming for us from the back.

"Hilarious," she said, and hung up.

Dianne said, "Johnny? Are you near the 241?"

"I'm on Green River Road. Eight minutes out." I got on the Harley.

"The humans have lost their minds," Dianne said. "Big party in Borrego Canyon. Otherwise known by social media idiots as Skull Canyon this year. About fifty cars. At least one accident and injuries. Pham and Jekel are coming up from the south Toll Roads. EMT ETA fifteen minutes."

I got back on the 91, riding along the Santa Ana River Canyon, and flew up the on-ramp into the mountains. The Toll Roads wound through the Santa Ana Range, which rose along the coastline and sloped down to the ocean.

Hundreds of canyons along the Toll Roads—when my dad brought me to Limestone Canyon or Santiago Canyon, back when I was a kid and we visited his rancher friends, I'd see the wide fissures in the earth worn down by streams and floods, if it was an old canyon, settled and farmed. The freeway was mostly empty, and I was already exiting on Santiago Canyon Road, which ran along the base of the mountains all the way to the southern part of Orange County. But a few minutes later, a stream of cars—lowered Hondas, Beemers, modified Camaros—passed me going the other way, racing onto the freeway headed south. The engines so powerful I could feel their vibrations in my chest. I let them go. At least thirty of them.

I had to get to the injury crash. They got a free pass, and they knew it.

Borrego Canyon was three miles in, a dark stand of eucalyptus trees and a chain across a dirt road. But the two stumps had been knocked down and the chain thrown to the side. Corona meant bored kids, parties in places like this. I went slowly up the first curve. My dad told me that back in 1900 some rancher from Wyoming had decided to raise sheep here—borregos—and had a herd of fifty. It was a year of drought, and the sheep were half starved, eating creosote and brittlebush, which made them sick, and then one big rain came, flooded the whole canyon, and washed them into a deep arroyo, where they drowned. The rancher went back to Wyoming, the canyon kept its name, and every twenty years or so kids heard the story. I approached the old ranch gate, a high wooden arch. Instagram shit. These idiots had gone into the arroyo, found a bunch of skulls, and nailed them all around the wood. Lots of photo ops.

Justin Pham and Rob Jekel pulled up in the Explorers. They followed me, and we raised dust into the night air. They'd probably never been here before—I knew the big curve into the old ranchlands. In the flat area where the corrals had once been, the glitter of hundreds of broken beer bottles, the smell of fireworks, and deep scours of tires where the kids had been drifting and doing doughnuts. I could hear pounding electronic music. A Honda Civic overturned like a black june bug in the arroyo at the far end.

I got off the bike, removed my helmet, and put on my mask. Made my way down into the arroyo. The roof was smashed hard. The car must have been doing some stunt and flipped high up before it came down onto the rocks, leaning on the driver's side. The passenger window was smashed open. Deep shoe prints in the damp silt of the arroyo, where someone had jumped out. His friend had fucking abandoned him.

I leaned into the broken window. The driver was upside down, dangling from his seat belt, holding the sleeve on his left arm.

Saturated with blood. It was dripping onto the seat beside his ear, and he tried to turn his face.

"Can you breathe? Can you breathe?" I shouted over the music.

He shook his head. His face warped from being upside down. Justin leaned in with me, said something in Vietnamese. The driver shook his head again.

"We gotta get the car up first, or he's gonna suffocate," I said. "We can't wait for OC Fire. Too far up in the canyon. Justin, get in there to hold him up."

Justin climbed into the passenger seat. Rob and I went to the back of the Honda, where it was lighter, and pushed up. Our boots sank in the silt—we only got the car a few inches up.

Justin shouted, "More!"

"Shit!" Rob hollered loud. "One, two, three!"

We pushed up again. Then two people ran out of the chaparral above us, and I said, "Rob, down slow."

We both pulled our weapons.

Two boys. They called out, "No, no, it's our friend! Don't shoot!"

"Fucking idiots!" Rob muttered.

"Hurry up!" Justin shouted. "He's gonna bleed out!"

The boys stumbled into the arroyo and crouched under the trunk.

"One, two, three," I said.

We lifted the Honda two feet up, and Rob said, "Go, Frias, we got it."

I smashed the driver window with my flashlight. On the other side, Justin was holding the kid up so that the seat belt wasn't cutting into his chest. The blood was dripping through the kid's fingers. I held his chest with my left arm and cut the seat belt with my knife. He was a kid, but his body was heavy when he fell. I pulled him out the window and laid him on the sand.

The Honda was lowered to the ground. Then one kid ran out of the arroyo. Pendejo. I headed into the brush and caught him at the old ranch fence, tackled him before he could try to climb the splintery wooden rails.

I got him at the knees. But I fell onto a rock, and my arm got tangled in an ancient roll of barbed wire near the fence. The rusty points went through my uniform sleeve.

I wanted to punch him—for leaving his friend to maybe die. Nobody from my neighborhood would do that. But I only put the restraints on him, hands behind his back, and stood him up. "Where the hell are you three from?" I said.

He shrugged. White kid, long brown hair falling over the top of his face, shaved on the sides.

"It's not like we can't find your TikTok," I said, marching him back.

I put him on the ground next to his friend.

Rob said, "This one's from Long Beach."

The sounds of the fire truck and the ambulance echoed up the canyon toward us. Justin had put the driver on a tarp, with his head elevated. A tourniquet on his left arm. Justin said something to him in Vietnamese, and sighed.

"He said he came up here by himself. He was trying to turn around and he didn't see the ditch. Nothing else. He doesn't smell like alcohol," Justin said.

"He's embarrassed. Pissed that he's probably all over Instagram already," Rob said.

I went back to the car. Broken bottles of Topo Chico—that's what had cut his arm. His phone resting uncracked on the ceiling of the Honda. Just fine.

"MIJO, YOU'LL BE forty in December, but your back is already fifty," my father said to me when I'd gotten home from the twelve-hour shift. I had two gashes on the underside of my forearm, five stitches in one and two in the other. Bruised ribs from the rock. But I didn't want to tell him I'd spent an hour at the ER along with Trinh Bui, who was seventeen, who had finally cried when his mother showed up. He'd cried into her shoulder, and she'd cried on the back of his neck, where his hair was fresh cut.

I was thirty-nine, my father was sixty, but I was his only son. His only child. His only living blood kin.

The morning sun was hot on the sidewalk where I was walking out my back, kicking my legs like a tío dancing drunk.

"Thanks for the reminder," I said into the phone. "How old is your back, viejo?"

He laughed, and I could hear the cows behind him, their songs of walking out into the hay he'd scattered. Heifers and calves.

"Did you have to hang the canvas for some shade?" I asked. "Hot as hell today."

"Sunday was a hundred and thirty in Death Valley, Johnny," he said. "Close to the highest ever recorded, eh? Saturday was a hundred and eight up here. Pues, today supposed to be a hundred and seven."

The sun was gold in the jacaranda trees at the end of the block, near the empty field along the Santa Ana River. A red-tailed hawk was flying straight along the sidewalk, as if the old white cement were a creek bed. He was skimming so low I could see the feathers above his eyes, like brows. Eyes round like those of a ghost surprised to see me. The wings tilted, and I swear he was laughing—he wasn't hunting; he was just cruising down this stripe of land because he felt like it. Nobody else was walking.

Nobody was out at all, on a summer morning. It was hot—but that wouldn't have stopped the little kids on their Big Wheels. Not the viejas watering their roses and lemon trees, with tissues hanging from the sleeves of their dresses like little flags. Not my neighbors, who should be gathered around a truck that wasn't working, hood up and four dudes bent inside looking at the hoses and filters. On Jacaranda Court, one long block of thirty houses all close together, three generations of Romeros would be looking at that engine, and I would bend my head in there, too. Because if you didn't, that was messed up. *Why you walkin' by so fast, Frias? Que onda?*

Corona made all of that enough to kill us.

My father said, "My back is fine. Because I ride Jefa. Not a Harley."

True—riding a horse was different from riding a motorcycle for twelve-hour shifts. Two of our guys were down with corona, so I had only one day off a week.

"I know," I told my father. "I'm walking it out right now."

"Larette and Grief, they're okay? After the corona?" he said. "Their son, he's okay?"

Grief and his wife hadn't been to the ranch since New Year's, when we always set up a telescope in the hills for Dante to see the stars.

The way my father said *their son*. He'd been wanting to say *your son* for all these years, and I'd never gotten married.

"Yes, they're all fine now."

"Mijo, you're coming today, eh?" His voice sounded worried.

My father and the two ranch workers who'd helped raise him—they were seventy-eight—couldn't come down to Santa Ana because of the virus. I took supplies up there Mondays.

I said, "Tortillas, cerveza, queso y crema." They had plenty of coffee and Coke. "Cebollas."

"Cacahuetes," he said. "For Ramon."

Ramon Vargas, when he got nervous about the heat and the calves, would sit and eat salted peanuts in the shell. Calmed him down. His zen was cacahuetes.

My father said, "Sunday and still no church. No misa, no conchas, no somebody else making coffee. Nothing."

"I know."

The hawk went about three feet over my head. The light caught up under his wings and tail. Gold and red, his feathers glowing like he was showing off. But he didn't give a shit about me. He was crazy. He was high, like everybody racing down the freeways at night, blowing through the red lights on the avenues. I turned to watch him—or her. The hawk went straight down my block and lifted off to ride up on a current like someone in heaven pulled a string.

MINE WAS THE middle house of a triplex. Three square houses built in 1925, each with their own narrow driveway and wooden garage at the end. My house was stucco painted pale green like nopal skin. A red tile roof. The birds liked to build their nests under the openings. On the west side of my house was Albert Chagolla and his family—light blue paint, with his work truck in his driveway. He installed AC, and he'd been running overtime. On the east side was Rose Becerra's pink house. She had so many flowers and trees you could barely see her windows; she had birdcages along her wall, full of canaries. Rose's birds were chattering soft in the heat when I rolled open the old-fashioned sliding doors on my garage.

My classic 1976 Chevy Cheyenne truck, all my tools in the old red Craftsman cabinet along the wall, the one my father gave me when I turned twenty-one and got the CHP job. I opened the little refrigerator with Modelos for when Manny Delgado and I worked on cars. Manny had finally gotten la corona—he was home, not in the hospital, but I hadn't seen him for two months. My garage smelled like hot nothing. Like lonely.

I checked over the tires on the motorcycle, just like every morning. Dusted off the body and seat with the chamois cloth. We took care of our own bikes in CHP. I'd had this Harley for five years. I wiped the dust from Borrego Canyon off the fenders.

I closed the sliding doors, took off my jumpsuit, and threw it in the washer I kept out here. Everything—boxers, too. I washed my face in the old metal sink, wet down my hair, threw the towel in the washer, started it up. Every cop I knew, every firefighter, every nurse and EMT—we'd all set up our laundry and even showers outside. Keep the virus away from our families.

My only family was up on the rancho. The fewer people you loved, the fewer people could disappear. Or die.

I PUT ON jeans and a T-shirt, moved the old truck out to the driveway.

Music was coming from the Romeros' driveway now. Old-school Art Laboe soundtrack. Sly, Slick, and Wicked confessing their feelings.

Rudy Romero and his brother Leonard came out to the curb to get some tools from Leonard's truck. Rudy lifted his chin at me. Leonard lifted his Tecate and said, "I'ma drink one for you, homes." They both laughed.

I said, "Drink two." The Romeros were kings of the block. They never slept. Just drank beer all day and coffee all night. They kept an eye on everyone, twenty-four seven.

I sat in the barber chair, the sliding door open, and closed my eyes. All the secret gatherings of guys in their garages. Their classic cars. The Romeros had guys working back there, on two 1963 Chevy Impalas for the Viejitos car club. The white guys I saw looking up from open garage doors on Bristol Boulevard, two classic VW Bugs and silver-haired dudes sitting on lawn chairs beside them. They couldn't have car shows this summer, but I'd see vehicles lined up in back parking lots of the Elks Lodge or the Legion, or a Wienerschnitzel parking lot, and men standing around looking at the chrome and the fenders, the hoods up so they could talk about the engines. They were saying fuck corona—they had to be together. I wondered about women—because it was men I saw who couldn't stay away from each other. I'd bet it was Joan Dimian's husband who wanted to go to the secret party out in Palm Springs. And he was still there.

Had she kissed her stepmother?

The air conditioning had blown her words to me. Her frozen sadness, I guess. If the virus was in her mouth and nose, it had drifted hard into my face—but I had to hope my mask and helmet and the Santa Ana wind already hot on the freeway shoulder had kept that shit away.

I'd get up and make coffee in a minute. Just close my eyes for a little while.

I MUST HAVE slept about an hour. The humming of all the AC units in a row behind the houses was like beehives. Once when Manny Delgado and I were small, on the ranch, we went into an arroyo where bees had colonized a hollow pepper tree, and they came out like a black veil through the sun. My mother had a black mantilla. She wore it when the babies died. Twins. My sisters. They were four months old. They shared a coffin. The palest pink. I was five. I threw two roses, and held my mother's hand.

I came up out of the dream like a rope was pulling me from the dirt. The phone. The ringing.

Grief. He was driving. I had my phone set up so that people's faces showed, for when I was working on the rancho and couldn't look down more than a second.

He said, "Johnny, there's a bull on Carbon Canyon Road. Right on the county line between San Bernardino and Orange. Blocking the traffic. San Bernardino CHP called me. I'm up here in my truck, and this animal is huge. It has a brand. You're the only one might know."

"Where are you?" I asked him.

"About two miles east of Sleepy Hollow," he yelled. "Black bull."

"It's gotta be Dick Wolf's bull," I said. "Dick had to open his ranch gates last October when we had the big fire. He never found two heifers and that bull. I'll get my dad and we'll come up. Don't go near him." I got out of the barber chair and looked at my custom Jalisco-made vaquero boots on the floor. "His name is Cabrón, okay?"

"I knew you were off today. I figured you could ID the brand. CHP has Carbon Canyon Road blocked both ways now, and there's probably five hundred pissed-off drivers already. They're trapped in here. Can you make it in here on a fire road?"

"Yup," I said. "Don't get out of your truck. My dad and I will be there in half an hour. Don't try to tranquilize Cabrón. Larette will kill me if you get hurt."

I TOOK THE two boxes of groceries from my kitchen and put them in the truck bed. Started up the Cheyenne. The Chino Hills stretched east to west for thirty miles, big round geologic formations I'd learned when I was twenty, at city college. Miles of grassland and chaparral, cottonwoods and sycamores that grew near the springs. Carved with deep, long canyons every mile or so from the scour of creeks and rainwater and old floods. Canyons only people who lived around here knew. Until social media—like Borrego.

The Santa Ana River ran along the base of the hills, and the only way to get across the river here was Gypsum Canyon Road; I drove over the Gypsum Canyon bridge and through the strip mall and stores, gas station, fast-food places. I turned east into the new development called Paloma Hills. About three hundred beige two-story stucco homes that had been built shoulder to shoulder on forty acres of land sold off by the railroad. It had been empty canyon and field for my whole life, where Manny Delgado and I hunted rabbits. Now there was a tiny pocket park and a clubhouse in the middle of the development.

I came this way every Monday, and every Monday my father would say, "You hear any birds? Those people there, they call it Paloma Hills. No palomas now. They can hand each other crema por desayunos. If you sneeze someone says *Salud!* out the window because los vecinos are two feet away."

The new Paloma Hills Road led along the railroad tracks, which ran between the canyons and bluffs and the Santa Ana River. The paved street ended, and I bumped off onto a dirt road that ran along the tracks for about a mile. There was an old wooden bridge over the arroyo and creek that ran out of Bee Canyon. I looked up at that ravine, like I always did. An old man lived there, back when I was a kid; he kept beehives in white wooden boxes. Bees used to come rolling down out of there like smoke. But twenty years ago, when Bee Canyon was just a place where people went to get high and drink beer, I'd come upon someone evil. He tried to kill me, but I'd killed him. I'd been a rookie officer, only six weeks on the job.

His bones were buried in Bee Canyon—and I'd never told my father, or the Vargas brothers. I'd never told anyone but my training officer from years ago—Melt Olsen—and his brother, Bum. Those two men, sitting in their driveway like judges in plastic Walmart chairs, would keep my secret forever. They had their own secrets.

A quarter of a mile, and I came to the wooden bridge over Cuernos Creek. My mother's ancestors named that creek for the longhorn cattle they brought with them from Mexico, back in 1774. The creek bed was dry, and wild grapevines tangled up the rocks.

Past that bridge was the first ranch gate. Fuego Canyon, our place, wound into the hills for five miles. NO TRESPASSING, PRIVATE PROPERTY. We didn't have a sign for Rancho Anza. Nobody needed to come up here unless my father and the Vargas brothers had asked them to meet down at the gate. We sold cattle to two men only —J. B. Loveland in Ontario, who supplied meat markets throughout San Bernardino, and Ed Valadez, in Vernon, who supplied carnicerias throughout Los Angeles. All that carne asada, the tri-tip and T-bones and flank steak. That was our steers.

I got out of my truck, unlocked the ranch gate, drove through, got out again, and closed it behind me. Snapped the big lock shut. If somebody wanted to hunt illegally, or a homeless guy wanted to set up a camp, or a potential thief wanted to steal from the barns, they could cut the lock. But it was a long way up to the ranch, and my father had slept light his whole life. With his Winchester .30-06 rifle beside him. His father's gun, from 1950, when his father was in Korea.

I drove slowly to limit the dust on the leaves in the orange grove. Down here close to the river, my father took care of thirty acres of Valencia and navel oranges, stock from some of the original citrus planted by the first people on Anza Ranch. We hadn't had rain for 139 days. The trees needed pruning. Their branches were almost meeting over the long furrows of irrigation. My father had turned on the water last night—I could smell the wet in the soil, see the dark stripes in the dirt.

Rancho Anza. Six hundred acres left of the ten thousand that the first Anza got after California was divided up by the Spanish and Mexicans. But my mother's people were the Yuma Indians who brought Juan Bautista de Anza's party up from Mexico through the desert and then across all the rivers to this place, back in 1774. My mother's six-times great-grandmother rode a horse with her husband on that trail.

Since 1945, this land had all belonged to the last Anza. Mrs. Dottie Anza, who still lived up in the big adobe house from 1845, at the top of the canyon. She was 103 years old. I had to keep corona away from her.

Past the eucalyptus windbreak and the irrigation pump system that brought water up from the river, I turned into the dirt clearing next to the old barn. Not a bright red barn like in our books from school or movies about the Midwest. Ours was half adobe bricks, covered with thick whitewash we sprayed on every two years, when Mrs. Dottie came down to watch. Half redwood siding gone black with age. And the big structure in front covered with palm fronds. The ramada, where we worked and hung out when it was hot, like now. No one was in the morning shade. Past the clearing was a narrow dirt lane, and the ten little wooden houses built in 1910 for the ranch workers.

My father still lived in the first house, closest to the barn. With the memory of my mom. The Vargas brothers lived in the one across from him. And the windows were still washed on the house where Manny Delgado's family used to live. We were born the same year, me and Manny. But the Delgados left when we were sixteen. Manny and his dad and son came up now and then to hang out—and his dad liked to sit in there. In our ghost town.

It was almost 9:00 a.m. My father and the Vargas brothers had been up since 4:00, I knew, checking on the cattle, making sure there was water in the stock tanks.

"Pa!" I shouted toward the barn, and he came out, wearing his Stetson and sunglasses. He took one box from the truck. The other was for the women up at the Anza house.

My father and the Vargas brothers didn't eat chicken. They ate beef every day, from the two big freezers in each barn. If I brought food from my neighbor Rose, posole con puerco or birria de chivos, they would eat that, but they'd never cook it. They ate eggs and frijoles for breakfast, tortillas and coffee. They drank orange juice from navels they pulled off the trees. For lunch they had frijoles, carne asada, and tortillas. They ate tenderloin or sirloin steak cooked with red sauce and rice for dinner. Every day. Corn and tomatoes and cilantro that they grew in the plot behind the barn. Mrs. Dottie's caretaker, Diana Monroy, cooked the same food—beef.

Inside the barn was Manny's fridge—my father always said it was the best present a human ever got. Manny ran Rialto Classics, a custom car shop where he restored any Chevy you brought. From a 7-Eleven closing down in San Bernardino, he'd found a commercial refrigerator case, with two big doors and five shelves, and brought it here. I moved the bottles of Mexican Coke to the middle shelf; my father unloaded the Modelos. I put the dairy and vegetables and eggs on the bottom. In the small freezer not for meat, I put a box of twenty paletas from La Michoacana. My dad looked longingly at the coconut ones.

"Where's Ramon?" I asked.

"Up there at the tanks. You eat?" he said.

"No," I told him. We'd have to take the ranch truck and big trailer, and two horses so we could rope the bull and get him into the trailer. Grief couldn't tranquilize something that big and move it. "We gotta vaquero first. I think Cabrón just showed up."

"Cabrón?" My father laughed. "Dick's Cabrón?"

I laughed, too. Dick Wolf was about eighty-five years old; he'd been born on the next ranch over, which was now mostly the nature preserve. He was the generation between Mrs. Dottie and my father. But Dick's parents were born in Wisconsin. In his whole life, Dick had learned about seven Spanish words. Four were food—*burrito, taco, enchilada, churro*. Two were probably from *Gunsmoke*—*mañana, siesta*. And one was *cabrón*.

But when my mother died, Dick Wolf had brought my father $500 to help pay for the baby-blue coffin. When our septic tank started to leak, Dick had his son-in-law, a plumber, come out and empty the tank and seal it again. Dick loved my father and the Vargas brothers because they loved horses.

My father's people had come from Jalisco in 1880, when the ranches needed vaqueros to take care of thousands of acres of land and cattle. My father's grandfather had come with his sons from the mountains near Guadalajara, five men all recruited by the Americans who'd bought land. My father was born in Chino, on one of the old dairy ranches, in 1959. He was raised speaking Spanish, dropped out of school after the eighth grade to work the dairy. My father knew everything about horses and cattle. He'd braided his first reata from rawhide, when he was twelve. He taught me to braid my first one when I was twelve. His father had braided one when he was eight.

"We better saddle up Mano and Jefa," he said. "Go get the trailer hitched."

My father would do anything for Grief Embers.

I PULLED THE ranch truck around and backed it toward the trailer, which was always at the side of the barn. The horses were out in the corral already—my black gelding was Mano; my father's palomino mare was Jefa. On my day off we usually rode up to the acreage at the top of the ridge, where the Vargas brothers were now. But we hitched the big stock trailer to the truck and checked the ropes and chains. Then I grabbed the rake and lifted in two flakes of alfalfa hay. If it was Cabrón, he'd been eating dry foxtails and wild oats for months. He might even be delirious and dehydrated from yesterday's record heat. He had to have found a spring somewhere in the hills, to have survived all this time. We could use fresh hay to get him into the trailer, if we were lucky.

"We can take the fire road along Blue Ridge, out toward Sleepy Hollow," I told my father. "I'll call Grief when we get close."

We loaded the horses into the trailer. I put up the gate to keep them from the hay. I drove up the ranch road, past the eucalyptus windbreak protecting the houses and barn. When I was small, the smooth-skinned trunks had looked like giant white bones in the moonlight. The bark had since been charred into black satin that gleamed even brighter now in the sun. It was that fire, started by a sparking muffler on an old truck, that raced up into the hills and made Dick Wolf open his gates to let his stock run for their lives. I'd been up here with hoses, watching the big Sikorsky helicopters suck up water from the river and spray it in huge plumes like white feathers brushing away the flames. Half of Dick's land had burned. Ours, only the eastern edge. We'd gotten lucky. Dick had had a heart attack, and after the fire he'd moved to his daughter's house in Yorba Linda. He told my father he had a quarter of an acre to mow, and a plumber's truck to wash. He kept saying he was coming back, but his daughter wouldn't let him. He'd hired a caretaker for the ranch.

"If this is Cabrón, Dick's gonna want to see him," I said to my father.

My father nodded, looking at the fire road ahead. "Veinte años, you brought Grief here the first time. Pensas, I remember thinking, Dolores, mujeres name for that, but no man named Dolor. José, Josefina. Juan, Juanita. Your mother."

My mother. Antonia. Her father Antonio.

Women were named for flowers. Liliana. Rosa. For emotions and dreams. Soledad. Paz. Alma. Caridad. Esperanza. Dolores.

"I guess men don't get named for feelings," I said to my father. "Not in Spanish."

THE FIRE ROADS carved into the earth by the county and the state branched out all over the Chino Hills, beige and dusty like pale vines on top of the ridges and reaching tendrils down into some canyons. My father had taught me to ride this land with him when I was seven. We'd be on a small trail and come across a secret spring that made a burst of green between two huge boulders, or a long flat series of stones that still held perfect round holes from back when this was Serrano land and women sat here with a view of the world while they ground acorns into flour.

Today the earth was scorched and golden, the brittlebush skeletal, like coral stuck outside the ocean.

"Shit, where are we gonna put him?" I said to my father.

He laughed and got on the two-way radio he kept in the truck. "Sergio!" he shouted. "Encontraron al toro. Sabes, Cabrón. Sí. En Sleepy Hollow. Necesitaremos un corral. Sí."

Sergio and Ramon would quickly put together a strong enclosure with the Bulldog movable pipes and wire we used to build corrals. My father told them I was with him, and we had the horses. He had looped both reatas onto his lap and kept softening them with his big hands. That meant my father was nervous. We had two hundred head of cattle, longhorn and black baldy, but we had only one young bull, named Rana because his face was scrunched like a frog. Rana had been raised by my father from birth. We hadn't had to deal with a big mean adult bull in a long time.

What did Melt Olsen used to say? I watched the next ridge come up. South. *This could go south real quick.* Melt taught me to speak American. We'd be on patrol and he'd say, "Well, Johnny, cold as a witch's tit out here, two a.m. and that Camaro's weaving around, so he's gotten himself pie-eyed at the watering hole. This could go south real quick."

Why did they pick south? Why was south bad? Shit, north was cold.

My father pointed to the next ridge and said, "Past there." I turned slowly onto the fire road that traced the next canyon. "Recuerda, así es Carriage Hills. I bet Cabrón went to see them rojas. The English cows."

He was right. We came around on the road, dust rising up behind us like a long snake. Scattered big estates built ten or fifteen years ago, with pools and wrought iron fences and artificial turf laid out like weird green puddles of antifreeze. Golf holes. But to the east, facing the wildlands, was a barbed-wire fence. Two shaggy, red-coated white-faced cows stood there staring at us. Herefords. Bred for England. Probably wouldn't run if a mountain lion came cruising down this road right now.

Wait—would their genetics even know a mountain lion, if they were English cows? England only had foxes. How many generations would it take before their cow blood figured out California?

"Mijo!" my father said. "Watchate!"

We were close to the highway now. Car horns blaring. The fire road gave out onto a cul-de-sac and I bumped the trailer slow onto the short street. Only two estates. But at Carbon Canyon Road, the cars were a solid line, the sun glinting off miles of doors and windows and chrome.

Carbon Canyon ran all the way from Chino, on the other side of the mountains, San Bernardino County. It had started out as a path worn by Serrano and Tongva feet, and then mules and horses. Then ranch roads. And now it was a local highway winding through the wide gap in the hills cut by the big creek, ending down in Yorba Linda, near the old oil fields. Thousands of commuters used the road for a shortcut from freeway to freeway. Cabrón had fucked up their morning. Big-time.

"Grief," I said into my cell phone.

"Damn, Johnny, you took forever. I got one SB deputy ready to shoot this bull. And people got guns in their cars, man. Where are you?" His voice was rough—corona had messed up his lungs.

"Carriage Hills Road. There's a ranch here. My dad says the bull was probably heading this way. Look at your GPS."

He was quiet for ten seconds. People were hollering in the

background. Then he said, "We're quarter of a mile up from you. Ride along the road."

I knew every inch of Carbon Canyon. That section was blocked in on both shoulders with cliffs and oak trees.

"We gotta get the trailer on the highway. Tell CHP to radio to the west lanes. Run some cars off onto side roads, and then open up a break for us to pass through. We'll park right here." I told my father, "It's probably the two Dannys. They'll open it up."

Danny Schmidt and Danny Avila—they worked day shift out of Santa Ana Division. I'd seen them coming in this morning.

The cars began to back down slowly, until we had an opening. I swung the truck and trailer onto the highway so that they were blocking the cars in case the bull came toward a little Prius or Mini Cooper. He'd toss them into a tree. The hills rose up around us. The bull would be coming downhill. It was like a rodeo chute, but millions of dollars' worth of cars instead of wooden rails.

"Dad," I said. "Corona."

I took out the bandannas from the glove compartment. Black. He washed and ironed them every weekend, like his father had back in the day. We tied them tight around our faces. Bandidos.

Jefa and my father went first, my father's reata loose in his hand. I followed on Mano, my own reata circled at my thigh. It was the first thing I'd learned to do when I was eight—throw the lariat at a post a hundred times. On a Saturday. Then do it again on Sunday.

The horses smelled the red Herefords up on the hills, tossed their heads and snorted a little, and swung around to look back at the trailer, then lifted up their eyes to the road. The exhaust—what did that smell like to horses? Jefa was named for her temperament—bossy and didn't take shit. That's why my father had loved her for fifteen years. She moved cattle around like she was a queen and they were her subjects. Mano was my own goofy black horse, a gelding who followed his mother loyally wherever she went.

But now we were trotting past idling cars, windows open, and people saying, "What the actual fuck? Desiree, there are fucking cowboys here now. OMG, I'm getting this. This is gonna go viral." A hand came out holding a phone, filming us. Of course.

"Are you serious? They called some Mexicans to fix whatever is going on up there?"

"Fuck, they can hear you."

"They probably don't speak English."

"OMG, they look like fucking bandits in an old movie!"

Phones went up in every window. All I could see was knuckles and thumbs, bright-painted fingernails with jewels, screens flashing, sunglasses.

One girl looked up at me, wide-eyed. I looked down and said, "Make sure you put this on your Finsta."

I spoke English. I could habla American, too.

Jefa figured the cars were bullshit. She didn't even look at them. My father was talking to her. She kept her head level and trotted up the highway.

Mano always followed Jefa. Just like I always followed my father. Mano snorted a few times at the horns honking, the people yelling out the window, but if Jefa didn't care, he couldn't let her hear him being nervous.

Then the horses smelled the bull. Their heads went high. Nostrils open wide, chuffing that odor out like they wanted to pretend it wasn't there. We slowed, coming up behind a CHP Explorer parked sideways to block the road. I didn't recognize the officer. He'd never recognize me, in jeans and boots and black Resistol hat, black bandanna. He had his windows cracked, was talking on his radio.

The bull was wheeling around in the space between two bluffs along the highway. He had about fifty yards to work with. Grief was parked in his Animal Control Services truck, facing us, where he'd come from the east. Someone in the passenger seat. Two San Bernardino County sheriff vehicles behind him. They'd done a good job, getting the bull trapped where there was no canyon or creek to escape into. He swung his head toward us. He smelled the horses.

The deputy facing us forty yards away was out of his unit, in stance, with his rifle pointed at the bull. Probably scared shitless. His patrol car was sideways on the highway—he'd been first on the scene when someone called. His passenger door had two huge dents. The bull had hit him hard.

Grief saw us and held up his hand. He better be telling the deputy that if he shot this big-ass animal, they'd have to move fifteen hundred pounds of muscle, at dead weight, off the highway.

My father and I did this all the time on the rancho, when young steers went running off into a canyon and got wild. Teenagers. We didn't need to signal each other. But this was Cabrón. The brand on his dark flank. A jagged lightning strike with a sideways L.

Lazy Lightning Ranch.

Black hide rippling with muscle in the sun, snot flung off his nose like watery ropes. His wide horns out to the side. He'd been free for months. Living like a king in the hills, doing whatever he wanted.

But he was thin around his haunches. He hadn't been eating that good. That was the thing about cattle—big shoulders and heads, but get them around the ankles and they went down just like big men did when you spun out their feet. I'd had fights with big, tall men when I was young, when Manny Delgado and I used to box and get in trouble, and Manny was much shorter, but always went for the ankles if someone fought dirty. He used to laugh back then and say, *Once we're both on the ground, bro, we're the same size. Except I don't play.*

My father and I had to get the reatas over Cabrón's head and around one hind foot. My dad pranced up Jefa in a circle to make Cabrón's eyes move different, swinging the reata so perfect that the bull stopped for a moment. I went the other way. My job—I shouted "Hey!" to get him to look back at me and turn. He did. I swung my reata and got ready. That sound. The whistle of leather. When I was a boy.

Cabrón circled around and tried to make a break for the road shoulder, the buffer of sand, and my dad's reata floated over his head and the horns. He'd allowed for the horns—he'd roped longhorns thousands of times. The reata tightened fast, and Cabrón swung back toward my father. I sailed my reata toward the bull's back legs. Ridiculously small for his body—damn. Not a long, tall steer, like I'd been roping for years. The reata fell a few inches short, on the road. Shit. I had about ten seconds to do it again. Do it right. Or Cabrón would take my father out.

My father was moving Jefa around in a circle, the bull jerking his head and twisting, jumping sideways in that ridiculous and amazing way huge animals do to try to make a rope disappear. I pulled back the reata and coiled it again and twirled it over my head—threw it into the right place on the asphalt—directly under his belly—and Cabrón's left hind foot stepped into the loop.

I pulled up hard. He twisted and leapt for a minute. I was praying the deputy understood—the bull was done.

But in that moment when Cabrón was in the air, I knew what I was really scared of—the deputy with the rifle saw a wild animal and two Mexicans. One flick of the finger on the trigger, if he figured we had fucked up in law enforcement eyes. I had those eyes. I always had to calculate danger to the public. If this deputy shot at Cabrón and missed, we were fucked. Cabrón would lose his shit, the horses would lose their shit, and the bullet might hit my father. Or me.

Jefa pranced sideways, and Mano pranced the other way—they knew exactly what to do, they'd done this a thousand times with steers and heifers. Cabrón went down on his forelegs. My father whistled three times—like a whip of sound. *Wee you wee you weep.* He thought Cabrón would remember Dick Wolf's whistle. The exact sound Dick used for the bull. But Cabrón had been wild for a long time. He shook and shivered, and we needed to keep him going, like heading down the road was his idea. He raised himself up, and that was the moment—if he'd decide to charge my father, who'd have to dance Jefa out of the way in a narrow space.

My father whistled the twirl of sound again. Cabrón stilled like a bird had landed on his head. My father sent out that piercing whistle like another reata, looping toward the bull's ears. Then Cabrón started trotting, his head still tossing, but his legs moving him down the asphalt.

My father and I were like satellites attached to him. We watched every muscle, and the cars, exhaust trembling in the air around us. I heard two doors slam. Grief and the deputy would follow us. CHP would manage the traffic.

Grief let out the fast two-note whistle I knew so well. For me. He and Manny and I had called each other that way for twenty years—in a fight, or on a field, at a party when somebody was coming for us. *Wheet wheet.* It meant, *Let's go, I got your back.*

The horses cantered like we were in a regular canyon on the ranch, bringing in a steer. Mano's ears never stopped moving—the right one would swivel back to me, when I said "Buenobuenobueno" and ran my palm fast down the side of his neck, because he heard Grief's truck behind us, the radio crackling. The left ear was facing forward, listening to Cabrón.

We moved smoothly, my father never looking back, and I hoped Cabrón would smell the fresh alfalfa hay. He was hungry. The trailer was just ahead. The bull loped up the ramp and inside, and we let go of the ropes. He went all the way to the front, bent his head immediately to the green grass.

"Like his first cerveza on a hot day," my dad said, laughing. I got down off Mano and handed the reins to my father. Grief's truck stopped behind me, and he jumped out fast. Together we went up the trailer ramp and shoved the heavy gate to close in the bull. Locked it on the sides.

I was out of breath. I said, "Damn, man, you got me workin' before breakfast?"

But Grief didn't laugh. He didn't say anything about buying me biscuits. He bent forward and put his hands on his knees. His Animal Control Services uniform had as much heavy gear as I wore on shift. Sweat glistened like rain had fallen on his hair.

Grief was black and Cahuilla and Serrano and Spanish. When we first met, we were sixteen, playing baseball against each other in high school. He and I looked so much alike that people thought we were cousins, except my hair was Mexican and Yuma straight, and I kept it short and shiny with pomade, and Grief's hair was curly and he kept part of it in a braid down his spine.

Now he tore off his medical mask, his forehead covered with dust from this morning. He looked up at me. Then his legs buckled and he knelt in the trailer. He looked like he was doing that yoga move. Child pose?

I bent toward him, and he whispered hoarsely, "Gotdamn corona, man. Wrecked my joints. My knees. Elbows. Shoulders. Everything hurts like hell."

The other Animal Control officer, the young woman in uniform, said, "Lieutenant Embers, are you okay?"

"Tell her I dropped something," he hissed at me. "Shit."

My father was still holding Mano's reins. He said, "'Sta bien?"

"He's good," I said, standing.

Grief slowly pulled himself up by the metal railing along the trailer. "Man, you never smelled a bull's bad breath? That smell can take you to your knees. No joke." He was breathing shallow and fast.

The San Bernardino deputy walked up behind us, the rifle slung behind his back by the strap. He was about thirty, brown hair buzz-cut, square cheeks, big forearms like he used to play baseball.

He lifted his chin. "That your animal?" he said to me. "Do you speak English?"

I pulled the bandanna down to my neck. Folded my arms. "CHP. Santa Ana Division. Off-duty," I said. "Lieutenant Embers knew we could take care of your problem. Bull belongs to a rancher named Dick Wolf."

"How do you know that? How do *I* know you're not gonna take it somewhere else?" He stood with his legs apart in stance again. He thought I was lying. Like I didn't know that stance.

I put my boots in stance, too. I laughed. "I know the Lazy Lightning brand. We're gonna kill a bull and sell the meat? Who the hell would eat Cabrón? I'm out of the 675, bro." I started to move my hand—and I froze.

Because for the last four years, I'd known it would be crazy to reach for my badge, always in my jeans pocket when I was off-duty. Now that the leader of the free world called me a bad hombre. A dirty Mexican who'd figured out there was no wall. I never knew when a deputy or a driver or a random white dude on the street would claim I was reaching for a weapon—before he shot me.

Grief stepped forward and said, "McKnight, I told you I was calling a pro from CHP." The sweat drops on his forehead were like shiny beads, and one slid down into his eyebrow. "We're lucky Officer Frias came. We got this. Go back and help with the traffic before one of those commuters kills somebody."

McKnight stared at my father, then at me.

I said, "Johnny Frias. Night shift for eighteen years. Call the two Dannys out of 675 who are probably down there on the entrance to Carbon Canyon Road by now. Thanks for your assistance, Deputy. See you around."

He gave me thirty seconds of hard look. I gave him my sunglasses and nothing else. Just like I did drivers who tried to go big dog on me. Pues no soy perro. I put my badge on my shirt pocket.

Grief was leaning against the ranch truck now. I tried to imagine how the virus had invaded the cartilage of his joints, a strong guy six feet exact, like me, weighed 187, like me, our joke that 187 was code for *murder* and we'd never die of heart attacks because we stayed at 187, we were in good shape. But he was in such pain that I could see it deep in his eyes, like they say. His eyes black, like mine. Tiny flecks of gold.

SEVEN ♦ Noontime Rider

MONDAY. FIRST DAY OFF IN TEN FOR LARETTE AND CHERRISE. Larette would have paid $20 to take a shower in her bathroom at home, where she could open the window and see the branches of the big oak tree. Seriously. It was 10:00 a.m. and already had to be ninety degrees inside the Mallard.

She looked out the little window—of course Cherrise was on the phone, pacing in circles near her own trailer.

Larette would have paid $50 if it could be Thursday and Dante was at baseball practice for three hours and it was Grief's day off, and he'd come in after his own shower and say something ridiculous like "Uh, Mrs. Jones? Do we got a thing goin' on?"

That used to be Thursdays. Every Thursday last fall. Because the house had been built in 1880, and it was small, and there was only one bathroom, and Dante could hear everything. He was ten when he started Little League Thursday practice. Then eleven. Then twelve. Larette used to whisper to Grief, "We need to add on a big room for us."

"En suite. That's French for 'put the tub in here with y'all,'" Grief would say, looking at whatever design magazine Larette had brought home from the hospital waiting room.

Last fall. She and Grief hadn't slept together since the end of June.

Dante took a shower there every day, she hoped, but since he was thirteen and couldn't play baseball or have a girlfriend because of the damn virus, maybe he didn't even shower as often as he should. She didn't know shit about her own son.

She texted him a blue heart. **Dodgers 2nite.**

Nothing back.

Just what he and Raquel accused Cherrise and her of doing. Ignoring them. This wasn't motherhood.

Last night, Cherrise and Pam and Larette drinking another cup of coffee, holding their phones scrolling the list of all the things they hadn't seen or done or replied to, not even with a heart or a thumbs-up. All the children and friends and teachers and neighbors.

Dante sent, **Can U tell dad we need cereal he's not answering. He went 2 rescue a dog on the freeway**

Pam's mother: **Should I just plan Christmas now or are you coming home? It sounds awful out there in California.**

"Thanks, Mom," Pam said. "Yeah, plan Christmas on August 16. Please. I'm not trying to make extra money at all."

Cherrise's daughter, Raquel: **Mrs Hua says I should order this book on Amazon for school so I have poetry not on my phone can we do that plz mom.**

Mom. Srsly. I need to use the VISA.

Mom. It's like midnight plz say yes.

Then Cherrise put down her head in the break room and cried. When Larette went around the table in the two layers of protective gear and bent to put her arms around Cherrise, the swishing of their blue gowns, Cherrise whispered, "No one says *It's midnight, please say yes to me* like they used to. You know."

Cherrise's husband gone eight years.

Larette said, "I know. I know."

◆

OUTSIDE THE TRAILER now, Cherrise put one hand on top of her head, buried it deep in her curls, like she was trying to keep her brain inside. Larette put on her sandals. Marisol had put a mason jar on the table, with a bouquet delivered last night.

Thank you, ICU Angels. Thank you for Everything. The Family of The Midnight Rider. He'll make it home.

Roses and baby's breath and the bluest delphiniums. Larette touched the white stars inside the deep blue. Then her phone actually rang. Not a text.

Johnny Frias. He hasn't gotten corona even though he leans his face into all those windows, she thought. Well, shit, he must have it now. Is he in the hospital already or calling to ask me which one to go to? I have to see where there might be beds in Santa Ana during this fucking surge . . .

"He told me not to call you," Johnny said softly.

She sat up like a needle was at her back. "Who?"

Dante? Ten days ago, Dante had been outside trying to watch the Perseids meteor shower, and there was some guy trying to steal copper wire, and he pointed a gun at Dante. Grief had to shoot him with the tranquilizer rifle from his work truck. Shot him in the shoulder. Grief was at work now. Why would Johnny be calling unless there'd been an accident?

"Grief. His knees and elbows. He can barely move. We had to catch a runaway bull."

"Stop fucking with me, Johnny Frias."

There was a strange pause during which she heard nothing but a bunch of cows, and then someone laughing and saying, "Dios mío, es Cabrón! Cabrón!"

Then Johnny said, "Can you bring him some meds? We're at the ranch."

"What the hell is he doing up there?"

"I wasn't lying. We caught a bull. For work. But he almost fell. He can't really drive, Larette. Not right now."

Grief was trying to keep life normal at home for Dante, but he couldn't even grip the wheel on his county truck. What the hell could she bring? Prednisone? Tylenol?

Cherrise was still walking in circles, talking. Raquel was losing her mind. Cherrise was losing her mind. She'd washed her long hair—the wet curls were drying so fast Larette believed she could see them rise up off Cherrise's shoulders in the heat. They'd both taken showers, and joked that after wearing PPE all night, they'd like to just sit in the trailers naked for a few hours.

"I'm on my way," Larette said to Johnny. "I disinfected. Have the gate open, keep those old men away just in case." She hung up, then told Cherrise, "Grab two masks and a scarf. You're coming with me."

Cherrise said into her phone, "Raquel. Sweetie. I'll call you back." She put the phone in her pocket. Did two more circles and then stopped abruptly. "I'm like a damn dog chasing my tail."

Larette said, "No, baby, Grief says dogs are mad at their own ass because they think it's comin' for them. You're like a tiger in the zoo. Slow and crazy. Come on."

THEY TOOK LARETTE'S old Honda Accord. The plague wagon, Grief and Dante called it back in March, when people wouldn't touch their own groceries or doorknobs. She'd wiped down the whole damn interior constantly. Now she hadn't driven it for a month.

"Rick made me start it every week," she said, listening to the engine catch. "He was right."

Cherrise said, "Raquel thinks Rick wants to marry me or some shit. She's so pissed when she hears his voice. Jesus. I can't bring her back from the desert if there's no school." She put the seat back a little more and stretched out her legs. She'd painted her toenails Dodger blue. She said they were going to watch part of the game through FaceTime tonight. She and Raquel had always watched every game, wore their jerseys, painted their toenails together. That was a girl house.

Larette had a boy house. She said, "Dante and Manny III are fine; they'll play Minecraft after school. We bought the fancy telescope, so Dante's got his constellations to see."

She drove toward the freeway, the heat shimmering along the San Bernardino streets. In the rearview, she could see the cut in the mountains where the cars were headed over the Cajon Pass to Vegas, like corona had evaporated and it was time for blackjack together and fuck the world.

"Lolo called this morning," Cherrise said. "She found sand on the bathroom floor. And they take their shoes off at the front door."

"What?" Larette looked over at her.

"Raquel's been going outside at night. The first time she did it, she wanted to call me, because there's no service in the old house. It's too far in the back. But now she's been disappearing for two hours."

Larette said, "Maybe she's watching TikToks or texting her friends all night. Dante's been texting me at two a.m. Kids can't sleep, they're so anxious, right? It's like he's testing to see if I'm thinking about him."

Cherrise nodded. "Yeah, I think Raquel's testing me, too. But she and her STEM friends live life online. Raquel's climbing out of a window wandering around in Oasis. Not playing Minecraft safe in her room."

Larette headed onto the freeway, drove over the Santa Ana River into Rio Seco and then toward Corona. She missed her front porch, with pillars of river rock, her kitchen, with her coupon box. Raquel must miss sitting on the couch with her mom, doing her homework. They had only each other.

She still made the red beans and rice her mother and

Cherrise's had loved. Everyone in their family was descended from one woman—Marie Therese—who had been a child when she ran into the woods to escape slavery, back in Louisiana. Marie Therese had lived to be 104, but Larette's mother was only forty-eight when she died, and Cherrise's mother had disappeared when Cherrise was only five. Turquoise was her name. Twenty-two years old. Found somebody else and a better life—never looked back.

"I mean, Raquel will get A's like she always does," Larette said now. "You're a great mom. I've heard you quiz her a hundred times."

Cherrise didn't answer. She was already asleep, her head leaned against the window like a little kid, her left hand palm up on her thigh like she was waiting for someone to give her a coin. Larette felt a sharp prick of annoyance in her chest. Then she thought, Well, if she was driving, I'd sleep, too. Like our moms were taking us somewhere good. For ice cream 'cause it's so hot.

SHE'D BEEN LYING to Grief for weeks, she thought, while the freeway ran parallel to the Santa Ana River past Corona. We tell each other everything. Omission is lying. That's what we taught Dante. But I can't tell Grief about Jerry Jansen, his body shuddering. Rudy Magana's hand lifeless in hers, like cement. How the heart stopped beating, the lungs were drowned, and the skin turned shiny. The lips cracked. The women crying in their cars for those lips.

She didn't want him to look at her differently. Her hands on him. Her own lips, on his.

THE OLD MEN always said they wouldn't tell the truth about what happened on the battlefield because no one would ever look at them the same way again. One time, she'd been at a house party with her mother, when she was small, sitting behind a folding chair. The old people were all from Louisiana. One old man was telling another man about how he ran a bayonet through a German soldier somewhere in France, and the soldier still spit at him and called him a name, and so he ran the blade four more times. *One time for each of us. 'Cause it was four of us out there in them field. How he know that word? He say it all wrong, but he say it like he mean it. I kill him like I mean it.*

Larette had never been able to look at that old man the same way again. He was her mother's uncle Enrique. He had handed her a bowl of gumbo and she was terrified at his hands, which had run sharp metal through skin and organs.

People were right to keep that kind of truth inside. Grief found dead animals on the road, he euthanized dogs and cats and even burros and horses, and he told her about the animals that mattered to him. Like the burro. He'd almost cried over that burro.

She couldn't tell him about the body bags. This was war. How it felt to zip up black plastic over the face of Rudy Magana. Beth Beverly at 3:27 a.m. Jerry Jansen at 4:42 a.m. His body had fought so hard that he shook uncontrollably and turned bright red and then purple, and his hands floated up from the bed like ghosts and then dropped onto the sheets.

She'd always told her husband everything. Everything. Since they married. How it felt to see him with blood on his boots. How much it hurt when she was pregnant and the baby kicked her kidneys. How she was scared when crazy guys in Phelan pulled guns on Grief when he came for their dogs.

But not now.

The first one she sang to was Jerry Jansen. She'd sung to him for three weeks, until last night. Caroline Jansen was the one who'd recognized Larette from Rialto Community Players. Larette couldn't tell anyone, even the other nurses, how it felt to sing to someone in a coma, to sing over and over for four minutes, an extended verse solo behind two layers of masks and over someone who had a plastic tube like a snake breathing for him, someone whose sister was convinced that he could hear Larette's voice comforting him with the song he'd listened to most while he was a groundskeeper for thirty years at Cajon High School, carrying around a transistor radio on his riding mower, playing the Allman Brothers. *I got one more silver dollar . . .*

Jerry Jansen's labored breathing, his kidneys shutting down, and his legs swelling up so the brown hairs on his feet wouldn't lie flat. He wasn't riding on his John Deere mower.

His sister with her pink sweating face, her blue eyes and silver hair, her own feet swollen in her sandals from standing in the parking lot staring up at her brother's room. "My only brother," she kept saying. "He was a badass, and then he settled down, but that was his song."

So Larette sang it to him, "Midnight Rider," the whole song, and then she went into the bathroom and broke down.

All three of them with secrets. Grief's joints on fire. Dante alone for hours with his screens, seeing god knows what, everything in the world he shouldn't see.

For boys, the virus attacked the heart. After last night, she wasn't even going to let Dante come to CamperWorld.

From the passenger seat, Cherrise murmured something in her sleep. Larette drove faster, looking at the dried gold grasses of the Chino Hills, which rose in steep slopes ahead. A bull? Loose up here?

She had prednisone tablets in her bag, and Aleve. That was all she could do for the joints. Grief refused to go back to the pulmonary specialist, and his breathing was still not normal. The pneumonia. She worried about his kidneys. His pride.

Maybe with Cherrise here, he might let go of some stubbornness.

The mountains, the river winding to her right, cottonwoods and willows and the water sliding past, hidden. She hadn't been anywhere for six months, the world reduced to dark hallways, each ICU room lit up like an aquarium with one person inside swimming through the air trying to live, each door sucking controlled air at her entrance, then back down the hallway and down the stairwell to the parking lot, dark and dark and dark.

WHEN SHE GOT off on Gypsum Canyon Road and headed toward the ranch road, Larette could see the charred marks from the wildfire last October. Black sections of the foothills mixed with the fading watermelon red of fire retardant. Grief and Manny had come on their motorcycles along the dirt roads to help Johnny and his father with the flames.

She went over the bridge, and Cherrise woke up, said, "Where the hell are we?"

"You'll see," she said. The ranch gate was open. Larette rounded the curve toward the first barn and the ranch houses, an explosion of scarlet and gold bougainvillea everywhere. The vines had grown into fantastical shapes over the ramada where the men usually sat, had nearly covered the old ranch houses on the east side of the dirt road, and even grew thirty feet upward into the eucalyptus windbreak. The bright bracts glowing in the sun, translucent as if lit from within.

"Jesus, I've never seen anything like this," Cherrise said.

"Johnny's mother planted the two vines back in 1980, when he was a baby, and his father usually keeps it all trimmed. Like neat tunnels. But I guess he's got a lot to do."

"Like a fairy tale," Cherrise said. The ten small wooden ranch houses were ancient, each with an old board porch in front, twined over with the vines.

"But with more dust," Larette said. "Where's Grief?"

"Wait—who's this?" Cherrise said in a soft voice, looking straight ahead.

Johnny got off an ATV and came toward them, long-sleeved Henley covered with dust, black boots and a black bandanna hanging around his neck. He walked like a cowboy. Hips never moved. They were the center of gravity. Just those bowlegs kicking out. His hands and wrists powerful. Wide chest.

Grief walked the same way. Baseball, motorcycles. But Grief wasn't with him. "That's Johnny," Larette said.

"Wait—I think I remember him. He looks good. Didn't he stay with Dante when you had corona?" Cherrise said.

Larette was suddenly angry again, the same anger that kept rising up in her throat these last weeks, these last days hot and scouring like someone had pulled a tube from her chest, too. She was over all of it.

She said, "He met Ronald once." Shit. Larette couldn't take the words back. Johnny and Grief and Ronald had gone to a Dodger game once.

But Cherrise didn't notice. She said, "He's not married? He's a player?"

"I've known him since we were eighteen. I think he believes everyone's gonna die on him."

"Shit, that's how we're supposed to feel!" Cherrise said.

He pointed up the road and headed back to the ATV.

Larette felt the hot go back down to linger at the place between her breasts. That long sternum bone. The one cardiac surgeons sawed in half to get to the heart. "Yeah. He lost his mom. Like you."

None of them had any idea where Cherrise's mother was—whether she was alive. Before Larette's mother died, she said to Larette, "I miss Turquoise all the time. It never goes away. You gotta know that about your cousin. Just listen if she talks."

But Cherrise never talked about it.

"He takes care of his dad and the people up here on the ranch. Horses. Cows. And he's a cop. CHP."

Cherrise looked at Larette. Those three letters. The men who'd found Ronald, at the accident. They said they'd never forget it.

Now Larette felt terrible. She followed the ATV up the winding dirt road, through more trees, past the ancient adobe house where the old lady lived, shaded by three huge sycamores, the family cemetery behind it. Weird to have your whole family right behind where you were sleeping.

Then the big barn and corrals. Two horses tied to a rail. Grief's white Animal Services truck up above the corral. The doors that always held an animal each. Like a terrible ice cream truck, she used to think when she was small and the dogcatcher came to pick up a stray. Each dog and cat and raccoon slid into its own metal compartment.

Where the hell was Grief? A young woman was behind the steering wheel.

Now Cherrise said, "Larette, is that a bull? Are we getting out?"

Johnny's father and the two old men leaning on the metal corral were watching the black bull. Like in a cowboy movie, their arms on the top rail and one boot each on the bottom rail.

The bull snorting and ducking his head and circling around. Trying to figure out how to escape. Just like us, she thought.

Johnny's father turned. "Larette! That's Cabrón. Your husband saved his life."

Larette stared at this ugly animal, and Johnny's father could see her disgust.

He said, "Pendejo bull that one man loves, ey?"

"Baby?" Grief called from the dark. He was sitting on one of the weathered wooden chairs in the big barn. Saddles and halters, even traps hanging from the walls. Big rusted metal jaws.

Larette almost went to her knees, at the rough fear in his voice.

She said to Johnny, "That's Cherrise. My cousin. You met her a long time ago. She's night shift with me at Our Lady."

Grief's uniform covered with dust, his hair and even his long lashes, his perfect eyebrows. Fuck six feet distancing. She picked up his wrist. Took his pulse the way her mother used to take hers. The way old nurses still wanted to do if the blood pressure cuff didn't work. 110. Too fast.

"Even my knuckles hurt."

"Why didn't you tell me?" She knelt before him.

"Because I don't think we can fix it. You think you should be able to fix it."

"What if I can?"

"What if you can't?"

She had to be careful. Even with him. People who came up the road with their kid having fallen off a bike and scoured away half the skin on their knee—*I ain't got the money for no ER, girl, can you fix him up?* People sitting in the stands at the Little League games when a kid fell and held his arm and someone said, *Mija, go down there and see if it's broken, por favor, just check his wrist and tell me do I gotta take him out of the game.*

"We have to go back to the cardiologist, the pulmonary specialist, and the orthopedic guy."

"When? We ain't got two minutes, Larette. You know this. Work is crazy. The animals have lost their fear. This is your first day off in forever. When? Right now?"

Larette closed her eyes. She could hear the bull banging against the metal pipes. Johnny came into the doorway, Cherrise beside him.

"What the hell is that?" Cherrise said, pointing up at the big trap.

"Bear," Johnny said.

"Seriously?"

He laughed. "This old white dude gave it to my dad. Said he

trapped the bear up in Arrowhead and then he ate it. Back in, like, 1920."

The bull threw himself into the metal pipes. The bear trap above them.

Larette said, "You two risked your lives for a fucking bull that wants to kill you. We just want to be alone for one single hour, watching some stupid home-renovation show in an air-conditioned room, and have nobody trying to die, okay?"

"Is that what you two were doing when I called you?" Johnny joked.

"Johnny, right now you don't know shit about what we do."

She knew it was wrong the moment she said it. His beautiful forehead, with the little scar like a ladle from when someone had thrown a rock at him, his beautiful cheek with a scar from an orange-tree thorn. He shook his head.

"We had a long night," Cherrise said to him.

"Every night's a long night," Johnny said. He went out the barn door. Cherrise followed him.

"Larette," Grief said. "This isn't you."

"I'm taking you home."

"Officer Wright is in the truck. She's waiting for me."

All these people. This kicking bull. Furious. Grief had that burro with an arrow gone all the way through him last week, wandering and wandering, and when Grief finally brought him to the rescue place, the burro died not because he'd lost blood but because he hadn't been able to sleep for days. Hadn't been able to lie down and rest. His heart stopped.

Grief needed more tests. His heart might be damaged. No rest. His pain.

Johnny's father came inside the barn. "Grief has been hurting," he said, the *r* slightly rolled like in Spanish. "You brought him something, right? For the pain?"

She was instantly ashamed. Hernan Frias was sixty, limping

on a bad left knee. The two old men behind him were in their seventies. Their hands huge and gnarled with arthritis and broken bones healed badly. Their faces lined with years of sun, like rays burst in fans around their eyes. Identical looks of pure worry as they watched her.

"Grief, he's like my son," Johnny's father said.

"Yes, I brought him something. I hate to see him like this. It makes me a little crazy." Her face burned like she was five. In trouble.

"Loco in the cabeza, just a little," Ramon Vargas said, smiling at her with his big wide face. He was the older by five minutes. His ancient cowboy hat with dark gold sweat stains like mountains growing from the hatband. He made her feel even more ashamed. "August makes todos a little loco. Pues, corona, too."

"We used to call them Johnny-loco and Manny-loco when they were mocosos," Sergio said. He always spoke second. Just how it was.

"Take him down to my house," Johnny's father said. "I have coffee in there. An extra pillow in the closet. Let him rest for an hour. I hear what you say. Just rest for an hour."

GRIEF LAY ON the bed in the tiny ranch house. Larette heated up the coffee in the old Pyrex pot on the stove. They drink it darker and darker all day, she thought. Just like my mom used to.

Johnny had gotten his CHP voice out and told Officer Wright to take the truck back to Animal Control in San Bernardino. He said Lieutenant Embers would fill out some paperwork here about the morning's incident and the traffic control, and then he'd bring the lieutenant back to the office. He didn't look at Larette.

Larette found a blue mug. Everything was clean, but it was a ghost house. Tiny kitchen. Card table covered with a blue cloth. Just like what Marisol had back at CamperWorld.

The small bedroom held Johnny's father's bed, a wooden table with an old clock radio, and a little fan. Pictures of his wife on the walls. Black hair and black eyes shining silver in the old strip from the county-fair photo booth—her lipstick red, a silver cross around her throat. Picture of the old rancho with a family, pictures of old vaqueros. A Virgen de Guadalupe candle on a shelf, and a wedding photo.

Grief sat up, and she handed him the hot washcloth. He said, "That prednisone. Last time it made my chest feel less like waffles." He ran the cloth over his face, his neck.

She sat down on the edge of the old double bed. She felt hot tears coming.

"I miss you, Larette."

He held out his arms and she lay beside him. He smelled like hay.

"I couldn't stand up," Grief whispered, sleepy as a child.

"No." She ran her fingers along his temple, left trails in the dust of his hair. Fucking bull. She said, "So I came out of work three weeks ago, this woman comes up to me, I realize we've been FaceTiming in the ICU. Her brother was my patient. She says she recognized me from Rialto."

Caroline Jansen, her round face and faint freckles, silver hair cut like two big commas beside her cheeks. Retired sixth-grade teacher. Exactly who would come to see a community theater musical.

When she told Cherrise that night, her cousin had laughed. "You locally famous, girl!"

"Yeah, but Dante makes fun of live theater," she'd said to Cherrise. "Says a dog on TikTok has two million fans that wait all day for new content, and I'm up here practicing for weeks to sing for a few hundred people."

But Caroline Jansen had said, "You should be on Broadway. But can I ask you for a favor? Please."

They were standing ten feet apart, near the hedges that surrounded the hospital parking lot, the asphalt full of vehicles and people sitting everywhere in lawn chairs and along the sidewalk. Waiting. Waiting.

But she couldn't tell Grief any more, because he was asleep.

SHE LET HIM rest for almost an hour. Then she woke him up. Her sundress lifted around her waist. She whispered, "Your uniform is filthy. You need to take it off."

He couldn't lie on top of her, because his shoulders and elbows and wrists hurt so bad. She knew. His knees. Men didn't think about how many joints had to work to make good love.

"That's not a requirement, baby," she said. "I mean, this other part's working."

They could never do this in the Mallard. And Dante never left home.

She lay on top of him, fitting her body to his. The only man she'd ever fit her body to. "Gotta be fast," she said into his ear, just like she used to in the old truck.

"Jesus, Larette," he said. "Don't say that."

"Makes you think we're eighteen, right? Real fast. Like that. So nobody will know."

In the bougainvillea outside, an entire chorus of little birds all singing different songs that somehow went together.

"No noise from you, sir," she said into his throat.

SHE TOOK HIS jumpsuit into the bathroom. There was a door to the outside—because Johnny's father had built this tiny add-on years ago. Before that was an outhouse and pump. She shook out the dust and hay from the uniform.

"I gotta get back to work," he said.

When they went outside, Larette said, "I can't believe it's noon." Johnny got out two more folding chairs under the ramada.

She knew they were embarrassed for her—not because she and Grief had been inside for an hour. But because she'd been so angry, like when Mariah yelled at someone, and then they all ended up in the same room when a patient went into cardiac arrest, working elbow to elbow with Mariah when she'd just called someone a lazy ass.

So Larette did what they did at work, when you had to keep on. The people in the room were who you had. She said, "Johnny, Cherrise, I'm sorry I was a bitch. I'm having a kind of panic sometimes. I swear, we hold all these pills in our hands, and I wish I could take one Ativan now and then. Just one, to calm me down. But I'm scared."

Grief sat down slowly in the metal chair. He said, "My back feels better."

Johnny raised his eyebrows. "I bet it does."

Then they all started laughing.

EIGHT ✦ Mexican Coke

JOHNNY FRIAS CAME BACK FROM THE BARN WITH TWO more bottles of Coke. "My dad's gonna make mulitas in about an hour," he said. "We can eat." They were sitting under the palm-frond ramada, and it made her want to cry, for her own dusty, neglected ramada at home.

Cherrise said, "Wait—baby mules?"

"You never had a mulita?" Johnny said.

Cherrise looked fire at him.

"First time for everything," he added, recovering fast.

"Or the last," she said.

I don't cook, she thought, not like Larette. I don't sing. I don't speak another language—only me and Raquel's secret language. Talking shit about everything. No idea how to talk to anyone else. Especially a man.

Larette had her arms around Grief's waist now, her face gleaming and flushed and golden. "We have to move into the shade. Come on, you bowlegged man," Larette said to Grief. "You're lucky my mama liked you."

"*I love me a bowlegged man*," Grief said. "That's what her mama told me."

Cherrise rolled her eyes. But when they were in the deeper shade under the palm fronds, she said, "I was telling Johnny about Dante and Raquel. How much they hate virtual school."

Johnny Frias had actually looked into her eyes while she talked. Now he said, "I can't believe they have to worry about keeping their faces happy."

She said, "The girls do. The boys can look like shit. But the girls have to smile. That's what Raquel says. She says they wear makeup and smile, and she wishes she was a guy."

They all four looked at the hills beyond the windbreak. The golden dry grass, the ebony burned tree trunks. Cherrise got up and walked toward the eucalyptus—suddenly she couldn't stand sitting there, Larette and Grief fine now, holding hands, and Johnny Frias watching her.

Out in Mecca, where Ronald had grown up, there was a eucalyptus windbreak between two date groves where they'd ridden his horse, the first time she went to see his family. His auntie Lolo said, "But how did you meet this beautiful girl? Did she come in to play the slots, eh?"

Everyone laughed. Ronald said, "No, she doesn't gamble. She's a fighter."

Cherrise looked at the scarlet bracts of the bougainvillea vines tangled into the trees. Larette was talking in her low lovely voice, which she had used to lull Cherrise to sleep when they were small, after Cherrise's mother disappeared, when Cherrise slept in Larette's bed. She'd watched everything her cousin did—got good grades, went to nursing school—and so she did the same. She was only twenty-one, working at the casino with people who fainted because they'd been gambling for twelve hours, drinking margaritas, hoping the next slot would make all the noise. In the casino's medical suite, Cherrise would start an IV, and women would whisper, "Can you hurry? I gotta get back out there and win so I can pay my rent."

One night, a pair of guys targeted an elderly woman, watching her win, following her out to the parking lot, knocking her down for the purse. But the woman fought back, and Ronald Martinez had tackled the two men with another security guard. Cherrise rushed out to help the woman, who was trying to sit up and hit them again.

"No, ma'am, your arm is injured!" she said

But the woman replied, "Órale, I want to see those pendejos on the ground. Show me."

The young men lying on their bellies, handcuffed, so skinny in their black sweats and T-shirts they looked like they'd melted into the asphalt.

Cherrise said to her, "Like you threw water on them—Wicked Witches of the West, they're powerless now."

And the woman laughed and laughed, holding her heavy purse to her chest, her elbow dripping blood. Cherrise laughed, too.

Ronald asked her out the next night. He said, "You talk the right kind of shit to make people happy. I never met anybody like you."

Now she was just tired. She missed her own ramada, in her own yard, with Raquel. Even missed talking about the transmission methods, the animals, the birds, all Raquel's biology homework.

Cherrise walked back to the group in the shade. Sat back in the wooden chair. Awkward. She said, "So that was a bear trap you had up there? We had a patient last month who said he ate bear for a week when he was ten. He lived up in the mountains in Wyoming. He was, like, eighty. He said bears were full of parasites and he didn't want to eat it, but his dad said the fire cooked them out. He made his son eat a plate of fucking bear, even though he threw up. His dad said he had to survive in the world."

"Dude told you all this in his hospital bed?" Johnny said.

Cherrise gave him a look. "We're with patients for days and weeks. This man loved to talk. He said, *Whatever was in that bear beat up whatever's in corona. Maybe it started in a bird, right? Maybe the bear in me beat the bird. I don't know. My wife will be happy.*"

Larette said, "That was Harold Layton. He walked out of there on his own. Tough old man."

Cherrise touched her cousin's arm, stood, and went into the barn. Finally, they could relax for a moment. "You got the Mexican Coke, the good stuff." She leaned into the open door of the giant refrigerator.

Johnny had followed her inside. He said, "Feels good, right?"

The ATV came down the road, raising dust. Johnny's father. He handed Cherrise's phone to Larette, and Larette jumped up and came into the barn, too, just as Cherrise was saying, "This feels like heaven," and Johnny was popping off the bottle caps.

Larette said, "She's right here, baby," and handed Cherrise the phone on speaker.

Cherrise held out her hand. Fourteen missed calls. So many texts she couldn't count them. She said, "Raquel?"

"Mom! You're missing the meeting!" Her voice was panicked and angry, almost hoarse. She'd been crying.

Shit.

"I didn't have my phone, Raquel."

"That's what kids say when they're lying to their parents, Mom. Try to be more imaginative."

"Wow. Mrs. Hua's doing a good job."

"Mom."

"I dropped my phone because no pockets. I'm not in my scrubs right now."

"Yeah, sounds like you're in heaven, Mom. Drinking a cold one," Raquel said.

"Baby, what meeting is at lunchtime?"

"The science careers one, with Mr. Espinoza!" Raquel almost shouted. "He's doing special lunchtime Zooms for us and our parents. Where are you, even?"

Johnny raised the Coke and walked outside.

"Helping your uncle Grief. With Larette."

"Really? Wow. Cool. I didn't want to be a biologist anyway."
She was gone.

Cherrise walked out of the barn. The ramada so much bigger than theirs at home—a worktable covered with saddles and other gear. No wind chimes. She closed her eyes. Raquel waiting for her to come home, the blue silk robe flying in the wind when her daughter shook it out, the lemon tree glowing in the sun, the slivers of light on the cement, just like the ones at her feet.

NINE ✦ A Little Dreaming Is Dangerous

RAQUEL WAS LOGGED ON FOR THE MONDAY LUNCHTIME career talk. Akisha and her mom. Leilani and her dad. Marshall and her mom and their two French bulldogs sitting on their laps. Three of the boys—Gagan Mansour, the twins Tyler and Creed Johnson—all wearing black beanies and shit face, their eyes all over the place trying to play their games. Their parents clearly Zooming from work, with fake backgrounds of some city with buildings.

Her mother still didn't appear. Because she was in heaven with some guy. Having a beer.

The group chat texted, **R! U look amazing!**
The hoops from A
Fire
Slay the desert
Did U go 2 Coachella yet?
What if U C where Bey stood
Or Taylor
OMG send pics when U go

But she knew they were thinking, Where's UR mom?

Fuck this. Raquel texted Dante. **UR dad ok? Mom said she&Auntie were helping him**

No answer. He was probably playing Minecraft with Manny. Lunchtime.

She tried again. **U have lunch career zoom 2moro. Freshmen R Tues**

2moro is Tues.

So UR alive. Nice. UR at home in UR bed. I'm dying here

UR not dying. PPL are srsly dying

True—his parents had been really sick. Now she felt bad. Mr. Espinoza shared his screen and smiled. She texted quickly, **OK but does UR mom talk about it**

The trenches shell shock they don't talk look it up

WTF?

Nothing. Mr. Espinoza lifted his hand—Uncle Grief said it was like the old *Gunsmoke* TV shows where people lifted their hand up like *Don't shoot*. Everybody waved back all smiling like— fuck this, like they were in some old preschool video about how to be friends. All fake. Acting. We have to act all the time. Every fucking minute.

The three boys didn't. They got to sit in their beanies and never wash their hair and never smile and look like shit because they stayed up all night playing games. Because they were genius and gonna be coders anyway and never have to talk to anyone.

She was in the extra storage room at the date garden. Nice and cool. Behind the heavy door were trays and trays of dates keeping at fifty degrees. She had on a black tank top and her painter pants, and her big hoops Akisha had sent for her fifteenth birthday. Real gold, from BaubleBar. Akisha and her mom had signed the card. She hadn't seen Akisha IRL since March.

She smiled a little and lifted her hand. Kept the screen muted because lunchtime meant her aunts were laughing in the packinghouse. Behind her was the beautiful tablecloth Auntie Lolo had hung on the wall; someone had made it back in the 1950s when the packinghouse was super popular with movie stars and tourists. Pale yellow cotton and pictures of palm trees, burros pulling little carts full of golden dates, and the Salton Sea all blue in the distance. Lolo had put a white cloth on the old metal table where Raquel sat. On the floor were some ant traps because the flat cardboard boxes were stacked against the wall she faced. She'd been helping assemble a hundred boxes a day for shipping.

What if a scorpion saw a ripe date on the floor and thought it was a big-ass insect and stung it and the stinger got caught in the sticky fruit and the scorpion was just, like, caught there and died?

She kept the smile as long as she could. She didn't look at herself while Mr. Espinoza talked about extra credit for bio, and how research would contribute to careers in the medical fields like new medications, but also how biology was essential to the very survival of the human species and the planet, like look at coronavirus and avian flu and how the world was one big petri dish.

Akisha and her mom sat with perfect posture at their marble kitchen island. Leilani's room was all fairy lights and her own art, her dad sitting next to her in a rattan chair, hunched over awkward with his chin on his hand. Marshall's dogs were very cute. They cocked their heads at the same time and everyone lost their shit in the group chat.

Mr. Espinoza talked about research they could do even if they couldn't leave the house because of safety protocols. He talked about how virtual school might be temporary, but their brains could find active ways to look at the world through science.

For the first six minutes, Raquel knew she'd see her mom's face pop up in a rectangle.

Cherrise Martinez, RN. Her mother was always separate from her. Clearly in the fucking Mallard. Stupid name. Why would someone want to tow around a duck? Her mom's workspace was the tiny table, and her mother had hung fabric, too. She'd found a mason jar and put flowers on the table. Like they were together.

But no.

She stopped video for a minute, like she had to go to the

bathroom. She was disappeared. Her face. So tired of smiling. All the time. It actually hurt.

And that made her miss her mother even more. Deep in her chest. When they first started virtual school, her mother rolled her eyes one day after a meeting and said, "Some people's faces are just smiley, right?"

Raquel had laughed and said, "Yeah, their mouth just looks like that all the time."

"Like the Joker," her mother said.

"Seriously?"

Her mother shrugged. "We don't have that mouth. My mom didn't have that mouth. Men used to say, *You better smile, girl, if you want to get a man.* My mom would just lift up her chin and cock her head like, *Have you lost your mind?*"

Raquel watched Marshall's French bulldogs do exactly that at the screen. Side-eye all day. Marshall was smiling and smiling with her brown hair in two braids, and their couch was blue and their wall had pictures in silver frames.

Raquel was invisible.

We don't have that mouth, her mom had said. And Raquel had said, "We have resting—"

"Nope. No," her mother said. "There's no resting bitch face. That's not a thing. Because there's no resting bastard face. Right?"

"Yeah," Raquel said.

"We just look like we're serious, baby," her mother had said.

She started video again and smiled. That's why it was fucked—she loved Mr. Espinoza, and he loved seeing her. He wrote on her scorpion paper that she was truly thorough and also inventive and that those were good qualities for science. She typed in the official class chat, *My mother is working an extra shift at the hospital today, but I'll tell her about the careers tonight.*

She stopped video again. She didn't text Dante—she called him. She didn't want anyone to see the words.

"What?" he said.

She could hear the Minecraft sounds. "Where's your dad?"

"At work."

"He's not hurt?"

"He has long Covid. I guess today was hard."

"Why?" She watched the hands going up for questions in Akisha's and Marshall's videos.

"You're always mad at your mom. I'm not mad at my dad," he said.

His dad.

"Do you hear yourself?" she hissed into the phone. "Think about it." Good. He'd remember she didn't have a dad.

She ended the call, maximized the Zoom meeting, and smiled for the last two minutes. She was sleeping where her father used to sleep.

Dante texted, **Sorry. About UR dad. I didn't mean it like that. The trenches in war. Look it up. My mom keeps saying sorry she isn't normal. Prolly UR mom 2.**

FIVE MORE MINUTES.

Her aunt Ruby opened the door to the storage room and said, "Madam, your lunch. You didn't come out."

A burrito wrapped in foil. A tamarindo soda.

Raquel said, "I had a school meeting."

Ruby smiled. "I'm glad my kids are too little to go to school yet. But we have big orders today for Al-Hijra. We'll take a ride to deliver." Ruby knew Raquel was going crazy.

Raquel nodded. She ate three bites of the burrito. Chicken, beans, rice, cheese, onions, sauce. Her dad had three sisters. Ruby worked here, with Lolo, during the harvest and packing season. Rita and Rosie cooked lunches for the field-workers all around Mecca—their food was so good they could open a restaurant, but they delivered two hundred containers a day to the vineyards, the beets and broccoli and peppers, and Rita delivered lunch here to Lolo's, too.

The women in my family are badass, Raquel thought.

She texted Joey. **Can U tell UR cuz I need a ride 2 the cemetery 2night I want 2 C my dad**

Then she put down the phone. Scared.

AUNTIE LOLO ALWAYS rested for an hour after lunch, before she went back to the packinghouse. She was on her bed, but when Raquel came inside, she said, "Raquelli. Come see me."

On the adobe walls were hung pictures on a long wooden board. Lolo's only daughter, Leatrice, had died of cancer when she was thirty. In her high school portrait, she had long straight hair over her shoulders, perfect eyebrows, red lipstick. She was beside Raquel's grandmother's kids—Robert and Ronald, their long braids, and the three sisters, with hair blown big around their faces.

"I want to give you something for your birthday," Lolo said, patting the blanket beside her.

She took Raquel's right hand, started to slide a ring onto her middle finger, but the knuckle was too big. "Look what a hard worker you are," Lolo said. "Your right hand already thicker than the left one. You help your mom, eh?"

Raquel nodded. She held the ring in her palm—a gold band with a small ruby glittering in the center.

"Leatrice, I got her this ring when she graduated from high school," Lolo said. "You can wear it now. Try the other hand."

The ring fit on the ring finger. The wedding finger, people called it.

Lolo held Raquel's hand and said, "It looks perfect. Make you remember you belong. We fished with rock traps in that sea, down there. Salton Sea. Your mom's people, in Louisiana, they were Houma. They fish with baskets. You are both." She patted the hand with the ring. "I'm glad you're here."

WHEN THE PHONE finally lit up—*Mom*—it was almost 2:00. Raquel was in English class, she didn't answer. The phone lit up twice more. *Mom*. Then her mother texted, ????

Mrs. Hua was reading poetry, and Raquel didn't want to disappear. Mrs. Hua always looked nervous, like they wouldn't like the poems, and Raquel loved to hear her read.

She texted back the same ???? Then she turned her phone over. She stayed in her Zoom square and smiled. Every day Mrs. Hua read from their book—*Poetry of Nature and Resilience*.

"This poem is by Paulann Petersen," Mrs. Hua said. "'A Sacrament.' Close your eyes, if you feel comfortable."

> Become that high priest,
> the bee. Drone your way
> from one fragrant
> temple to another, nosing
> into each altar. Drink
> what's divine—
> and while you're there,
> let some of the sacred
> cling to your limbs.
> Wherever you go
> leave a small trail
> of its golden crumbs.
>
> In your wake
> the world unfolds
> its rapture, the fruit

of its blooming.
Rooms in your house
fill with that sweetness
your body both
makes and eats.

Wow, Akisha put in the class chat. *The golden crumbs are pollen.* Marshall wrote, *Yeah. The bee is anthropomorphized. I love that.* Leilani wrote, *I love the metaphor of the flower like a temple.*

Raquel didn't know what to say. Then she wrote, *The bee has to be male. There's only one queen.*

Mrs. Hua said, "Good point, Raquel. But the language of the last stanza seems very female, doesn't it? Why?"

Raquel thought about her mother on that voicemail—crying for Larette. Her mother went from room to room tending to strangers, touching their bodies, looking into their eyes. Watching them get sicker and sicker. Raquel hadn't looked up *the trenches* yet. But people always said brother in arms. Like in the war. Never sister in arms.

Then her mother and Larette went home. To the Mallards. Rooms in your house fill with sweetness. But they were alone. They had seen somebody die.

She knew they had.

On the Zoom, everyone was looking at her. She looked at Leatrice's ring. Lolo's only child. A dead daughter. She shivered. Then she wrote, *We don't know anything.*

Everyone looked freaked out. Not in their smiles. In their eyes. Akisha bit her lips, like *Raquel, seriously?* Raquel wished she'd unmuted and said the words, because then someone could make a joke, but now her words just sat there on the screen. No one added thoughts, so they stayed on top. *We don't know anything.*

Then Mrs. Hua said, "That's true sometimes. But let's look

at the lines. The poet is saying that we can have the divine even in the ordinary. Even in our houses. Because we keep all that—gold—inside us."

So the hive is gonna get harvested and the honey gets taken away, Tyler wrote.

The point is bees eat their vomit and so do we, Creed wrote. *My mom loves honey.*

Raquel looked at the boys' T-shirts and beanies. Adam's apple. That's what her mother told her the bump in their throats was called. Cartilage. *No Eve's whatever. Nope,* her mother had said.

The wolf eyes. Her mother never lied.

Her mother wasn't lying now. She wasn't even around to tell the truth.

SCHOOL WAS DONE at 2:30. Raquel didn't text her mom back.

Instead, she looked at the texts from her friends. She texted, **Going 2 Coachella 2nite. Will take pics so cool**

Joey would be working in the dates today. But his cousin worked at night. He'd be awake. She texted Joey again: **Can UR primo take me 2 the cemetery 2nite? & then 2 Coachella so I can show my friends**

Nothing back. She went to find Ruby.

The conveyor belt was loud, and there were people everywhere. The Orozco family worked harvest at Lolo's every year. Mrs. Orozco and her sisters and daughters—five in all—wore white headcovers and masks, like pharaohs in the desert. Mrs. Orozco stood at the start of the conveyor, spraying the trays of fresh Barhi dates with water. Then she dumped the trays onto the wide belt and rubbed them soft with a towel, cleaning them like babies. The dates went under a dryer, and then under more towels Raquel and Ruby had pinned with big clips to the conveyor. The dates came out shining and yellow, and Mrs. Orozco's daughters,

Ana and Alia, picked out the bad ones real fast, throwing them into a box. Then their aunt stood at the end of the belt with boxes, pulling dates into each compartment and leveling them off.

Auntie Lolo's boxes were beautiful, white with yellow suns and green trees, and red letters that said LOLO'S DATE GARDEN, PREMIUM ORGANIC DATES. Lolo herself stood with the second Orozco aunt, closing the tops, touching the dates to check one last time for perfection.

Lolo looked up and said, "You have to get to FedEx, Ruby."

Raquel helped Ruby and Lolo load up the van. The orders and paperwork already filled out by Ruby. It was so hot.

Lolo stopped to wipe her face with the wet white towel she kept around her neck. "Ninety-eight boxes today. Look at the mosques where we send them, Raquelli."

The addresses on the orders—L.A.; New York; thirty going to an address in Dearborn, Michigan; twenty going to an address in Detroit. Boxes going to London, Paris, Saudi Arabia, Yemen, and Dubai.

"When I was little," Lolo said, looking at the trees close to the packinghouse, "people would come here to buy dates. Right here we would have all the dates for people to taste, and we would decorate the tables with those cloths in your room. Movie stars—they would come from Palm Springs. Old people from New York. Everybody was old to me back then!"

She closed the van doors. Auntie Lolo's arms were still strong. "Now we have to mail them. If we didn't have Ruby, we'd be in trouble. But your dad, he'd be happy to see you here. Your mom, when she comes, she'll be proud of you."

RAQUEL GOT INTO the front seat with Ruby. The Salton Sea glittered blue in the breeze. In the distance were the Barhi palms. Raquel could barely see the crane lifting Joey's father up to the dates. She imagined her father going up the ladders, before they had the crane.

Was her father watching over her, like people said? She thought about him for hours, in the old house, in the trees.

They drove onto Highway 86, up through Mecca, Thermal, and Coachella, then into the city of Indio. The polo grounds where the festival was in April were somewhere around here. She could just ask Ruby to take her?

No. They had to get back to work. Ruby pulled into the FedEx shipping place. She and Raquel carried two boxes at a time onto the loading dock. They had to do PE for school, like push-ups, and they didn't have to video it yet, but if the school didn't believe they were exercising, they'd have to get their parents to document throwing the ball or whatever.

Work wasn't exercise, though. Two separate things.

She and Ruby unloaded the last boxes, and Raquel was covered with sweat. Ruby kept two wet hand towels in a little cooler in the front seat for this. Raquel leaned her head back and put the cold towel over her face. It was 114 degrees. Even with her eyes closed, she saw red for a long time.

But she sat on the edge of the loading dock while Ruby was inside. Scrolling on her phone. Akisha had made a new TikTok already. She was wearing all light blue, dancing to some old song called "Blue Skies," and her Chihuahuas were looking up at the ceiling in her room all quiet, which was weird. Akisha must have put something up there. Maybe she taped treats to the ceiling? How did she think up everything? How did she see the whole scene before she filmed it?

Then Joey texted. **Beto said 10 2nite. U can't go without me. Meet at the shed**

Ruby came out and said, "Okay, we're good. Let's get some Takis for you before we get back to work!"

Raquel felt so guilty. She put her phone in her pocket. Ruby knew she and her mother always ate Takis at night. Raquel hadn't had them in weeks. She wanted to buy food for her dad, but she couldn't ask Ruby for that.

LOLO FELL ASLEEP with the TV on to *The Great British Bake Off*. She said she liked their voices. Just before ten, Raquel went quietly out the bathroom window.

The date-blossom shed was an old wooden building where Señor Ortiz kept the long broom-like sprays of the palm flowers in spring, to gather the pollen. Joey was inside, in the dark. Last spring's extra blossoms lay on the shelves like ghostly golden tails of giant birds, trailing over the side. Raquel touched the strands, dry and papery. Joey said, "You don't know shit about Beto. He's— That cabrón isn't safe for you, okay?"

Raquel bit her lips. Was Joey safe? He had to be. His family and hers—they were right here. Together. She said, "It's just this one time. I have to see my dad."

The truck pulled up slow, no headlights. "Abuelo went home," Joey said. "But we gotta be careful."

She sat in the passenger seat, and Joey got in the back of the king cab. Beto said, "You're wearing that to take pics?"

Her black Dodgers T-shirt. Her ripped jeans. She held the bag of Takis. "We're going to the cemetery," she said.

He drove down the dirt road, passed the sign, and turned onto the asphalt. She didn't want to look at Beto. She stared out the window, at the vineyard where people moved up and down the rows wearing headlights on their caps. Trucks and cars were parking along the road, facing the rows to light them further. Two women came out holding crates of grapes and set them on a flatbed. Then they were gone.

"We live in there," Joey said. A big arching entrance with bougainvillea, red even in the dark, a sign that said SOLIMAR SHORES.

Mobile homes inside, lit up, with men sitting on chairs outside, embers of cigarettes. The place was huge—the fence, covered with more bougainvillea, went on for a long time.

"Not me," Beto said, like that place wasn't shit. He was driving fast now that they were away from Lolo's. "I got an apartment in Mecca." He pointed toward the mountains to the east. "Over there."

Then he was swerving onto a narrow dirt road, between more fields where people were walking down rows of tomatoes, lit up by headlights. He kept going, past a darkened chapel, and she remembered the place. She and her mother had met all the family here for her father's birthday three years ago, when he would have been thirty-five. A small blue truck was parked near the cemetery gate. Beto stopped, and Raquel opened the door and jumped out. She didn't want them to come.

A man watched her from the blue truck, his window down. "You kids better not be here to party," he said. He must have been about fifty. He lifted his chin. "That's my mom out there. You need to be respectful."

Raquel was terrified. The cemetery was lit by the stars. A woman sat in a sports chair, looking at the sky. The man glared at her, like it was her fault. She held up the Takis and said, "These are for my dad. In there. Ronald Martinez."

He nodded. "Ronald. Rest in peace."

She went through the open gate alone. The woman didn't look at her. Raquel headed toward the far end of the row of headstones—her father's was black shiny marble, next to an uncle who had died in 1943, buried with a white stone cross, and then Leatrice, Lolo's daughter, buried in 1979, with a pink marble headstone.

Her father's picture was in his stone. RONALD ANTOINE MARTINEZ, 1982–2012. ALWAYS IN OUR HEARTS. She sank to her knees in the sand, still hot from the day. He wore his Dodgers cap, his smile was wide, his hair was in two braids down over his shoulders, and his Adam's apple was even a little dark dimple in his throat. His eyes were hers.

"Dad," she said, and bent down to cry. She didn't care that Beto and Joey were watching, or the man in the truck. Her father's grave was outlined with white rocks, like most of the others.

Planted into the earth were blue plastic flowers, and along the base of his stone were three bottles of Corona gone dry, the limes wedged inside now hard little curves. She put the Takis there. Chili lime. She whispered, "There's no one at Dodger stadium. No one at the casinos, I guess. No one at home. I miss you. I don't even know what you'd be doing right now."

He was watching her. She believed that. But she was seven when he died—what would he think, seeing her ride in the truck with Beto and Joey? He'd probably be pissed. He was security. He'd call them fools.

She looked over at the older woman, still watching the stars. She believed something. Raquel looked up at the night sky—you could see so many more stars here than at home. But they didn't tell her anything. She edged closer in the sand to her father's face. She touched his cheek. The stone still warm, too.

SHE DIDN'T EVEN want to drive to Coachella now. "You can just take me back," she told Beto, who put the music on loud when they left the cemetery grounds.

"The polo grounds are only twenty minutes," he said. "I can't go the rest of the week 'cause I got double shifts. And this pendejo can't drive."

Joey said, "I got my license!"

Beto laughed. "But you don't got a car, fool." He drove fast through the dark, on the same highways through the fields. Raquel kept seeing her father's eyes. His grin. She remembered the ramada. The machete. Him holding her while she reached up to chop a frond and how they ducked when it fell nearby, the sharp thorns like shark teeth all along the stem. He held it up for her, and she touched the points. *Be careful, like a magic spell if you prick your finger*, he said, laughing. *Like Sleeping Beauty!*

Did he say that? Was she making it up? She couldn't cry again. Not in front of Beto. She took three deep, slow breaths like her mom said she did when she was panicked at someone's bedside. That made her want to cry more. One breath. Two. She was headed to Coachella. Her friends wouldn't believe it. They sped through the dark, the same way she had gone with Ruby. That made her feel shitty, too. She was supposed to be excited. Akisha and Marshall always talked about going to Coachella someday.

Beto drove into the lights of Indio, and only a few minutes later he pulled around to a tiny dirt road leading into a darkened area. Raquel peered out the truck window. Neighing—two horses were talking to each other. "This isn't Coachella," she said.

Beto said, "Yeah, this is where they keep the horses. I met all the guys last year. I made two grand in two weeks in 2019. Didn't make shit this year 'cause it was canceled. Corona better be over soon."

End of July, her mother had said when she first went to the trailers. Now it was almost the end of August. What if corona was never over?

Beto drove into the darkness, and they all rolled down their windows. Raquel could hear the horses making their snuffling sounds.

A man came out fast, and Beto said, "Rogelio, que paso? It's me, bro. Just showing my girl here."

Rogelio was an older man with huge hands, wearing cowboy boots and jeans. He nodded.

"I'm definitely not your girl," Raquel said.

"You are right now," Beto said, driving slowly through the stables, into the polo grounds. Fairy lights hung in the trees, huge lawns with sprinklers going, the drops like pieces of gold flying everywhere in the dim light. The swing—it was huge, bigger than she could imagine, hanging from a giant wooden structure.

She got out of the truck and started taking pictures with her phone—the light was weird, and she had to stand far from the swing, and it looked smaller in her pic, and then the sprinkler came around and hit her hard with water. Akisha would know how to make it look right. Shit. It was too dark. Joey called, "You're gonna get wet."

Beto came over and took her phone. "That's perfect," he said. "Go sit on the swing and I'll use mine. I got a new iPhone. Better pics."

Joey grabbed her phone fast and put it in his pocket. He shook his head at Raquel. But she couldn't prove she'd been here unless someone took pics. She climbed into the swing, her legs sticking out awkwardly.

Beto said, "Take off your shoes and sit sideways. Like a model. Not a little kid."

She unlaced her Pumas. Dropped them to the ground. Joey was shaking his head behind Beto. Like, *Don't*. But she sat sideways and imagined Akisha—she bent her knees, let her head fall back. She felt stupid.

"Good, good!" Beto hollered from ten feet away. "You look great."

"You're not a fucking fashion photographer," Joey said.

"No shit," Beto said. "Take off your shirt, you got a black bra on, that's cool."

Raquel sat up fast, her hands shaking. Joey came over, and she jumped down and grabbed her shoes.

"I thought you wanted good shots for TikTok," Beto said.

"I have to go home," she said. "Before Auntie Lolo wakes up." She looked straight at Joey.

He said, "Let's go, Beto."

Beto was furious. "Fuckin' wasted my time, bro," he said.

Raquel shivered from the sprinkler drops, even in the heat, and she sat as far away as she could from Beto in the truck. She kept her face in the window, thinking of her dad's spirit out here somewhere, watching her, because her mom didn't know anything about her now.

TUESDAY, SHE SAT in class, listening to everyone, watching their faces. She didn't even want to look at her blurry pics of the empty swing. The group chat was all about earrings and hair and Leilani's new paintings and Akisha's Insta. Raquel just sent emojis.

After school, she did homework on her Chromebook in the office near Ruby.

"Lolo's Date Garden," Ruby said when the phone rang. "Yeah, we can get them to you today. For Al-Hijra, right?" Ruby printed out another order and said, "Okay, Raquelli. This order we deliver. Deglet Noor, Medjool, Barhi, and Halawi. A big family, they order every year for Ramadan and Eid al-Adha and Al-Hijra." Her aunt's lavender nail polish was chipped in tiny little dents at the edges, like a caterpillar had nibbled at her fingertips. Ruby added, "She always says when you been fasting, the first date is like treasure on your tongue."

Raquel googled Ramadan and dates. The Prophet Muhammad had broken his fast with dates. That's why people still did it. She closed her eyes. She and her mother had the dry disks of the sacrament put on their tongues at Our Lady. White papery flesh.

She wrote a new doc with all the dates for Muslim Holy Days. She could expand it later to all the countries and what people ate when they broke their fast. That would make a good thing to write for Mr. Cardullo for history. Extra credit.

Ruby said, "Come on and help me with this one."

Raquel followed her into the other room, where Lolo and

Mrs. Orozco were making custom boxes. Lolo's hands moved fast, lining up the dates in perfect rows in the boxes. Ruby handed her the order—*Fatima Mirza in Palm Springs.*

Lolo said, "Raquel, go get a tray of Medjools, please."

Through the plastic strips and into the refrigerated area, Raquel shivered, bending down to get the cardboard tray labeled MEDJOOLS. The aroma of so much sugar. She stood there, feeling her body tremble. Her mother said corona made her patients burn up with fever, and yet the nurses were shaking in the climate-controlled rooms of the ICU.

Shit. What if her mom had corona? That's why she wasn't texting.

"Raquelli?" Lolo called. "Hey?"

Raquel carried out the tray. Her aunt had put four huge plastic platters on the packing table. Four kinds of dates—they started arranging them in patterns like a mosaic. A big flower.

"Here," Lolo said. "You do the Barhis for the center of the next three."

She watched them finish the first one so that she could do it right. Barhis yellow and round, like the pollen. Then Medjools fat and glossy and almost black. The Deglet Noors long and brown with papery skin. The Halawis round like pearls at the edges.

"Here," Lolo said again. "We make one small box for a present for this family. Three kinds of ripe for Barhi. First is right now. Khalal. Just picked."

The thousands of round yellow dates she'd carried. She picked up the fresh date from her aunt's palm. Crunchy and a little sweet, like an apple.

Ruby handed her one with crumpling skin. Soft. "Rutab. Ripe." The date was kind of gross—but sweet inside.

"Tamar—like butterscotch. People love this one so much," Lolo said. The last date was dark brown, like candy.

Lolo looked over at the Orozco family along the conveyor belt, and the forklift moving boxes of Barhis brought in from the trees. She put her hands on her hips and stretched her back.

"All that work. For these little fruits. But I see people, when they used to come here. Somebody kneel and put their forehead on the earth and pray, right there outside in the parking lot when the sun going down. Then they all sit at the picnic table and open the box. A little kid will taste this one. A grandma. The baby taste it and first time, right? The grandma taste it and she remember home."

Raquel almost cried, she felt so guilty about the nights, sneaking out. Especially last night. If Lolo had seen her on the swing, she'd have been so worried.

Lolo knew. Her dark eyes looked into Raquel's and she said, "This is your home right now—okay? So don't get in trouble."

Ruby handed Raquel the plastic covers to fit over the four platters. She said, "We gotta get on the road."

RAQUEL WAS STARVING. They were passing a field of baby watermelons. A man turning a faucet and water spilling into the rows like mercury from a thermometer. Her mother had kept an old thermometer from her granny, back in Louisiana. Her mother's grandmother had been a nurse, in 1890 in New Orleans, where people used to get yellow fever. Transmission: mosquitoes.

She said, "Auntie, I'm so hungry. Can we go to the store?"

Ruby laughed and said, "Lolo doesn't understand snacks, right? 'Cause she lives on coffee. Hot coffee when it's a hundred and twelve, for reals. Come on."

At La Chicanita Market, a school of whole fish stared at Raquel from the case. Swimming on ice. A woman turned with a plastic bag—three tilapia at her hip. Beto worked at the fish farm.

"Gotta be fast," Ruby said, holding up a twenty-dollar bill. Raquel grabbed Flamin' Hot Cheetos, Doritos, and Takis, her mother's favorite on a hot day. She wouldn't cry. She wouldn't cry in front of strangers at the thought of her mother holding that one bottle of Corona and eating Takis.

She and Ruby shared the Cheetos on the way to Palm Springs. When they got to the huge white house set into the side of a rocky mountain going purple already in the afternoon shadow, Ruby got out her Clorox wipes and they cleaned the red from their fingers.

"What if we could see the fucking virus like Cheeto dust?" Ruby said. "So convenient. Just walk around wiping off every doorknob and everybody's fucking elbow when they cough in their arm, right?" She looked at Raquel. "I know. We can't wipe the air."

They pulled up their masks and carried two trays each toward the massive wooden door. They could hear music inside. Ruby had to text that they were leaving the dates on the bench beside the door, then head out quickly.

Raquel imagined corona lingering in the entryway, on the doorknob, on the flowers in their pots, if someone had just gone inside—she thought of her mother, taking off her clothes, the silk robe, the spiders. The ramada quiet. The house empty.

TEN ✦ Your Body Is a Temple

LARETTE KEPT THINKING OF THE BULL. THE LITTLE BACK legs. The muscles. The skin. Rawhide—tanned hide—cowhide boots. Not bull hide. The bull fathered hundreds of kids who got killed for steaks and burgers. His whole job to be a dad, and he wasn't.

She and Cherrise had felt so guilty for not answering their phones yesterday. And Cherrise hadn't been herself at all on shift. She wasn't even interested in food, just drinking Arizona. Was she thinking about Johnny? Definitely sparks between them. Cherrise deserved some fun. Maybe she was worried that Raquel would freak out about a man.

Now, midnight on Tuesday, they were in the break room. Five of them, the most allowed in the room, each sitting at a different table, facing one another. The bag of food and the paper plates in the center like some weird offering for invisible gods.

Silvia Vasquez, the new traveler. She was from Brownsville, Texas. Pam had left for Indiana today. Mariah had been losing her mind all shift, they were stretched so thin. And Marisol was too quiet, but nobody wanted to ask her what was wrong.

The surge was real. More patients in the gift shop, in the chapel. "The triage tents are too crowded," Mariah said. "You got the regular ER cases too close to the Covid. Unless they put up another tent on the other side." She got up and put food on a paper plate.

"Too far to walk," Marisol said.

"Gift shop. The chapel. Wait till Labor Day. And Halloween."

Cherrise put both her hands around her fourth Arizona can. "Day of the Dead," she murmured. "I keep thinking about the cemetery, in Mecca. Where Ronald and Robert are."

Silvia said, "Your brothers?"

Cherrise gave her a quick look, over the mask. "My husband and his brother. My brother-in-law died in Afghanistan. IED. That was the first time we heard something wasn't called a bomb."

"I don't even remember what it is now," Mariah said. "Internal explosive device?"

"Improvised," Larette said. "Like homemade. Grief always said it's weird how it's called that when it's somewhere else, but homemade bomb if it's here."

They were all quiet, staring at the food. Rosie's chicken and waffles.

Cherrise hadn't even joked that she never cooked. Now she said, "Closest Raquel's been to her dad, for six months. She wants me to quit so she can come home."

Larette said, "Grief asked me to quit, too."

Mariah sat down and said, "Well, shit, nobody at my house wants me to quit. They don't make any money, and they like it when I'm not around."

Marisol wasn't talking. Larette felt it—Marisol just wanted to be outside. Smoking more than one cigarillo. In the trees.

Larette was eating a chicken thigh, taking apart the bones. Like her mom used to do. "Something's wrong with me," she said. "I swear I wanted fried chicken for breakfast."

"Your body is a temple," Mariah said. She was eating a drumstick.

Chicken and waffles, syrup and hot sauce, macaroni and cheese, greens.

Larette said, "Yeah. A temple of destruction. At home I always cooked healthy. Roasted me some salmon with Brussels sprouts and potatoes. Always ate my beets. Can't even look at beets since I got sick. Not happening."

Silvia Vasquez said, "My destruction is chicken, too. Pero chicken enchiladas. All that cheese. The flour tortillas soaking up the red sauce. Cholesterol and diabetes in one perfect package." She took a wing.

Like all travelers, she had fit in immediately, except Cherrise was a little wary. Silvia was hilarious. Long hair in a ponytail, her eyebrows plucked perfectly, the line from PPE red on her forehead, and on her forearm a tattoo of a normal pulse, the whole jagged line of leaping red and blue from her elbow to her wrist. For her to remember she was alive, she said, for her two girls at home.

Mariah said, "Remember Natalie King's mom?"

Cherrise said, "Natalie in the lab?"

"The phlebotomist?" Silvia said. "The one we saw in 3404?" Travelers had to learn everyone fast.

Mariah said, "Yeah. Her mom and her aunt were famous in Neonatal before they even called it Neonatal. They were from Oklahoma. Natalie's mom was the first woman I ever met who was big and said, *Fuck it.* I mean, the equivalent of *Fuck it.* She said, *Every day of nursing is hard. Give yourself one treat. Or you won't make it. Because in the old days, we wore all white, and our shoes and our caps, and they'd call us Nightingales.*"

Mariah said, "She told me, *Have your one candy bar. Or your one doughnut.*"

"I'm so fucking tired of doughnuts," Silvia said. "I was in Seattle two months, and every day doughnuts. I wish someone would bring conchas."

Larette said, "Oh, you're in San Bernardino now, baby... People bring conchas." She had almost said, *Norma Magana will bring conchas.* For weeks, Norma had brought the pink-and-white ones. Like sugar pillows.

Who was the first person to put together chicken and waffles? Roscoe's was famous. But some woman probably did it first. Genius. Larette always ate a thigh. Because it was a sacrament. The skin. The pockets where the batter collected along the vertebrae into salty, crunchy perfection. The tiny piece of liver you could say was your iron. The dark meat holding edges of more crunch. The two bones. *Make the doggy cry. That's what my grandpa used to say*, Grief had told her.

She put down the bones. Ten minutes left. She said to Cherrise, "Our moms didn't grow up eating fried chicken like us, remember? They had gumbo and po'boys and dirty rice."

"Yardbird," Cherrise said softly. "Grief used to call it yardbird."

"Chickens kept people alive during the Depression, my mom told us," Mariah said. "Eggs. Cows and sheep died in the dust."

Silvia said, "For real, pollo is life. Enchiladas, tacos, tamales. Caldo when you're sick."

Marisol was quiet.

"This is our MRE," Mariah said. "Thanks to Cherrise." She made her voice like a child. "What did you do in the war, Daddy? I killed people. What did you do in the war, Mommy? I tried to keep them alive one more day."

Mariah always went too hard, even for us, Larette thought. So she said, "Even though this chicken is amazing, it's not Marisol's adobo chicken and rice, Silvia. We get that on Sunday."

"Did you make it when you were little?" Cherrise said, her eyes haunted.

Larette realized, Damn, Cherrise is thinking about her mom, too. Turquoise. Turquoise used to joke that she and Larette's mother had to catch the chickens in the yard, back in Louisiana. She'd say, *You two girls just go on to Kentucky Fried, you never know all them feathers in your hands.*

What did Cherrise remember?

Then Marisol said, "We never have chicken except special. We live in the forest. We eat the snake. We eat the little bird. We don't have chicken because the dog get them."

Everybody was quiet.

"Rice," she said. "We eat the rice. Sometime we eat grasshopper." Then she stood up and smiled at Cherrise. "But I like the wing." She grabbed a wing from the bag, and some greens.

They only had a few minutes left. Masks back up, trash in the container, hands washed. Sanitized.

"Squirrels," Silvia said. "My dad talks about eating rattlesnake and squirrels back in Texas when he was little."

"Your body is a temple," Mariah said. "Let's go stand at the bedside and see the destruction of the temple. Utter desecration."

ON WEDNESDAY, CHERRISE didn't come out of her trailer at all. Larette could hear a movie playing on Cherrise's laptop in the morning. Men's voices. Maybe Cherrise was just texting Raquel.

After lunch, Larette looked in at the little window by the bed—she could hear Cherrise's phone playing the wave sounds she liked when she slept. But by 4:00 p.m., when it was time to stretch—they were doing stretches before shift now—she knocked twice. Nothing. She went inside, and Cherrise was wrapped in a blanket on the little bed, shivering even though it was sweltering in the Mallard and her scrubs were soaked through. She'd tried to get dressed for work.

Larette hadn't had the chills like this. The new variant. Cherrise's whole body was shaking, her teeth chattering. It was 105 outside today, and her cousin couldn't speak because her jaw was busy trying to keep her alive by crashing her molars together. Larette didn't even think—she put her arms around Cherrise and rocked her, said, "It's okay, it's okay, I got you, come on, calm down. Shhhh. Shhhh."

The heat of Cherrise's face. Her eyes huge, unfocused. Another wave of chills, strong as an electric shock through her body. Her hair shook against Larette's cheek.

Only three blocks. Insane to call EMTs. But Larette did, because even though she and Marisol had already had this variant, Silvia had just arrived Monday.

Rick stood under the crape myrtle tree, hands on his head like a little kid, his face all trying to keep the tears in, saying, "I woulda taken her if I knew! I just serviced her trailer!"

But he hadn't had it yet, either. Larette held up her hands to keep him away, while Joseph Tamayo and Mike Connelly wheeled Cherrise the few feet to the ambulance. They were babies, only twenty-seven, shaved heads and wraparound sunglasses. Larette saw them every night. Joseph always shook his head and said, "Twelve hours straight I bring in dudes who say they aren't sick."

Cherrise was on the gurney, half conscious, still in her scrubs, trying desperately to turn onto her side and curl up to keep warm.

Larette said, "Two minutes, and I'll be right there."

Cherrise held out her hand. Larette put her fingers together in a fist and cradled it.

Cherrise said, "The phone. Raquel."

"Don't tell her," Larette said. "She's too far. Too scary."

Mike lifted her inside and said to Larette, "See you there."

ELEVEN ✦ Lift

RAQUEL TOLD LOLO SHE'D CLEAN THE PACKINGHOUSE AFter dinner. She wanted the Wi-Fi.

She kept refreshing her phone to see pictures of her mom and her, in June. In the yard, with the machete, cutting down weeds. On the couch—toenails painted blue. Then she found the photos of her dad they'd shown her here, in Oasis. Him when he was seven, on his horse. His straw cowboy hat. Him up in the date palms, on an old wooden ladder.

Last night at the cemetery, his face in the marble. She could touch both of these pictures but not her mother's skin, not her father's face.

Mom. I went 2 C Dad last night. I miss him.
Sorry I didn't text U back

Nothing. She wiped her eyes. Her mother was so mad. She swept the area around the conveyor, the discard dates that had rolled under tables, three blue latex gloves like sad jellyfish at the edge of the wall. Her mother and Larette said they sweated so badly under their gloves that their hands were wrinkled like they'd been in a bathtub for hours.

That made her think of the old bathtub at home, and the picture her mother had taken of Raquel and an actual rubber duck. She'd been laughing so hard and slapping the water to make him bob up and down.

She shivered again in the AC of the packinghouse. Scrolling through her phone—so many TikToks. Dads dancing weird grinning routines in perfect sync with their daughters. Whole families with their feet moving like things that belonged to other bodies. The girls had long hair that spun out, and the moms were smiling the whole time like everyone in the world was auditioning for some giant school play.

A new TikTok from Akisha. Her Chihuahuas going nuts to "Single Ladies (Put a Ring on It)," the Ring doorbell making them lose their minds. Somehow they all leapt up at the front door and then twirled around over and over like ballet dancers. Akisha stood in the middle of them with her arms folded, cocking her head like *You bad boys.* She wore a white sundress, her skin was shiny with glitter body mist, and her braids were fresh. Then she held up dog treats shaped like rings and smiled like a queen, and the dogs stopped and looked at her.

#PandemicPooch #PandemicPuppies #LifeInLockdown #EverythingIsBetterWithDogs #ThisHappensAllDay #ChihuahuaPrincess #Covid2020 #SurviveCovidWithGrace #MakeItWorkPeople

Already 55K views and 3K comments. *I live for these every day. You make lockdown livable. OMG you're so beautiful, please DM me. Please DM us for fashion collabs.*

Raquel put down the phone. She wrote the botanic specifications for the six different types of dates. She pulled up a world map to see all the places where people celebrated Al-Hijra, the places on the boxes she and Ruby took to FedEx. Dubai, Egypt, Saudi Arabia, Yemen, Morocco, Iraq, Iran, Turkey, France, Germany, England. Detroit, Michigan. Yorba Linda, California. Fremont, California. Los Angeles. Santa Barbara.

The back door of the packinghouse opened, and she froze. Joey? Beto? She hadn't heard the truck.

Auntie Lolo said, "Raquelli. Time for bed. Teenagers are nocturnal. Like raccoons. But everyone has to sleep." Her aunt looked down at the computer screen. "You're writing about us? For school?"

She smiled so big that Raquel could see the three teeth on the left side of her mouth that were edged with gold. Rappers had gold teeth. But her aunt was the real old school.

THURSDAY IT WAS 116 outside. She could barely stay awake for school. At lunch, she went outside to help Ruby put boxes into the van. Fewer orders today. The sweat dried four times on her forehead and in her hair. She checked her phone every five minutes. Nothing from her mother. She texted Larette over and over. **RU guys OK?**

After work, she drank iced tea in the shade with Ruby. Out by the Barhi grove, she could hear music and somebody laughing. The crane and the lift—where Joey or his father went up. She hadn't texted Joey since they'd gone to the cemetery.

Ruby said, "When we used to go up on the ladders at night, your dad said it was like seeing the bottom of heaven. All the stars. He couldn't see them in San Bernardino. Everywhere he went was bright—especially the casino."

Raquel stood up fast so that she wouldn't cry. She said, "I have a school meeting."

The teachers sent reminder links for 6:00 p.m.: "The first parent-teacher meeting is for all students in all grades for our valued STEM Academy families, to discuss the possible continuation of Virtual School for the academic year 2020–21, and expectations and guidance for students, teachers, and staff."

She'd texted her mom the Zoom link again in case she hadn't had time to check email today. She emailed it, too, to her mom's personal and work emails.

Nothing.

She texted her aunt Larette—nothing. Dante—nothing.

She sat alone in the packinghouse, remembering when her mom would come to Arrowhead Elementary for assemblies. Back then she always worked normal day shift, 7:00 a.m. to 3:00 p.m., came in her scrubs to pick up Raquel from school. They got tacos from Mitla and then went to the auditorium.

At Raquel's fourth-grade open house, as her mom stood in the doorway to the classroom, a man said to his son, "Check him out, he got on a new wife-beater, musta gone to Kmart."

Her mother had lifted her chin and said, "Why would you think it's okay to call it that?"

The father stared at her, so surprised. He said, "That's just what they call it. Don't mean nothin'."

Raquel's mother was still wearing her scrubs, her hair in a high bun, and she cocked her head to the side and said, "What if we ladies had a shirt called a dick-smasher? You know? Just what we called it?" Then she took Raquel's hand and they sat down in the little desk chairs.

Her mother was a badass.

She couldn't cry. All the Zoom squares started lighting up. At 5:58 p.m., Raquel logged on in the storage room. She'd washed her face, wetted her curls and put them up in a messy bun, stuck a sparkly butterfly pin in there from Leilani, wore her hoops and a clean white blouse. She fucking hated every minute.

No *Cherrise Martinez, RN*. But her mother would never miss a meeting.

Raquel felt a chill go through her, sharp as an ice cube run down her back for a joke. No joke. Her mother was sick. It had to be that. She'd never be mad at me, Raquel thought.

She shivered again, started video but kept her mute on. The chat burst into waves of everyone showing off. Fuck this.

Mr. Espinoza introduced himself for bio. Mrs. Hua for English. Mrs. Wilson for math. Mr. Cardullo for history. The teachers with their fake backgrounds that said the school name, had a picture of the entrance, all professional. What were their houses like?

If students put up a fake screen, like a beach or mountains, then you knew they didn't want you to see their messy rooms or whatever.

Akisha and her parents together in their screen. Leilani in her room, her parents in their living room. Marshall and her mother and their dogs, on their patio. Then Dante and Uncle Grief. So Auntie Larette and Raquel's mom were working.

Somebody in the ICU must be dying. Again. Now she felt bad. Raquel could picture them crowding around the person in the bed. Her mom had said there would be four of them all working together, the doctor, her and Larette, sometimes a pulmonary specialist, all the tubes and machines. How did her mom do it—hear someone's last breath?

Then everyone on Zoom was smiling.

Zoom was so much worse than being in person. Instead of an auditorium, where her mom could walk in ten minutes late and sit in the chair Raquel had saved for her, there was nothing.

The screen was filled with squares now.

Akisha's mom said, "Raquel, I know your mom is working long hours. Our heroes! The nurses and doctors saving lives every day."

"And night," Akisha's dad said, all hearty, smiling.

"And where are you, Raquel?"

"I'm at my aunt's house right now," she said. "In Coachella."

But no walking away to end the convo. **OMG, you look amazing**, in the group text. **Raquel, welcome!** in the school chat below.

The desert looks very tropical! Marshall's mom commented.

WTF? Focus. She looked down at her phone again. **Where RU? MOM**

She looked up and unrested her bitch face and smiled. She unmuted her screen and said, "Sorry, my mom just called and there's an emergency at Our Lady. They're trying to save someone's life. I have to go, see you all tomorrow." Before Dante and his dad could say anything, she disappeared.

IT WAS 6:29 p.m.
  She texted Joey. **I need UR help PLZ.**
  He texted back immediately. **I work til 10. Meet me @ shed.**
  Raquel's heart felt like it was shivering inside her chest. She had to make this happen.
  Her mom and Larette said people died in their cars. On the way to the hospital. Corona happened that fast to their bodies.
  No.
  She put some clothes, her laptop, and her cords in her backpack. Deep in the desk drawer, there was an old Christmas card from 2008. She tore off the blank back and wrote, *Auntie, please don't worry. I went home for now. I HAVE TO SEE my mom.*
  She put down the pen. She should write *I love you*. She and her mother never said *Love you!* in that casual, hurried way Akisha and everyone else did. Her mother always told Raquel, *I ain't gotta say that—because you already know.*
  She wrote *All my love* like a poet would.

OUTSIDE, WALKING THROUGH the heat was like walking through water. Boiling water. Lolo's old thermometer hung on the side of the equipment shed. Ninety-two.
  She found the men and the lift easily. The music drifted through the Barhi grove, all the way near the water. She stood in the next row and watched them for a long time. Sometimes Joey's abuelo played old mariachi or ranchera music on their little speaker, set up on a wooden crate at the edge of the row. But tonight it was the same music Mr. Garibay and his brothers played when they were working on cars in the driveway—oldies. Art

Laboe. She heard his voice saying, "Well, we're out here in Palm Springs, sending love from Betty in Madera to her husband, Spider, in Delano. She says don't let no one get you down."

Joey's father was up in the lift, wearing not his cowboy hat but a white pharaoh head covering and a black bandanna over his face. Joey was driving the lift, wearing the same thing.

His father reached under the paper covering to turn the bunches and check if the dates were ready. Then the machete flashed. Once. He moved to the next bunch. Same. Then Joey brought him down, the lift full of cut bunches.

"Que paso, mija?"

She flashed around. Joey's grandfather was behind her. Of course. The trees. That first night—Joey following him. He wore his white cowboy hat and a black bandanna over his face, a wet towel around his neck. Like Lolo.

She stepped into the row near the flatbed and said, "I came to see if you needed help."

Joey's father laughed. "That's nice. But you can't carry these, mija. Too heavy."

Joey just stared at her. Then he lifted his chin. "We're trying to get ahead for tomorrow. Way too hot again."

Joey's father unloaded the bunches onto the low flatbed. His grandfather cut each individual stem with pruning shears, laid them like necklaces on a towel. Joey took each strand and flicked off bad dates onto the ground, then held up the stem and brushed the whole thing with a paintbrush. Fast, turning it, thoroughly, bringing it close to his eyes in the light from the lift.

He laid the strand in a box. The ones she and Ruby had been making all day.

"I can do that part," she said, stepping close to the flatbed.

"What shoes she got on?" his father said, and Joey looked down.

"Boots."

His father shrugged. "Okay, mija. But I'm trust you to do it right—take off anything looks bad, or Señora Lolo will catch you." He reached inside the truck cab and pulled out a flat, clean pharaoh hood. Raquel stuffed her hair inside.

"You look like an alien with a big head," Joey said, and grinned. "All your hair. Any of these dates look bad, I'm saying it was you. The rookie."

THEY WORKED WITHOUT speaking for two hours. Moving down the row from tree to tree, Joey's father going up, Joey moving the lift around four times to each side, the bunches laid delicately on their sides. Raquel and Señor Ortiz pulling out the too-ripe soft dates and those marred by insects. I still have to ask about the insects for my report, she thought, brushing the dust from the center of each strand. The life cycle of dates. The different types of trees. The pollination process—good insects and harmful insects.

When they were done here, she'd tell Joey what was going on, and they'd borrow the truck. It was four hours round-trip. He'd be back fast. With the money.

"THE LAST ONE for tonight," his father said. She had no idea what time it was. He handed her the machete and his leather glove.

"You try one time." It was always weird when you couldn't see someone's mouth behind the bandanna but you could hear that they were smiling.

Like he thought she'd have trouble, or that she'd be fine?

"I'll do it," he said, motioning for Joey to move from the driver seat of the lift.

Joey turned off the speaker and put it in the truck. Then he stood in the center of the row. She opened the gate and stepped onto the metal mesh platform. Three sides of a rectangle. She put the machete by her feet, held on to the railing, and rose slowly into the air.

The bark of Barhi trees not trimmed. Sharp slanted, slashed fronds every few years. No way you could put ladders on these. Then she looked past the trunks toward the Salton Sea.

This is a secret, she thought, staring out at the vast shimmering water, which smelled so bad and looked so beautiful. The sea of trees all around her—fronds tossing in the hot breeze, glinting silvery, too. She was at the bottom of heaven. Her dad. He called it that. He'd been up here. Looking at this same water, these mountains. Lolo's people's mountains.

My people.

My mother.

Breathe. Breathe.

"You too scared to cut?" Joey called. "You never had a machete?"

Fuck him. She had her own machete at home; it was her brand. But that didn't work. She called down, "I like my dad's machete better."

She reached under the paper. The bunches seemed bigger up here. Something flew out and hit her in the mouth. A moth. Glanced off the bandanna and into the air. Raquel felt around the top of the bunch. The dates had to be hard but nudging into ripe.

She pulled off the paper and it floated down like magic to the earth. Held the machete, and the gloved hand on the thorny stem. One slash, or Joey would laugh. She let out her breath. Sliced hard onto the stem, and the bunch was so heavy it pulled her sideways. She lowered it to the tarp. Didn't look down.

Joey's father whistled. "Bueno, eh, Papi?" he said to his father, and Joey's abuelo lifted his hand. Thumbs-up.

"Come down," he said.

The lake, the trees, the trunks, the earth. Joey reached in and grabbed the single bunch. "Like you would do that all day," he said, and put it on the flatbed fast. He grabbed the shears and cut each strand. She walked to his father and gave back the machete and glove, and his father turned off the lift. The loud engine stopped. Everything stopped for a minute. Raquel heard coyotes far in the distance, in the hills.

Joey finished the last bunch and put the box onto the second flatbed, loaded with boxes. His father started that truck and drove down the row toward the packinghouse. His grandfather drove his little white truck farther into the rows, like he would never go home. The lift and the work flatbed stayed where they were.

Joey said, "Hop in."

The old golf cart. That's how they ran back and forth to the packinghouse for supplies or food. She held tight and he bumped down the row.

AUNTIE LOLO WAS in the packinghouse, of course. She and Señor Ortiz seemed to sleep about two hours a night. She watched them put the boxes in the cold storage room. The plastic strips slid back and forth on Raquel's shoulders when she ducked inside.

Then Joey's father talked to Auntie Lolo for a minute, and she said, "Raquelli. No more homework. Half an hour."

Joey said, "I'm gonna call Beto. He said he needs some help tonight."

His father's eyes narrowed, over his bandanna. "He's paying you?"

Joey nodded. "He's gonna give me a ride home."

His father lifted his chin. "Watchate. Not past one."

He drove out of the parking lot in his old brown Bronco. Joey and Raquel sat on the two metal folding chairs by the equipment shed. He got out his phone.

They sat in silence for a long time. The coyotes. An owl. Then the little white truck came slowly out of the rows and went through the parking lot onto the road.

JOEY DROVE THE golf cart down the side of the dirt road. She smelled the fish long before they got there. The Salton Sea was dark. Stripes of starlight here, and the fish farm was down another long dirt lane. Round ponds and pumps, and the smell was so strong it felt like they were passing through the mud themselves.

Beto's truck was parked outside a long, low shed. He came outside, wearing a jumpsuit and black rubber boots, carrying buckets. Raquel looked inside. Pellets of fish food. He put the buckets onto an ATV with a flatbed attached and came over to them.

He looked at her. Holding her backpack. Still wearing the head covering from Joey's father. "Only one drives the truck is me," he said. "You gotta wait till Saturday."

"I can pay you a hundred and twenty-eight dollars," she said. "I have it in San Bernardino."

He laughed. "That's a weird number."

Raquel wished he could see her resting fuck-you face. "It's an accurate number. Cash."

"Fucking attitude for a jaina," he said.

Joey said, "Chill, Beto. I'm taking her home."

"Not in my troca, bro. Look at you in the fucking golf cart. That's your speed." Then Beto looked at Raquel again. "Why you going back? You got a fool to see? Besides this fool?" He nodded toward Joey.

Raquel stared at him. "My mom's sick."

Joey got out of the golf cart and held out his hand. For the keys.

Beto zipped down the jumpsuit. Of course he had a white tank top underneath. "You got a stepdad? I don't want some viejo busting up the troca."

She pictured her mother, in the tiny desk at school. The dad who wouldn't meet her eyes. She pictured her mother saying, *Oh, I'm wearing a dick-smasher. I got it at Forever 21.* She had to be tough like her mom. She said, "That was four questions. My limit. Bro."

Beto motioned to Joey, and they walked away, talking. Joey shook his head, but Beto said, "Only way, primo. Tell her they better be good."

Then he handed Joey the keys.

He called out, "You got two hours to get there. Two hours to get back. It's eleven. I get off at six. Don't mess up the trokita, or I'ma make you regret it. Fuck around and find out." Then he looked at Raquel. "If she don't have the feria when you get to San Bernardino, you know what to do."

THE TINTED WINDOWS made everything look like she'd entered a different world. Joey drove slowly through the darkness onto Grapefruit Boulevard.

She didn't look at him for a long time. *Tell her they better be good.* Beto meant pics. She knew. But she trusted Joey. The money was at home.

He got on the freeway. Rancho Mirage. Indian Wells. Palm Springs. It felt like last year that Raquel and Ruby had delivered the platters.

She had a million texts in the group chat. Nothing from her mother or Larette.

Finally, she said, "Your cousin."

"He's a culero about the troca." Joey looked at the gas tank. "He didn't even fill it up. I got twenty dollars. Till we get to your house."

Raquel said, "I wouldn't lie. Not to you." Then she looked out the window into the desert, glowing pale in the night.

TWELVE ✦ Wishing Well

SHE COULDN'T MOVE. HER BACK AND SPINE PULSED WITH pain. Her head felt like all the Seven Dwarves were using their hammers and picks trying to get the fucking treasure out of her skull. Raquel had laughed so hard at them. Sleepy. Dopey. She was five when they went to Disneyland. They stayed in the hotel—Ronald had gotten a weekend package from someone who won big at the casino.

She could hear his voice right now. *Come on, we gotta get you workin' here. We could bring Raquel all the time.*

But she was falling asleep again. The witch with the green apple. Green? Red? Snow White. Sleeping Beauty. The teacups. Her heart felt like the teacups. Like it was spinning inside her chest.

She licked her lips. Swallowed. Nothing in her mouth. Her lips were closed.

Cherrise couldn't even lift her hand. She moved her tongue. Touched the roof of her mouth. No tube. She was breathing. From the bottom of the well. Like looking up. Was she ever in a well? The well of wishes? She'd never been in a well. Just in the movies they had wells. Raquel threw a penny into the well, at Disneyland.

✦

LARETTE STOOD BESIDE her, whispering, "Cherrise, I'm right here."

Cherrise opened her eyes.

Tom Jacobs, the ER supervising physician. His brown hair, brown eyes, brown glasses—always smiling in the parking lot where the patients were lined up on gurneys. She squinted up at him, behind his face shield.

"We're moving you upstairs," he said. "We think you're good, nothing secondary. Not yet. We just gotta monitor you. Get that fever gone. Hydrate and sleep, okay?"

So weird to see Larette's eyes looking down at her. Not across the bed.

Hydrate. She kept telling Raquel to hydrate, out in the desert. "Raquel."

Larette said, "Don't tell her yet. Not till you're out. You don't have it bad anyway. Maybe one more day and you're out."

"Her daughter?" Tom said.

"Yeah, she's staying with relatives because of the surge."

He said, "*This* surge. There's gonna be another one. Like, five more. Think about it—Fourth of July. Labor Day. Jesus—Halloween. Thanksgiving is gonna—"

"Don't say that," someone said.

They were leaving the ER ward. The gurney moved and every bump sent a sharp pain into her back. People said Covid camped out in their spine. It's in my lungs, mija. I can't breathe. It's inside my head. I can't think. It's in my back. It hurts.

So tired.

A WINDOW. FACING south. Second floor. Regular ward. The sun was going down, so it was late. People came and went. Marisol in the daytime on her break. She sat in the chair by the bed. She said, "I work in the day this week. My sister Jasmine coming."

Marisol held up her phone.

Pam Ott on FaceTime. "Cherrise! I'm so sorry you got it. I miss you guys. I can't come back—my husband and my mother-in-law are too scared to let me go. This new surge. I have to stay here."

They disappeared.

Cherrise said, "Raquel."

Marisol said, "Larette have your phone. She bring it for you soon."

She closed her eyes. "You still 104," Marisol said. "You sleep."

MARIAH BALL IN the chair. "I was worried that first night. You were like the ones skating between a hundred five and a hundred two. You didn't drink a fucking thing, did you?"

Cherrise said, "I was in the trailer. Sleeping. Too tired to get up."

"I know," Mariah said.

She was funny. She sat like a guy in the low chair. Her knees round like little plates in her scrubs. Disney scrubs. Mariah went to Disneyland all the time, with her son.

"Your patellas," Cherrise said.

"Patellae," Mariah said. "On our tests, right?"

"Is Stan Earley still up there? His knees are so big."

"He's still there. Getting bad, though."

"Marisol is working in the day?"

"She keeps having meetings with someone. Top secret."

"Who did you smoke with?"

"Just Larette."

"Nobody knows. Not Grief."

"Yup." Mariah stood up. "What's yours? That nobody knows?"

"Tequila," Cherrise said. "But that's not the same. One shot. But everybody knows."

"Yeah. And tequila doesn't keep you company. Like a cigarette."

NATALIE? WAS NATALIE taking her blood? Cold swab of alcohol. The needle. Natalie's eyes behind the plastic shield.

Dr. Yoon. His forehead smooth, with the one line below the PPE. His black eyebrows like two crow feathers lying straight.

He said, "We miss you upstairs. But you're lucky. A fairly mild case of the new subvariant. You should be good by tomorrow morning. But when you're released, you'll have to rest two days before you come back to us."

"Even more lucky!" Larette said. "Two days off. Jesus."

Lucky. Cherrise was lucky, so now she'd have to feel bad about that, too.

Wait. What was today? The window was dark.

Dr. Yoon and Natalie left.

"It's Wednesday," she said to Larette.

"It's Thursday," Larette said. "Thursday night. Almost midnight."

Cherrise sat up. Her head filled with sand. "Thursday! My phone. You have my phone."

"Cherrise, I texted Raquel a few hours ago. I haven't heard back from her yet. I just told her to call me. I messaged all her teachers, too. I'm a mom, okay? I got this. You need to rest. Think about all those texts from patient families that first day—I had to transfer all their contacts to Silvia and Marisol and me."

Cherrise held out her hand. "Larette."

Raquel's texts from Monday, when they were at the ranch and Raquel was so pissed about Cherrise missing the lunch meeting. Seventeen messages. Then Raquel hadn't responded for a whole day. She started texting again Tuesday night. Cherrise had been on shift, but she was already dizzy and hot.

The last two: **Srsly Mom! U sent me out here 2 the end of the world & UR the 1 acting like this**

Then, at 11:52 p.m.: **RU OK? Plz don't ghost me**

A needle in her heart. Cherrise looked up at Larette. "You didn't tell her where I was?"

"I didn't want her to lose her mind," Larette said. "They're teenagers, her and Dante. Half the time he doesn't even respond."

"He's a boy! Two days ain't shit for a boy not to talk to somebody. That's like a month for Raquel. Damn, Larette, you didn't . . . you didn't get to make that decision. For me."

"You were half unconscious until a little while ago, okay?"

Larette had that look, though. Even when we're grown we can tell when we fucked up. Larette wasn't telling her something.

Larette said, "I dream about somebody taking my phone away! The patients, the updates, all of it! I wish my phone was in the trailer under the bed. I'm so tired I wish the phone would fucking evaporate."

"I do, too! But that's not how it works!" Cherrise said.

"She's gotta be asleep now," Larette said. "Here, let me have it. I'll bring it back to you at six, before I go off shift. We can call her before school. But you have to rest, and you won't sleep if you have the phone."

Cherrise said, "Let me check voicemail, in case she called instead of texting." She saw so many missed calls and voicemails, all patients or spam. But three from the desert area code. Lolo Martinez.

Cherrise, it's Lolo. I don't know what's going on, but Raquel is gone. She didn't say anything to us. I asked Ruby, but no. Call me at home.

Cherrise it's ten p.m. We talked to Gonzalo Ortiz. I don't know if you remember him. But his grandson is gone, too. They must be together.

Cherrise, it's eleven. Maybe you are at work. Try to call her and see what's going on. Being out here was hard for her, but we thought she was doing okay. Let me know, please.

Raquel was gone.

And Lolo thought Cherrise didn't give a shit.

"Larette."

No texts or missed calls from Raquel since late Wednesday.

The panic leapt in her chest and the machines went crazy. Her blood pressure and heart rate. She could feel the valves. *Thump. Thump.*

"Larette! You didn't tell her, and now she's gone. Lolo says she's gone. With a boy."

"Cherrise, calm down, I'm so sorry. She must be trying to come home. I'll call Grief right now. He'll go out to the desert."

The machines. Bryan Bradford, the shift nurse, came running inside and said, "What the hell?"

Cherrise was trying to yell. She felt the Gulliver lines. Like they'd joked about. She said, "Yeah, call Grief. You guys can be all, wow, how terrible? Dante would never run away. Because Grief is there. And you're a perfect mom. I'm a fuckup."

"Now you're delirious."

Bryan was at the machines. "Calm down, Cherrise. Like you tell everybody else. Larette, give her some water."

Cherrise licked her lips. Her head. Filled to bursting with a loofah. Dry loops. "Don't give me shit, Larette."

She reached over and got the cup. Wished it was tequila. Raquel thought she didn't care at all about her. Lolo, Ruby, they all thought she was a fuckup. A shitty mom.

She looked at Larette, her eyeshadow vivid, her dark liner still intact. Of course one curl edging out of the PPE like a tendril arranged for a photo shoot.

"Must be nice, cuz. To be perfect. Grief never gets mad at you. Dante all happy just playing his games, looking at the stars with his new telescope. He'd never run away."

Larette leaned close to her. "Dante barely speaks to me. He's the one who doesn't answer my texts. He says I picked strangers over him."

"Raquel says the same thing. But you treated her worse than a stranger! You told Norma Magana more than you told my daughter!" Cherrise's heart thumped again. Harder and harder. So angry. "You can't protect everyone by not telling them shit! You didn't even tell her a lie. You gave her nothing. Nothing!"

"Cherrise, you're—" Larette cut herself off. "Your blood pressure is one eighty-three. You have to breathe."

Cherrise whispered, "You shoulda called Raquel the minute you brought me in."

"I didn't want to scare her."

"Yeah, we were all scared when you got it, but everybody knew where you were. ICU 3112. Because I was there and I told them. Just like we do for everybody else. For total fucking strangers, Larette. You're like my sister, and you didn't even treat my baby as good as you treated those asshole families. The ones that hate us and say it's not real."

Larette said, "She's a baby. It's too much. We'd never call a kid to tell them."

"There's nobody else to call. Just me and Raquel." She looked away from her cousin. At the wall.

Everything went quiet. The beeping of machines. Cherrise could hear the blood pulsing in her brain. Her throat.

"You have me," Larette said softly. "All of us."

"Not the same. You didn't get to choose. You should have known." She turned her head to face Larette again. "If I died, you'da had to drive all the way out to the desert to get her, and they'd have to move me from here, and she'd never have seen me again. For real."

"Stop," Larette said. "You weren't gonna die."

"How the fuck did you know? We get patients die in the lobby! In the car out there! So fast. You didn't know."

Bryan came back in with Dr. Jacobs.

Cherrise whispered to Larette, "I don't cook, I don't sing, I don't give a shit. I'm just good at Raquel. And now she's gone. So get me out of here so I can find her."

"I already texted Grief. He can take off work and go look for her."

When Larette was gone, Cherrise closed her eyes. Monday. The barn. The bear trap. Monday night they worked. The fried chicken. Everybody was eating it and Cherrise already felt like shit. She kept thinking of the bear trap, that night, and the guy who said he ate bear and didn't get sick. All the patients above her. Mariah pissed about being short on shift. Raquel out in Oasis. Crying. She'd been crying. Now she was gone.

Raquel didn't care about boys. She had just turned fifteen. The boys at STEM were like Dante. They only loved Minecraft and Call of Duty.

Who was this boy? Did she know him? Did he know Ronald?

Where would Raquel go? Home. She wanted to come home.

THIRTEEN ✦ Calimesa

RAQUEL WAS SHIVERING IN HER HOODIE. JOEY LOOKED over and said, "You don't have to be scared."

"I'm not scared."

"I'm not Beto, okay?" But what if he was, and she just didn't know it yet? No. They were cousins, but completely different humans. Just like her and Dante.

He drove slowly, carefully, both hands on the wheel. Her mom always drove with just her thumb, at the bottom of the steering wheel, because she said that's how Raquel's dad drove, and he taught her mother. She'd never had the money for a car until she started working at the casino.

"I'm just scared about my mom." What if she was so sick—so sick they might not make it to Our Lady in time? No.

"I can't believe how many cars," Joey said. "It's, like, almost midnight."

"It's almost Friday now," Raquel whispered.

Joey didn't hear. "Everybody's fucking racing on here. All those rich pendejos from Palm Springs and shit."

They'd left the desert, passed the dinosaurs, passed the casino at Morongo. So many cars swerving past Joey, who was driving slowly—white lowered cars, black lifted trucks, everybody racing in all the lanes, and then big trucks like Amazon and FedEx in the slow lane, and guys weaving around. Joey got scared—she could tell. He tried to stay in the slow lane, and then three black cars came up behind them, going fast. One cut right in front of the truck, and Joey swerved onto the shoulder for a moment. Drove slow for about five minutes before two more big Amazon trucks passed and the windows shook hard.

A few minutes later, the truck sounded like it was exploding. "What happened?" Raquel said. "Are we out of gas?"

"No!" he shouted. "I don't know!"

He pulled over to the shoulder again. The wind was fierce, and his Raider hat blew off his head. He ran along the embankment to grab it, and she rolled down the window—the tinted glass gone, and now it didn't look like TV. The big trucks blasted past, shaking the doors. He threw his hat inside.

"Fucking flat tire," he said. "We're almost on the rim already. Beto's gonna kill me." He looked at the huge billboard above them. "We can't change it here. We'll get hit. We gotta make it to Calimesa. I remember that's where my dad got gas when we went to L.A. once."

The sound was terrible, and he drove so slowly that Raquel was sure a car would plow into them. But they made it to the exit, where they could see a gas station.

He parked at the edge of the gas station lot, and they got out to look for the spare tire. Nothing. She couldn't believe it, but Joey's eyes filled with tears. That was all she could see, beneath the Raider hat and above the bandanna. He said, "I'll be back. Lock the doors."

People went in and out of an encampment in the huge oleander bushes along the frontage road. The sudden blue flame of lighters, red sparkle of cigarettes. Two men lit cigarettes for two women with their own embers. When Joey unlocked the door, she jumped.

He handed her a Coke with ice. He didn't look at her, kept his eyes on his phone. Finally, he said, "We're fucked. All I have is a twenty. My dad says always have a twenty just in case. The Coke was free. The guy saw us out here with the flat." Then he put his forehead on the steering wheel. "I can't call my dad. Or my mom. I can't call Beto. I don't know what the fuck to do. We gotta get a new tire. And the rim is for reals messed up. Beto's gonna kick my ass."

Raquel said, "How much is a new tire? I have three dollars on me, and a hundred and twenty-eight at home."

He shook his head. "More than that."

"I'm sorry I texted you."

He shrugged.

She said, "I can't call my mom, she's sick. That's why I have to go home. I can't call my Aunt Larette. I don't want her to know—not like this."

She looked up Our Lady on Google maps: 20.2 miles away. What if her mom called? Raquel's phone was at 10 percent. They couldn't run the engine to charge it. They already needed gas.

Then Joey said, "What if Beto has a tracker on here—in case somebody stole the troca? If he comes out here with his friends—shit." People came and went at the gas station. "We can't stay here."

She texted her mom. **RU OK? Plz don't ghost me**

JOEY WENT INSIDE to charge their phones in the bathroom. He told Raquel to stay in the truck. "Too many crazy people around," he said. "Take the keys. You gotta have the windows open 'cause we can't run the AC. But lock the doors."

Four big trucks parked at the gas station. Two Amazon trucks, one FedEx, and one that said Woodrell Trucking. The men didn't get gas—only food from the minimart. Then they drove across the street to park in an empty lot, raising plumes of dust.

A truck pulled right next to her—a long shiny black trailer with no company name. The driver was a guy about the age of her uncle Grief, with a wide belly and chest, a silver goatee, and a tanned brown face. He came back from the minimart carrying a bag of food. When he opened the door to the cab, a dog barked, and he snapped on a leash and the little dog sailed out like he was diving into a lake instead of landing on the parking lot.

He ran straight to her door and barked up at her. But he was grinning. Like a baby clown, with a big ruff of white fur around his neck, and a golden body.

"He's fuckin' famous, eh?" the truck driver said, grinning at Raquel, too. "He's a corgi. My wife runs his socials—he's got Tik-Tok and Instagram. I take pics of him when we're on the road. He's got so many followers I don't even know."

Joey came walking fast toward them. He must have been watching from inside, trying to keep an eye on both her and the phones.

The guy turned and said, "Órale, mijo, Raider nation! That game last week was fucked up, eh?"

Joey nodded, looking like he didn't trust this guy. Raquel figured she could get out and pet the dog. He put both front paws on her knees and she rubbed his head.

"You guys look just like me and my wife. We got married when we were eighteen. How long you two been married?"

Raquel looked up at Joey. His face. Why would— Oh. She was wearing Leatrice's ring, from Auntie Lolo. On her left hand. She didn't say anything.

Joey said, "A month."

"I seen you got a flat, mijo. You okay? You need some help?"

Joey rubbed his hands over his hair. He said, "My primo's truck. I got a nail or something. The rim's messed up."

"Here," the man said, handing the leash to Raquel. "His paws are gonna get too hot. You gotta carry him like a damn baby."

She scooped up the dog, and he lay in her arms, still grinning crazy with his pointy black nose and his pink belly. The guy knelt down by the tire. "Yeah. A big fucking roofing nail. These are Kumhos—you got a spare?"

Joey shook his head.

The guy whistled. "The rim is bad. These are black Hollanders. New ones about two-fifty. Órale, mijo, where you headed?"

Raquel said, "My mom's sick. She works at Our Lady in San Bernardino, and I have to go see her. Tonight."

He shook his head. "You gotta let her know not tonight. It's past midnight. Too late to do anything now. But I can help you tomorrow after I pick up another car. I got a 1958 Chevy Bel Air in there now." He pointed to the black trailer.

Joey said, "My uncle's favorite. He loves those."

The man grinned. "Pues, I'm transporting it for this rich pendejo up on the hill over there. But he's broke from the shutdown, and now he wants to sell one more car. He told my boss to send me back up there tomorrow. Never comes outside. I talk to the Ring, eh? He ain't been outside since March." He pointed to his cab, and Raquel could see the gold writing now. Ray Allala Customs. "I'm taking two cars from one millionaire here to another millionaire in San Jose. So tomorrow we'll get you a tire and get your rim fixed."

Joey said, "I don't have money for that."

Raquel said, "We could pay you a hundred and forty-eight dollars."

Ray Allala laughed, and his dog barked twice, short and sharp. Laughing, too. "I should be halfway home by now! This pendejo's making me spend the night in my truck, instead of with my wife. He won't know if I charge three hundred extra. I know a guy in Fontana who can fix this rim. Drive after me 'cause you can't sleep right here. It's not safe." He nodded toward the trees at the edge of the gas station.

Joey looked at Raquel, holding the dog. She knew what he was thinking. *This ain't a Hallmark movie. No shit. In Calimesa?*

Ray Allala held up his big-ass phone again and she thought he was going to show her a car. But she heard ringing on speaker and then a woman said, "You better be careful on the 5 calling me, viejo."

He said, "Mujer, look." He turned the phone toward Raquel and the dog, Joey beside her. His wife said, "Who did you find now, Ray?"

"They got a flat. They look just like us, eh?"

The woman's face was small and brown, her makeup perfect, her hair shiny and black, and she smiled big at Raquel. "Except you got curly hair, mija!"

"They need a rim fixed," Ray said. "I gotta pick up the Shelby tomorrow, so I'm gonna help them out."

"Be careful," she said. "With my baby boy."

Raquel said, "I love your dog. What's his name?"

"Chulito," the woman said. "Because I'm Chulita."

JOEY WINCED LIKE every inch the truck went on the rim was painful in his body. They drove in the cloud of dust behind Ray Allala's truck, to the vacant lot on the other side of the frontage road. Seven trucks parked there, and four more in a long line on the road itself. Raquel thought, Cheaper than a motel room, and no virus in your own truck.

Joey had charged the phones to 30 percent. She tried her mother's number one more time, while the dust settled on the windshield like magic. Bad magic. But it made the bright white of the freeway light a little dimmer. Straight to voicemail again. Larette—same.

It was past 1:00 a.m.

Joey said, "I hope he's not some serial killer. I don't know what the fuck he's got in the trailer. Maybe it's not a car."

Raquel said, "His wife looks like she runs the world, though," and he laughed a little bit. "And the dog, right? We don't have a choice. If we sleep here, and he's gone in the morning, whatever."

Joey said, "If he turns into a freak and comes at us, I got something."

"Well, okay, but I have this." She opened her backpack and took out her flashlight/stun gun. The last time she'd used it was for the scorpions.

That felt like months ago.

Joey rolled his eyes. "Whatever. You get in the back."

She opened the door and got into the back of the crew cab, carrying her backpack for a pillow. Then with both doors shut, and the dust, and the tinted windows, it was hazy dark. Joey reclined the driver's seat, and she lay with her feet behind him, curled on her side, facing the seat that smelled like fish.

SHE'D FORGOTTEN ABOUT peeing. The Coke. She woke up. Suddenly remembered Joey's grandfather peeing against the palm trunks, Joey following him. Shit. She wasn't gonna tell him she had to go. And she couldn't go against a tree.

She slid her feet slowly from under the back of his seat. Picked up the flashlight from the floorboard in case there was a coyote. She opened the door quietly, and the light came on. He didn't move. She eased it shut and started running toward the gas station.

Barely made it. Her mother and Larette always joked about how many gowns and scrubs they had to pull up and down to pee and how they barely made it. Her jeans were so loose she didn't even unzip. Just slid them down.

When she came back out, the cashier looked at her. Fuck him. She reached into her pocket for her three dollar bills and bought the last two churros rolling in the heater. Put them in a white bag and, when she got to the door, started running again. Coyotes.

Just when she crossed into the frontage road, two men and a woman came out of the oleander bushes. The woman was carrying a lantern. One of the men was on a kid's bike, with a Big Gulp cup in his hand. She made it to the vacant lot, but he cut her off fast on the bike. The other man came up quick, his cigarette glowing red, and stepped in front of her. The trucks roaring past on the freeway blew away his words at first.

He said it again. "That your brother in the truck?"

Raquel could smell him. Weed and dirt. She took another step and he mirrored her.

"Does your mommy know you're out here?" The man laughed. "You're worth about three hundred dollars, little girl."

His face was creased deep in the forehead and on the sides. He was missing teeth.

The woman said, "I'll take care of you, little sister. Don't worry."

Your mommy? Fuck this. She felt a rage so hot she wanted to kill him. She heard sounds like sharp laughter from the vacant lot. No. Barking?

Her mother always said, *Look at everything first. Listen. Don't talk. Look at the body, that's what we do. The eyes—all red? Pupils too dilated? Are they on something? Look at their skin—kind of yellow? Pale gums?*

"She's got a good rack under that big shirt," the man on the bike said. "Cinnamon girl."

Raquel looked at everything. The man on the bike, the man in front of her, the woman between them. No weapons she could see. She took two more steps, and the man in front of her grabbed her left arm. He was the boss. His fingers dug hard into her muscle, pushing it into the bone. She dropped the churros, pulled out the flashlight/stun gun with her right hand, and pushed both buttons. Aimed for his nuts in the jeans.

The device crackled and pulsed.

But he laughed. Said, "You think you're funny? You think that shit's gonna hurt me?" He grabbed her by the top of her hair and pulled so hard she saw black. His fingers so strong he dragged her head to the side. She thought her neck would break.

"Let her go!"

It was Joey, running across the lot, holding something up. She couldn't see what.

Then she heard a dog barking. A door slamming. A *shuck-shuck* sound.

Ray Allala said, "Let her go, cabrón, or you get a shotgun in the face."

The guy laughed again. "Really? 'Cause her face is next to my face."

He must be so high, she thought. He pulled even harder until she felt his whiskers against her neck. She kept her eyes on Ray Allala. He aimed the gun, but he didn't move.

A shot came from behind them. The front bike tire whistled. Another shot. The back tire. The bike fell and the man, still holding the Big Gulp cup, raised his hands. The woman ran.

A window was down on a big truck parked on the road. "This ain't TV, asshole. Fuckin' get away from her."

All Raquel could see was the rifle, pointed at the guy with the bike. "Your friend goes first."

It was quiet. Another shot. Into the Big Gulp cup—it flew into the bushes.

The man let Raquel go. She stumbled and fell to her knees.

"Now head down the road. Or I take you back to Arkansas in this trailer and nobody'll even find your fuckin' bones. I'll feed you to the pigs. Walk."

The man backed away, facing the truck window.

The other man picked up his bike and carried it. He yelled, "He'll be gone in the morning, bitch, and you got a fuckin' flat tire and no money. We'll be back."

Raquel was on her knees. Her scalp burning. The flashlight in the dirt. The truck driver she couldn't see fired once more. The bullet thudded into the pepper tree just ahead of the men. Joey was beside her. He dropped the thing he'd been holding on the ground and put his arms around her. But he was crying.

"CALMATE, CALMATE, YOU'RE good," Ray Allala said to them both. "I got you."

He lifted his chin toward the truck from Arkansas. Woodrell Trucking. A pale hand came out and made a fist in the air. Then the window glass slid up.

Ray Allala said, "Get in your truck, mijo. Calm down. Drive up in here."

He opened the back door of his trailer, pulled down two metal ramps. Joey was shuddering like you did when you cried too hard. Raquel hadn't cried. Her face was hot and full of sand. Her arm hurt. Her neck hurt from bending.

"Joey," she said. "It's okay."

"Fuck that," he murmured. "I didn't do shit."

Raquel now saw what he'd been holding. His machete. He picked it up, went to the truck, and put it under the front seat.

"We're going in his trailer?" he said. "What if he's a fucking serial killer?"

The wife. The dog. She looked at the Instagram fast. Pictures of Mrs. Allala holding the dog, of Ray Allala sitting with the dog in the front seat of fancy cars, the dog's paws on the wheel. Both of them grinning the same.

She said, "His wife said *Who did you find now*, like he helps people out. He's that guy."

Joey drove slowly, the rim thudding, up onto the ramps, and the metal pulled the truck into the trailer. The shining beautiful car in his headlights, facing them. Ray Allala walked up into the trailer and fastened heavy chains to the wheels of the truck, and straps to hooks on the side of the trailer. Then he said into Joey's window, "Órale, go to sleep now. You can keep the windows open. The trailer's ventilated. You're okay, mija. Pues, in the morning you can sit with the dog, and we'll get a tire and fix that fucking rim."

He closed the back door.

It was black inside. She left the flashlight on. She whispered to Joey, "I almost got us killed."

He said, "Stay up here in the front."

She reclined her seat a little. She didn't want to be on her back. Her hair. The man had left his dirty viruses and germs in her hair. She took Joey's bandanna from his hand and wrapped her hair. He reached over and held her fingers on top of the cup holder.

Then the engine started up, the whole trailer shaking, and the truck began to move.

"Shit," Joey said. "Now we're fucked."

Under the wheels below them, the gravel of the lot. Then asphalt, smooth. They went a long way. Then up a hill. Turning. Turning. Joey got out the machete. Raquel held the flashlight.

No. They were fine. He wouldn't hurt them.

The truck turned one more time, slowly, and came to a stop.

Ray Allala slid up the trailer door, climbed into the trailer and came to Joey's window. "Those culeros would come back and fuck with the trailer for sure. They were watching everything we did, from the trees. I never have to pull the trigger, not when I make that shotgun sound. And I don't want to start now."

Joey said, "Thank you, Mr. Allala." But he had the machete in his hand, under the seat.

"We're up high now. Come see."

They stood in the open trailer door. A narrow street, high up in the hills above the freeway. The lights blurry below in the heat.

"Go to sleep," he said. "Only thing up here is bears and raccoons, eh? If there's a bear, Chulito will go crazy. Don't worry."

He left the trailer door open, jumped down onto the road, and after one soft bark from Chulito, everything was quiet.

Joey took her hand and closed his eyes again. But Raquel felt the other fingers imprinted in her arm, and her hair.

FOURTEEN ♦ You Know Better

SHE'D NEVER BEEN OUT HERE ALONE. LARETTE LIT UP THE Lucky Strike, blew smoke into the branches. The security guard was new. He stood between the tree and the street, staring at his phone, the colors reflecting off his glasses in the dark.

Larette closed her eyes. When Cherrise was a freshman, she'd wait for Larette in the theater during rehearsal, doing homework in the seats, and they'd take the bus home in the fall dusk. As they walked up to the apartments, every window would have a TV on in the same place—all the laughter or car crashes or music videos sounding through the windows, kids laughing or singing along. The smell of Downy from the machines in the laundry room near the stairs—no matter what time of day or night, the washers and dryers were always going. All the moms trying to keep up with the laundry.

Cherrise would say, "I miss my mom. I only remember, like, three things. She would sit me up on the dryer and put our socks in little balls and fill up my lap. Say we'd never have stinky feet."

Larette pressed the paper towel to her eyes. The dog Marisol sometimes left food for watched her from the opening in the hedge around the trees. Larette took a deep breath. She'd fucked up. She lit another Lucky Strike. Her mother smoking them. Cherrise's mother shaking her head and saying, "Topaz, that shit ain't good for you. You know better."

I knew better, she thought. Cherrise might never forgive me. Never. Friday at 4:00 a.m. Where is Raquel? Who is this boy? What if he's taking her somewhere far away? What if she met someone online and she's going to meet a grown-ass man who'll kidnap her?

She'd text Grief in two hours, when her shift ended. She'd tell him not to say anything to Dante. No. He'd lose his mind, and he didn't need any more worry.

Raquel could already be home, waiting until later in the morning to call her mother. Maybe she really had known somehow that Cherrise was sick?

Way back then, on the apartment stairs, Cherrise's mother said, "Lucky Strikes—Topaz, that's what the men smoke. Girl, you know better!"

And Larette's mother said, "You still a baby. You don't know nothin' yet! You been at Our Lady five minutes."

And after Turquoise was gone, and Cherrise came to sleep in Larette's bed, one night they heard a neighbor saying outside the window, "I don't believe she'd leave that little girl. She loved that baby with all her heart and soul. She'd never go."

Larette realized then that *heart* and *soul* were two different things. You could love someone with all your heart, but what about your soul?

Grief loved her with both. Cherrise loved Raquel with both. Larette was messing up big-time with both her husband and her cousin. Keeping secrets.

Dante loved her so deeply that he stayed awake every night to text her and fell asleep for a few hours before school. He'd never run away.

Would he? She breathed the smoke so deep inside her lungs that her heart felt the warmth. Heart and soul. What if Dante knew Raquel was gone? No way she could text her own thirteen-year-old son and ask what their classmates knew.

The kids knew everything about everything, and she knew nothing, Grief knew nothing; they only knew all these bodies with toes and paws and tails and the remnants of tails when she and Marisol turned them. The tailbone. Coccyx. Deep inside the clefts of the buttocks she wiped.

All those years she'd wanted to be alone, and right now she was alone for twenty minutes and it felt like she would die. She stared at the dog. The dog stared back. Pissed at her? Patient? Waiting to bite her when she got up?

It was strange to miss Marisol so much. She was working day shift all week, doing something mysterious in the evenings.

The bench. The trench. You have to trust your men in the trenches—isn't that what guys said in the movies? Now maybe Cherrise wouldn't trust Larette. She wiped her tears on her wrist. Fucking 2020. Fucking coronavirus.

She breathed in the Lucky Strike. The moon in the west. Dante knew the precise moment of sunrise and sunset every day. The position of each constellation for the day of the year. His journals. He wrote them by hand before he added the data to his laptop. In case of total breakdown, he said.

Total breakdown.

Smoke rings. Her mother saying, *What if a dude could make a smoke ring real small and you could stick your finger right up in it? In the air!*

Larette and Cherrise tried to put their fingers into her circles of white, in the night. But the ring finger was too awkward. Only the pointer finger, as her mother called it. Then when they learned *phalanges* in nursing school, they never saw the hand the same way.

She'd talked Cherrise into nursing school. Talked her into coming here, after the accident when Cherrise didn't want to go back to the casino. And in March, she'd talked Cherrise into working nights and overtime during Covid, to make extra money for the secret college funds they'd started for the kids. They were putting in $200 a month. One of the school moms—Akisha's mom, what was her name? She and her husband had started their college fund for Akisha when she was in kindergarten. "Damn," Cherrise had said. "I'm always behind. Leilani's parents started three funds for their kids when they were born. With grandparent money and their own."

"Then I'm behind you, cuz," Larette said. "I'm in line. Sign us up."

They were going to tell the kids and Grief when the school year was over. They had expected to have a good chunk then.

Mariah appeared before her. "Earth to Larette. It's too quiet out here." The dog barked once, short and deep, and melted back into the hedges. "Jesus, he scared me!" Mariah said, lighting her cigarette.

Larette took one last pull and then put out the butt in the sand. No cigarillo from Marisol.

Mariah said, "I stopped in to see her. She's been crying. Said you knew why."

Larette said, "Her daughter. Mariah, I think Cherrise and I better move to days in September. The kids."

Mariah nodded. She'd be pissed later, if Larette was serious. But not here, at the benches.

"You know, my first husband was a tree trimmer for the city," Mariah said. "Every weekend some friend had a tree emergency. Fire clearance up in Waterman Canyon, or termites, or whatever. We had the kids. He'd get home late, smelling like Coors and Camels." She blew out smoke. "But God forbid a nurse should drink beer or eat bad food or smoke. My second husband was my daughter's bio teacher in high school. Mr. Hike up San Jacinto or San Gorgonio on the weekends. I'd hike ten miles with him, and if I slowed down for five minutes, he'd be all, *It's because you poison your body!* He bought us Fitbits, and I fucking killed him on every single category during the week."

Larette looked at Mariah's Crocs. "Nurses know better, right?"

"That's what everybody says. We gotta be perfect. But my kids fucking hate me. Not because of Covid. They just do. I'm fat, I dress like shit, and I want to sit on my couch when I get home and watch *Homestead Rescue*. I'm not an Instagram mom. Larette, you know what they call those kind in England? I had a patient show me once. Yummy mummies. My dad would say, *Holy moly that's not good*."

Their phones lit up. They both looked down.

"Jesus," Mariah said. "My kids sending me shit. The patient families. All of it. The fucking hashtags. #MomLife. #PandemicLife. #PandemicPajamaLife. I hate that one. My kids stay in their pajamas all day long."

At that, Larette closed her eyes. She saw her mother, Topaz, in the amber silk pajamas she bought herself for Christmas one year, and Turquoise, Cherrise's mom, in the bright sky-blue set. Her mom had gotten matching sets for the girls, and Cherrise wore her silky pants long after her mother had disappeared, until the knees wore through into fine mesh.

She had to help find Raquel.

PART THREE

FIFTEEN ✦ Track

I'D BEEN OFF FOR THREE DAYS SINCE I CRACKED TWO RIBS on that rock in Borrego Canyon, chasing the kid. My duty sergeant, Hubie Vaughn, was pissed when he called to check on me and I told him I'd have to build a new corral on Friday at dawn.

"When my dad calls I'm on the Harley, and I get off shift and go straight to the rancho," I said. "Twenty hours with no sleep so many times this summer. It's gonna be a hundred and three up in the Chino Hills today, Hubie."

"We're down two again on night shift," he said.

"I've been working doubles since March," I told him. "I'm not going to Vegas. I'm moving a bull named Cabrón."

Hubie sighed. "I'm putting you on doubles Saturday through Monday," he said. "Wish I was up there building a corral."

Hubie was fifty-five. When I first started at the Santa Ana Division, he told me his father was from Comfort, Texas, grew up on cattle ranches, and Hubie used to go every summer. If I said cows and horses, he was cool. If I said Vegas, he'd lose his shit.

But I never said that. If Cherrise called me, I wouldn't take her to Vegas. I had it figured out. I'd ask if she wanted to go to San Diego. Just far enough away that nobody could call us in an emergency and expect us to be there in half an hour.

She hadn't called me.

I hadn't talked to Grief since Monday.

But my father had said, "We need you up here, mijo, in the morning."

Grief texted to say he had to do a follow-up check on Cabrón for the County Animal Services, paperwork saying the bull was in a safe enclosure, couldn't escape, and was being treated humanely. Dick Wolf was coming to meet us, too, at 6:00 a.m. He missed Cabrón.

SUNRISE AND THE heat already hung in the eucalyptus windbreak near my dad's house. I unloaded a case of Modelo Negro and a case of Mexican Coke into the big 7-Eleven cooler in our barn. A twelve-pack of the tamarindo soda the Vargas brothers loved. Hurt my ribs like hell. At least the twenty tortas I brought from my neighbor Rose were lighter.

My father came up the ranch road on his ATV, leading Grief's county truck and Dick Wolf's old Bronco. I got into the Cheyenne and followed them up to the big barn at the top of the ranch.

Mrs. Dottie was there. Her caretaker, Diana Monroy, had driven her across the road from the old adobe house built in 1845. Adobe bricks with layers of thick white paint that turned chalky but didn't chip off, red tile roof that had sections busted, where birds loved to nest. Mrs. Dottie didn't want anyone coming up here to fix anything, except us. My dad would have to find the old tiles in the big barn. But it hadn't rained in forever. The long porch with wooden railings and jasmine vines tangled all around them. In normal times, Diana took Mrs. Dottie down to Santa Ana on Fridays to get her hair done, to go to Mass, to get groceries. But since corona, they hadn't left the house. The priest came up twice to give them communion. I brought supplies. That was it.

But Mrs. Dottie had her binoculars, saw everything, and had no trouble keeping track of the accounts and the cattle.

"Dick Wolf's bull," my father shouted. "Cabrón."

"Claro que sí," she said, like he was a child. She was tiny, with her white hair in a bun, with a dress and those heavy black shoes old ladies wore. Binoculars around her neck like jewelry for a giant. Her eyes were black, and they saw everything. "Richard."

He got out of the Bronco and nodded.

She nodded back. "I pay for the hay y todos. You pay later. Don't take Cabrón."

"Es al infierno," my father said. "Tenemos mover el corral."

She nodded. "Y Rana?"

Our other bull.

My father laughed. "Rana, siempre contento."

She humphed a little. "Happy bull. Pues, Cabrón es puro longhorn. We keep him until you go home, eh?"

Dick nodded.

She turned for the car, her hand so gnarled on the cane knob it was like a little blind animal sitting there. But Mrs. Dottie loved watching all the horses, and her cattle. She wished she were still out here riding with them.

THE RANCHO WAS divided into four parts: the orange groves by the Santa Ana River; then the ranch housing and our barn and corral; then up here the adobe and the big barns and corrals that stretched on the acreage down to Cuernos Creek, which was dry now; finally, above us, the six hundred acres of pastureland in the higher hills. My father kept a temperature gauge on a pole in the shade near the barn, but he always knew within two degrees how hot or cold it was.

"Already eighty-nine," he said. "Vamos."

For the horses, we had one big wooden corral. But we had

movable pipe corrals everywhere, mazes that only we knew. Cattle pens where we kept heifers or steers for sale or when they were sick. Rana's corral was farther up the slope, in the shade of two pepper trees. But a hundred yards away, Cabrón was still in the rectangular Bulldog corral the Vargas brothers had put together in a hurry when we brought him here Monday.

He'd done a lot of damage, banging against the metal pipes. We all walked over to see him. Even in this heat, he leapt into the air like it was the rodeo and one of us was on his back. He had hops—he twirled himself two and three feet off the ground, and when he landed, his hooves carved more holes in the dirt around the stock tank. He fucking hated being caught.

Dick Wolf said, "You old son of a bitch. You was home on the range, and then you wasn't."

He shivered when he heard Dick's voice. Swung his head around at us. His eyes huge and dark—not brown, not black, not anything but an oblivious shine saying that he despised what he saw. He'd been free, out there for months, even if it was hot and he was hungry, and he'd been able to run full speed, break tree branches, and rest where he wanted in the shade.

Just like everyone I saw speeding on the freeways at night, eyes wild and something calling them. Being locked up made them hear, Screw this, do what you want.

Sergio, Ramon, Grief, and I started putting together the bigger corral, another hundred yards down the slope toward Cuernos Creek, under two of the oak trees for shade. Cabrón was showing off for Rana, who gave no fucks about the old dude. But we figured if Cabrón had more shade and even some fall acorns, he'd be a little less—cabrón.

My father unloaded the Bulldog sections with the forklift, and we fastened them together in a huge square around the two trees. We had to stop and rest every hour, drink a Coke from the cooler we had in the shade. Pee in the dry creek bed. Sergio and Ramon wore their oldest Levi's, almost shredded at the knees. Their short bowlegs, powerful chests, and big square panzas under the long-sleeved orange shirts I'd brought last year. The same ones we all wore, so we could be seen. "Like the hunters used to wear," my dad said, the first time I showed him the shirts, at the Santa Ana swap meet.

"This is what everyone buys now, so you don't get hit by a car," I said. "All the road crews, everybody."

"They're cheap," he said. "Get four, eh, mijo?"

By the time we finished the new corral, it was ninety-four degrees. Just after 10:00 a.m. We sat panting in the shade by the barn. We ate the tortas, drank one more icy, peppery Coke, and went to finish the alley to get the bull down there.

Alley fencing let us move the cattle easily. We used sections of heavy schedule 40 pipe, all the bars horizontal for longhorns, so they wouldn't break their horns on a vertical bar. We made a seven-foot-wide hallway so that Cabrón would have room to run but couldn't turn around. This one was a straight shot, from the gate of Cabrón's current prison down the slight decline to the larger corral. We carried the pipe sections into place, locked them down tight, and attached the alley to the gate of the new corral. My father would open that gate—we'd dumped a load of fresh hay in there for him to smell, and we'd installed a metal stock tank for water.

Grief, my father, and Dick stood near the new corral. Dick was bent like an old cowboy, his face hard and lined. *Clint Eastwood*, we always teased him.

But without the money, he always said.

Ramon opened the gate. Sergio and I hung on the alley—we had a gate to close halfway down, in case Cabrón panicked, backed up. The whole point was to keep him cruising, not stopping—like everything was his idea.

Ramon guided the bull with a pole toward the gate. Sergio's

elbow was inches from mine. He spit onto the dirt in the alley. He smelled of twin, I always thought. They had eaten everything the same, worn the same clothes their whole lives. When I was little, they smelled of beer, garlic, and tobacco, when they'd smoked Marlboros. Now I smelled old man—still garlic and onions, smoke, but also pee and the orange shirt that he wore four or five more times after it should have been washed.

"What if it never rains again?" I said. We had our gloved hands on the gate, ready to swing it after Cabrón passed. The metal bars like a barbecue grill.

"Mijo," Sergio said. "You think it was never hot? It was always hot."

Cabrón didn't move. Just stared out at the hills. Not even looking at us.

Like, *Fuck this pendejada.*

Dick Wolf whistled, down there at the other corral. The loop of sound like when we caught the bull on Carbon Canyon Road. Dick Wolf's whistle. Two more times. Nothing. Dick walked back up along the alley, whistling. The massive head turned. Those long horns dipped. They're like our eyebrows, I thought, the way they show feeling.

Dick said, "Like a damn mockingbird. But I'm out of breath."

He whistled again and again; Cabrón circled and then saw the open gate. Trotted down the alley, almost past us, Dick whistling at the new corral now. Then silence. Cabrón stopped dead, looked at us. I got off the pipes, but Sergio was slower. Cabrón looked like he saw a snake in front of him, planted his front feet and kicked the middle gate. Sergio flew sideways and landed in the dust.

Ramon shouted and ran toward us. Cabrón took off for the new corral, and when my father slammed the gate, the bull threw himself around like he was covered with biting ants.

I made it to Sergio, who lifted himself up like nothing had happened. But his whole body was shaking.

Ramon knelt beside his brother, whispering, "Calmate, calmate."

Sergio looked at me, his big square face, his forehead two colors. Hat fallen behind him. Never saw him without his hat.

He said, "Mijo. The shirt. Cabrón don't like orange, eh? Too close to red."

His left wrist hung broken.

THE VARGAS BROTHERS shared their small house across the lane from my father's house. The same tiny kitchen, two-burner stove, old enamel sink. Square wooden table I had made in high school, with two wooden chairs. Two new recliners we'd bought them for Christmas last year. Cup holders they loved. The small flat-screen TV. The rancho had a satellite dish.

The pictures on the wall—the Vargas parents, one each holding a twin boy. *February 10, 1948*, the spidery white ink said along the bottom of the photo. Mrs. Dottie's writing, I realized suddenly, for the first time. I didn't come in here very often and stare at stuff. *Martin and Ofelia Vargas*, the wedding photo to the left said. I picked it up—*Los Nietos, California*. Mrs. Dottie's writing, too. The parents had never learned to read or write—they'd died in a truck accident when the twins were about twelve. The boys had stopped going to school. They stayed right here, and the rancho people watched over them, cooked for them and washed their clothes—my mother's people.

In their bedroom, Sergio lay in his twin bed. Ramon sat on the edge of his.

"He can't go to the hospital, mijo," Ramon said to me. "Corona everywhere. No."

We'd cut off the orange shirt. His left shoulder probably cracked. But his left wrist definitely broken.

But Sergio said, "No ire, Johnny. No ire." He wouldn't go down the hill.

"Get the tape," Ramon said to my father. The same thing he'd said hundreds of times, for all of us. Tape and tequila and IcyHot. I'd bought five rolls of hot-pink pressure tape from Rite Aid in spring, when Ramon's ankle was bothering him.

Ramon took me out to the porch. He found two small, flat pieces of wood, about ten inches long, from an old citrus crate. He sanded them quickly, smooth and golden, brushed off the dust, and poured rubbing alcohol over them, into the dirt by the porch.

Grief finally said, "Are you crazy? You gotta get an X-ray at least. Let me call Larette and ask if she can help."

I said, "Head down by the road—the service is better there."

But I followed Ramon inside. They both shook their heads, not much different from the bull.

"No hospital," Ramon said.

"No corona," Sergio said, faintly.

They'd never been to the hospital. They'd never go even if it weren't for corona.

Ramon had my father hold the one slat under his brother's hand and wrist. The other on top. Arranged the hand flat, Sergio wincing, then taped the whole thing carefully.

Then Ramon said, "Bring the medicine, mijo."

In the kitchen cupboard were four plates, four coffee cups, four spoons, four forks, four knives. Exactly how it had been in 1950. I took out the bottle of Tylenol, the bottle of Patrón.

I already smelled the IcyHot. I had to bring ten tubes a month. They were addicted to IcyHot. My father filled a coffee cup half full of Patrón Gold. Three Tylenol Extra Strength. Ramon sat beside his brother's bed.

When I got back out to their yard, with tools everywhere, Grief's face was like stone. "Johnny," he said. "Cherrise's daughter, Raquel. She's gone. She's with some guy. Larette wants us to check the house in San Bernardino, and maybe head out to Coachella if we can't find her."

"Where's Cherrise?"
"At Our Lady. She's got corona."

I FOLLOWED GRIEF'S county truck to the Animal Control offices up in San Bernardino. Sat in the parking lot staring at the arrowhead formation in the mountains.

Pneumonia. That's how corona killed people, didn't it? Drowned them. I slammed my hand on the dashboard. My mother had died of pneumonia, coughing and coughing, in our little house, while I lay on the couch staring into the bougainvillea that covered the front window. All the people from the rancho back then kept bringing caldos, liniments. And finally my mother stopped coughing.

I'd never wanted to love anyone, because they'd die.

Grief was at the window. "Come on," he said.

He'd changed into jeans, boots, and a T-shirt. But he carried a duffel bag into the truck. I knew he had a tranquilizer rifle in the bag. He put his badge into his front pocket.

He said, "This way, at least people might answer our questions. Although I don't know who the hell you're supposed to be."

I didn't know who the hell I was supposed to be. Cherrise clearly wasn't interested in me, but I couldn't stop thinking about her. And even if that hadn't been true, a teenage girl was out there somewhere trying to get to her mom.

"Head to Our Lady," Grief said. "Larette's working a double shift, because they're down two nurses. Cherrise and somebody else."

I drove to the hospital. When Justin Pham and I had to escort the EMTs with the kid from Borrego Canyon to Hoag Hospital, the ER entrance was crowded with ambulances. At Our Lady, they were lined up like cows at the trough—six of them, waiting to drop off patients.

I looked up at the blank silver windows. Larette and Cherrise patrolled the hallways like I did the freeways? I'd only been to the ER a few times, never upstairs in my life.

Grief called Larette, but she didn't answer right away. "She's got patient families calling every minute, and the surgeons and doctors all text each other for where the nurses have to go," he said, looking up there, too. "I know we got crazy, Johnny. I got whole packs of feral dogs colonizing empty office parks and shit. You got—"

"Whole packs of feral dudes racing each other on four lanes of the 91 trying to kill whatever slow grandma is finally out on the road," I said.

"Yeah, but up there—it's different."

A text chimed in. "She said Cherrise won't even talk to her. She's angry that Larette didn't tell Raquel she was sick. Raquel and this boy must have left in the middle of the night."

It was almost 2:00 p.m. now.

"Two hours from the desert to here. She should be home," Grief said. "Let's go backward."

SINCE I WAS a kid, I could track animals—my father and the Vargas brothers taught me how to see pawprints—coyote, mountain lion, bobcat, raccoon. Hoofprints—cow, deer, wild pig. Each kind of boots from someone who might be trying to steal a calf, way back in the day. Hikers in the hills.

Grief was just as good at animals. I'd helped him many times. We paid attention to every detail. But he didn't have to find people very often.

When I started law enforcement, I got just as good at finding people. I'd found a man who'd been throwing rocks onto the freeway, back when I was twenty-one, scouring the earth with a team of trackers. CHP had the ability to track phones, follow vehicles, and use GPS to lay spike strips on freeways to disable cars. But how do you find a fifteen-year-old girl?

Grief gave me Cherrise's address. "Do we ping the phone?" he said.

"Does Cherrise have a tracker app on her daughter's phone?" I asked. "Does she follow all her movements? Half the guys at my division are dads—they're obsessed with knowing where their kids are at every minute."

Grief shook his head. "Cherrise doesn't roll that way. If she wasn't on shift, and Raquel wasn't at school, they were together all the time. They ate together, they hung out. Raquel didn't go anywhere, except our place, or Dante's games, and then we were all together."

"Well, we could find her friends, look at their socials. That's how my friend Rob checks on his daughters. Did she report Raquel missing?" I said.

"Johnny, Cherrise is barely coherent right now. Her fever is a hundred and four, down from a hundred and six, but she can't talk."

"Does she have pneumonia?" I said.

"I don't know," Grief said. "Larette says fever, severe headache, joints on fire. That shit hits us all different. Larette and me, our lungs. Other people, their kidneys, whatever the virus feels is vulnerable. Dante says it's like *The Avengers*. People just disappear."

CHERRISE LIVED IN a wooden bungalow in San Bernardino, painted blue with yellow trim. Long gravel driveway. Grief checked the garage window for her car. Still there. No one in the yard. Dust everywhere on the patio, no footprints or shoeprints. Raquel wore Pumas, Grief said. Cherrise, too.

Dust on the washer and dryer she had put outside—just like mine. No fingerprints—only the perfect star-shaped tracks of a possum. The house was like an oven. No one had been here for a long time. Dust like a tiny sand dune in the bottom of the white sink. Grief went down the hallway, and I stopped at the pictures on the wall.

Cherrise and her husband wearing Dodgers jerseys, at a game. Her curly hair all over her shoulders. Then they were holding their daughter at a game, she was about three, wearing her own jersey, her dad's big leather baseball glove up in the air like they were going to catch a home run.

The daughter looked right at whoever took the photo. Big dark eyes, she wasn't smiling, she looked like she was just waiting for the damn ball to come her way. Tough kid.

"Nobody's been here," Grief said, coming back into the kitchen. "We gotta go out to Oasis."

ON INTERSTATE 10, you could drive from Santa Monica to Florida. I stayed in the middle lane. Grief was looking at his phone. "Can't call Dante and ask if they been texting—he'll freak out. He loves Raquel even though he'd never say that shit. They're the super nerds. All science. No common sense."

We went past Calimesa, Morongo, Cabazon, and into the long stretch of desert—Palm Desert, Rancho Mirage, Indian Wells, some of the wealthiest places in California. Then Indio.

I said, "Remember we came out here for baseball tournaments? Those guys laughing at us when we thought we'd pass out on the field from the heat?"

Grief said, "Those desert dudes didn't mess around. I almost fainted, and they laughed their asses off."

My dad had brought me here a few times. He lived in Calipatria one summer with his father, in a camper, when he was only twelve. His family needed extra money, so they worked cotton. He said he and his father would stand in the heat and stare south, to the border, but they never went to look at the fence. My father told me, "I've never been to Mexico, because mi abuelo said there was no one left on their old rancho. Way up in the mountains in Jalisco."

Grief said, "Johnny. Turn here."

I headed down Harrison Road. All the streets here named for Presidents, Grief said. The road was lined with fields and date palms, a few gates and signs for mobile home parks with names like Desert Shores and El Sol. Then Lolo's Date Garden. An old wooden packinghouse. Six cars and trucks. A tiny adobe home at the edge of the palms. We parked and stepped out into the furnace of afternoon.

Cherrise's daughter must have been losing her mind out here. We pulled up our bandannas to cover our faces, put on ball caps. The adobe was a little cooler, with the window AC roaring. The woman named Lolo had to be in her eighties, but she wore jeans and a T-shirt that said LOLO DATES. Her hair in a long braid wrapped around her head. She sat at a kitchen table with a younger woman, and stared at us.

"You look like train robbers," she said.

We stayed about eight feet away and pulled down the bandannas. Took off the hats.

She said to Grief, "My nephew Ronald called you brother-in-law. You were at their wedding."

He nodded. "We'll find his daughter, ma'am."

But she frowned at me. "Who is this?" she said, folding her arms. "Who are your people?"

She was very small, so I lowered myself down to a crouch so she could see me. I knew what she meant, too.

"My mother's people were from Loreto. We think Yuma and Kumeyaay," I told her. They came in 1774. With the Spanish. They passed through here."

"Ah," she said. "I see your forehead." She waited.

"They went to the mission in San Gabriel. My mother's five-times grandmother married a Serrano man. Like Grief's three-times grandmother married a Serrano man."

Lolo said, "You live in San Bernardino? San Manuel?"

I shook my head. "Chino and Santa Ana. My father's father was from Jalisco. Bracero."

She said, "Your hair is too short."

I said, "I'm a cop."

She raised her eyes. "You look like robbers from the old days, but everyone looks like robbers now. Joey and Roberto, too."

She had written things on a yellow piece of paper.

She said to Grief, "Raquel liked to work out in the dates. She worked with Joey Ortiz. They like each other. They were working late last night. We have five golf carts. Now only four. Joey's father, he went looking for one of the cousins. Roberto. He had the golf cart at his trailer. He's been in trouble, that one. But Joey loves him. Roberto works at the fish farm, up there." She slid across a small card. Christmas card. Taped together, and writing on the back.

Grief read it. "Raquel says she went home to see her mom. Okay. So she might be riding with these two guys? Joey—where are his parents? Can we talk to them? Maybe she's at their place."

Until then, Lolo had seemed okay. Her cheeks were round and smooth, and the deep lines fanning out from beside her eyes went up, into her forehead, and down, around those cheeks. Like fancy scrolled tattoos.

But now she put her hands over her face. She said into her fingers, "His father and his abuelo are working in the dates. His mother is home with the daughters. She never comes here, but she came this morning. Crying. All of them crying. Just waiting for him to come back. I never believed Raquel would do something like this."

WE DROVE SLOWLY on the service roads around the date garden, trying to not raise dust, not get too close to the workers. There were three trucks, one with a lift, men working the tops of the palms, lowering bunches of dates. A flatbed full of boxes. So the kids met out here.

"They took a golf cart to the trailer park, then," I said. "She can't be staying in there with the other guy, right? Roberto?"

I drove down the road only half a mile, into the entrance for Solimar Shores. Five long rows of mobile homes, twenty on each row. ORTIZ on the mailbox in front of one, with flowers and a Virgen de Guadalupe altar in the little yard. A pink bike. That must be Joey's parents. Up and down a few other rows, slowly. The other ORTIZ was at the far end, five single-wide homes from the 1950s. A white one with red rust around the windows and doors that had dripped for years, like brown icicles. Nothing. No golf cart, no truck, no Virgen. Just orange buckets in the dirt driveway, and tools.

Back on the road, Grief said, "Pull over here. I've got service now."

We were surrounded by vineyards, long green hallways filled with people wearing head coverings, snipping grapes, and putting them in crates. Golf carts everywhere—a guy wearing the exact same bandannas as we were stared at us from his cart, carrying water.

Grief said, "Can you call one of your dispatchers to check these guys for priors? We don't know shit before we roll up into that fish farm."

The darkest wet dirt mixed with dead fish—we could smell it. I looked up the road.

I called Dianne Howard—she was working days now. "Amiga, can you run a name and city for me, see if anything comes up?"

"You're off duty, Johnny," she said.

"Accurate," I said. "But I got a little problem."

"Damn, Johnny," she said. "Reason?"

"Stolen truck," I said.

"Where are you?"

"Oasis."

Dianne whistled. She had a good whistle. "A hundred and twenty today? Fine."

Roberto M. Ortiz. Twenty-one years old. Born Indio, California. Arrested for misdemeanor assault in 2019—a fight at a club in Coachella. Arrested for stalking in April 2020—a young woman named Brittany Mendoza. She refused to press charges. Great. He had a 2019 Chevy Silverado. License plates clean. No tickets.

I drove into the entrance of Star Fish Farm.

"If the truck isn't reported stolen," I told Grief, "and she's not reported missing, we can't even call county sheriffs out here. We're on our own."

It was like we had driven deep inside the center of some other planet. Dirt road past the office, which was a former house. No one came out. Grief said, "They've got eight ponds. They must ship everywhere. Look, two guys loading a truck."

We got out. The two men, who were older, stopped moving the orange five-gallon buckets into the back. Grief flashed his badge, and they looked worried. Wiped their faces with bandannas, pulled up the cloth gaiters from their necks to their faces.

I said, "No te preocupes. Sabes donde Roberto Ortiz?" I didn't want them to think they were in trouble.

Both pointed toward the ponds. We drove down the lane, passing the massive circles of water. They weren't black, close up—the darkest blue, roiling and bubbled. An ATV with a small trailer was parked in the center at the very end. Roberto was wearing a jumpsuit, not much different from my CHP utility uniform, and white rubber boots. Holding a bucket of what must have been fish food.

In the heat of early evening out here, in the Coachella Valley, the stink of the water and the mud, the fish poop, was like nothing I'd ever smelled. Out on the rancho, the wind just smelled like grass and cows. Here, there was no wind, the August sun hung red and purple in the west, and a thin crescent moon was already rising up past the Salton Sea. He turned when we slammed the truck doors shut. Headphones and a bandanna under his Raiders cap. Lifted his chin and shouted, "I don't sell fish down here. You gotta go to the office. Mr. Fan."

Up to Grief to decide the tone. He said, "We need to ask you some questions about Raquel Martinez, Roberto. And your Silverado."

The kid put down the bucket and folded his arms. He'd been asked a lot of questions before. He went straight hard stance. I had no stance—I was wearing vaquero boots and jeans. My cracked ribs meant if he wanted to run or fight, I was gonna be in even more pain. I got ready.

"Who the fuck are you?" he said.

Grief flashed his badge, but Roberto looked close. He lifted his chin at me. I just folded my arms, too.

"You're Animal Control. You want to know about the fish, ask Mr. Fan. They're not animals, though. They're fish. Fuckin' tilapia. The only animals here are sometimes hawks grab a fuckin' fish or a coyote waits for a stupid one to jump out."

Thousands of fish rolled in the water, hearing us talk. Swerving in big schools, with sharp fins that broke the water and then went sideways when the fish dipped back down. They were blue and brown and black and gray.

"What kind of tilapia?" I said. "Where are they from?"

"Blue," he said. "Israel. You undercover ICE for fish, bro? You want their papers, go see Mr. Fan." He pointed again to the office, out of sight.

I shook my head. "So you ride a golf cart to work today? Or did you walk?"

"What the fuck you care?"

"Where's your truck?"

He didn't move.

"You steal a golf cart from Lolo's Date Garden?" Grief said.

"It's not an animal, so fuck you," Roberto said. "Somebody lent it to me."

I took out my badge and said, "I'm CHP. And I'm here about your truck, and Raquel Martinez. Is she here on the farm, is she at your house in the trailer park, or is she with Joseph Ortiz Jr.?"

Now his face got a little scared. "I don't know anybody named Raquel."

"Give me your phone," Grief said. "Unlock it or I take it and throw it to the fish."

Beto was twenty-one. Priors for assault. Would he come at me first, or Grief?

Grief was about to get himself in trouble, so I said, "Fine. I'll call it in. Indio CHP about your truck, and Riverside County deputies about the girl reported missing."

He pulled the phone out of his pocket and unlocked it. A solid block of blue texts to Primo J.

UR fucked fool
where RU
fuck UR jaina
bring the troca now
U better have $$$ or pics

"Pics?" I said.

He maintained hard stance. "Somebody borrowed my phone. I don't know what you talking about. I gotta get back to work."

Grief took the phone from me. The veins in his forehead and

his neck were standing out. Back in the day, when we were eighteen, Grief and Manny and I could take on anybody. We fought CHP rookies that hated us, and bikers in the desert. But we were almost forty now. Grief couldn't breathe, and I could barely move.

He opened the camera feed. I stood close. In his hand were all kinds of girls. Lingerie. Thongs. Less. I didn't want to see this.

But we saw Raquel. She was tall, wearing jeans and a T-shirt. She had climbed onto a giant swing. She held her knees and threw back her head.

Grief threw the phone into the pond. The fish went crazy, the water boiling with bodies and fins and tails—like in a low-rent James Bond movie. You could throw somebody in there, and maybe they could stand up, but it would be hard.

"I don't even know where she is!" Roberto shouted. "She's with my cousin somewhere. In San Bernardino."

"She's fifteen," Grief said. "You're fucked. I'll be back."

I DROVE THROUGH the darkness of the fields toward the freeway. Cherrise had brought her daughter out here on July 5. Plenty of time for Roberto and his cousin to groom her for pics, or worse. She'd been sitting on that giant swing like a little kid in a backyard. Until she threw back her head and you could see her figure outlined under her T-shirt. That's what these guys saw.

Grief said, "The date garden. The golf cart. They rode in the golf cart to Roberto's trailer? Does the other kid live there? Roberto's truck is still gone and he's pissed at his primo. And he want pics of Raquel. Like they're gonna traffic her."

"Is she vulnerable? Easy to fool?"

"She's a badass, like her mom. But she just turned fifteen, Johnny. She's a STEM kid. A genius. Never even been on a date."

Tracing. Tracking. We had ninety-seven miles of possibilities, all of them bad.

I got Dianne on the phone again. She called the provider and, by the time we were going back past the dinosaurs in Cabazon, got them to ping Raquel's phone.

"Johnny, we tracked her phone from Oasis to Calimesa, and then it just disappears. Either it's dead or somebody smashed it. I'm sorry, babe."

"Calimesa? Where's the last location?"

"Gas station and minimarket on Calimesa Boulevard, right by the freeway."

"When?"

Dianne paused. "Four nineteen. This morning."

IT WAS PAST 6:00 p.m. when we got to the gas station. The cashier, a young kid, had just started his overnight shift and had been working the night before, too.

Grief showed him a pic on his phone—Raquel in her Dodgers jersey.

He looked scared. "Yeah, I saw her. And her husband."

Grief said, "What?"

The kid lifted his palms. "She was wearing a ring, man. He was, like, all in love with her. You could tell. The way he looked at her. They had a flat and pulled into the parking lot, right there." He pointed out the sliding doors to an area of the big parking lot near a line of pepper trees. "Then they were talking to some guy, and they got in the truck and drove it to where the big semis park. That fucking tire was so flat you could hear the rim digging into the asphalt. They went across to the dirt lot on the frontage road."

Holy hell, did the Ortiz kid take her to where the trucks were? No way. Grief looked at me. Pics? Trafficking? I couldn't believe it.

The cashier said, "But then she came in at, like, four to—you know."

Grief said, "I don't know."

He looked embarrassed. Pointed to the bathroom.

"Then she bought two churros. She went out there and I heard some argument. Then I heard four gunshots. Like, spread apart. Like, whoever was aiming."

"I got it," Grief said, staggering a little against the counter. "I got it."

I grabbed his arm. "Come on."

We walked into the parking lot near the pepper trees. Smell of someone smoking weed, but no talking. We were being watched. The truck rim had carved a deep channel in the hot asphalt, all the way to the frontage road, and across. The dirt lot was huge, already lined with trucks pulled off for the night, drivers sleeping in their cabs to save money. Grief and I wouldn't say it. Girls hung around big truck stops to work. They climbed up in the cabs and had quick sex with drivers. I saw them now and then when I had to follow a semi into a rest area.

We sat there in the Cheyenne. No idea where to go. Grief said, "How am I gonna call Larette with this? How am I gonna call Cherrise?"

I didn't know what to say.

He put his hands on the dash. "Remember when I had to trap the two baby bears back in June? The mama bear got hit by a car up in Fawnskin?"

"Yeah." Grief had been in the newspaper for that.

"Took me five days to track them. Fish and Game, me, and a specialist from the county. We had to find her den, track them in the woods, calculate how far they'd go, all that. We could hear them in the trees, but we couldn't see which tree. We had traps everywhere, but we didn't know what they wanted to eat."

"Grief," I said. "This isn't—"

"My niece. Cherrise's only child. I have no idea how to find her."

Raquel and Joey had been parked across the street when the cashier heard gunshots. Then Raquel's phone stopped working. Where the hell could they be?

SIXTEEN ♦ The Night Already Begun

SUN FLOODED THE CAB. THE OPEN TRAILER DOOR FACING east. Her scalp. Her arm. Her feet were bare. She had curled up on her side, in the passenger seat.

Joey watching her. He said, "Last night."

Raquel said, "I don't want to talk about it."

She opened the truck door. Jumped down from the trailer. He followed.

A steep slope of dried grass and bushes dropped off from the edge of the road. Pepper trees in the canyon below. Ray Allala was walking the dog along the dirt shoulder. No sidewalks here. Just a big wrought iron security gate and a long white driveway leading up through a row of trees. At the top of the ridge was a red tile roof and a glimpse of white house.

Cameras everywhere on the wrought iron fence all along the road, and at the gate. The dog sprang forward and barked when he saw Raquel.

Ray's phone rang. "Mr. Winter. Good morning. Look forward to seeing that Shelby. Yes, sir. That's my son and his wife. No, they weren't here yesterday, because they got a flat tire. Yeah, they're driving up to San Jose with me. Road trip."

Raquel looked up the driveway. A man up there watching everything they did.

"Yeah, they're not on our socials. Just the wife and dog. Her brand, eh, she keeps it like that. But no worries—my son's just here to help me."

The way Ray said it—he wanted a kid. A son.

But the man up there in that house was Mr. Paranoid.

"You let me know when you're ready to move the Shelby. You know, the auction up in San Jose starts in a week. No, my son's not driving either car. Nobody touches the cars but me. Yeah, they're just following me. Yes, sir, you got the trackers in the cars; they'll be fine."

Joey backed the truck down the ramps again and onto the side of the narrow, winding street.

Ray said, "Raquel, you and Chulito can chill out down here. Joey and I will go see about the car. I'm gonna invoice Mr. Winter an extra three hundred bucks. This cabrón, he lost money, bitcoin or some shit. Órale, now he has to sell stuff. He just wants to fuck with me because his money fucked with him, eh?"

Raquel looked at Joey. He raised his shoulders about an inch, and she thought, I already know him. I already know everything about his face. He's still scared.

Ray said, "I called the Wheel Doctor, mijo. He'll come from Fontana. He'll be here by four, five. Usually this is too far for him, but he and I go way back, eh?"

He handed Chulito's leash to Raquel, went to the cab of his truck.

Joey ran his hands through his hair on top, smoothing it back. He said, "Five? My dad's gotta be losing his shit. Beto's gonna kill me."

Raquel said, "You can just go back home as soon as the tire's fixed. I'll get a ride with Mr. Allala."

He shook his head. "You said twenty-point-two more miles. That's just, like, one more hour, and I'm already fucked." He touched her arm. "That culero. He coulda killed us."

The fingermarks already turning purple. She held the little dog closer and turned away to get her backpack.

RAQUEL SAT IN the bed of Beto's truck on a blanket from Ray's sleeper, the dog curled into a tiny circle by her thighs. Friday. 11:20. Her class was reading poetry.

Her phone was dead. Her laptop was dead. No idea what Akisha or Leilani or any of them were doing. Reading. Texting.

She got out the poetry book. She read an excerpt by someone named Marcel Proust titled "The Day Already Begun":

> We say that the hour of death cannot be forecast, but when we say this we imagine that hour as placed in an obscure and distant future. It never occurs to us that it has any connection with the day already begun or that death could arrive this same afternoon, this afternoon which is so certain and which has every hour filled in advance.

Behind the black iron gate, the truck and trailer had driven to the big house. Joey had gone up there, too. Ray had no son.

The day had already begun, long before she and Joey got the flat, before the three people had watched her from the trees, before Ray had driven them here. How had this day known what to do? Why try if the day already had it all planned?

She was invisible. Really invisible, not just a black square but nothing. She was in the bed of a truck with a dog. Smelling like fish food. Her jeans filthy. Her hair—her hair. The asshole up on the hill was probably watching her right now, thinking she was pathetic.

Four times the gate slid open, then closed, then open, then closed. DoorDash. Amazon. Amazon. Two landscaping trucks that went up and stayed. She heard mowers, trimmers, blowers.

What were the men doing up there? Talking about cars? Fucking men.

She lay on her back, staring into the trees. Her mother—what if she wasn't sick? What if she was just really pissed at Raquel? Then it would be much worse that she'd run away. What if Raquel got to the house and her mother was there, in the kitchen, making coffee?

She finally cried, into Chulito's fur. He didn't mind. His round plump belly. He licked her hand, gave her side-eye. "Where are corgis from?" she whispered to him when she had dried her face with her shirt. "Chihuahuas are from Chihuahua. German shepherds—easy. French poodle. Where are you from?"

He looked at her like she was an idiot. He was from San Jose. Then he curled next to her again, and they both fell asleep.

SHE HAD NO idea what time it was when Mr. Winter finally decided to let Ray Allala take the Shelby. Whatever a Shelby was.

She just knew the gate slid open very slowly, Ray's truck came down the driveway very slowly, and she was glad she'd already gone down the steep slope into the shade beside a pepper tree and peed. Where she figured the cameras couldn't see her. Chulito had watched intently, but there was nothing Raquel could do about that.

Fucking males.

She wanted her mom. She wanted Auntie Larette. Akisha's laugh on the phone. Lolo and Ruby in the packinghouse. She could never go back there again. She'd messed up everything, and she was still 20.2 miles from home.

Joey jumped down from Ray's cab, and Chulito barked like he'd never seen him before.

Ray said, "Callate, he's good."

"That dude was crazy," Joey said to Raquel. "He comes out

in black sweats and sunglasses and a hat, like he thinks he's in a movie. Garage like a warehouse. Like, twelve cars in there. He's talking on the phone the whole time, but, like, we're nothing. He stops in front of each car like the person's asking about them. Then he has all this paperwork. Then he finally lets Ray put the Shelby on the trailer. Finally. Pendejo."

Raquel said, "So you know what it is? Or you just like saying the name?"

Joey actually grinned. "It's a race car. 1968. Ray said it'll sell for three hundred grand."

More than she could imagine. She said, "So you guys hung out and ate DoorDash?"

"Fuck no. Mr. Winter grabbed his food and went back inside and took two more hours to transfer the money on his phone. That's it." He smiled again. "But Ray ordered some tacos and horchata for us just now. DoorDash knows the way up here, for reals."

What would her mom say? *This fool just up here grinning at me, like I like him.* But even though she was so hungry she felt dizzy, she liked Joey. Pictured him and Ray probably peeing on whatever trees were behind the huge garage, with millions of dollars' worth of cars.

THEY SHARED THE tacos and horchata in the shade of the trailer, where the cameras maybe couldn't see them. Chulito got two pieces of carne asada. The sun was low when a van pulled up.

The Wheel Doctor looked like he could be Joey's brother. Skinny, a goatee, a T-shirt and jeans. But he and Joey jacked up the truck, Ray took off the tire, and they worked on the rim for a long time. The Wheel Doctor took it into his van, and it came out black and whole. The segments pretty—a black snowflake. Beto couldn't say shit to Joey.

Ray paid his friend, and they talked for a long time. Ray laughed, saying he couldn't open the trailer and show the Wheel Doctor the two cars—but the guy on the hill was texting Ray every two minutes.

"I got the fucking Shelby, nothing he can do," Ray said. "Traffic's bad right now, I'll get on the road when I feel like it. But mi reina—she wants to talk to you."

Raquel held up the phone. FaceTime—Ray's wife was on a couch. "I miss my Chulito. I heard he spent the whole day with you, mija. Look at the two of you!"

Raquel walked down the side of the road, carrying the dog like a baby. She said, "He saved my life. The dog. He did."

Chulita bit her lip. Her lipstick was dark brown, and her top tooth was very white. She said, "Ray told me. That dog, he's supposed to herd cows and sheep, eh? In England. He's the queen's dog, for reals. Mija, when I was little, we went to my abuela's house in Guadalajara. She had a guard dog on the roof, a German shepherd, he was so beautiful, but we couldn't even pet him. He just paced around up there all day and night. I could hear his claws. He was so sad. I wanted a little dog to keep me company."

Raquel burst into tears, and the dog barked. Her whole body shook, and she stopped walking, held him tight with her left arm and the phone on his face, not hers, with her right hand. The tears fell hot into her mouth and down onto her filthy T-shirt.

"Mija! What's wrong, que paso, you're okay, you're okay!" Chulita stood up and paced with Raquel, like she was holding the dog, too.

"My mom," Raquel sobbed. "She's gonna be so mad at me. She's sick and I've been gone for so long. My aunt's gonna hate me. My phone's been dead forever. I'm in so much trouble."

"Mija, mija, you're just late, you had some bad luck, it's not your husband's fault about the tire! A nail! Life's full of nails! You're her daughter, she's so lucky to have you, how can she be mad? Look at you. You're beautiful! I wish I had a daughter. Órale, tell those pendejos to hurry up. Don't let them keep you waiting. Me neither. Tell that man to bring my baby back."

Raquel nodded, and the phone went black. She wiped her face with the hem of her T-shirt. She went back slowly, hoping her eyes weren't too red. Joey looked at her, raised his chin. The new tire was on the truck. She laid the dog in Ray's oil-stained arms.

She said, "You didn't have to do anything."

He said, "Mija, nobody has to do nothing. Unless they want to."

THEY DROVE BEHIND him down the winding road, back through the hills, and into Calimesa, toward the freeway. She wouldn't look east, back to the billboard above the lot where the trucks parked.

There was an accident on the 10 freeway, through Yucaipa and Redlands. It took an hour just to go ten miles. Joey looked so nervous. But finally they were in San Bernardino. At the exit, Joey honked. Ray honked three times in reply. Then he was gone.

Almost a whole day to go the last 20.2 miles. Raquel leaned out the window, seeing the jumping colors in Mrs. Ralphine's window. Mrs. Ralphine slept in her recliner in front of the TV. But her own house was dark. No one here. Her mother must be in the trailer.

Joey had turned off the headlights. He drove slowly down the long gravel driveway. Raquel closed the truck door quietly and went into the yard. It was almost 9:00 p.m.

The back porch. The ramada. Raquel stumbled to the chair by the lemon tree, took off her mask, and stared at the empty hook where her mother's robe should be. Not in her backpack.

Joey stood at the edge of the yard. She didn't want him in the house. She was already in trouble—but that would make it worse, if her mother found out. "Can you just wait in the truck?" she said. "I'll go get the money."

She opened the back door with her key. Ducking into the hot darkness of the kitchen, she smelled nothing—no popcorn, no JLo, no coffee. She went down the hallway to her room. No AC on. The house was so silent and hot. The smell of cheese. She found it—one Cheeto on her dresser, a glowing worm. The money was in her softball sock. She counted it again and put it in her pocket.

But then she opened the door to her mother's room. On her bed, just the indentation of her mom's body in the pale green of the bedspread. Like after she took Raquel to the desert, she'd come back and taken a nap, but she was so hot and tired she hadn't even gotten in the sheets.

Raquel curled there in the shape of her mother's body. The faint smell. The JLo. She pulled her mother's pillow to her face. All those months of her mother standing on the patio pulling off her scrubs, throwing them in the washer, and coming in here to sit on this bed. The virus in her hair. In her eyelashes. The—cilia? Inside the nostrils? The tiny hairs to protect us, her mother taught her. Eyelashes are protection. Not for being sexy.

Her mother was either in the trailer or in the hospital.

SHE WASHED AND dried her face. She looked like shit. Her scalp felt burned—was that possible? The ring Lolo had given her twisted on her finger. She went outside to the truck. The windows were open. The front seat was reclined all the way back. Joey was asleep.

He must have stayed up all last night watching out, even though they were inside the transport trailer. His phone was still dead, in the cup holder. Raquel picked it up and took both phones into the kitchen to charge. They lay side by side on the counter. Like when she and her mom gave up for the night. Back when things were okay. When she did her homework on the couch next to her mother. If this were a normal year, would Mrs. Hua have given her class the same poems?

We think about death, the day already begun. This was the second night, already begun, and if she and Joey had known what would happen—would she have still run away? Run here?

They could have died. Or he could have gotten shot, and she could be with the people in the trees. Wishing she were dead.

She couldn't think like this. She grabbed a blanket, went back outside. The truck still silent. She spread the blanket on the wicker love seat under the ramada. Her favorite place to sleep in the summer. She was 4.2 miles from Our Lady. She could walk, in a little while, to CamperWorld. She closed her eyes.

HE SAID, "SOMEBODY stole my phone."

She sat up. Dark. The palm fronds rustling and crackling above her, in the wind.

She said, "No, it's inside charging."

She ran into the kitchen. Both phones lit up.

Her texts in long stripes. Akisha. The group chat. Her school. From yesterday.

Then Ruby. **Where R U? We're worried. Call me**

And just tonight, Larette. **Your mom's OK, sweetie. Your aunt called from Oasis. Where R U? We're worried. Call me.**

Joey's phone buzzing right now. Countless texts from Beto.
UR dead where R U
Did U get pics if not UR even more dead
Good pics this time bro
Fuck UR dead
The dead emojis.

It was 3:42 a.m. They'd slept a long time.

She took both phones outside. Joey was sitting on the wicker chair, rubbing his eyes. No hat or mask. His eyes were big and black in the solar light strands she and her mother had hung on the ramada. His cheeks had silvery tracks from when he cried. That felt like last week.

He said, "You sleep out here?"

She nodded.

He said, "My clothes. Changing that tire." He looked down at his Dodgers shirt, his jeans. "I need a shower."

He'd protected her. He'd cried. Now he had to go back home and face Beto.

All her fault. "Wait here," she said.

She went quickly into her bedroom. She found a pair of black sweats from when she played softball. They were big and loose. Her own Dodgers jersey. Size L.

On the back patio, she said, "Go take a shower. Leave your clothes outside the bathroom door. I'll wash them fast."

She opened the back door, took him down the hallway, and when his hand came out to drop the clothes, she put them in the washer. Tide. Express cycle.

WHEN HE CAME out wearing her clothes, she handed him the six twenties, the five, and the three ones. His hair was wet—he ran his hands through the longer hair at the top of his head, pushing it back. He handed the bills back to her, said, "Beto just texted me. He doesn't want money."

They stood on the back porch. The washing machine was finishing. Spinning. "I have to dry your clothes," she said.

They sat on the folding chairs on the patio, looking at their phones, while his clothes dried. Then he went inside and changed.

When he came out, he looked exactly as he had when they left Oasis. Except he wasn't the same. Like Mr. Espinoza and her mother had taught her, she and he both had changed the neurons in their brains. Inside their skulls. She looked at the side of his face. His jaw. His cheek. They might remember totally different things. Or maybe exactly the same scenes.

He lifted his chin. Looked at the palm trees along the back fence. "The first time we saw you, Beto said you were fine, and I said, no, you were beautiful. He said we've had the troca two days and he would charge pics." He wouldn't look at her.

Raquel knew what he meant. "OnlyFans," she said.

She and Akisha had looked at OnlyFans. Girls on Insta who advertised. *Head over to the dark site*, they said. *Slide in my DMs.* Guys were constantly DM-ing Akisha, asking her for pics, trying to recruit her for videos, for whatever. She said they asked for OnlyFans all the time. "It's so nasty," she told Raquel once. "They say, like, *Only the waist up*, or *You can wear a school uniform*, or all kinds of stuff. They want to see my feet. It gives me bad dreams."

Joey said, "I'm not doing it. For real. We been at the boxing club in Indio. I can fight better than him. He's meaner, but I'll be okay. So no." Then he took her hand. Picked up his phone and walked with her to the ramada.

She said, "Wait, you said no pics."

"I have to charge you something," he said. He put the phone on the chair and touched the screen. One of those oldies like Mr. Garibay played across the street. A guy with a high voice, singing, *Why do I feel this way, thinking about you every day, and I don't even know you?*

She'd heard this song. She said, "My neighbor plays this in his garage. Are you, like, sixty?"

He didn't answer. He put his hands on her shoulders.

Raquel said, "When guys sing like this, like, really high, what's it called?"

"Just—"

"Falsetto." What poem had that word in it?

"You don't have to talk all the time," he said. He slid his hands down to her back and started to move her in a circle. Her face by his shoulder. His chin right there by her cheek. His knee hit her knee softly.

Joey kissed her. Didn't stick his tongue in her mouth. Just pressed his lips. A little chapped. Moving soft on hers. He put his hand at the end of her spine and pulled her in tighter. He stopped kissing her and moved his head so he looked past her shoulder.

When the song was done, the next one started right away—a woman's voice—and he bent down and kissed her one more time. Fast. Then he let her go and silenced the phone.

He said, "Órale, we're cool. Because you're never coming back to Oasis, eh?" Then he walked to the truck and got in.

SHE RAN INSIDE. Akisha had never kissed anyone. Leilani and Marshall always talked about how they didn't want to ever share germs and guys only wanted head. But Joey had only ever been kind to her—from the moment he spread his shirt on the cistern. A lifetime ago.

She found one bag of Takis in the kitchen cupboard. Two bowls. She grabbed her backpack off the patio and ran to the truck. His arm was along the door, but he didn't look out the window at her.

She said, "Can you take me to where my mom lives now? It's four-point-two miles."

Joey said, "Because I'm already dead?"

Raquel said, "I can take the pics if you want. I will. So he doesn't—"

"He's not gonna kill me. Just make me work night shifts for him at the fish farm after I get done with the dates." Joey took the bowl of Takis. "I didn't think you took pics."

"I don't."

He nodded. "Cool."

She pulled up the photo of the trailers her mother had sent weeks ago. A big sign that said CAMPERWORLD behind them. Joey drove silently down her street, turned onto the avenue, and headed toward the hospital. She could see the four stories lit up in the sky long before they got there. At the corner with the CamperWorld sign, all lit up, too, she said, "Right here."

The trailers down there at the end of the street. The owner, who watched the nurses. Kept an eye on them. Kept them safe. We don't look safe, she thought.

Joey turned off the truck. The night was deep in shadow, in the alleys between buildings. She slipped the money into the cup holder.

Arrived! the phone said. All triumphant and impatient.

Joey looked down the street. "Dead end," he said.

She reached up to kiss him on the cheek, but he'd leaned a little forward to look out the windshield, and her lips landed on the side of his neck. Hot and salty. He froze. Then he shivered like she'd put ice there.

"Damn," he said. "That makes it worse." He shivered again.

She could taste his skin.

He said, "Security cameras up there on the sign and the fence."

She slid out of the truck and closed the door quietly. She walked toward CamperWorld. She didn't look back.

THE ONLY OTHER buildings were a storage facility with two dogs that came rushing to bark at her. Then a wall of golden blocks, a big iron gate, and a sea of RVs for sale.

The Mallard. That's what her mother always called it. The trailers were lined up ten feet apart, along the curb at the back wall. There was a rogue baby oleander growing under one trailer. In a crack of the asphalt. Four potted red geraniums and some other flowers by the metal steps of the only trailer with lights on.

She moved slowly past the camera. Would the owner call the cops for one homeless person? Which trailer was her mom's? Was she in there asleep?

The smell of chicken from the one with the flowers. A woman opened the flimsy metal door and stood on the black steps. She wore magenta scrubs, black clogs, and full makeup. Magenta lipstick, perfect eyebrows, her brown skin contoured and highlighted. She squinted behind glasses and said, "You Raquel. Why you out here? I see you every day on your mom phone. You with grandma. She don't tell you come." She slid her mask up over her mouth and nose then. Looked at her phone. "Today is Saturday. Five a.m.!" She shook her head.

Raquel thought fast about the things her mother had mentioned. Indiana, Sacramento. Pam Ott, Marisol Manalang. Pam liked apple fritters. Marisol made amazing Filipino food.

The woman said, "You mom better now, but still sick. You cannot see her. Nobody go in her room. Only us."

Raquel felt dizzy, and she looked up at the dark sky. The stars. The CamperWorld sign so bright. She fell to her knees. Her mom had corona. Her dreams had told her. Her father had told her, up in the date palms. Her mother's body—kidneys, heart, lungs. The things her mother never kept from her.

"You okay? You hungry?" Marisol put her hand on Raquel's shoulder. "Raquel. The camera, he watch us. Rick. He own the CamperWorld. You have to be visiting nurse." She lifted Raquel by both elbows, facing her. "You just get here from—San Diego. Pick up your backpack. Go stand." She pointed to the last trailer.

She came with a plastic bag and a key, opened the door of the trailer, handed Raquel the bag.

"Wipe your whole body. Wash your hair in the sink. Put on the scrub. The mask. Everything. Wait for me."

The trailer was hot. A little oven. Pictures of a very pale woman with long brown hair, thick eyebrows, a man wearing hunting gear, and a little boy. Pam Ott. Her son was Jonah. He was five. Indiana.

The plastic bag held scrubs, clean and folded precisely. Raquel put on the light blue pants and big shirt with hundreds of tiny teddy bears. She retied her Pumas.

She texted her mother. **RU OK?**

Suddenly her phone rang, and the screen said *Mama*.

Her mother said softly, "Hey, baby. I didn't forget you. Larette had my phone. Where are you?"

She didn't sound mad. Did she know Raquel had run home?

"You have the virus," Raquel said.

Her mother tried for normal. "How you gonna tell me what I been doing?"

"I can hear it. It sounds like . . . like you swallowed paint. A whole gallon of paint. Don't lie."

Her mother said, "I'm going to call you back."

"No!"

Raquel held the phone away from her. It went black. Then it lit up again with her mother. FaceTime. A hospital bed. Her forehead looked almost yellow, she was so pale. The three tiny beauty marks beside her mother's left eye seemed darker. A cap covering her hair. Her hand was snaked with an IV.

"First day everything tasted like when I was little and I found a penny," her mother whispered hoarsely. "I remember that. I was about five. Larette dared me to lick it clean."

Raquel said, "Why didn't you call me?" The tears slid into her ears and she shook her head.

"It happened so fast. I had a fever. Felt like somebody hammered a spike into my head. I fell asleep in the trailer and I never got up."

"Who took care of you?"

"Larette. She called the EMTs." Her mother stopped talking. She swallowed a few times. She licked her teeth.

Raquel had no idea what she was allowed to say. She couldn't say, *I went to see Dad and now I miss him more, which is messed up. But I knew you were sick because you're all I have. It's just you and me.*

Raquel said, "Did you think you were gonna die?"

"No." Her mother answered too fast. She was definitely lying.

"What does it feel like now?"

Her mother breathed heavily and tried to laugh. It was like the shudder when you're done crying. "You know those cement deer Mrs. Ralphine got in the yard? I swear it's like two of those are on my chest. I dreamed they were talking to me. They had spots and you know only the babies have spots." She was whispering now. "I can't think. The babies."

Raquel said, "Fawns."

"Yeah."

Then Raquel said carefully, "When can we go home? I can take care of you."

"Baby," her mother said. "I'm almost done now. I get out in two days. But corona's gone crazy here. It's only going to get worse."

"Mom," Raquel said.

Her mother's eyes closed. Her arm, lying on the sheet, was so thin. Raquel could see the bones like marbles at her wrists.

Raquel said, "How did you get it?"

"I just got it, Raquel. So many patients. It was my time."

Raquel said, "You always tell me everything. Seriously."

Her mother said, "Yes, Raquel." She was whispering. "You tell me everything, too. Where are you? Lolo and Ruby are so scared. Where did you go?"

Raquel pictured the transmission. She'd been close to the feral people. She'd been with Ray Allala and the Wheel Doctor. She'd just danced with Joey Ortiz. Kissed him. She had to isolate now.

She said, "You get to go home now, right? Not to the trailer. Home home."

Her mother said, "Soon as I get the letter to clear me, from the public health department, I have to work. Like Larette did. We're desperate, baby."

"Back to work?" Raquel couldn't believe that.

But another voice said, "Okay, Cherrise, you gotta put that down now."

Her mother slid away like a wind had blown through her room. Larette had the phone. Larette wore two masks and her hair was in a mushroom, and her whole body was covered in a white jumpsuit with a thin blue plastic gown.

Larette's voice sounded like she was under a blanket. "Raquel! She made it through. The worst is over. Don't worry. You just stay put. Snug as a bug in a rug, okay?" She moved to the door. "Where are you, sweetie?"

Raquel ended the call. They'd make her go back.

The trailer door swung open. Marisol was all masked up, with a cap on now. She said, "Here. You eat. So you don't faint."

She handed Raquel a container. Two hot pieces of chicken with rice. Soft and salty and sweet. The best thing Raquel had ever tasted in her life. Marisol handed her a water bottle.

"Drink. You put on the cap, too. I take you. Your mom get mad, but I take you."

Raquel fitted the mushroom cap over her head.

Marisol said, "You are—who?" She looked up at the sky. The moon. "Luna. You Luna from San Diego. You the traveler come here while Pam is go home to visit."

They walked down the middle of the street, Marisol five feet away.

At the corner, Marisol said, "Look that guy watch you. Suspicious."

Joey was still there, the window open. He could see the trailers. He met her eyes, and then lifted his chin. The window slid up, and he drove away.

"Ah, that you boyfriend," Marisol said, walking fast in the clogs.

"Just my ride," Raquel said.

"You can lie maybe five day to Rick, about you work here," Marisol said. "But me? You don't lie about the boyfriend. Too easy."

An ambulance roared past them, the looping red sound like a lariat over Raquel's head. Marisol said, "Look—so many people. Don't go near."

The hospital parking lot was full of vehicles. People were sitting in lawn chairs on their truck beds, people were sleeping in their cars, standing on the grassy median holding phones up into the air. FaceTiming—Raquel could see nurses talking on the screens. Patients sitting up in bed. Her mom, Larette, Marisol—nurses were the only ones all these waiting people had to tell them the truth. She saw her mother standing before the washing machine, her hair soaked with sweat from the cap. Her fingers wrinkled from the gloves. Her mother, standing next to someone's bed and speaking to all these people who stared at Raquel now. *He's getting better. He's keeping the fever down. Hang in there.*

She followed Marisol through the maze of vehicles. Her mother touched hundreds of people. Their faces and hands and feet. All their parts. Wolf eyes. *I always tell you the truth.* Her mother had been doing this for months. Sleeping in the little trailer.

A woman saw Marisol and Raquel walking past and said, "You guys are the heroes! Thank God for the nurses!" She reached inside her car and brought out a gold box. Chocolate. "My sister's in there," the woman said. "Can you take this to ER? They saved her."

Raquel carried the box. She felt foolish. Then a few people whistled and clapped. Marisol lifted her hand. She kept walking fast. In a half-hidden courtyard with a rock maze, Marisol pointed up. The windows lit up silvery-blue in the night.

"Second floor. Room 2208. I text Larette now."

Raquel stared at the second stripe of lights. Her mother would be so mad. We don't lie. First rule. Raquel stared so hard at the reflections that she felt dizzy. And then a sliding of material in one window square. Someone was pulling aside the curtain—she saw a burst of color like a little tropical fish moving in the glass.

SEVENTEEN ✦ **Desperado**

AT 3:00 A.M. ON SATURDAY, LARETTE HEADED INTO THE break room. She drank the last of the coffee from her thermos. She knew she was going to have to sing to Stan Earley. His body was failing. Tonight. She felt it.

She wanted to run down to the second floor and see her cousin. But she had nothing to tell Cherrise. Grief and Johnny hadn't found Raquel.

It was all her fault. She should have just told Raquel the truth.

Nobody in the ICU waiting room. She pushed her forehead against the window. All the vehicles in the parking lot. The waiting room of the world now.

She faced west, toward Rialto, Pomona, L.A. Her own house, down Base Line, somewhere in the distance. She could place it by the light atop the cement plant in the Lytle Creek Wash.

She pushed open the heavy door and headed down the Mariana Trench of the hallway.

SATURDAYS USED TO be her favorite during a show. Grief and Dante would sit in the front row, nervous for her, not because she wouldn't know the lyrics or sing better than anyone else but for her costume and makeup and movements. Trip and fall—every singer's worst fear. Gowns and period shoes. She'd joke that anything except surgical booties was fine with her, but even low heels took a lot of getting used to when she had to move across the stage while singing.

She leaned on the counter at the nursing station. She would be forty on December 27. All year, she and Grief had been saving for her big birthday trip to New York. Three days in a fancy hotel. Three nights of Broadway. Three midnight dinners in three different restaurants.

Not now.

Mariah glanced up and said, "Cherrise doing okay?"

Larette said, "Seems better. Maybe they'll discharge her tomorrow?"

Mariah shrugged. "Not our call. Nothing is our call. With Marisol on days this week, thank God we have Ola and EJ." Ola Namukasa and EJ Johnson, from the rotating nurse staff. She pointed up at the board. "You got Crescencio Sotelo. He's been awake a few hours now. I think it's better if you tell him about Rudy Magana."

"Shit."

"Yup." Mariah swiveled her chair around and started typing again. "It's all shit."

ACROSS THE HALLWAY, she looked into the window at Crescencio Sotelo. At his feet. He wiggled them now. He had come out of the coma last night, at 10:00, the tube had been removed from his tracheotomy, and the hole in his throat was covered with dressing and tape. He couldn't speak yet, couldn't eat yet, but he was sitting halfway up. Looking at himself like people did, as if they expected a leg or foot to be gone.

If they were diabetic, that happened.

She put on a new gown and gloves and face shield. She'd had him since the first night, and hadn't always thought he'd make it.

His temp was 106, his blood pressure was 192, his oxygen level was so low he should have been dead. But he was one of those men whose body contained something that wouldn't stop fighting—and Dr. Yoon had said, "It's still mysterious, how the virus attacks different organs and systems, and this patient kept sending reinforcements."

Crescencio Sotelo looked up when she opened the door, lifted his arms draped with the IV lines like, *'Sup? You ready or what?*

She had to laugh, behind the mask.

Now Larette bent close to him. "Mr. Chencho," she said. "That's what your wife told me to call you. It's nice to finally meet you."

His mouth shaped words, though no sound came out. "Thank you, mija. I'm so fuckin' hungry. What you got?" He looked for a cart. Like she brought him a steak.

"Jell-O," she said. "Jell-O and juice. But that's not till eight, okay?" She patted his big hand. She and Marisol had rubbed off the green candy-flake paint over a series of days, with alcohol. Only that little finger left. She said, "I'm going to check your trach, and the respiratory therapist is coming to check your lung function."

His lips said, "Dolores. I heard you."

Larette stopped. "Your wife. I'm going to update her."

She was only inches from his face.

He said, "Did she tell you? About us?"

Dolores had asked her to sing. She'd looked at Larette on FaceTime and said, "Chencho was eighteen and I was nineteen and every day for two weeks he picked me up in his old car and asked me to marry him. My dad was from Michoacan, eh, he hated Chencho's lowrider and the music. Please sing. Please. When he gets out, I'm gonna bring you dinner for a month. Enchiladas, posole. You tell me, mija."

She'd sung The Fuzz's "I Love You for All Seasons."

Chencho closed his eyes.

Larette closed her eyes, too. Imagined she could only hear.

The monitors beeping, the blood pressure cuffs on his legs inflating and deflating, even the buzzing of the lights. Had he heard her singing, wherever the coma had held his senses? His soul? All the suspended souls in all the rooms here, in the hallways. All of the consciousnesses here and everywhere right now—slipping and sliding through the membranes and bones, hesitating. Waiting.

She trembled in her gowns, feeling the heat of her own skin around her. Containing her. She breathed three times. Slow. Lungs and heart and blood. Aerate. Aerate.

She opened her eyes. Touched his little finger, with the green paint. She had to tell him about Rudy Magana. She said softly, "We have to talk about the Imperials."

He opened his eyes. The Imperials Car Club—he and Rudy, the classic 1964 Impala they had to get done for a show. But Chencho worked nights at the Petco warehouse, and he'd carried the virus to Rudy's backyard. It was their wives who told Larette how they found their husbands one day apart, each lying on the kitchen floor in their houses only three blocks from each other.

She told Chencho slowly, softly, about Rudy. That he'd been four doors down the hallway. That he had hung tough for days, but he passed on August 13. She said, "It wasn't your fault. Corona is no one's fault, Mr. Chencho. It's like nothing we've ever known."

Chencho couldn't speak, but he could cry, it looked so painful, huge ragged breaths and sobbing, tears streaming into his ears, but he couldn't stop himself, his face crumpled like a child's, until Larette patted his shoulder firmly, again and again, saying, "You have to breathe, okay? Just slow down and breathe. Nothing's our fault. Nothing. You can't think that way."

The words rang in her ears. She breathed so hard that her own mask felt like fur against her lips, like a paw smothering her, a hair caught inside, no, the fraying of the fabric, a paw trying to shut her up, because everything did feel like her fault.

3:42 A.M. SHE and Mariah and Silvia filled out paperwork while they ate at their separate desks. She missed Cherrise and Marisol. Silvia had green GladWare. She'd ordered DoorDash at CamperWorld—tortas from Tacos Ricos. Mariah ate beef stroganoff from her red GladWare. Larette ate a PayDay bar and an orange. She drank chamomile tea. She waited.

AT 4:09 A.M., in room 3012, Dr. Yoon looked up from Stan Earley's back. "A big man," he said.

The three of them had to turn him from his stomach to face up. They lifted in tandem, Larette sliding her hands under his pelvic bone on the right side, Ola Namukasa on the left. The way they did every human, to straighten out the legs. And each time, Larette felt the curving cradle of thick bone that supported everything inside. The first time she turned her baby son over so he could sleep on his stomach, the tiny bowls of bone that held Dante together there, spindly legs and flat frog belly.

In the hallway, they took off the PPE and dropped it into the container. The diaphanous blue gowns settled.

Dr. Yoon said, "I will call his son in Hesperia." He looked out the window at the end of the hallway in which they could only see themselves. He said, "This was the promised land, for the Mormons. When they came, they planted more wheat and corn and fruit trees than anywhere in America. A Mormon man told my mother that, when we first came here. He told her to go up the old Mormon Highway and she would find paradise. Hesperia." His brief smile. "Paradise. Parasite. I remember when I learned the difference in the words."

"YOU OKAY?" SILVIA said, beside her.

Larette nodded. But she wanted Cherrise. She couldn't even text her that Stan Earley's body was failing. He was leaving. Cherrise and Larette had liked him.

The lights below them, in the windows. *Day is done, gone the sun, from the lake, from the hills, from the sky.* Beth Beverly had been cremated. Lisa Beverly had sent a thank-you card to the ICU.

Stan Earley was sixty-nine, had been joking the first day in the room, said to Cherrise and Larette that he'd have drunk more expensive whiskey if he'd known that cheap whiskey would do this to him. Then he went down. Never regained consciousness. His kidneys had ceased to function, and his body was swelling, his legs and feet grotesque under the sheet. His broad chest rose and fell heavily, his lungs full of edema.

"COPD for five years, heavy smoker," Dr. Yoon read from his phone. "I talked to the second son. Mike. I think we have half an hour for him to get them all together."

Fifteen minutes later, Larette assembled the four sons of Stan Earley on FaceTime. It would be easier for Dr. Yoon to talk to them while she held the phone. She'd not shown them their father. The four of them in their boxes—Ricky and Bobby together in Calimesa, Ronnie and Mike in Hesperia—all with shaggy brown hair and blue eyes. She asked about their father. He was born in Hesperia, up near the mountains; he'd been a long-haul trucker his whole life. Their mother had left and moved to Utah ten years before, after the last son, Ronnie, graduated from high school. Their father had been alone since.

Larette offered. She said, "I can sing to him, so he won't feel alone. What's his favorite song? The song you think he'd like to hear?"

A long silence. Then Bobby, the eldest, said, "You won't know it."

"Try me," she said gently.

"'Desperado.'"

She was so tired. She cast about in her brain. She said, "The Eagles."

All four faces nodded in unison.

"I love that song," she said.

Dr. Yoon came into the room. It was time for them to see their father. Dr. Yoon knew. He said, "We must make a decision now."

Larette turned the phone toward the bed.

Stan Earley was yellow and purple, he was not their father, his fever was spiking again, he was a body possessed by a demon, he bucked and settled and bucked again, and they cried in the hoarse way men sounded on her phone. They asked for him to have only morphine for the pain, for the other machines to be disconnected.

Larette went to the break room for five minutes. She drank more chamomile. She played the Linda Ronstadt version on her phone. One of the most beautiful songs of all. She put new coveralls on.

Silvia added morphine to the line, and they began to disconnect all the lines and tubes except that one.

Silvia said, almost shy, which was not like her, "I could never do it. Sing like you do." She took away the catheter tubes. The waste bags. They pulled out the snake of intubation. Silvia wheeled aside the suction machine for the techs to disinfect.

Then Larette was alone with Stan Earley.

She wasn't going to sing about his prison being in this world all alone. She wasn't going to sing about his pain and his hunger. Just what she could.

It's hard to tell the nighttime from the day . . .

He would take another breath. Catch. Take. The air inside the room cold and whooshing. His soul was leaving slowly. His skin turning from bluish white to yellow, waxy, she could see each time the essence of a human fading from the tissues. Heart monitor the only one left on. The green line pulsing gently, rising, falling. She loved Linda Ronstadt's voice, the tremolo, the sweet perfect scour in her throat. Larette aimed for it, trying to regulate her own breath.

She refused to sing the last words of the song. It was never too late. His sons loved him.

It may be rainin', but there's a rainbow above you . . .

His skin the palest yellow now, his teeth with silver glinting at the back, his huge forearm swollen with edema and the sunspots stretched to brown flakes like Raisin Bran.

She touched the spots gently and said, "So this is the arm that hung out the window of the truck, this is the arm that felt all that sun, wherever you drove, Stan, I bet they called you Stan the Man, all your friends, and your sons love you so very, very much, I bet you taught them to drive, right, you taught them everything you knew."

Then he was still. There was no breath. But his heart kept beating, and she remembered that he had a pacemaker, and that Dr. Yoon would have to cease the beating with his cell phone. So she stayed there, her blue gloves brushing back his dark gray hair from his forehead over and over, waiting for the door to open.

SHE COULD BARELY stand when it was done. She went into the break room and put her head on her arms. Mariah didn't come after her. Larette listened to the clicking of the vending machines.

Then she went to the second floor.

And she leaned against the wall beside Cherrise's door. Couldn't go inside. She and Cherrise had never had a fight since they were little, when Cherrise's mother had never come home, when she'd left them for someone else, and Larette's mother went next door to get Cherrise's things.

Cherrise was four. Larette was seven. But Auntie Turquoise had bought Cherrise way more clothes than Larette's mother had bought for her. So many dresses crowded the closet, and all the stuffed animals, too. Larette's mother didn't go for stuffed animals. She said they attracted moths and bugs.

That first week, sleeping in the same bed, Cherrise kicked Larette in the back. Again and again. In her sleep. Larette finally pushed her cousin off the bed onto the floor and shouted, "Stop it! Stop it! You don't get to kick me!"

Her mother rushed in and popped Larette on the back of the head. She picked up Cherrise, who wasn't crying, just staring at Larette with angry eyes, and took her into her own bed.

I feel petty, Larette thought. Foolish and petty. Bad combination.

Cherrise's room dark. No staff. Cherrise held up her phone. She was FaceTiming. The silver-blue light made her look even more gaunt. Cherrise had the strange corona-face they all recognized now—you'd been sleeping forever, but there were still haunted smudges under the eyes and even at the temples, as if darkness had gathered there, while the rest of your face was too pale, no matter how light or dark your skin.

Cherrise was saying, ". . . I have to work. Like Larette did. We're desperate, baby."

Larette knew immediately from the softness of the voice that she was talking to Raquel.

Cherrise looked up at Larette. Tears gleaming.

Larette put out her hand. "Raquel! She made it through. The worst is over. Don't worry. You just stay put. Snug as a bug in a rug, okay?" She moved to the door. "Where are you, sweetie?"

But Raquel had disconnected.

Cherrise said, "Where is she?" The tears sliding now.

"She didn't say, she must have gone through a dead zone. She'll call back." Her own phone buzzed five times in a row. "I have to check on Chencho Sotelo. He made it." She wouldn't tell Cherrise about Stan Earley. Not yet. Then she put her head on her cousin's blanketed feet, for just a moment. "So hard. I miss you. I do."

She stood up fast and went out the door.

MARISOL TEXTED HER half an hour later. **Go to check Cherrise.**

Larette flew down the stairs. Why would Cherrise have texted Marisol?

She opened the door. Cherrise opened her eyes.

Look outside, Marisol texted.

Larette pushed the button for FaceTime and slid open the curtain. Down on the grass near the rock maze was Marisol, handing the phone to another nurse. Who?

No. It was Raquel. She lifted her face to the window. Wearing scrubs. "Can I see her on FaceTime again, Auntie?" Raquel said.

Larette handed Cherrise the phone, said, "Your baby's right there. Outside, with Marisol."

Then Larette fell to her knees, dizzy, unable to breathe. Like she was praying at the side of their bed when she was a child.

Raquel said, "Mama?"

Larette pressed her forehead into the hospital blanket.

EIGHTEEN ✦ CamperWorld

IT WAS LIKE A PARADE, AT 7:23 A.M., WHEN THE NURSES came out of night shift. Nurses in light blue, purple, green, and teddy bears and sunflowers and cats, the younger nurses in black pants with neon stripes like a track team. Their backpacks and bags and thermoses.

Raquel stood outside the hospital with Marisol, who left her then and went inside. Larette was in the parade. Larette wore apricot-colored scrubs, and the tiny woman next to her wore turquoise. Her name tag said Silvia Vasquez.

"I *cannot* with you," Larette said, holding up her hand. "I'm not able to hug you right now, Raquel, I can't yell at you, I need some food, so just—just walk, baby. You have to isolate again."

"I know," Raquel whispered. "Five days."

When they got to CamperWorld, Larette said, "You only went in Pam's trailer to change, right?"

Raquel said, "I slept on her bed for two hours."

Silvia took a big breath, opened her door, and said, "Me vale madre, Larette. I got it."

"I'm coming," Larette said, then turned to Raquel. "Sit your runaway butt down on the curb." She left and came back with spray, paper towels, and disinfecting wipes.

Larette and Silvia opened the windows in Pam's trailer and

cleaned it fast. The sharp scent of lemon and bleach drifting out almost made Raquel cry again. This morning Raquel had leaned against the dryer at home. Joey standing there. She was so hungry. In Pam's trailer, Marisol had left a purple container with *MM* written on it in black marker. "Breakfast for you," she'd said.

Silvia came outside, her forehead beaded with sweat above her mask. She sat on the curb a few feet away. "Puro pinche Saturday," she said. "I'm going to bed."

"Thank you," Raquel said.

Silvia rolled her eyes. "Your mom would do anything for me, mija, I'll do anything for her."

Raquel said, "Didn't you just get here?"

Silvia said, "A week in that ICU? That's like twenty years in a war." She went up the two little steps to her own trailer, just as Larette came down the two little steps of Pam Ott's trailer.

Larette said, "Okay. Look. You got five days until Jasmine comes. The new traveler. I can keep an eye on you during the day. Maybe your mom gets out tomorrow. But, Raquel—she comes back to her trailer, and she rests for two days, and you can't even open that door. You can wave through the screen."

Raquel lifted her arm and pretended to wave—like the queen—rolling her eyes.

Then Larette said, "Baby girl. What happened to you?"

She was staring at the bruises on Raquel's left arm. The waving one. The four fingermarks were huge, purple-black. His hand—she hadn't thought it was so big. Raquel pulled down the sleeve of the scrubs. Joey. Joey had seen it. No one else.

Raquel said, "Nothing."

"Did this boy from the desert hurt you, Raquel?" Larette said, holding her hand to her mouth.

"No, he would never hurt me. A guy grabbed me in the Arco

store because he thought I was stealing two churros. But I had the money."

The lie came out so fast. So easy.

Then Raquel went inside, closed the trailer door, and locked it. She sat at the tiny white table. She ate the four little fried rolls of meat and vegetables. They were the best thing she'd ever tasted. There was more chicken in the brown sauce, and rice. Heaven.

She took off the scrubs and folded them carefully. She put on a T-shirt and shorts and got into the small bed at the front of the trailer. She curled on her side in the fake-lemon-scented sun and closed her eyes.

SHE SLEPT FOR fifteen hours. When she woke up, her mother's trailer was gone.

She put on the scrubs, panicked. Went outside. Her mother's trailer, the Dodger flag in the window, was near the CamperWorld gate—the guy named Rick was power washing the Mallard. Her mother must be coming home.

But when she texted, there was no answer.

Larette and Silvia came out and waited for Raquel. She put on her backpack over the scrubs and walked behind Larette, so that Rick would believe she was a nurse named Luna. In the parking lot at Our Lady, people were staring up at the windows, holding signs. WE LOVE YOU CARLOS and GET WELL SOON GRAMMA and WE MISS YOUR YELLING SO COME HOME JACK!!

Silvia went ahead, and Larette leaned close to Raquel. Her eyes above the mask were all red. Was she tearing up?

"When your mom got sick, I found her in the trailer. I know you guys haven't talked about it yet. She was sweating and had a fever. I called the EMTs and they drove her here. I should have called you right then. But I thought you'd be too scared, and you'd freak out. You're fifteen. You had the right to feel however you felt. Dante's younger than you, and he's a boy. Totally different. And it's just you and your mom. If I had told you the truth, instead of treating you like a little kid, you could have come here and held up a sign for her. Saying whatever mean shit you wanted."

Raquel said, "I'da wrote TAKIS AND TEQUILA AWAIT. HURRY UP."

Then someone started a car right beside them. A little blue Kia. A woman was holding her phone and crying. She put the windows up even though it was hot, then started screaming.

Larette said, "That's what we do. Me and your mom. We have to tell people. She hasn't told you about that, and you haven't told her how you got here, and I haven't told Dante enough, either. We gotta work on that, okay? I have to go, baby."

Raquel touched her arm. "Dante says you guys are, like, in a war and you'll never tell us."

Her aunt put her fingers on Raquel's fingers, for just a moment. She said, "We have to figure it out ourselves first. Like those poems your mom said you're reading. She read me the one about the bee. How he brings pollen everywhere. Dante makes me read all his freshmen poems, too. He had one about an old fish like a warrior. Maybe your mom and I have to figure out how to tell you the story. It might take a while. Okay, wait for me."

Raquel stood exactly at the spot near the rock maze. Only nurses and doctors and all the other people in hospital uniforms were here. She was a nurse. Not a single person had questioned her yet. Her phone buzzed with her mother's face, the curtain slid away, and her mother stood at the window with Larette.

Raquel said, "I'm not leaving. I mean it. I'm not a little kid anymore. I want to be right here if you have a relapse."

"I know you're worried, Raquel, but you can't stay there."

"Mom. I can't live without you."

The beeping of machines from inside. The faint music and slamming doors of the parking lot behind her.

Then her mother said, "Baby girl. One more day. Be careful how Rick sees you coming back. But he'll keep watch over you."

RAQUEL WAITED FOR Marisol on the other side of the street. Two men were sitting in canvas chairs on the sidewalk, in the shade. On the little metal table between them a lantern. Like camping.

Like the lantern the woman had been holding in Calimesa. When the three people came out of the trees. Like they were camping.

Only Joey and I know that story, she thought. And Ray Allala. And the stranger from Arkansas. He saved my life, and I'll never see him again.

Before this, her mother had known everything about every day. All the boring stuff—Akisha brought sushi for lunch, Marshall and her mom were going camping at the Grand Canyon, Raquel got an A on her history test. Now her mother knew nothing about entire weeks. Raquel knew nothing about what her mother might have said to a woman screaming in a car.

The beginning of secrets. She stared at the windows of Our Lady. Not lies. Secrets. Wait—secretions were liquids leaving the body. Secreted. But secrets—just thoughts held inside, nothing actually physical, memories, fear, whatever else.

The flashlight in her hand and how he'd laughed. The fingers in her hair pulling so hard her scalp felt like it had tiny bubbles under the skin. He whispered so the others couldn't hear, *Caught you. Wait till I pull your hair for real, bitch.*

She heard him even now. Even though she'd washed her hair twice.

The sound of the bullet hitting the tree.
Never even find your bones.
Joey's eight-pack. His flat bones coming from his sternum. His phalanges holding on to hers when they finally fell asleep.

His mouth.

His scapulae when he turned away from her and cried without a sound. *Angel wings*, people liked to call them. But her mother and Larette always said, *Call bones by their right name, and that's the beginning of knowing about the body. The truth.*

How could Raquel ever tell her mother all the truth?

SUNDAY MORNING, HER mother came back to CamperWorld. She waved at Raquel, who stood outside Pam's trailer. Her mother went inside her own trailer, and for a few hours Raquel lay in silence, listening to the wave sounds her mother played on her phone to help her sleep. Waves, sirens, barking dogs, and a mockingbird—Raquel could hear it all.

Noon was quiet. Silvia, Larette, and Marisol were sleeping. Raquel checked her phone every few minutes. Texts from everyone. But not Joey.

She heard tapping at the flimsy metal door. Her mother's eyes were better. But her voice still wasn't the same. It came from the middle of her throat. Like something was lodged in her trachea. Or her chest.

"I just want to be outside in the sun," her mother whispered. "Come on."

They sat ten feet apart, in plastic chairs under the big sycamore, looking up at the arrowhead in the mountain. The white rocks pointing down toward San Bernardino. Her mother whispered, "I wish we could go for breakfast burritos and take a walk up by Strawberry Creek."

Raquel felt five again. In the best way. She said, "But we can. As soon as you feel better."

Her mother smiled and said, "I feel better. Except my forehead. The pain just sits there."

Her forehead was too pale, too soft, and still had a faint brown line from all the PPE.

Then her mother said, "So who brought you here? Tell me the truth. Marisol knows. She knows everything. She has powers, Raquel. But she said this is between you and me."

There was no sense lying. Her mother knew Oasis, from the old days. Raquel said, "Mr. Ortiz, the older one? His grandson. Joey."

Her mother looked at the mountain. "How old is this Joey?"

"Seventeen. He borrowed his cousin's truck. He was nice, Mom. He drove me here and dropped me off."

"Uh-huh. Dropped you off and sailed into the sunset."

"No. It was, like, five in the morning. He went back home. I gave him the money I'd been saving for Christmas."

"From your bedroom. He went in the house? Into your room?"

"Mom. Seriously? You're the one hanging out with some cowboy at a barn."

Her mother shook her head. "Good deflection."

"I went inside and got the money. He stayed in the yard. Then we drove here."

"And that all took how long? It takes two hours to get here from Oasis. You were gone for two days."

Music came on in Marisol's trailer, and Marisol stepped outside, walked to the chairs. She said, "My sister Jasmine coming early, Cherrise. Tuesday. She drive from Sacramento. We tell Rick Schneider one more trailer."

Raquel's mother said, "No. We can't keep lying. We'll get Pam's trailer ready." She looked at Raquel. "I guess it's your trailer. For one more day."

Her mother had made up her mind about something. Raquel could see it when she stared up at the mountains.

Then her mother said, "Come on. Let's get two sheets and lay on the grass. Under the tree here. For just an hour. Like when you were little. Getting some sunshine."

PART FOUR

NINETEEN ✦ Trench

ON SUNDAY NIGHT, AUGUST 22, LARETTE GOT TO OUR LADY half an hour early and went straight to check on Chencho Sotelo.

But he was gone.

A woman was in the bed, intubated. Larette checked the wall. Genie Wilson. Admitted at 5:10 p.m. Larette studied her face. One box braid had fallen out of the cap over her hair, a gold bead at the end. Larette tucked it back into the cap. The still hands on the sheet. Fingernails freshly painted pink.

How could she feel suddenly alone? She went to the break room. Sat there in the bright light. Rudy Magana, Beth Beverly, Stan Earley. Their hands in hers. Their lips soft when she swabbed the water inside for comfort. The soul was supposed to be inside the heart. *We pray like this*, her mother said. *Hold your hands before your heart. Your soul.* Their breath, their souls, their blood. No priest, no mother, no husband, no dog beside them. This whole building filled with souls, always, the babies crying in Neonatal, the men sitting in the ER holding their broken arms or bloody faces with stoic dignity or anger or trying to joke about the pain—like Chencho would be doing even now, wherever he'd gone to rehab.

She couldn't miss them. Not now. But she did.

Cherrise would be sleeping in her Mallard now, and Raquel in the next trailer. Was Cherrise still angry with Larette for keeping the truth from Raquel? She picked up her phone, looked at the cascade of texts from Dolores Sotelo. The phone calls. Larette couldn't just text to see how Chencho was doing. That's not how it worked.

When patients were gone—either way—they were gone.

If they wanted to be in touch, they would.

For the first four hours of shift, she was restless. She went to the end of the hallway several times, when she couldn't breathe. But it wasn't just her lungs. It was her heart. Racing. Feeling as though someone were stepping on her sternum. A heavy shoe. Like she was lying flat on her back, not standing at the hermetically sealed glass, looking out at the lights trembling in the heat.

Marisol found her there. "Come. Ola cover for you. We have twenty minutes. In the trench."

THEY SAT ON the benches. The tree trunk smelled of fresh urine. Lovely.

Marisol lit Larette's Lucky Strike and then her Swisher Sweet. "Why you so scared tonight? Raquel safe. Cherrise is home."

"I can't breathe." Larette exhaled. "So why am I doing this?" She studied the ember.

Marisol took her puffs. She lifted her left hand to the security guard at the edge of the grass, watching the street, watching them. She said, "You say breathing. But I see you hold your hand here." The center of her ribs. "That not the lungs, Larette. Something with your heart. You need EKG and stress test. You tell them schedule you."

Larette stared at the white puzzle-bark of the ancient sycamore. She listened to her blood. Marisol was always right. Always. Her heart was pounding all the time, and when she wore the PPE and masks and walked in the hallways, it was all she could hear. Her heartbeat. Deep inside her head. She heard it in the pillow, when she was trying to sleep.

When she was crunching ice on her molars, or hearing the soft crackle of the lit cigarette, like now, the beating was faint.

"Marisol. How do you always know?"

Marisol said, "I don't always. But I look. I don't know the people like you do, I don't have to talk like you with them. So I look at you. When we turn the patient over, you get dizzy now. Have to run outside when we done."

She was right. Some nights when they turned a big man who was gasping, she remembered her own panic, the impossibility of pulling in a breath, as if a grown man sat on her chest.

Larette saw it. That night. She'd been walking home from the corner market, carrying a small sack of groceries for her mother. Rice? A five-pound bag. Half a pound of shrimp. Two onions. Summertime. Maybe nine o'clock. At the vacant lot off Base Line Street, a big man had knocked her down on the grass parking strip between two palm trees. The bag flew. He turned her over roughly, put his knee at her breastbone, and when she screamed, he said, "Crush you like a bug, you little bitch, you don't shut up."

Pushing her into the earth. The grass at her ears. The tiny rustling of whoever lived in the blades, crawling toward her hair.

He put his other knee on her arm. His hands at his zipper.

Screeching tires at the curb. A door slammed. The sound of something hitting him. A landscaper, it had to be, Larette turned her face to the side to see his boots shaggy with wet grass. The big man fell off her. She saw a shovel, resting by the boots. Mud dried like chocolate.

Now she said to Marisol, "I panic when I can't breathe. 'Cause this man jumped me. When I was thirteen. Sat on my chest."

Marisol nodded.

"Someone jumped out of his truck and hit the guy in the head with a shovel. Jesus. That sound. The guy fell off me. I got up and I couldn't breathe."

She hadn't even looked at their faces. Either of them. But the man with the shovel had said, "Get your food. Go on home."

The two onions had rolled onto the sidewalk. Her mother would ask where the onions were. When Larette bent to pick them up, she was just as afraid of the man with the boots as she'd been of the other man. She ran.

Marisol blew out smoke. "Look," she said. "The dog."

The big black dog. Short hair. White blaze on his chest. Sitting at the edge of the grass, watching them.

"I know," Marisol said.

"What?"

"I smoke this because I don't have pipe. Because I like the tree here. In San Bernardino. I fourteen in the forest. My mother send me out for meat from my aunt house. And a man catch me. A bad man."

Larette could see that, too. A narrow path? Trees? "I'm so sorry, Marisol."

"I try run home, too. But nobody come." She pulled in two more long breaths from the cigarillo. "I have a baby. She born too early. She die."

"Oh, Marisol."

"She bury back in the forest. Behind my mother house. When we come to California, I fifteen. I think about that baby. I don't want no more. So I have my three sister. My dog." She blew out smoke and put the cigarillo stub in the sand ashtray. "I have my grandmother pipe. She give to me when we go. She tell me smoke every night to chase away the aswang. The spirit. If I out in the night."

Larette finished her cigarette. She had seen the bruises on Raquel's arm. Clear and defined as though the man's hand had been dipped in ink when he gripped her skin. How dark the deep circles of black and pain had been on the inside of her own thin arm from the man's knee. The bruise on her chest from his other knee.

The shovel. Had he died? Had he lain there? Had the stranger buried him—with that same shovel?

She stood up. The security guard waved at them. Marisol took something out of her pocket and put it on the ground. When they were twenty feet away, Larette looked back. The dog was eating.

"Chicken," Marisol said. "For the aswang."

THERE WERE SO many ambulances lined up at emergency, and so many new cars in the parking lot, they had to weave through the vehicles. Marisol went first, Larette behind her, the open windows of cars where people snored, listened to the radio, talked on their phones. Without warning, a big SUV door opened in front of Marisol, and Larette almost bumped into her.

A woman got out and said, "You two work here, right? I've just about had it with this shit. You people are keeping my fiancé hostage up there. He doesn't have the fucking virus. He has the flu. Regular flu. I need to know who to call because nobody will give me an answer."

Marisol and Larette backed up in the narrow channel between cars. The woman came toward them. No mask. Her skin was tanned too brown, her hair way too black, her teeth way too white, her lips huge, and her eyes were—purple, in the harsh parking-lot lights.

They stared at her.

Marisol said in her fake nice voice, "What your fiancé name? Where you from?"

The woman said, "Why are you asking where I'm from? Where the fuck are you from?"

Marisol's shoulders lifted and fell with her deep calming breath.

Larette said, "A name and a home address can help us identify a patient, ma'am."

The woman said, "His name is Thomas Lunzi, and it's none of your fucking business where he lives. For your government records or whatever. We were at the casino and he got sick and it's been a day and a half. I'm tired of this shit!"

Marisol said smoothly, "We go to work now, we can check for you."

But the woman didn't step back. She came forward again.

A black blur raced past Larette's legs and leapt at the woman, who fell against the bumper of her SUV and began to scream. The dog kept moving, leaping one more time gracefully over the hedge near the sidewalk, and disappeared.

Larette couldn't believe it—Marisol grabbed her elbow and they backed away and went down two more rows.

When they got to the entrance, Marisol said, "The aswang."

"The aswang," Larette whispered.

Marisol said, "I go work somewhere else soon. Time to go."

Larette couldn't say, *Please don't leave me. Not yet. Not until Cherrise doesn't hate me. Please don't make me sit outside alone.* She said instead, "Sacramento?"

Marisol actually smiled, behind her mask. You could always hear how the words were shaped differently when someone's lips were smiling.

"No. Maybe not far. Maybe you come work there, too. I take you to see your friend. Sotelo."

Thomas Lunzi's fiancée was out there somewhere in the parking lot.

Marisol read her mind again. "She have too much spray tan."

"Her eyes were purple. Like, amethyst," Larette said.

"Contact," Marisol said. "Her fiancé, he sad when he see her real face. If he stay alive."

Larette walked beside her to the stairs.

TWENTY ✦ Tequila Tuesday

I STARTED WORKING MY DOUBLE SHIFT ON SATURDAY—and during my breaks kept checking my phone to see if Grief or Larette had texted me, to say Cherrise's daughter had made it home. I kept remembering Grief throwing Roberto Ortiz's phone into the pond, the instant boiling, the sound like a stone. All those young girls in his photos, down at the bottom with the mud.

On patrol, I passed Limestone Canyon, Blind Canyon, Borrego Canyon. My blood and Trinh Bui's soaked into the sand there.

Cherrise's daughter could be with this Joey kid, in the truck, hiding in some canyon while Roberto found another ride and showed up, for whatever these guys were planning. Grief and I couldn't search everywhere.

On the 91, I drove past Bee Canyon at least ten times a night. That ravine where I'd shot the man who'd been raping a young woman—she'd run away. I'd gone with my service weapon to shoot at cans, because I wanted to be the best at the range—and when the man came at me with a knife, I shot him in the chest. Buried him in Bee Canyon. He was bones now.

I was alive. That young woman—she'd trusted the guy who took her there. Raquel was only fifteen. Where was she?

I always thought I didn't want to get married, because it's too hard. I'd have to tell someone about Bee Canyon. About how it felt to see my mother, dead in her bed. I'd never wanted to lose the love of my life—like my father had. But having a kid would be even scarier—to lose your child?

Finally, Grief called me at 11:00 a.m. "She came home. She showed up at Our Lady, and she saw her mom through the window. That's all I know."

"We could drive back out there," I said. "Roll up on these Ortiz kids."

Grief said, "Let's wait till she tells Cherrise what happened. Maybe Cherrise will get released soon. Raquel has five days of isolation. Wherever the hell she was."

It was like high school, no idea if I should call. I kept seeing Cherrise's mouth, the two indents in her cheeks, how she laughed in the barn. All I did was work and sleep. I could leave a message saying I was glad both she and her daughter were okay.

But I didn't.

ON TUESDAY AT 2:00 a.m., I'd just gotten coffee at the 7-Eleven off Gypsum Canyon Road, and when I got back on the Harley, heading up the 91 toward Yorba Linda, I heard the Kawasakis. They'd been racing every night, and none of us had caught them.

Three box cutters slicing the dark. Coming from behind me, from the east. Custom Harleys were deep, guttural engines, like snarling chainsaws cutting through the air. Kawasakis were high and sharp zippers opening the sky, like spaceships from another world. I moved to the slow lane, revved up to eighty-five, but shit, if they were racing all three lanes and came up on me, I was fucked.

They were flying west, through the Santa Ana Canyon. The sound bounced off the sheer cliffs and walls along the freeway. I could see the bikes coming up on me now, in my side mirror. The leader was on a Kawasaki Ninja 650, bike worth eight grand, top speed two hundred. Bright green, the color young guys liked, and he was wearing the skull mask over his whole face, under his matching helmet. The color of caterpillar blood. Behind him was a white 450 with a black windshield. Getting his ass left. Just behind him another white 450. No chance.

I kicked up to ninety in the center lane. I knew they were heading to the 241 through the Santa Ana Mountains. That bright green shot up the swerving on-ramp lanes into the hills. He thought he was a god. Probably twenty, hadn't had corona, and figured this was the best time of his life because of the empty lanes.

I had just made everything better. A cop getting left in the dust.

I cued up the Bluetooth and said into the mike hanging around my neck, "Rob, Justin, green Kawasaki Ninjas. A 650 and two white 450s coming on the 241. Those same assholes."

Justin said, "I'm on the 55 at Lincoln. Shit."

The Tahoe could get up to 130. He was at least fifteen minutes from where I figured they'd be coming out.

But Rob said, "I'm on the 5 at El Modena. I'll head over to the 261. They're probably heading to Irvine or Newport. I'm gonna bust their asses."

Dispatch would call Irvine PD and OC Sheriff.

"They're hitting about a hundred and ten now. We got ten minutes, tops," I said, then added, for my mother, "Gracias a Dios."

I went up the long curve into the mountains, hoping a deer or coyote wouldn't pick this time to cross. The moon was almost half full, showing the limestone eroded into long pale wrinkles of earth, like thousands of candles pressed into the dirt. I kicked up to ninety-five, stayed in the center lane, and prayed also that nobody cruising along to the beach in a Camry or Prius was gonna die.

When I got up to the second crest near Jeep Trail, I saw their taillights disappearing down the long decline toward Blind

Canyon. Even as I was holding at ninety-three, I knew each canyon. The wind whipping past me, and last year, I would have loved this—taking the Harley up to the limit, the lanes empty. The dream. But not now. I expected to come up the next rise near Santiago and see mangled bikes, or flames, or a truck flying off into a canyon. Years ago, I'd found a girl already dead in Santiago Canyon, her surfboard flown off into the rocks when a deer leapt up and hit her car, and I crawled to both of their bodies in the brush.

Three red pinpricks far in the distance, past Blind Canyon. One far ahead. The Ninja 650 just fucking with the other riders. Like tiny animal eyes in the night, then they disappeared.

Too fast. Too smart.

Rob and Justin would never see them. The Kawasakis would get put back in the fancy garages in whatever mansions the parents of these guys lived in. And they'd schedule the next race on their socials. YouTube or TikTok were the only way to catch them, eventually, because that was the thing about everyone being alone—they all had to brag about something. Prove they were still the shit.

I got off at Santiago Canyon Road and took a breather with my mask off. The smells of creosote bush and the purplish bells of jimsonweed. Back on the Toll Road, the shadows of the canyons and the silvery brittlebush all bones from the August heat.

IN THE MORNING, when we were finishing up paperwork, Hubie Vaughn, the duty sergeant, came over to me in my folding chair outside. Handed me a fancy beige envelope. It smelled like lavender. My name in black cursive writing, and the division address.

"Frias. Either you're invited to a wedding on Balboa Island, or you got a badge bunny who sends letters," he said.

Justin Pham rolled his eyes. He said, "I just get hate DMs on my Instagram. From the girlfriends of guys I pulled over. They send me some shit."

Hubie frowned. "You got that letter Friday, Pham. In Vietnamese."

Justin lifted his chin at me. "The mom. From the fool in Skull Canyon. He got out of the hospital. She said thank you."

I could see the kid hanging upside down, his hair held together by pomade but dangling sideways by his forehead. The borrego skulls more than a hundred years old, starring in TikToks.

Hubie and Pham both stared at the envelope. Return address also in cursive. *Joan Dimian. Newport Beach.*

The card inside was thick, with her name at the top.

Officer Frias,
   Please accept my apology. My casual insistence on speaking with you when I could have been a carrier for coronavirus was very rude. I did not enter my stepmother's suite. I did not, in fact, contract the virus. But my flippant tone, when you, too, have lost your mother, was inexcusable. I hope you remain well in these dark days.
                                                              Joan Dimian

Hubie was hovering. "You got a fan in Newport?"

I put the card back into the envelope and stuck it in my utility pocket. "Nope," I said. "Pham got a letter from a mom. I got one about a mom. All cool."

AT HOME, I put my uniform in the washer, sat in the barber chair, and held the framed black-and-white snapshot of my mother I kept out in the garage. For company on a Tuesday morning like this. She was with four other women in a line at the orange packing company, all of them smiling behind their wooden crates of Valencias. They had long hair, those dark wings blown back from their faces, and they wore dark lipstick and heavy eyeliner. My father had taken the Polaroid. My mother was nineteen. Before I was born. They met at a dance in the old colonia called Las Flores, in Placentia, where the citrus workers had settled in the 1900s.

I fell asleep in the barber chair, like always, my ribs more comfortable than when I lay on my back in bed. The garage door open, the sounds of morning sparrows, and the hawk far up in the sky, either for real or in my dream.

AT 1:00 P.M., Grief called. "Cherrise hasn't texted you, J?"

"Nope," I said.

"Well, Larette said even though you and I can find a runaway bull but not two teenagers in a black Silverado, they want to meet us at three." He paused. "It's Cherrise's birthday."

So a couple of hours later, Grief and I were looking at the fifteen wooden picnic tables arranged in the big half-acre dirt area under giant mulberry trees behind the Eagles Lodge in San Bernardino. The Eagles had set up an outside bar on the big shaded patio attached to the old building so that the lodge could survive during the pandemic. TEQUILA TUESDAY! the sign said. SIX FEET SAFE!

"Safe," I said to Grief. "What a weird word. You got *save*, and *savior*, and then *safe*, *safety*."

"Here we go," he said, rolling his eyes. "Deconstructing English."

"American," I said. "Not English. *Safe* where you keep the money. *Safecracker*. But you can't *crack* iron. You just open it. You *crack* the code."

"Been watching too much TV again, Johnny?" Grief said.

"My ribs," I said.

About twenty people were spread out at the tables. Safe. I'd kept my distance last night from the 2010 Pontiac LeMans nosed off the 91 freeway at Green River Road, where a good Samaritan had called the EMTs after the driver went unconscious from corona, where the tow truck driver and I imagined the cloud of virus still hanging in the air, and so waited for five minutes to get the car hooked up, hoping the passing trucks blew enough wind to send corona into the Santa Ana River. The driver was thirty-nine, from Riverside. His big smile, his cornrows, powerful neck with one vein visible in his work ID—Big Five warehouse. I put his wallet in a plastic bag, delivered it to Circle City Hospital in Corona.

The security guard watched me roll up on the Harley and said, "Ironic, eh, bro? Corona in Corona. All fucking night."

We'd parked in the Eagles lot—Grief's county truck and my pickup—and picked a table, ordered Modelos.

Four guys rolled in saying, "We got the dogcatcher here, man? I don't want no mapaches or zorillos coming out that truck. And it's fucking hot, homes, do they got AC? I hate those fucking zorillos, but they shouldn't die like that, bro, that's not right."

Zorillos—nobody liked skunks. People would rescue a mapache, a raccoon. But not a skunk.

Larette and Cherrise were a half hour late. We were finishing our second Modelos. Not lit. Just working a little buzz where you can keep going and still think, and function, but you're trying to take the mean edge off the end of the day. Grief and I never got to do that now, never got to have a beer at night in my garage and work on our motorcycles.

He said, "Something's wrong with Larette. They been working nights for too long. Why doesn't she want to be home? It's not just we were both sick. It's something else."

"Nights are weird," I said. "You get used to it, like a strange family. I see the guy who makes me coffee at 7-Eleven twice a night, more than my dad."

Grief put down the bottle. "I don't want anybody else being her night family. What if there's a doctor wanting to be her night husband?"

"That's crazy," I said, looking at the entrance. "They're here."

I finished the Modelo and took a deep breath. I didn't want my first conversation with Cherrise today to start with why we hadn't found her daughter. They stood there for a minute, looking for us. Both wearing scrubs. Cherrise's hair in a bun like a crown on top of her head. She looked different. Her cheekbones. You couldn't lose weight from bones. They made her face more like a heart. She saw me. She lifted her chin. Smiled a little. A tiny move of her mouth.

They came over to our table.

"Are you both faded?" Larette said.

She sat next to Grief. Cherrise next to me.

"You didn't call me," I said to Cherrise. Damn. I sounded like an eighth grader.

"That's accurate," she said.

I said, "Can I buy you a drink?"

She said, "I saw the attempt at a thought process there. That's what you came up with?"

Then she laughed. Her forehead shiny with sweat.

She said, "It's like a furnace inside the trailers. And I just had Covid-19. Not 18 or 17 or 16. Whoever the hell got those earlier versions. So yeah, I'm not supposed to drink or do anything to jeopardize my health."

"Cherrise," Larette said.

"See what I'm wearing? For my birthday? My only clean clothes. I have to get back to work tomorrow night, right, cuz? We're heroes. The nurses. Everybody holding up signs in the parking lot saying thank you and bringing us so much coffee and doughnuts we could swim in the coffee and float on the doughnuts. Like—"

Then she stood up, swayed, and almost fell.

I jumped up to catch her arm, and then I almost fell. Because my ribs moved wrong.

"Like the lifesaver rings?" I said.

"Yeah," Cherrise said.

"I got you," I said, holding her up.

TWENTY-ONE ✦ **Mexican Candy Shots**

ALL CHERRISE HAD DONE SINCE SHE WAS DISCHARGED from Our Lady was sleep and talk to Raquel outside. At night, she looked at her daughter's silhouette in the other Mallard.

How would they tell each other anything? Raquel had been with Joey Ortiz for two days, somewhere. Cherrise had been in a barn with Johnny Frias. Last Monday afternoon. Just before everything went to hell.

"You should take it easy," Johnny said.

Cowboy clothes again. A pearl-snap shirt? Sitting all stiff and straight up, like he just got off a horse.

At the tables closest to theirs, four roofers with tar on their boots. Then four cement guys with boots gray and sandy. August heat—they probably started work at five and got off now.

She said softly, "I did everything right. I sent my girl away, and maybe she hates me. We're living in the fucking Mallards and we still almost died. I'm having tequila."

"Good choice," Johnny said.

"My neighbor Mr. Garibay told me the reason he never got corona is because he washes his throat twice a day with tequila," Cherrise said.

But then she felt her heart race again. Her house. How would she get Raquel back to the house, keep her safe?

She stood up and said, "Be right back."

In the bathroom, she stared at herself. A good mom wouldn't be here. Not today.

She'd washed her hair this morning, dried it in the sun, listening to Raquel speak every now and then in her Zoom classes. Her curls gleamed black and brown and copper. She'd put on the scrubs and gotten ready for the parent-teacher Zoom meeting at lunchtime. But sitting in the trailer, in the dim hot light, made her feel as though she was drowning. Watching the other parents in their curated rooms, their fancy plants and pictures, their coffee mugs and never-ending smiles. She and Raquel in separate screens. Smiling, too. No resting-tired face. Mr. Espinoza talked about environmental research careers, about forests, watersheds, animal species, and survival.

Now she splashed water on her face, dried it with a paper towel. A good mom would get a different job. She could work remotely, doing billing—and make shit money. She and Larette could say, *Sorry, all these strangers are breaking our hearts.* Even Raquel and Dante knew their hearts were broken—they'd never seen Rudy Magana or Stan Earley, but they knew.

My mom left me, she thought, turning away from herself. I had a big . . . rift. Inside. Like a crevice and the rain just goes down in there forever but it's never filled up. Then I left Raquel in Oasis. Like I didn't know any better.

Raquel had put in the meeting chat, *My mom's birthday is today! Thanks for coming, Mom.* Like Cherrise was in Bermuda, not twenty feet away in a fucking RV. The other moms all wrote, "Another trip around the sun! Congratulations!"

I don't want to go around the sun, she thought. I want to get lit and flirt with this man. Then go home to my patio. I have no mom. No dad. No granny. I have to figure out how to get Raquel home.

◆

HALF AN HOUR later, she'd had the one shot of Don Julio, Grief and Johnny were on their third Modelos, and Larette was sighing.

Johnny Frias. A little scar like a ladle above his left eye. He was watching her.

Larette said, "You and Grief wouldn't last one hour on the ICU. Every room is a shit show. Every machine is going off—people lose kidney function and lung function, and their blood pressure just spikes. You two wouldn't be able to even keep the tubes straight."

Grief said, "I have to know every kind of cat—you know how many damn breeds there are? Maine coon cat. What the hell is that, here in Rialto and stuck in a tree? Then I gotta catch five raccoons in somebody's attic. Bring me that damn coon cat." His face changed fast. Got hard. "Then I gotta figure out why some jerk spent a thousand dollars on a fancy Bernese mountain dog that should be in the snow in Switzerland, and he tied it to a tree in August in Rancho Cucamonga and let it almost die."

Johnny tried to lighten it up. "Okay. I have to know every mile of nine different freeways. Last night? Three Kawasakis going a hundred and thirteen miles an hour, on the 241, and I couldn't come close to catching them. Then an hour later, dude in a 2020 Avalanche, lift kit, rolling on 33s, he's got the DON'T TREAD ON ME bumper stickers. Pissing on the side of the 91 in Fullerton. Told me I was an agent of the federal government trying to regulate his urine."

Grief laughed softly, his arms relaxed around Larette, wrists just up under her breasts in the scrubs. Johnny was next to Cherrise, being careful.

She shivered, even in the dappled heat under the trees.

"You okay?" Johnny said. He was watching everything she did. He didn't look drunk, either. But his eyes showed some kind of pain.

Larette said to Cherrise, "You tell them, cuz. They think they have it hard."

Cherrise reached forward and touched Larette's hand on the wooden table. The morning Raquel showed up outside the hospital window, Larette had knelt on the floor. All the dirt and virus on that floor, from all their booties. She'd knelt beside Cherrise's bed after Raquel walked away with Marisol, and she'd said, "I'm sorry, so sorry. I never know what to do or what to say now. Never. Nothing works. Nothing I do."

They'd never told anyone anything that happened at Our Lady. Larette didn't tell Grief. Cherrise didn't tell Raquel. About these last six months.

She said, "You guys look up. You look up at the tree where the cat is, at the overpasses or whatever. You can see the fucking sky. We look down at the numbers on the machines, and we look down at our phones 'cause the families want FaceTime, and we look down at the body."

"The feet." Larette stared across the picnic tables at all the roofers. Their work boots.

"All these men and their secrets. The diabetic gods attack the feet." Cherrise turned, close to Johnny. "The whole world is in the body. We have to see every small thing. One spot on somebody's back. People do drugs between their toes. They have yellow in their eyes, and their family doesn't even notice." The jaundice. Wolf eyes.

Larette said softly, "They have blood in their work socks and they don't want their wife to know, so they throw the socks away and buy new ones on the way to work the next day. We end up taking their toes. Their feet. Those guys work so hard. But now with corona? They have . . . Everything fails. Just—everything."

Grief didn't say shit. Because he knew his own body.

Cherrise whispered, "When someone's in a diabetic coma for ten days and their legs swell up and their kidneys can't process all that liquid? After we get them stable and they wake up and we start diuretics, the water comes out of their toes. Like, all around the toenails. They start hollering for us."

Grief and Johnny looked about like she'd expected.

"How the hell does that even work?" Johnny said.

"You wanna know?"

He shook his head.

Grief said, "Great. We get to debate the ruination of human and animal bodies."

But Cherrise was looking at the mountains behind San Manuel. So gold and calm in the heat today, they were like some version of heaven.

The casino only a few miles away. She'd never say this: Her husband, in the car, after the drunk driver had hit them head on. A CHP officer like Johnny would have seen him. But Cherrise had never seen him again. They told her not to look. And she didn't. Closed casket. Never to see his mouth or hair or hands again. Never.

Raquel imagined her father, too. Cherrise knew it. Raquel was obsessed with the body, the biology of disease, the skin and liver and tongue. Once they went to a party with tacos de cabeza and tacos de lengua.

"How can we eat that?" Raquel said, and started crying.

Cherrise had taken her to the car and said, "We ate chitlins and neckbones and head cheese when we were little," she said. "All we had was the bad parts of the pig."

Raquel had said, "I'll never be that hungry."

Cherrise had said, "No, baby. You won't."

But her daughter would never have a father again.

Then a woman came out of the Eagles back door with a tray of drinks. She put down the tray on the table nearest theirs and stopped. Staring at Cherrise, then Larette.

"I saw you," she said. "Just like that, with your scrubs. You're nurses. You FaceTimed my tía." She pointed at Cherrise. "You gave us the updates every night." Then Larette. "And you sang for my tío. Rudy Magana. It was you." She sat at the empty table and started to cry into her hands.

Two of the roofers jumped up and came over fast. "You okay, mija?" They glared at Grief and Johnny. "Bro, que paso?"

The Eagles didn't fuck around.

Cherrise had been here only once, when Ronald's friends had a kickback. She said, "We work at Our Lady. We—we were the nurses for her uncle."

"She sang my tía's favorite song for him," the woman said, pointing again at Larette. "When he was in the coma."

No one moved. Grief just stared at Larette.

He still had no idea. Of course. He had no idea that Larette stayed in the patient rooms alone, singing, brushing back hair from a forehead turning paler and paler, holding Rudy Magana's big fingers like she was a little girl, singing Mary Wells over and over. None of us know, Cherrise thought. Larette singing through three masks, her face shield fogging up, Cherrise watching through the window as her cousin's body vibrated with the effort.

The woman wiped her face with bar napkins. She said, "My mom has six sisters. Norma was the only one didn't get married yet, and she was in love with somebody, but we didn't know who. I used to sleep in her bed at night and she'd tell me how she did her hair and put on her makeup, she for real ran to catch the bus on Base Line, and she worked in a bank on Base Line and Mt. Vernon. Rudy came in every Friday with his money. That's who she loved."

Rudy Magana. His skin soft as silk—at the end. Sixty-two years old. On his stomach, his toes wedged into the sheets like those of a baby in a crib.

The woman said, "My tía heard in the parking lot that there

was a nurse who sang for people, so they knew someone cared about them while they were in the coma. It was you."

Cherrise felt the hot breeze shift in the mulberry branches. Larette's face across from her. She couldn't tell Grief. How it was hurting her now. Making her so sad she stayed in the bathroom alone for ten minutes afterward. How every night she smoked.

"You ladies did that?" the bigger man said. He wore a work shirt—Cardenas Roofing. The other guy wore the same shirt.

Larette said, "Yeah."

He said to the server, "Mija, Mexican candy shots. For the table. Make 'em strong, eh?"

In a few minutes, she brought a tray of shot glasses. "Real strong," she said.

They held up the drinks. Bright pink—with a darker swirl of hot sauce inside like a red tornado. Lime wedge on the side. So many virus possibilities. Tajín powder dusted on the rims.

They touched glasses, all four together, the chili powder fell onto their wrists, and they drank. Fire and watermelon, tequila and lime.

TWENTY-TWO ◆ **Sacrament**

LARETTE STARED AT HERSELF IN THE BATHROOM MIRROR, the sound of the Eagles bar staff calling out to one another beyond the door. How would she explain it to Grief, now? Six months of keeping it all inside, the lyrics to all the songs echoing in her head every moment she was away from the hospital. She used to practice for *The Wiz* or *The Sound of Music*, singing her songs over and over, and then at the theater the notes and lyrics flew out into the audience, she always imagined, the lines she'd perfected leaving the stage and the elaborate sets, leaving her body in an imaginary woman's costume—a witch, an Austrian nun, a librarian, Dinah Washington way back when she did a Women of Soul revue.

How could she describe the hospital room to Grief when he'd been in 3142, in the ICU for two days, and she never left his side but he didn't know she'd been there, and she'd not sung for him, only held his hand and whispered their entire lives together like a story? She'd always made him sing back to her, since high school, and when he lay there with the fever, delirious, all she could do was whisper.

Paper towels from the dispenser. Just like the hospital. She wanted her own soft towels. She wanted to go home.

They were waiting in the parking lot. Johnny watching her warily, Cherrise reaching out to touch Larette's hoop earring, which had gotten turned sideways.

"Always perfect," Cherrise said. "Forever."

Grief was leaning against the chain-link fence, his hands in his pockets, exactly how he'd always waited for her when he was done with baseball practice and she was late coming out of the theater. Larette felt the strangest little leap of joy just behind her sternum.

Just then a car pulled up, and a woman got out crying.

"My niece called me," she said to Larette. She stopped abruptly. Six feet away. "Look at you. You're so beautiful."

Norma Magana. Larette crossed her wrists over her chest—like someone was aiming a punch at her heart. The niece peered out from the Eagles doorway. Larette began to cry, too. She felt the tears slide down as if she were onstage and she couldn't wipe them.

"You must be her husband," Norma said to Grief. "She's an angel. Her voice goes all the way up to heaven. You're so lucky. And I hope you both never get this, because . . . because it takes the best."

Grief was frozen, staring at Larette.

Norma said, "God sent you here to the Eagles, because I didn't want to text you. I wanted to ask you in person. We been waiting for the funeral home. The memorial is in September. We want you to come. It's safe, it's outside, we have a car for you to ride in. Please, can you come say goodbye to Rudy? Mi familia, it would mean everything to them. Because you saw him last. You got to touch him, you were holding his hand."

Larette uncrossed her arms and ran her wrist across her eyes. "I'll talk to my husband, Mrs. Magana," she said. "But I'm honored that you asked me. That you came here. I'll text you."

Norma Magana got back into the car. She put her head on the steering wheel and sobbed, just like everyone in the hospital parking lot.

Larette went to Grief. She put her head against his chest, like she always had after practice, and his arms went around her.

She said into his collar, "Sometimes I don't want to be an angel. All those people. In the parking lot, in the ER, in the hallways. Right here. Everyone you see on TV, banging pots and pans, everyone doing parades, it's so nice. But then I have to be all alone with—their breath. Their breath just—it slows down and it's terrifying every time. And your breath. What if you get it again? Look at us right now—we sat outside and I loved it."

"But all these people," Grief said softly. "You needed some time away from the old Mallard. And some tequila. You gotta come home. Please?"

She could hear Norma Magana driving away. Hear the humming AC of Grief's work truck. The animals inside. Some of their raccoon or possum or dog souls already gone. Others waiting. Waiting. She kissed the chili powder on his lips.

TWENTY-THREE ✦ **Lovebirds**

GRIEF CALLED TO ME, "SHE'S GONNA DRIVE ME HOME, Johnny. Officer Wright's coming to get the truck. You lovebirds better be careful."

Cherrise said to me, "Very funny. I'm taking you to my house for some coffee so you don't have to give yourself a damn citation, okay? I live three blocks from here."

The four roofers came out and said, "You fools are lucky, eh, you got some badass wifeys right there." They actually took off their hats and held them to their orange shirts, and nodded to Larette and Cherrise.

Damn. I never got mistaken for married.

My ribs. Getting up in the passenger side of my own truck felt wrong. I hadn't ridden on this side of the bench seat—ever. I bought the truck when I was nineteen.

But Cherrise didn't turn the key. She said, "This is either a classic that means something to you, or an old-ass vehicle 'cause you're cheap."

"Don't hold back," I said.

I hadn't been faded in a long time. If that made me a stupid pendejo, well, fuck it.

But she was watching her cousin. Grief was holding Larette so tightly, like he did back when we were eighteen, playing baseball.

I couldn't believe I was jealous all of a sudden—the way her head fit perfect into his shoulder, how his hands went exactly the same place into her hair.

Cherrise took a big breath and said, "She's okay. They're okay."

She drove slow and careful out of the Eagles lot. Usually women talked at me. Nonstop. Cherrise didn't say shit. Did she still watch the Dodgers? Was that the worst thing to bring up?

She was the one waiting. For me to say something. But all I could do was watch her drive, her hair smelling like coconut, her chin lifted up while she concentrated.

The little bungalow was dusty, in the daylight. I'd been here Friday night. She drove down the long gravel driveway, parked back by her garage, took me in the side gate. Now I saw the backyard in the sun. A ramada, just like we had by the barn. The palm fronds were old and dry, desiccated by the heat.

She went to the little patio by the back door and said, "Well, shit, I haven't been here in so long. Somebody took my robe."

She touched a hook on the wooden pillar. "Who would steal that?" she said, leaning on the washer. "Look at these fingerprints in the dust. Somebody ran the washer." Opened it, and then the dryer. "I smell Tide. And look. Lint in the filter. What homeless woman would come wash clothes and steal my robe?"

"Your daughter's not here?"

Then she smiled. "You're law enforcement. I can't tell you where she is."

"Wait, what?"

"She's barely fifteen. She can't live here alone while I'm in the trailer." She cocked her head at me. "You'll see. Or you won't."

Then she unlocked the back door. I followed her through the house. Empty and hot and sad, like when Grief and I had checked it. I hadn't noticed the picture in the hallway of her daughter on a horse, with her dad.

"Your husband rode?" I said.

"He's from Mecca," she said, staring at the photo. "Torres-Martinez reservation. His uncles had horses. They used to ride all the way to Palm Springs for fiestas back in the fifties. He took Raquel through the Mecca Hills. Those canyons."

"She could come ride at the rancho," I said. "You saw the horses."

She didn't answer. She opened the second bedroom door.

IT JUST ABOUT killed me to sit on the edge of the bed. I'd put on the pearl-snap shirt so I wouldn't have to lift my arms, but I left on my Hanes. She stood there, frowning at me.

I said, "You might as well see."

She lifted up my undershirt. The pink tape. "Sexy," she said. "Just like work."

I unwrapped the tape. The bruises were still deep purple. "Five and six are cracked." I said.

Cherrise said, "How'd you do it?"

I told her about Borrego Canyon, the kid in the car, the kid running.

She said, "But seriously? If you can't bend over, I gotta pull off your boots. Like we're in fucking *Gunsmoke*."

She did. Like my mom used to do for my dad.

She put two pillows for me on her bed. I lay on my back and she was beside me. Only my boots and her Pumas on the floor. The overhead fan clacking and clacking. It needed oil.

Cherrise said, "I wish we could be anonymous. Like in a movie. But we can't go to a hotel. Everything's deadly."

I felt the tequila wearing off. I was tired, too. I said, "Well, I can just take you . . . home. To CamperWorld."

She got up. I'd blown it.

She said, "Neither of us can get a DUI. We're public servants. Let me make the coffee. You worked last night. I have to work tomorrow night."

I heard her in the kitchen. The coffee smelled strong, like my dad's Bustelo.

She brought in two beautiful mugs with orange poppies. "A patient gave me these. Long time ago," she said.

The coffee was like nothing I'd ever tasted. "Damn," I said. "This is good."

She looked sad, though. "Community Coffee. What my mom and Larette's mom used to make. From Louisiana." Her voice was strange. She lay on her side and ran her hand all over my face. I closed my eyes. Her hand was like a feather skimming over my mouth. My neck. My chest. She traced my collarbone. My ribs.

She said, "Nice. Aside from the carnage."

I said, "Nobody else has been here?"

She looked at me. "In this bed?"

Shit. "I meant in the house."

But she said, "I went to Dodger Stadium. Three years after Ronald died. I was there in the daytime, when Raquel was at school. She was ten. And I just wanted to walk around. You know how beautiful it is over there."

"Yeah," I said. Elysian Park and Dodger Stadium were like gardens.

"I met this groundskeeper. He took me on a tour. His crew had four guys. Very cool. Cactus, agave, all the trees." She closed her eyes. "He was divorced. I was a widow. We went out for six months. But—he didn't like Raquel."

"Why?" I said, careful.

Cherrise smiled. "She treated him like shit. She's smart, and she's got her ways—like me. She didn't want him to like her. And he was thirty-five, I was thirty-one. He wanted his own kids. Not somebody else's kid who might hate him."

Her voice had gotten softer and softer.

"Are you too drunk to do that math? I'm thirty-six today." She touched my jeans and said, "I haven't seen anything that worked for a while. Nothing works in the ICU. So you have a low bar. But I can't take a chance on your ribs and then you start crying and I have to call EMTs and they'll know me. Come on. We're going outside."

I sat on the patio. She unloaded clothes from her backpack, started the washer, leaned against it.

"I still feel hot, inside. From the virus. Like I don't want to be closed in," she said. "The trailer's killing me."

The sounds of a loud TV next door. I saw a woman in the window, then the curtain closed. Old-school music coming from the garage across the street—a song by Thee Midniters.

"Do you hear Larette singing to people?" I asked.

She shook her head. "She's alone when she does it. Every time, we can hear their monitors speed up. The patients hear her. The charge nurse and I watch their pulse and heart rates, and they always beep faster. They hear her."

The sun came onto the porch and touched my ribs. I got up and leaned beside her at the washer. Real close.

Cherrise said, "I'm making up my mind about you. But I have to think about Raquel. You'll see why. I told Larette we gotta switch to days, we have to be home nights for the kids."

I said, "Yeah, that's good. Except I work nights. So I won't see you."

She smiled. She had those cheeks that lifted high when she smiled for real. Her eyes were brown and green. She said, "Well, you can break something else and come to Our Lady in the day. I'll meet you in the parking lot." Then she leaned over and put her mouth right at my ear and said soft, "But I'm coming to your house next time. So make sure we have the same day off."

"Hey," a man hollered from the driveway. "Who's in the yard? Whose truck is this?"

Cherrise said, "Good. The system's working."

I moved away from her and got ready for whoever it was. A

man about my dad's age came around the corner of her house, holding a sawed-off pool cue. Good choice. He could either smack me in the head or poke me in the throat.

"Mr. Garibay," Cherrise said. "It's okay. This is Johnny Frias. He's a cop."

The man stood there, still frowning at me. I felt stupid in my Hanes.

"He don't look like a cop. And his truck was here last week when you were gone. Mrs. Ralphine gave me the license plate. She got binoculars now."

Cherrise said, "He was here checking on the house, with my brother-in-law."

"They looked like burglars," her neighbor said, glaring at me.

She said, "He's got broken ribs from chasing a suspect, so I was just helping him out."

She led him down the driveway like I wasn't even there.

I DROVE TOWARD Our Lady. "Maybe your daughter would like to go to a Dodger game? Would that be cool?"

Cherrise laughed. "Cardboard fans in the stands? Like everybody says, puro pinche 2020."

At CamperWorld, we walked toward the six trailers parked at the end. A guy came out of the gate in a golf cart, looking fire at me. Three nurses wearing scrubs came out of different trailers and stared at me from a ten-foot distance.

"Marisol, Silvia," Cherrise said. "Wait, you must be Jasmine." She waved at one in black scrubs.

The woman named Marisol wore bright crimson scrubs, a ton of makeup, and black hair in a tight bun. She pointed to a cake on a table and said, "Happy birthday for Cherrise!" Then she studied me. "This the dad of the boyfriend?"

"Of who?" Cherrise said.

I saw Marisol's face close down. "Nothing."

She thought she'd seen me. Or someone who looked like me. Interesting.

Cherrise said, "This is Grief's best friend, Johnny. Larette asked him to give me a ride back."

Marisol put out two Arizona iced teas for us. She said, "Jasmine come early."

Cherrise bit her lips, like that was bad. She said, "Okay, we'll clean the trailer."

Jasmine said, "Thank you. My sister's the OG. She was the only one born in the Philippines. The oldest of all four of us girls. She used to bandage us up when we got hurt, and she was only, like, twenty. Our parents were working in a care home and they were always gone."

Marisol's face changed—she said, "They help the people die. We suppose to help them live."

Cherrise said to me, "We told you and Grief. At the Eagles. We tried to make you see."

Then the last trailer door opened and another nurse came out. Purple scrubs. Hair like Cherrise's in a high bun. Beautiful, angry black eyes, and very young. But she wore a wedding ring. She stood by her trailer, no mask, staring at me like she would kill me. Not keep me alive.

"That's Raquel," Cherrise said.

The same girl who'd been on the horse, smiling?

"Wait, your daughter's a nurse?"

"She is right now," Cherrise said.

"I don't get it."

"You don't have to. She can't stay at the house alone, and I was sick. So Rick over there—the guy on the cart? He thinks she's a traveler nurse. She's been here since Saturday, now she's gotta leave." Cherrise sat down fast on a folding chair. She must have been ready to collapse.

Her daughter walked over to us. "Seriously?" she said, looking fire at me. "This is the cowboy?"

Cherrise said softly to me, so no one could hear, "The only thing that made sense today was Mexican candy shots."

I said, "Not me?"

She whispered, "Maybe you."

TWENTY-FOUR ✦ *Perdoname*

HER MOTHER SAID SOMETHING TO THE COWBOY. JOHNNY Frias. He lifted his hand and said to the nurses, "I heard some stories today—you're all ten times tougher than me." Then he nodded to Raquel and said, "Good to meet you." And he walked away.

Her mother just shook her head and smiled.

Silvia said, "You got lucky, Cherrise."

Raquel waited until the old truck left the cul-de-sac. Then she stood beside her mother and said, "I already disinfected the trailer with bleach wipes. All my stuff is in my backpack. All Pam's stuff is in those boxes."

Marisol pointed to the three boxes beside her trailer steps. "Raquel is a good packer. She make this like balikbayan."

"Balikbayan?" her mother said.

Raquel was proud now. She touched her mother's shoulder. She said, "The boxes Marisol and Jasmine's family send to the Philippines for their family. Rick's gonna mail them tomorrow. Because you and I are going home. Right?"

Her mother said, "We have to go somewhere else first."

THE SUN WAS gold and red in the west when they passed the exit for Calimesa. Raquel hadn't thought about the billboard for Jack in the Box, or the stand of pepper trees, that she would see at the place where it all happened. It was across the freeway; she could see the trucks lined up in the big dirt lot, more parked on the road, the gas station sign. Then they were past it.

One nail on the side of the freeway. They would never have stopped here.

When they got to Oasis, everyone would still be working the dates. They'd all see her. All Raquel could think of was how many times she'd have to apologize.

Did she have to say she was sorry to Joey? She wasn't sorry. She'd almost gotten kidnapped. She wasn't a kid. *Robando*, Ray Allala had said to his wife. *This guy fucking tried to steal her.* She and Joey could have been hit by bullets. People thought they were married. She'd danced with him. She'd kissed him.

What had Joey told his father?

Her mother didn't speak. She just drove. The AC was roaring, the radio on to the Dodger pregame show.

"I only asked him to take me to Our Lady because you were sick."

Her mother looked at her for a moment. "I believe that. But he should have known you were only fifteen. His father, Lolo, Ruby, they're all upset."

"I'm the one who lied," she said, when they went through the forest of tall white windmills past Cabazon. "By omission."

Her mother finally said, "Plenty of omission to go around. Larette should have told you I was sick." Then she said, "Did you catch up from school? You missed two days."

"I'm doing extra credit for bio and history. I finished math and English."

She had texted Joey on Friday night. **Thx 4 saving my life. I'm ok. U?**

Nothing.

Saturday she texted, **RU ok? Is he mad? Yr primo**

Nothing.

She texted him again now. **I hope UR ok.**

Nothing.

She looked at the photo burst on her old phone, the pics of her on the giant swing. She'd almost finished her makeup report for Mr. Espinoza. The botany of date palms in the Coachella Valley. The first trees were Deglet Noor, from Algeria, brought in 1919. She'd saved a newspaper picture of Lolo and her sister, Sofelia, Raquel's grandmother. Standing in front of the packinghouse, 1962, pointing at the sign, smiling wide. Beautiful eyes, high cheekbones, dark lipstick, hair in braids hanging long over their shoulders. Just like hers.

Her mother got off at the Indio exit. The wind blew dust across the hood of the car when she pulled into a gas station.

Raquel reached over and said, "You just got better. I'll pump the gas, Mom."

When she reached for her mother's purse, her mother said, "Raquel! Look at these bruises!"

Her sleeve had ridden up. The four fingers outlined purple and green on the front of her upper arm. The thumb on the back. The thumb had hurt the deepest—our fucking thumbs so powerful, she thought immediately.

"Joey did that? What happened?"

Raquel kept her voice steady. It was so hard. She said, "Joey would never do that. We were at a gas station and an asshole grabbed me, and Joey made him let me go."

Her mother had lifted her arm gently, was looking closely at the bruises. "A stranger did this?"

"A man."

"Oh, baby, you must have been so scared."

"In the parking lot," Raquel said. "He thought I had some money, but I didn't. I was scared. I had my flashlight, but the stun gun didn't work. But Joey—Joey waved his dad's machete around. From the dates."

Half the truth. Is this what she would do now?

Her mother said, "A machete? He just had that in the truck?"

"Yeah. In case."

"Jesus, Raquel." Her mother stared at her.

Raquel put the nozzle into the hole and listened to the gas. Bruises. The blood rushing to remove the dead and damaged cells. Her scalp. Could a scalp be bruised? If you cut it, there was blood. Under all her hair, something had happened. Between her scalp and her skull? Her mother would never see that. No one would—except Joey. He knew, but he didn't know.

No one would know unless she told them. She'd never had anything big like this, like the whole two days, the rifle, sleeping in the truck cab, the security cameras watching her. Nothing. Only Joey knew. And she'd probably never talk to him again.

The gas hissed. She'd touched the thumb bruise several times. The pain was weird. The pain was supposed to keep her from hurting the tissue again? *Blood is always busy.* Her mom had said that when Raquel was, like, ten. *Blood never, ever stops, it runs around the whole body.* Her mother had lifted Raquel's wrist, showed her the veins. The vein in her temple. The jugular and femoral arteries. *If someone gets cut here . . .*

Her mother had said, *Blood only stops moving when it clots. It's trying to prevent the rest of the blood leaving out of the injury.*

Raquel pulled out the nozzle and two drops of gas fell at her feet. Secrete. Secretions.

She couldn't even tell her mother one part of the secrets yet—because then her mother would worry even more.

When Raquel got back into the car, her mother said, "Tonight we're moving back home. I'm gonna work one more week of night shift, while they figure out the schedule, and Mrs. Ralphine and Mr. Garibay will be watching the house with you in it. Then I'm taking off a whole week. And then I start days again."

"Seriously?"

Her mother had to laugh, just a little. "I feel sorry for anybody who tries to sneak around. Mr. Garibay has a new sawed-off pool cue. Impressively menacing."

Raquel reached over and put her arms around her mother. She cried into her mother's collar, the scrubs that smelled strange. No perfume. Her mother's robe was rolled tightly in the single box of Raquel's things, the box Marisol had given her. *You keep one pair scrub, so you remember how it feel. When you in the parking lot. When you think you want to do stupid shit, put on scrub and don't do something scare your mom, eh?*

Marisol five inches shorter than Raquel. Arms folded. Something scary in her eyes. Like she knew everything, and she never lied.

HER MOTHER GOT onto the old Grapefruit Highway, and Raquel remembered driving with Ruby toward Palm Springs. Would Ruby forgive her? She twisted Lolo's daughter's ring on her finger. When her mother got on Avenue 66, passing the vineyards with people moving down the hallways between grapevines with trays on their shoulders, Raquel remembered Joey saying that everyone was getting sick in the fields. What if he got corona, and she never saw him again?

Her mother turned abruptly onto Martinez Road. "I'm not ready to see them all. Not yet. Let's go sit with your dad for a while. I brought him some things."

Raquel cried into her palms.

Her mother said, "Take this—he'll remember when you were a baby, and you left tears on his shoulder."

A blue T-shirt. Los Angeles Dodgers 2020. And an L.A. baseball cap.

✦

THERE WAS NO one at the cemetery. She and her mother walked through the paths, past graves from the 1880s with simple wooden or stone crosses inscribed with names to shiny black marble headstones with photos. Like her father's.

Her mother spread a blanket from the car near his smiling face and said, "Ronald, I forgot how hot Mecca gets in the evening."

Her father grinned from his stone.

Her mother said, "Almost time for September baseball, baby."

She put the T-shirt on the earth near the empty bottles of Corona. The bag of Takis she'd left must have blown away. *You never move someone else's love*, her mother said the first time Raquel came here. She remembered that so vividly now, not like coming here last week.

Her mother said, "Get six rocks from over by the fence, Raquel." And when she brought them, her mother anchored the shirt and took two bottles of Dodger-blue nail polish from her purse. Silently, they painted the stones with sparkling blue flowers and crosses and hearts. Her mother finished first and lay on the blanket, staring at the darkened sky, while Raquel blew on the stones.

AT THE PACKINGHOUSE parking lot, Raquel saw the little white truck and Joey's father's old van. The men must be in the last part of the Barhis.

"Ruby said Lolo's in the house," her mother said, getting out. "She took a break."

A break? Lolo never took a break. Raquel followed her mother to the house. It felt like a year ago that she'd gone out the window. The little ceramic burros by the front door.

Her mother called, "Lolo? We're here!"

And Raquel couldn't move. She'd lied. Run away.

"Raquelli?" her aunt called from inside. "Come on."

Lolo was at the big table, sorting green beans into piles on newspaper. And Sofelia was snapping them into a bowl.

"Cherrise!" Grandma Sofelia said. "These are your favorite, eh, I remembered. I bought them when I heard you were coming." She stood up. "You had la corona and you lived. When I heard, I thought, we can't lose you, too."

Her mother hesitated, said, "Don't worry! We disinfected, we're both clean."

Sofelia held out her arms and Raquel's mother ran into them. Like a little kid. She started crying. Her mother never cried. She cussed. She stared you down. She put her head on Sofelia's shoulders, crying like she was her own mother.

Raquel had never seen anything like it.

Her mother sobbed to Sofelia, "We went to see him. We took him gifts."

Lolo said, "Raquelli, come give me some sugar. Stop worrying. I'm not mad."

"SNAP OFF THE little end with the stem, and then snap in half," Lolo said.

Raquel was surprised at the pop when she broke the bean in half. She dropped the little stem on the side of her pile. Like her mother did. Her mother loved green beans from Rosie's, but she never made them at home.

Her mother's eyes were swollen. She had hugged Lolo forever. Raquel's mother didn't have a mother. Lolo didn't have a daughter.

Raquel waited.

Sofelia said, "We're making these to take home to Mecca. We can eat with everyone. If you can run away and be around strangers, you can sit six feet apart and see your people."

Raquel tried to snap each bean in exactly the same halfway place, to stay calm. But they were each different.

"All this work, to keep you alive, keep me alive, and you could get somebody else's child killed," Lolo said softly.

"What?" Raquel looked up.

"Joey thought you were sixteen. He's seventeen. If somebody call the police, he's kidnapping. You are— What is it, Cherrise?"

"Underage." Her mother bit her lip.

"What if Joey had seen a cop chasing him and panicked, drove crazy?" Lolo said. "What if the cop had shot him? He's their only son."

Raquel actually shivered, in this heat.

Her mother said, "It's my fault. I should have talked to her. I didn't even know about this boy."

Then they were all silent, the pop of the beans like rubber. They popped and popped. She couldn't just get up and walk away. Run to her room like a baby. Because that wasn't her room. It was Lolo's room again. Where her dad had once slept. *Tell the truth. Always the truth.*

Raquel said to her mother, "I knew you were sick. I could feel it." She looked at Sofelia—Ruby's mom. "But when Ruby and I delivered all the boxes, I was so happy. We were in the car. Like me and my mom. That made me feel worse."

"Then why didn't you ask Ruby to take you to San Bernardino?" Lolo said.

"Mom said everybody calls corona the plague. So we're like the plague people. Ruby has kids. And she could bring it back to you, Auntie."

Lolo said, "I was just afraid. For you. Because Leatrice, when she got cancer, that was two years, then she was gone. Then Robert was gone in a minute. Ronald gone in a minute. Now that I see you every day, you're somebody else to be afraid for." She wiped at her eyes with the back of her hand. "I lay in the bed in here and look at all those pictures. I don't even have a picture of you." The wall of photos.

Then Raquel's mom said, "Those are all senior graduation portraits, Lolo. Raquel's only a sophomore. Despite the fact that she apparently looks and acts like she's grown. Senior year, we'll have one of those. But how about we take a picture of all of us today, in Mecca, on my phone, and I'll get it developed into a poster. Frame it and bring it out here. One for you, one for Sofelia."

Grandma Sofelia smiled big. She was younger than Lolo, her hair silver and black, pulled tight into a perfect bun on top of her head. She wore big hoop earrings and blue eyeshadow, and she smelled of Jean Naté, like Raquel remembered.

She said, "Look at Cherrise going fast on those beans!"

Raquel watched her mother's fingers move. Her mother's wedding ring, thin and gold on her left hand.

"Me and Larette did this all summer when we were little. My mom and her mom loved them some green beans in the summer. We bought them at a stand out in Rialto. Every couple days in July. Larette's mom cooked them down with bacon and onions."

Now her mother was crying, but not an ugly cry. Just the tears rolling down her face and splashing onto the newspaper. Big drops like rain.

My mom. She never said that.

No pictures on their wall at home except a single mall portrait of Larette's mom and her mom's mom. They were teenagers. They had big crunchy curls from gel, and a lot of makeup. Topaz and Turquoise. *All the girls in our family before us got named for precious stones*, Larette used to say.

"I don't know anything," Raquel said, tears sliding down her face, too. At least she didn't cry ugly. She cried beautiful like her mom. I don't know anything. *We don't know anything*, she had written that in the chat, about the bee poem.

Raquel pulled off Leatrice's ring. "Auntie Lolo. You gave me this. It's how me and Joey were okay, when we got a flat tire."

The small ruby sparkling. She pushed it across the table. Lolo picked it up and slid it onto the first part of her ring finger. But it stopped at the big knuckle.

Raquel said, "This really nice man, he was parked beside us. Ray Allala. He moves expensive cars. He thought we were married and he got us a new tire because he said we looked like him and his wife when they got married."

Sofelia started laughing. Then Lolo.

"You and Joey Ortiz? Married? You're children. Was the man blind?" Lolo said.

Raquel said, "We had on our masks."

"So you got old eyes?" Lolo laughed. "An old forehead?"

Sofelia said, "Ah, your father sent him. The car mover."

Even Raquel's mom was laughing. "You're tall like your dad. And you got resting-don't-fuck-with-me face like your mom. I guess that makes you look eighteen. Jesus help us."

Raquel wasn't going to tell them anything else. Not yet.

SHE WENT TO the bathroom. She looked into the bedroom at the fan, the old dresser, the window. The scorpions, wherever they were, stayed hidden.

They rode in the golf cart toward the music. So hot it was like driving through gold. Liquid gold, the heat sitting heavy and wavering and thick in the palms. They went up the rows to where the lift was working in the Barhis. Joey was at the top, with the machete. He looked down. What could he see? Raquel tried to remember, from when she had been up there so high.

He wore his black bandanna, his black Raiders cap, and a flannel shirt. He turned around and cut the next bunch, lowered it to the blue tarp at his feet.

Señor Ortiz and Joey's father came around the other side of the flatbed to keep an eye on Joey. They stood in the humming hot shade in the next aisle of palms, away from the flatbed and the men brushing the dates, laying them gently in rows.

"I'm so sorry, Mr. Ortiz," Raquel said to Joey's father. She turned to his abuelo. "Perdoname, Señor Ortiz," she said.

Mr. Garibay had that tattoo like a necklace around his collarbone. *Perdoname, abuela* and praying hands. Beto had that tattoo on his forearm. *Perdoname, mami.* A picture of a woman.

Joey's father folded his arms. He pulled down his pharaoh mask and looked right at her. He said, "It would be better if you didn't work with us. That night. We were happy you want to help. And then you run away."

Her mother was silent. This was on Raquel.

"I'm so sorry. Joey could have been in trouble. I didn't think about that."

He said, "You could ask me to drive you to San Bernardino." He turned to her mother. "Joey told me you were sick. I would drive her. I remember Ronald. I love to work with him. But she don't ask."

Raquel's mother said, "They don't talk to us, right?"

He looked surprised. "They don't talk! My wife, she cry for two days. His sisters cry. They think he's never coming back." He turned to Raquel. "Joey, he is my only son. He is—everything. Beto, that's not a good kid. He try to fight Joey on Saturday."

She nodded.

But Joey's grandfather stepped forward and took Raquel's hand. He held up her palm for her mother. "Callos en su mano, sí?"

Calluses?

Then he said something else in Spanish to her, and nodded at Joey's father, who told her, "You are a Martinez. Different for you. This is your land. But you are study to be a doctor. Joey want to work here forever."

But his abuelo was smiling, saying something else. "You can come back to work, mija. Next summer. You are hard worker. Lo mismo de su papi. Ronald like the machete. You like the machete. Maybe too much, you like the machete."

He dropped her hand and patted her on the shoulder. Then he went back toward the flatbed.

Raquel's mother said, "Joseph, I'm so sorry, too. I feel responsible. I shouldn't have left her out here."

Mr. Ortiz took off his hat and wiped his forehead with the bandanna. The deep indentation on his skin.

Raquel's mother said, "Oh, Jesus. We have the same mark."

She pointed to her forehead. The dark line from her PPE was still there, even after her days away from Our Lady. She was putting cream on it every day.

"From the—" He made gestures like putting things on his head. But it looked like he was casting a spell on himself, and he realized it. Started laughing a little. He never laughed.

Raquel's mother laughed, too.

Joey had stopped cutting the bunches. He was listening, up close to the sky.

PART FIVE

TWENTY-FIVE ♦ **Subacute**

ON SUNDAY, AUGUST 30, MARISOL KNOCKED ON LARETTE'S trailer door and said, "Come on."

They went east, away from Our Lady, down the wide avenue that led toward a hill at the edge of the city. Marisol pointed up at a building Larette had seen many times—but never explored. Spanish-style, almost like a castle, set into the side of the hill.

At the entrance to the long driveway was a sign: Rosary Subacute Care.

Larette had to take her time walking up—it was steep. She felt her lungs protesting and expanding, as if the hot daytime air was worse than smoke, and she said to Marisol, "No more cigarillo."

Marisol shrugged.

Two long single-story wings were built into the hill, white plaster walls with big deep-set windows. At the center of the complex was a large round building three stories high, like a castle tower, tile roof laid in a beautiful circular pattern. They went through the big wooden door into the tower.

"I remember someone talking about this place," Larette said, walking past the old dark furniture in the lobby. Red tile floors, the thick walls. "This was for tuberculosis patients back in the 1920s, when they sent people from the East Coast."

Marisol said, "Yes, but now the owner, she is seventy-two. Tired. She want to sell to me and my family."

"What?" Larette followed her to the central part of the complex. An office, with the door closed, a kitchen with smells of hospital food and two women talking. Marisol stopped at the nursing station. Two women in scrubs waved at Marisol.

She said, "Naima, this is Larette. She work with me at Our Lady. She is the best under pressure. I hope she work here, eh? I bring her to see her friend Sotelo."

CRESCENCIO SOTELO WAS here, rehabbing in room 19. Sitting in a hospital recliner beside his bed. A nurse was beside him, taking blood. She filled up three vials.

When Crescencio saw Larette, he said, "I don't got no blood left! My heart's, like, outta gas!" and gave her a big grin. His voice was still raspy and faint. The tape over his trach wound was smaller.

Then the nurse set up the EKG machine. "Mr. Sotelo," she said. "You have plenty of blood. Plenty of jokes." She started sticking the tabs onto his chest. "We're going to get you in good enough shape to go home."

When the nurse wheeled away the EKG machine, Larette pulled over a visitor chair. "I actually missed you, Mr. Sotelo."

He grinned. "You know who got the most power in the world? Women when you're in a chair. For reals, mija. Like, when you getting your teeth clean, eh, and the lady's just talking and talking, about her kids, and you can't move, and you can't act like you don't give a shit because she got them sharp instruments, she's digging in your mouth and you have to make your eyebrows go up like, órale, I'm listening about your son training sheepdogs, or she might pretend to slip and that sharp shit will make you cry."

Larette said, "Well, your voice is certainly better."

He rolled his eyes. "And when you're in the La-Z-Boy at home and your wife starts telling you all the shit you didn't do yet, she's just tall over you and you gotta listen, eh?"

Larette nodded.

Then he whispered, "I heard you. That's why I'm telling you. You were by my bed, I couldn't see you, but you were holding up the phone and I could hear my wife talking. She was real little, like a bee. You told her don't cry 'cause crying don't change nothing for me. I heard you. I remember that. But then when I woke up, the other one was there. Your prima."

"Cherrise," she said.

"Yeah. She said I was out for ten days. In the coma. It felt like ten minutes. Like when I woke up, I had only did one thing."

Larette nodded. "What did you do?"

"I went to heaven. And my dad wouldn't let me in. He stood there with his arms folded like he used to when I was fucking up, when me and Rudy were running the streets. My mom was next to him. She wouldn't look at me. I could only see her hair. 'Cause her hair was up like for church. She always wanted me to go to church, but me and Rudy would go to the car shows on Sundays. We didn't give a shit about nothing but them Impalas. My dad wouldn't move. To let me in. Then I went backward. And I woke up with my throat." His fingers went to the trach bandage, and he whispered, "I heard you sing The Fuzz. I heard it."

Larette took a breath. As scared as during Stan Earley, all of a sudden. She'd never sung to someone who'd lived. Never. She'd sung, *I love you with the gentleness of a falling leaf on an autumn day.* Chencho was alive.

He whispered, "The leaf part."

She shook twice. Like a dog. Tried to recover.

Tears started collecting in his eyes. He said, "We used to hear it in my car. My dad was mad at me. Up there. Because I killed my best friend. He was telling me I have to stay here, take care of Norma and the girls. Mi palabra."

"You have to take care of your own wife. She's waiting."

He said, "I gotta get back to work. Finish the car in Rudy's memory. Paint his face and everything. I have to." Chencho held out his arm, covered with pressure tape. "And I'm putting his face right here."

ROSARY SUBACUTE HAD only thirty beds, instead of fifty or a hundred, like all the other rehab places in the area where Our Lady sent patients. The same family had owned it since the 1920s, but now they wanted to sell to the Manalangs—Marisol, Jasmine, an aunt who was an RN, and two male cousins—a respiratory therapist and a physical therapist. They'd been saving their money as travelers for six months—together, they could make a down payment and mortgage the rest. Together, they could run this place for the most part.

"But we need three RN," Marisol said. "If you and Cherrise come here, you have twelve-hour shift, but only four day. And we pay thirty-five dollars per hour. For you."

"You've got it all figured out," Larette said.

"I do math every day," Marisol said. "I can work Our Lady until Christmas. But Christmas will bring too much Covid. We know this—Dr. Yoon say it will be the worst. We cannot do this forever. At Rosary, we see the ones who live."

"I can't abandon Mariah," Larette said.

Marisol shook her head. "Mariah the general," she said. "You don't abandon. She get new soldier. When I was little, I hear the soldier talking all the time. They move place to place. We can move, too."

Larette threw her head back to the sun. She saw the stickers for the EKG on Chencho Sotelo's chest, like white moths landed on his skin. When her heart hurt, when she couldn't breathe—it was panic she felt. Panic when she ran down the ICU hallways for an alarm sounding, panic when she and Marisol had to do chest compressions, deep pain inside her own chest when the body beneath her began to buck and rise, while she and Marisol pushed again, again, for an hour.

She wanted to be home at night, with Dante and Grief. She wanted to cook beans and rice in her mother's cast-iron pot. She wanted to joke with people who were alive, even if they had to learn to walk again.

She said to Marisol, "No more smoking if I come to Subacute, okay? We have to stop."

Marisol nodded. "We find the tree here for a break. You think I am a traveler, and I go. But I stay. I will miss Swisher Sweet. For now."

They turned the corner to CamperWorld. The trailers looked so small, from here, in the daylight. The hitches like black snub noses on strange animals. The last crape myrtle blossoms drifted like pink snow along the curb.

TWENTY-SIX ✦ **Take the Dry from Sand**

THE FOUR WHITE HORSES WORE PALE BLUE RIBBONS IN their manes. They stamped their feet gently in the parking lot at Our Lady of the Rosary. The cathedral's doors were open. Inside, at the altar, Father Bill Deverell stood alone. Only Norma and her four daughters sat in the front pew while he said the mass.

Then the white casket was carried out by six young men—the husbands of those four daughters, and two nephews. White suits, white bandannas, and pale blue shoes. They transported the casket through the back doors of the white carriage and slid it onto the satin bed. The funeral directors closed the glass doors. The horses tossed their heads, and the carriage driver said something to them in Spanish.

Father Deverell was about fifty, with red hair and pink cheeks. He floated serenely into the back seat of the first Impala, holding a Bible, and an altar boy rode beside him with the censer holding incense.

Norma and her daughters got into the second Impala. The eldest daughter drove, her long black hair streaming down her back in the breeze.

Crescencio Sotelo was behind the wheel of the third Impala, Dolores beside him. He'd gotten home three days ago.

Grief was behind the wheel of the fourth Impala. Manny Delgado's prized 1964 pale blue lowrider, which he and Grief and Johnny had worked on for two years when they were young. Manny ran Rialto Custom Classics; he and his father, Manny Delgado Sr., worked on all the Impalas. No car shows now. He'd washed and waxed the car, with his own son, Manny III, and brought it here to the church.

Rudy and Chencho were lifetime members of the Imperials. Manny's father, too. They had all gone to San Gorgonio High School together. School colors blue and white.

The tops down, all forty convertible Impala lowriders in line at the parking lot and along Arrowhead Avenue near the church, waiting for Rudy to lead them to the cemetery.

Five representatives from eight car clubs. Imperials, Dukes, Viejitos, Rickshaws, Suavecitos, Berdoo Shifters, Fontaneros, and Over the Hill Gang. All with their gold or silver identifying plaques displayed on their cars.

The four horses began to walk. Rudy Magana rode down Arrowhead Avenue, and the cars followed him slowly. Manny texted, **Now.** Grief turned on the music, and so did every other car. *Hoo, hoo hoo . . . Well, here come the Nite Owl.* Like a real bird singing in the day.

Everyone on the sidewalks stared. Men whistled and hooted back. Trucks and cars on the busy avenue stopped. People came out of stores to watch the white horses and the stately floating carriage, in no hurry.

Larette reached for Grief's hand. "I'm glad I don't have to sing this one," she said. "I'd probably sound like a parakeet."

He looked astonished. "Oh, my wife got jokes again?" he said. "I been waiting." He kissed her softly on the cheek, so he wouldn't mess with her makeup.

THE PROCESSION ROLLED toward the pioneer cemetery. The cemetery gates were open. Every moment of this could be illegal, but who would challenge them? The motorcycle escorts led them into the asphalt circle at the center of the old burial ground, and the first twelve Impalas parked there. The rest of them parked in the lanes that led to the center. When all the engines were silent, all the phones turned off, all the stereos quiet, Father Deverell and the altar boy stood in front of the monument. The mortuary director had set up two standing microphones, and two speakers.

Father Deverell looked up at the trees, the soft Santa Ana winds tossing the branches just a little. "These breezes are the same ones that touched people here long before I got to San Bernardino," he said. "Rudy Magana's family arrived here in 1870. The family of his best friend, Crescencio Sotelo, arrived here in 1892. Many of you are lifetime residents of this place. And me—I came here in 1982 from County Kerry, Ireland, and found that San Bernardino was just like my birthplace. A homeland of strong faith, love for family, food, and beer. Instead of Irish whiskey, I learned from the Maganas and Sotelos and so many of you here today to drink a shot of tequila from my granddad's old whiskey glass."

Of course, somebody had to whistle through his fingers, and someone else said, "Hush."

Father Deverell said, "Norma and her family have finally been able to say farewell to their beloved Rudy inside the church. Though they were separated at the final moment of his passing, he was not alone. I delivered the last rites on my phone, with Dr. John Yoon kindly present. We now say goodbye to a loving husband, father, and friend. Norma has asked two people to deliver remarks. Crescencio Sotelo is first. Can you come to the microphone, please?"

He was already crying, supported by Dolores and his cane. She stood holding his arm at the microphone. Larette moved closer to Grief, shoulder to shoulder, her arms hot in long sleeves. Chencho looked at the carriage, wiped his face with a pale blue bandanna, and then looked at Norma, sitting in the car. She was crying, too.

"Rudy was better than me," he blurted out. "He was a better man. He never made nobody cry, like I did. I made a lotta people cry, but Rudy, he always went and comforted them. We met at Our Lady of the Rosary in first communion and we wore white suits."

He stopped, leaned hard on the cane. Wiped his eyes again. Dolores whispered to him.

"We wore these little white suits, pues, if you saw them now they were like, the size of puppets, you know, some puppet on some fool's leg in a comedy show, eh? Me and Rudy. Then we went to San G together, we were in metal shop and auto shop, and we started working on ranflas. Pero, I just was good at painting and upholstery, Rudy could build anything, man, he could rebuild the whole engine, he made the cars run. It's my fault he's gone. I—"

He shook his head.

He said, "Back in the day, you gave somebody the flu and they said, *You cost me two days' pay, cabrón, you owe me fifty bucks!* But I killed him. How could God do this to us?"

He bent his head again, and men shouted softly from the Impalas.

"Don't say that, vato."

"It wasn't your fault, homes!"

"Don't say that about God!"

He looked out at them. "God shoulda taken me. Rudy was the best man around, and I'm sorry, Norma. I'm sorry."

He turned his back to everyone. He shook. Dolores helped him back to the car. He bent over, sobbing, and the priest waited. Dolores whispered to him, hugged him, and finally Chencho lifted his head.

"Norma would like Larette Embers to come to the microphone, please," the priest said.

SHE WORE A sequined white cocktail dress from some local theater awards show years ago. It still fit because she was so thin from working too much. Grief held her arm all the way up to the microphone. He wore a white tux. He stood to her left, and she slipped her left hand into his, put her right hand around the microphone stand. She said nothing, only looked straight at Norma and began to sing.

It would be easier to take the wet from water, or the dry from sand . . .

Everyone in the cars knew this song. From the oldest ones to the teenagers riding beside their dads or uncles. Nothing would change in this world, cars or songs or clothes or love—except the ones who were gone.

Than for anyone to try to separate us, stop us from holding hands . . .

Norma stared at her husband, in the carriage.

Grief's knuckles hot over her fingers. Holding tight.

In the silence when she finished singing, everyone looked at the casket, behind the glass.

Rudy's hands, she thought, with the iridescent auto paint like fingernail polish. His body. Then the darkness of the bag. The terror of the soul inside the refrigerated truck for two weeks—who would ever have thought the beloved would be stacked inside an anonymous trailer parked a block from the mortuary? Waiting, waiting?

Now the clean glass. The trees.

Father Deverell began to wave the censer so that the incense smoke wafted in the wind toward all of the cars, lifting into the sycamore branches.

"'The Lord is my shepherd; I shall not want,'" he recited. "'He maketh me to lie down in green pastures: he leadeth me beside the still waters . . .'"

Marisol's smoke, she thought. The smoke lit for the new baby to be passed through, in the forest where Marisol had lived, the smoke lit on the ground and the new mother placing herself over it, to cleanse the spirits from where the baby had left her body. She and Marisol and Mariah and Natalie, sitting on the benches, in the trenches, the cleansing smoke of the Swisher Sweet, the smoke rings Larette blew into the air for her mother, her mother who'd spent all that time cleansing the hospital corridors and floors and beds and bedpans, the caustic solutions and bleach and the fumes from mopping and mopping all gathered in her lungs to cease her breathing, and here was the sweet hot smoke of belief. Threading through the air around the carriage and into the reins, the four horses snorting softly, and then the last twist of white disappeared.

TWENTY-SEVEN ✦ Between Starshine and Clay

"ARE YOU SERIOUS?" RAQUEL SAID TO HER IN THE KITCHEN. Cherrise suddenly realized she could see it as a text—**RU SRS?** All those weeks of texting. Now they could argue in person.
"Yup."
"How many times can I say it? I'm not a little kid. I don't want to ride on your boyfriend's horse. I don't even have boots."
Cherrise laughed. "I've seen the man three times in my life. And yeah, you do have boots."
She dropped the tooled black cowgirl boots from her own closet onto the kitchen floor. She'd rubbed them down with Ronald's old neat's-foot oil—it made her sad, but she'd sat in her bedroom closet, so Raquel hadn't seen.
"We wear the same size now, right?" she said to Raquel. "So clearly you're a young woman. Who still has to respect me. I only wore these three or four times out in Mecca, because I wasn't a good rider. I just watched you ride with your dad."
Raquel was furious. Of course. "So why would I want to remember that and go to Mr. Marlboro's ranch?"
"Jesus, you are still a baby," Cherrise said. "It's Marlboro Man, that guy was white, and Johnny doesn't smoke, as far as I know."
"Mom, it's Wednesday! I have school!"
Cherrise said, "Grief and Larette are bringing you and Dante to the ranch after school, around four. It's a surprise for Dante.

He's put up with just as much shit as you have." She touched Raquel's hand. "Do you know how freaked out he was when you were missing? Grief said Dante wandered around all night in the backyard. Remember, it was only a few weeks ago those two meth heads were stealing copper from the tower near their house, and he saw someone get electrocuted. He needs something we can all do, just for him. It has to happen tonight. September 9."

"Must be stars. Meteors."

Cherrise poured a cup of coffee. "Plus, the last three weeks have been the hottest in history up in Chino Hills. Johnny and his father have spent days keeping their cattle alive, so I'm sure they can use some help."

She ran her hand over the old wooden counter. She used to think this kitchen was so small, but it seemed perfect after the Mallard. Every single thing in her house felt loved, even the old palm fronds she and Raquel had pulled down on the weekend from the ramada, with bird poop and splinters flying. Raquel wore a white pharaoh head covering and pulled up the bandanna over everything but her eyes. Cherrise stared at her and said, "Wow. They gave you that out at Lolo's?"

Raquel just kept pulling the stubborn fronds from the wooden frame.

Now Raquel took the boots into her bedroom. But she came out with something on a hanger.

Cherrise's blue silk robe. Wrinkled.

"Mom, I took this when I had to go out to Oasis. I needed it to remind me of you."

Her robe. She thought someone had stolen it from the backyard.

"I just wanted to be beautiful like you. I'm sorry." She laid the robe on the table. She said, "The boots fit. So fine, I'll go."

✦

CHERRISE HAD MOVED to day shift on Monday. Larette had one more week of nights—but she'd taken off tonight, for Dante. Mariah was so happy that Larette hadn't left yet that she didn't even talk shit about it. Two new travelers had moved into the RVs. Marisol and Jasmine were still at CamperWorld, saving all their overtime pay for the Rosary Subacute Care Home.

Larette wanted her to think about it—both of them working for Marisol. Cherrise had gone to visit Chencho Sotelo. He was playing Bananagrams with another patient, a professor.

"Professor here used to beat me," Chencho told her. "He had *croissant* and *baguette*—he's from New York. I told him, you get French, then I get Spanish. I got all the *z* words, mija. *Zapatas, zorillos, cerveza.* Órale, I'm winning now."

When they walked back to Our Lady, Larette said, "It might be nice to take care of people who could go home."

"Maybe," Cherrise said. "It's gonna get so bad after Thanksgiving, cuz. So bad."

Larette nodded. "But we have to take care of ourselves too. So we don't get in more trouble. You and me." She touched Cherrise's shoulder. "Ti-fille."

Cherrise stopped. What Larette's mother used to call her. *Ti-fille.* Little girl. Cherrise was so small when she went next door with her bare pillow, the pillowcase full of her clothes.

She stumbled over to the bench by the sycamore tree. Where Larette and the others had been smoking. The sun filtered through the big leaves. Larette sat with her arm around her shoulders. They had to dry their faces with the hems of their scrubs. Wiped off half their makeup.

"Well, now we look like shit," Cherrise said. "Good thing for two masks and a face shield."

Larette's mascara was smeared.

Cherrise said, "You and Marisol and Mariah and Natalie, you

all would come in so happy after you smoked. Like you'd been at a little party."

"The trenches," Larette said, looking at the tree bark.

Two ambulances turned into the ER bay. They both stood up.

"No more smoking," Larette said. "Everything looks different in the day, right?"

Cherrise put her arm through Larette's when they walked back. "Like going to school. When you told me first grade would be okay but no naps."

JOHNNY LIVED IN Santa Ana. Jacaranda Street, a long narrow lane of old houses and cars parked tightly at the curb. Two men in the driveway across the street from Johnny's address slid out like magic from under a car, on wooden dollies, and watched her park in the driveway. Johnny met her at the curb, lifted his chin at them, and they did the same to him.

He said, "They didn't come at you with a pool cue."

"Small mercies," she said.

Walking down the driveway, toward a green house, Johnny waved at the woman watering in a tunnel of flowers, birds chattering from her pink house. On the other side, a man was unloading tools from a truck at his blue house.

"Bro," the man called.

"Albert," Johnny said, grinning. He opened the garage door and showed her his setup. Just like hers. His blue jumpsuit hung from a hook on the wall. He said he threw it in the washing machine and disinfected at the garage sink.

His kitchen was old-school, with a yellow tile counter. Perfectly clean. They drank coffee and ate conchas, and she told him about the Starbucks, the doughnuts, the conchas in boxes left every day at the ER.

He said, "Nobody gives me anything but a hard time."

His bedroom was not like that of a messy single man. It was painted pale green. Two black-and-white photographs on the wall. A woman with an iguana on her head, like a crown, and a woman walking in a desert with hundreds of black birds. On his bedside table, a Polaroid snapshot in a frame—his mother, in the bed of a truck, smiling and waving at someone.

He took off his shirt. Bruises green and yellow on his ribs. Such a strange structure, she always thought, when she was pressing down on the chest to keep someone breathing. The skull hollow, the ribs and sternum protecting their organs. Pelvis the same for men and women except theirs held nothing compared to ours, really, she thought.

He had no tattoos. He had a lot of scars. Kind of a white dent on his shoulder. She said, "This one?"

"Fight. Dude with a sharp ring punched me. Grief and I were at a bar up in Sacramento, and some white guys didn't like us. We were in the CHP Academy."

"This one?" A long thin line on his left forearm, like white wire. "Orange branch fell and the thorn got me. In February. Helping my dad with the harvest."

"This one? And this one?" Two small white roses, like perfect blossoms, on his left shoulder blade.

"Last fall. We had a big fire, and we were all fighting with the hoses to keep the barn and houses safe, and two embers fell on my back. Burned right through my shirt. Grief smacked me with his shirt and put them out."

Larette and Grief. She and Johnny. Maybe it would work.

She took off her jeans. Her T-shirt. Her Victoria's Secret—black lace camisole and bikini, the set Raquel had laughed about back in March, when she still wore them under her scrubs.

"You wear those to work?" he said.

"Sometimes," she said.

"Damn," he said. "Do I get to see your scars?"

"No," she said. "Because they're not visible."

She lay her head on his chest and heard the heavy thump inside the ribs. Eight years since she'd lain on Ronald's chest. He always let her listen, even when it was hot and his skin was slippery from sweat. This was the only other man whose heart she'd ever heard. Not on a machine.

Johnny ran his hand down her spine, two times, three, and Cherrise said, "Like you're petting a horse."

"Like I'm calming down something I don't want to be scared."

"Some*thing*?" she said.

"Someone," he said. "Someone."

She said, "Well, I can't lie on my back since the hospital, because it's hard to breathe, and your ribs still look like that . . ." She motioned for him to sit up, against the headboard. She eased herself onto him, and he put his lips on her collarbone, and she put her hands on his shoulders.

"Now I can't breathe," he said.

"Good."

THEY SLEPT FOR a long time. When she woke on her side, with his hand on her hip, his eyes were open, but he didn't move. The birds sang elaborate conversations in the hedges next door. It was hot. For a moment, she imagined she was still in the Mallard. But it was hot because there was another warm person beside her. Not the thin RV mattress, where she'd awakened pushing down on an imaginary chest, failing and failing. Johnny's chest was rising and falling, and she pulled herself closer.

SHE FOLLOWED HIS truck to the rancho. She didn't want Raquel to think she'd spent the whole day in Santa Ana. Not yet.

They parked at the first barn. The temperature gauge on the tree said 101, and it was 2:00 p.m. So hot that she put her face into the big cooler like a little kid. Johnny had attached a trailer to one of the ATVs, and he put two big plastic crates on the back, tying them down with bungee cords.

"You want to see what we made for Dante?" he said. "We can finish setting up."

Those bowlegs. The black Henley already covered with dust. She rode behind him on the four-wheeler, holding tight. Her cheek against his back, the trees sliding past, the feel of his muscles. The ranch road wound up the canyon, and they came out onto a ridge high on the hill, a plateau where the land was flat—covered with chaparral and shrubs. In the open was a small shelter built of stone, with a wooden roof and wooden door so old the boards were black.

He helped her off the ATV. "This is where the men used to shelter back when they were watching the cattle and a big storm came. We come up here, my dad and me. Turn around."

She could see forever—down into the Santa Ana River valley, the freeway snaking far below, the mountains like giant golden mixing bowls turned upside down by the gods.

He said, "We watch the Disneyland fireworks from up here. We have to stay with the calves sometimes. We built this for tonight."

Past the stone shelter, on a clearing of bare ground, there was a large platform.

Johnny said, "We cleared the brush and put together some corral pipes. See the bottom? That's Bulldog sections like we have for the cattle. So the kids won't worry about bugs or lizards."

Cherrise walked around the big square—the pipe was two feet off the ground, formed as a base, and on top, there were ten long, wide boards. "Barn boards?" she said, and he grinned.

"Yeah, we keep them for something like this. We used to make big tables, back when the ranch was full, and we had fiestas." He put both plastic crates on the edge. "These were my favorites when I was little," he said.

Old woolen blankets, striped, with fringe.

"From Mexico," he said. "My grandfather brought them up from Jalisco in 1930 or something. They're warm, but not very soft. So I brought some quilts to put over them." He sat at the edge of the platform, wrapped his arm around her.

She thought of Larette, lying here. She thought of her pillowcase—her pajamas, her one pair of slippers, one pair of sandals. Her kindergarten books.

"You need pillows for Larette and Grief, because they can't lie on their backs either," she said to Johnny. "Their breathing. So we gotta ride up here again. 'Cause I like that ATV." She got back on behind him, said into the side of his neck, "Pretty sexy."

"Yeah, but I gotta be careful not to get a panza," he said. "So you can say that again."

SHE SAT ON the couch where he'd slept his whole growing up, where he said he still slept if he spent the night with his dad in the ranch houses. He made a fresh pot of coffee in the tiny kitchen, poured a cup for each of them, and filled a blue Dodgers thermos.

"Larette gave this to my dad for Christmas," he said.

The sun through the bougainvillea tunnels over the porch, making translucent shimmers of crimson that shifted in the wind. In his father's bedroom, his mother smiled above an altar with fresh roses in a jam jar. In the closet-sized bathroom, two toothbrushes were slanted in another jam jar on a shelf, *H* in black marker on one, *J* in red marker on the other.

Hernan—his father.

They drank the coffee on the couch, facing each other with

their legs side by side. She put her head back to listen to his mother's sparrows telling one another long stories in the flowers.

They heard Grief's old Apache truck laboring up the road, and she jumped up and said, "We'd better get back to the barn. I'll be in trouble."

He got up fast, laughing, grabbing the thermos, and they barely made it, hidden in a veil of dust raised by the tires.

WHEN RAQUEL, LARETTE, and Dante got out of Grief's truck, Raquel immediately held up her phone.

"There's no reception, right?"

"Not up here," Johnny said. "You gotta go down to the road."

Cherrise said, "But you can take pictures and make TikToks about your cowgirl life when you get home." Raquel rolled her eyes. "Think of your school friends doing this—saving historic cattle on a California rancho. They'd put this on their college apps. Pretty sure you can do that."

But Raquel looked fire at Johnny. She said, "These are my dad's boots."

Johnny said carefully, "Justins. Nice."

Cherrise realized she was standing maybe too close to him.

Raquel pointed to his chest. "Remember what you used to call that, Mom?"

He had on a white tank top and a flannel over it. Cherrise felt the blood in her brain, she could swear, moving like ferns inside her skull. Fucking Covid. Raquel was angry—but what was she talking about?

Johnny said, "My dad used to call them Hanes."

"Why?" Dante said.

He shrugged. "He spoke Spanish first, and so did I. When you're going between Spanish and English your whole life, you call stuff what it says at the store. He'd say, *Put on your ChapStick*, and take some Kleenex to your mom. He'd say, *Give me the Windex.* He'd say, *Put on your Hanes and Pendleton, it's cold.*"

Cherrise said, "Your dad had one, Raquel. A Pendleton."

"Yeah—Pendleton is wool," Johnny said. "From the old west. They used to be blankets, for Indians, back in Montana. The lady who owns our ranch, she has some old Pendleton blankets from a man who traded them here. In the 1800s."

Cherrise looked at Larette. "My mom was raised by her grandmother, and she spoke mostly French, so my mom went back and forth, too. Like, *turtle* was *tortue.* And *moth* was *papillon de nuit.* Butterfly of the night. Remember, cuz?"

"I haven't thought about that in forever," Larette said.

Johnny said, "*Palomas de la luz.* Doves of the light. That's how we called moths."

Like a poem, Cherrise thought. Come on, baby. Calm down.

But Raquel said, "Mom. This is the shirt that one guy called a wife-beater. At my school. You got mad and said a different name."

Cherrise said, "Oh, shit. I said what if women wore a shirt called a dick-smasher."

Grief laughed, said, "Sounds like you, Cherrise."

Johnny raised his eyebrows at Raquel. "Well, heck, I think I'll stick with Hanes."

Cherrise saw Raquel's chest rise and fall. Deep breaths. Raquel was trying to get used to everything too fast—her child had bruises on her arms, she'd been surprised by Johnny.

Then Dante said, "Can I see the bull?"

"Come in the barn and get some sodas first. We got a long afternoon of watering stock," Johnny said.

Cherrise put her arm around Raquel and said, "Let's get some dust on your dad's boots."

✦

INSIDE, SHE COULD smell Sergio Vargas before she saw him, resting on one of two cots set up near the barn door, under the bear trap she remembered. He opened one eye when she and Larette walked in, like a comic actor in a cowboy movie. Raquel and Dante stared at him, and he opened the eye farther. Damn, Cherrise realized, he never saw kids.

"The nurses, sí?"

Wells of darkness under the old man's eyes. His forehead silver with sweat.

Johnny said, "He broke his wrist. Cabrón the bull. But he won't go down the hill for X-rays."

Cherrise said, "You kids go up to the horses. We'll be right there."

Grief took Raquel and Johnny took Dante on the ATVs.

The old man smelled ripe. He lay on his back with his arm on a pillow. A homemade splint—two thin pieces of wood with pink pressure tape wrapped tight.

"Only way es no pain," he said to them.

Cherrise took his pulse with her fingers, old-school. Normal range. At least he doesn't have corona, she thought.

Larette unfastened his pearl-snap cowboy shirt. More pink tape on his shoulder. "Broken too?" she said.

He shook his head.

She unwound it. He could rotate it, but who the hell knew? He was seventy-something. His breath. The bottle of tequila on the little table beside him. This was fucking *Gunsmoke*.

"Mi hermano say one more week. Rest." He must have to be continuously mildly drunk to keep him from riding and working.

"Patron as medicine is hard on the liver," Cherrise said.

Sergio winced when Larette made him stand up and walk in circles.

"You gotta get some blood flowing," Larette said.

"And drink this whole bottle of water," Cherrise said, handing it to him.

They unrolled the makeshift cast. Carefully, slowly. The wrist was set with the wooden splints on top of the hand and below. Straight and perfect. Masking tape thick and precise.

"Ramon cut the wood," he whispered, eyes closed. "Mi hermano."

"Okay, caveman-style, but it seems to have worked," Larette said.

Cherrise saw five rolls of pink wrap lined up on another table. She started rewrapping. "Paleolithic style?" Cherrise said. "We're supposed to be specific, Raquel says, and not use gender. Also, her history teacher is very cool, even on Zoom."

Sergio pulled in his Paleolithic breath. Larette secured the end of the bandage.

"You should have gone down for X-rays, Mr. Vargas," Cherrise said.

He shook his head. "Sit en la sala and they cough, and I die."

He was right. Our Lady? Anywhere in Santa Ana or Anaheim would be just as bad.

He said, "Es my left hand. I have my right."

THEY WALKED OUT to the corrals.

Raquel and Dante were in the big corral, Dante on a smaller black horse, Raquel riding smooth around the arena on a big reddish horse, her back straight and hair flying behind her. Cherrise couldn't believe it. Ramon and Grief and Johnny's father stood like they did, one foot on the bottom rail. An old car, a woodpaneled station wagon, came rolling down slow from the long adobe house barely visible through the trees. A woman driving Cherrise knew instantly was a caretaker. How do we all recognize one another? she thought. Serviceable. Careful. Alert.

The caretaker helped out an older woman. Silver hair in a bun, sunglasses, silver earrings and a necklace with a crucifix, a housedress and pressure hose and black orthopedic shoes. She must have been a hundred. But she wasn't bent over, with a hump of curved spine. She walked straight and slow over to Johnny's father.

"Es la chavalita mas hermosa." She pointed. "She ride like me. When I was chavalita."

The caretaker said, "Mrs. Dottie, it's too hot."

"Cinco minutos," the old woman said.

She sat in the barn with everyone ten feet away, Diana the caretaker by her side. Dorotea Antonia Salvador Bautista de Anza told stories about when she still rode her mare Rosita, the mother of that red horse, Canela.

Mrs. Dottie held her wooden walking stick, her knuckles so swollen they were like saladitos under the skin. She said to Raquel, "I ride Rosita aqui, to the top of the ridge, and I see her. León de montana."

"A what?" Raquel said.

"Mountain lion," Johnny said.

"How did you know it was a female?" Dante said from the corner.

Mrs. Dottie smiled. "She have . . ." She took one hand off her stick and made a shelf into her dress.

Boobs.

Everyone laughed.

But then she said, "She hungry. To feed babies. I hear her scream in the night. She maybe catch conejos. But if she catch a horse, she can rest a long time."

Dante and Raquel had their mouths open. They could see it. The mountain lion, leaping onto the horse to bite its neck.

"La león, she is not . . . up." Mrs. Dottie held her hand above her head, open to the air.

"Like, on a branch?" Raquel asked.

Mrs. Dottie nodded. "Sí, she is on a rock. She is wait for me and Rosie by the water. She wait for the animales to drink. She look at me. Ojos verdes. I have la pistola. My papi make me shoot la pistola when I am ten. Twelve. I take la pistola from my leg and shoot."

"You shot her?" Raquel said.

Cherrise looked at her daughter's face—not closed, not angry. Stunned. Like when she was five or six, and something would surprise her so much that all those hundreds of muscles in her face would melt into wonder.

Mrs. Dottie laughed. "No! I shoot the tree. Tres balas." She held up three fingers. Bullets. "I know she can jump on me if she not scared. But she go and I go. We both run away." She pointed to the red horse. "You ride Canela up to that tree. Sicomoro con la corteza blanca. Las balas"—she poked a finger into the air—"inside."

"Why did you have the gun?" Dante said, very seriously.

Mrs. Dottie could hear it in his voice. She took a breath. "Because one man—he come for me. Five time. My father, he say no, she never marry. But the man, he come when I ride. So I have la pistola."

Raquel shivered as if someone had poured ice down her back and whispered, "Did you shoot him? The man?"

Mrs. Dottie's face was far away. So deeply lined like those of the women whose foreheads Cherrise washed with a wipe, the skin thin as Saran Wrap over their skulls. The man would attack her, carry her off, and if it was way back then, he'd get to marry her because she'd be—spoiled. Damn.

Mrs. Dottie said, "I shoot beside him. I am up on the ridge with las vacas. He come from his rancho, down there. I ride away from las vacas, and he come, too. Then I shoot the dirt. Beside his horse. That horse go up and he fall." She shrugged. "If he fall and die, I bury him and take the horse. I like that horse. Palomino."

"Jesus," Larette said.

Mrs. Dottie said, "Sí," and actually smiled. Like she would have enjoyed going to get the shovel. "Jesucristo!"

Cherrise looked at Johnny. He raised his eyebrows and nodded. She hadn't understood how this place worked. Although she was called Mrs. Dottie, she had never been married. She was just a legend. The land had been more important than love, for this woman.

Then Mrs. Dottie's whole face changed. Got hard. She stood up and said, "Demasiado caliente, Ramon. Ve a ver las vacas."

She was the queen of this place. She walked slowly with Diana to the station wagon, and when she passed Johnny she said something to him. Then she looked at Cherrise and Raquel, and lifted her hand.

GRIEF TOLD THE kids, "Johnny's ribs are broken. You guys have to hook up the hoses."

Johnny said, "That's a four-hundred-and-fifty-gallon tank on the ranch truck. We have to fill it up, and then you drive up there to fill the stock tanks."

Cherrise and Raquel learned how to pull the hose couplings to the pump, tighten them up, and feed the hose into the dirty plastic tank. Johnny's face was tight with pain, though—and something else. She didn't know him enough to see what it was. Maybe it was seeing Raquel ride, reminding him of how hard this might be. For both of them.

She bent to the hose—a giant IV. Another tube to check. The trees above hung still in the withering heat. Grief lifted bales of fresh hay into a trailer hooked to the ATV. The tank was full. Johnny turned off the pump. Silence. Like the hospital room when she disconnected all the catheters and IVs and waited for Dr. Yoon to come. To say something was over.

Johnny opened the truck door for Raquel. Said, "Your dad must be watching you ride. I always think my mom's still watching me ride, too."

AT THE FIRST pasture, he unlocked the gate and headed down the dirt road slowly, to limit dust and not stress the cattle. He said his father and Ramon had ridden since before dawn, checking on the heifers and calves up here, tossing down a little fresh hay, throwing buckets of water from the stock tank over the backs of any animals who seemed too hot.

"It was a hundred and nine yesterday," he said. "Look at all this water gone."

Raquel helped him pull the hose into the stock tank.

"Each cow needs about twenty gallons a day when it's like this."

The cows were bunched up in the shade under the oak trees. Some were in the creek bed even though it was dry. Black baldy, he called them. Sleek hides dusty and gold. The heat was so intense when Cherrise looked into the water, her eyes hurt, like there was nothing inside her skull. Her eyeballs—they didn't move. She leaned forward to splash the stock water onto her face—and it was icy, from the center of the earth. Raquel did the same.

WHEN THEY MET up on the ranch road, Johnny's father and Grief on the ATVs, Johnny said to the kids, "Do you want to find the sicomoro tree?"

Raquel stared at him. My child, Cherrise thought. Her hair in a huge bun and the dust settled in her curls.

Dante said, "You know where it is, right?"

"Sicomoro blanco," Johnny's father said. "You know that?"

Raquel said, "White. Like, white bark."

Grief said, "You two can get in the trailers. You never get to do that in SB."

The three ATVs headed up the long ranch road.

Dante shouted, "I see green up there! Like there's water!"

His braids gold with dust, too. Larette had redone them on Sunday—the baby hairs at his forehead were messy today, sweat dripping down his temples.

They walked single file into an arroyo with a sandy bottom to a place where everything was suddenly dark green—grapevines grew along the trail, and wild roses. Johnny pointed to the dripping water.

"The spring," he said. "They named it for the village that used to be here. Paashinonga. Before the Anzas came, Tongva and Serrano people lived here."

Raquel said, "Like the Cahuilla people. In Coachella."

Cherrise watched her.

"Grandma Sofelia and Auntie Lolo's people were there at the same time as this place."

"They were?" Johnny's father said. "Grief, your people are Serrano, sí?"

"We're probably all cousins," Grief said. "Not just Larette and Cherrise."

"We're sisters," Cherrise said.

"We are," Larette said. She'd been quiet, panting on the walk. She sat against a rock.

Then Dante shouted, "There it is!"

The huge tree was ahead of them, with the water trickling into a pool and a long flat rock on a ledge above. Where the mountain lion would hide. And the lion's great-great-however-many-greats-grandkids could be hiding up here—right now. Did Johnny's father have a gun? These guys probably always had a gun. Johnny's wide back was still. He was watching everything.

Our Lady's sycamore was half this size. This was the biggest tree Cherrise had ever seen. The white bark was mapped with puzzle pieces and knots and holes. The leaves were changing from green to gold already.

Raquel and Dante went closer to the tree, threw back their heads.

"How high would the bullets be?" Dante asked.

"The león de montana liked to come up here to drink. Wait for deer or rabbits to drink, and put their heads down," Johnny said. "I can feel your moms all nervous right now."

Cherrise said, "She's, what, a hundred? Mrs. Dottie. How old was she when she shot the tree?"

"Old enough for some jerk to come hunting for her," Raquel said.

"Maybe fifteen," Johnny said. "That's when she was supposed to get married. She wasn't supposed to be out riding. She was supposed to be having ten kids. To work his rancho."

Cherrise watched her daughter look up into the tree. Fifteen. She was so young. The leaves hid the bark way up there. Johnny said, "My dad says she put something to mark it. So she would remember."

The bark was flesh. Maybe Mrs. Dottie had nailed something there.

Raquel squinted. "I see a long piece of rope?"

Johnny said, "She tied her reata. Abajo. See it hanging from the branch? Good eyes, Raquel."

He looked at Cherrise. The first time he'd said her daughter's name to her. Like they knew each other.

"Where are the bullets?" Dante said.

Johnny said, "Tres balas. They'd be deep in the bark, right where the reata is. A secret, right? Except she told you, so she must respect you some." He put his arm around Cherrise's shoulders. "Now we gotta water the horses. And Cabrón. He's how we all got together."

THE HORSES STOOD in the shade of the corral, near the big barn. Raquel and Dante helped Johnny and Ramon throw buckets of water on Rana, the young bull, his face dripping, scrunched. Almost like he was smiling. Then they walked down to Cabrón's new corral and threw buckets in the general direction of the bull, who kept his ass to them.

It was almost dark. Ramon put on the barn light. Johnny's father had gotten out an ancient grill with a flat top. He put carne asada and onions on one side, piled them hot onto six tortillas at a time, added shredded cheese and salsa, and put another tortilla on top. Turned them over twice. "That's mulitas," Johnny said, who served them first to Sergio, sitting up on his cot, and Ramon, sitting on the other cot, facing his brother.

Then the kids. Raquel was looking at the leather lariats circled and hanging on nails in the smaller barn. Reatas—like how Johnny and his father had caught Cabrón.

Raquel said, "Mrs. Dottie. She's not a Mrs."

Johnny said, "Nope. But people had to think she was a widow. You couldn't just not be married. So she told everybody she'd gotten married and her husband died. Anybody who knows the truth would be dead by now."

AT 8:00 P.M., they took all three trucks to the top of the hill. The platform was covered with blankets and pillows. Five camp chairs were in a line nearby. Johnny had set up Dante's telescope on a big piece of plywood.

"Tonight is the peak for the Epsilon Perseids," Larette said.

Ramon moved two of the chairs farther away, near the old shelter. He and Sergio sat apart, watching nervously. They weren't used to people.

Johnny, his father, and Grief sat at the edge of the platform.

Dante moved the telescope around, said, "It's gonna record for later. This is so cool."

Cherrise lay staring at the darkness gathering from the center of the sky, falling to the edges, it felt like. Larette lay on one side of her, and Raquel on the other.

Raquel said, "I hear animals. Over there in the bushes."

Grief said, "Probably rabbits. They come out at dusk. The coyotes chased them already. Now the rabbits are moving around figuring out who we are."

"The coyotes are close to here?"

Everyone was quiet. Cherrise closed her eyes. Yes. Rustling in the bushes. Small rustling. What did they say about coyotes? You didn't hear them. They were too good for that.

"What if they roll up on us right now?" Raquel whispered.

Johnny said, "The coyotes are on the ridge over there, to the east. They know we have eight people. Too many for them. The mountain lion—there's one up here, but she doesn't want us, either. And we have the rifles."

Raquel sat up fast and twisted around to look at him. Cherrise turned onto her stomach and saw the dark outline of a gun propped on Johnny's knees, and one on his father's knees.

"Do you shoot that gun?" Raquel said, on her knees.

"I learned with this rifle," Johnny said. "We shot rabbits and deer when I was little. We were hungry. I have a handgun when I'm working."

His father said, "I shoot if a coyote tries to get a calf. But I don't shoot the coyote. I shoot the dirt to scare him."

They were all quiet. Dante moved the telescope.

Then Grief said, "Did that boy out in Oasis have a gun, Raquel?"

Raquel stood and jumped off the platform. "No, he's not like that. He's super nice." She walked over toward the Vargas brothers and looked up at the sky from there.

Cherrise felt a sharp tug under her navel—where her baby had rested. Her child had secrets now. This was the beginning. How much longer for telling each other everything on the couch, Raquel's feet in her lap, both reaching for the bowl of Takis?

Cherrise had secrets, too. Larette had been keeping so many things from Grief—but a few days ago they sang together from the sidewalk outside CamperWorld. "My Favorite Things," the first song Larette had ever made Grief memorize. But he sang, *Fried chicken and waffles, no more lost kittens . . .*

"Raquel," she said. "Come lie down."

And Raquel did. She lay beside Cherrise and took her hand. Cherrise took Larette's hand. Dante lay on his stomach at their feet, a piece of paper spread out on the wood, his tiny penlight moving. He said, "The peak is at ten. Best viewing is five a.m."

"Well, you get the peak," Grief said. "'Cause that will be the start of our descent. The old folks."

Dante rolled onto his back. He said, "We're here in the center. Perseus is right there." He lifted his finger to the right. "The moon is over there, to the northwest. Taurus is beside the moon. And Aries is behind us. The stars never change unless they die."

He was right. They were pricking out now, wavering in the heat.

Larette said, "Every time I sing a song, it's different. Even if I try to make it the same."

They were all quiet. Humans. Animals. Changing every moment even after their hearts stopped beating.

"Yeah," Dante said. "Everybody's all, *Why are you studying something stupid? Stars can't do shit for you. You should be coding,* 'cause they all want to work on games. But, like, Dad's animals die, and the people at Our Lady die. The stars, it's like a billion years, and then if they run out of hydrogen, they blow up into a red giant, and then a supernova, and then they're a white dwarf star. So they're still up there. Even if they're dead."

"Cheerful," Grief said. "In a way."

Johnny said, "My dad and me, we've been looking at the same stars forever. My mom saw them, and her great-great-great-grandmother. The same constellations."

Then Raquel got out her phone. "Dante. Mrs. Hua told us to find our own poem last week, and I found this one with a star in it." The blue light was almost blinding.

"Turn off your phone or our eyes will have to adjust again!" Dante shouted.

"OMG, calm down, baby boy," Raquel said. She closed the phone. "I remember some of it. Lucille Clifton. She looks like your great-grandma in Louisiana, Mama."

Then her daughter recited,

i made it up
here on this bridge between
starshine and clay,
my one hand holding tight
my other hand.

Cherrise tried to see the bridge—in the sky.

Larette said, "My one hand holding tight my other hand."

"Yeah," Raquel said. "Like, you have to make it up for yourself, and you have to hold your own hand. Because maybe nobody else is around."

But she lay back down in the darkness and lined up her arm tight against Cherrise's arm. Moved even closer. And on the other side of Cherrise, Larette kept their fingers twined, like when they had fallen asleep together in the summer on the blanket in the grass, back in the day when they were children, under the smoke rings and silver streetlights.

ACKNOWLEDGMENTS

For my family, four generations now: Rosette Sims, for taking care of me, for Angel and Calvin; Delphine Sims, Kunmi Jeje, and Ileriayode Brienz Sims Jeje, for making life infinitely hopeful and beautiful; Gaila Sims, for being a light of our ancestors and so much necessary American history; Dwayne Sims, for random outings and the Rubidoux swap meet; and my mother, Gabrielle Leu Straight Watson, for endless hours of Toblerone and memory.

Thanks to Marcia Bales, Jennifer Stewart, and all the traveler nurses I met, to the hundreds of medical professionals and every single person who works at Riverside Community Hospital, Kaiser Permanente Hospital Riverside, St. Bernardine Hospital in San Bernardino, Highland Hospital in Oakland, and Pomona Valley Hospital, who took care of my family, my friends and neighbors, both of my fathers, and thousands of others. Thanks to Raincross and all the staff there as well.

Thanks to my many families: All incarnations of the Michael Street Sims family, and the Jeje, Adewoye, Andrews, Chatham, Hamilton, Chandler, and Vargas families. Mario and Nancy Soria familia; Ray and Lilly Allala; Johnny, Rebecca and Lydia Orta; the Felix-Murrillo–Drake families; Kristin Calderon and family; and Sergio and Priscilla Delgado.

For the sisters who keep me alive: Holly Robinson, Teri

Andrews, Karen Wilson, Reiko Rizzuto, Kate Anger, Chris Johnson, Diane Taulli, Julie Greenberg, Deanne Edwards, Tracy Salyer, Julie Terrell, and Susan Tomlinson.

For the storytellers: Louie Lozano, Trent Chatham, Alfred Garibay, Dave Rogers, General Sims III, and John Sims.

I wouldn't be a writer without my first readers, the amazing and steadfast Eleanor Jackson at the DCL Agency, lifelong best writing friend Holly Robinson, firme Alex Espinoza (and Kyle Behen), veterana Helena María Viramontes, gangster lean Tod Goldberg (and Wendy Duren), Reiko Rizzuto, Ivy Pochoda, Viet Thanh Nguyen, Michael Connelly, Patrick Carroll, JT Lachaussee, Jackson Howard at FSG, and Blaise Zerega at Alta.

Special thanks to Jennifer Beals and Tom Jacobson, for changing everything and treating me like a queen.

This book couldn't have been treated more generously than by the team at Counterpoint/Catapult: the brilliance of Dan Smetanka, Megan Fishmann, Wah-Ming Chang, Rachel Fershleiser, and Pat Strachan. I would only write in legal pads if it weren't for you all.

Thanks to Robin Bilardello for the beautiful cover, and to Stan Lim for the author photo on my porch when it was 106 degrees. Rancho Cucamonga forever . . .

Gratitude for the music all day and night that keeps us in love and remembering who we are—at Radio Aztlan: Jorge "Mr. Blue" Hernandez and Darren "Aztec Parrot" DeLeon; the Art Laboe crew: Joanna Morones, Jimmy Reyes, Angel "Angel Baby" Rodriguez, Rebecca Luna, and in memory of Josefa Salinas.

For my loyal and loved Riverside Elks Lodge #643 and all the members who make a community work, who spend hours and days making banquet halls beautiful for hundreds of memorials, celebrations of life, weddings & quinceaneras & graduations, dances & birthdays & farewells—I love being in the kitchen with you. For my loyal and beloved First United Methodist Church of Riverside, where faith and family are steadfast—I love being in the kitchen with you all as well.

For my treasured colleagues at University of California, Riverside—Kim Wilcox and Diane del Buono, Sandra Balthazar Martinez, Rich Cardullo, Deborah Wong, Begona Echevarria, Jessica Weber, Elizabeth Watkins, Deanna Wheeler, Susan Brown, Benicia Mangram, Marcelina Ryneal, Tanya Wine, Mayra Hong, Summer Espinoza, Janice Henry, Monique Veloz, Yazmin Perez and Bryan Bradford, Kathryn McGee and Agam Patel, and Michael Jaime-Becerra.

© Stan Lim

SUSAN STRAIGHT has published nine novels, including *Mecca*, *A Million Nightingales*, and *Highwire Moon*, and one memoir, *In the Country of Women*. She's been a finalist for the Kirkus Prize, the Dayton Literary Peace Prize, and the National Book Award, among other honors, and received the Lannan Prize, the O. Henry Award, the Edgar Award, a Guggenheim Fellowship, and the Robert Kirsch Award for lifetime achievement from the Los Angeles Times Book Prizes. Her fiction has been translated into ten languages. She was born in Riverside, California, where she lives with her family. Find out more at susanstraight.com.